SENTINELS OF CREATION

SENTINELS OF CREATION

A Tale of Two Gardens

ROBERT W. ROSS

Library of Congress Control Number: 2017909366
CreateSpace Independent Publishing Platform
North Charleston, South Carolina

Cover Illustration by George Patsouras (www.cgmythology.com)

To my wife who is the love of my life, the guard at my back, and the partner by my side. She is my own Scottish lass who both loves and fights with equal passion. I'd have it no other way. Thank you Rachel, for saying yes those many years ago.

Chapter 1

PROLOGUE

Lucifer looked down as the surf foamed about his feet. He curled his toes feeling the moist sand seep between them, crouched, and gave his cuffed jeans another turn to ensure they didn't get wet from the spray. A few lonely bubbles popped through the wet sand and Lucifer absently scooped up a handful, then straightened. He wiggled his fingers letting it slip though until all that remained was the small sand crab.

"Hello little sand flea," Lucifer said with a smile as he continued, "I reached down my hand and removed you from all that you've ever known. Are you impressed? Are you fearful?"

The small creature waggled its eyestalks nonplussed and Lucifer chuckled. "Neither, huh? Well, my tiny friend I must tell you that—" Lucifer broke off as he felt someone approach.

"What do you have there?" came a female voice.

Lucifer sighed as he turned toward the voice. She was still several paces off and there was no moon, but the fallen angel could see her clearly while knowing she could not yet discern his features. She was tall and toned with long, flowing black hair that cascaded about her shoulders. She wore a bikini that accented every curve and a wrap about her hips that Lucifer noted drew, rather than deflected, attention.

As she continued toward him, he counted backwards softly to himself, "*Three...two...one...*" She paused staring at him, now close enough that the starlight bathed him in sufficient light for her to see him fully. He watched the expected intake of breath, heard her pulse quicken and saw her eyes dilate slightly.

Lucifer glanced over the woman's shoulder and up the dunes where tiki torchlight illuminated the gathering. He wondered absently what could have caused her to leave it.

The woman stammered, "I'm, I'm Sam. Samantha really, but some people call me Sam. I don't really know why. Sam's a boy's name and I am not a boy. I mean you can see I am a grown woman, right. You, um, wow, has anyone told you that you are a dead ringer for David Bowie. I mean 80s Bowie. You know, when he was so—" She trailed off as Lucifer's blue eyes locked on her.

"Hello Samantha. Yes, I can see you are, indeed, a grown woman. And, yes, I do get the Bowie comparison more than one might think." He tapped a finger along his chin and looked up thoughtfully, "However, it is worth pointing out that I looked like him long before he looked like me. As for your initial question, I was just talking with a sand flea, although I must confess he is not much of a conversationalist."

"Huh? Sand. Flea?"

Lucifer smiled. "You asked what I had in my hand?"

Samantha recovered slightly, "Oh, oh yeah."

Lucifer held out his hand. "Sand flea. Or Sand Crab. Mole Crab. They have lots of names. They hide beneath the sand as the tide comes in, but as the water washes over their little burrow you can see air bubbles if you look closely. I scooped the little guy out to have a chat."

Samantha smiled wolfishly and drew close sliding her hand inside Lucifer's open shirt and brushing aside the linen as her hand traced down his chest. "Wouldn't you rather talk with someone more interesting than a sand flea?"

The fallen angel took a half step back. He gently grasped Samantha's outstretched hand, turned it, and placed the sand flea in her upturned palm. Lucifer looked into her eyes and arched an eyebrow. "My dear, you have no idea how hard it is to find a conversation more interesting than one I could have with that little crab."

"Well, maybe you've been talking to the wrong girls. Or, maybe," Samantha drew close again while allowing the sand crab to fall and scurry away, "you should try doing something more interesting than talking."

Lucifer showed is teeth, "Oh, and what might that be, Samantha?"

"Oh, I don't know—"

Lucifer's smile broadened, "I think you do, Miss Trelane. But, don't you have a fiancé up above and isn't that your engagement party?"

Her expression didn't change at first and Lucifer just waited patiently. He saw the awareness slowly wash across her face and she seemed to shake her head slightly.

"Yes. Yes, my fiancé' is up there. David is up there. But you are so—"

Lucifer broke in. "David is up there and he will notice you are gone. You should return to him."

Samantha Trelane took a step back. "I—I should return to him. But I don't want to return to him. I want to stay with you."

Lucifer narrowed his eyes. "But, Miss Trelane, I do NOT want you to stay with me. It seems I am finding it harder and harder to be alone with my thoughts without one of you stumbling into me. How did you even come to this beach? There are no airports on this island."

The woman opened her mouth to speak but Lucifer silenced her with a wave. "No, this is faster." He reached out and held her chin between finger and thumb then stared to her eyes. She gasped slightly and her lips parted, but Lucifer ignored the reaction. A moment later he sniffed derisively, and turned back looking out to sea. "Chartered sea plane. I wish you had never learned to build those things."

"Come back to the party with me," She whispered softly.

"No."

Samantha became more insistent, "Yes, I want you to."

Lucifer whirled around and the young woman gasped as she stared into his glowing red eyes. "You want me to go back to your human party so you can introduce me to your human lover and tell him that we are going to run off together? You are glamored, Samantha, because your little ape brain can't properly comprehend me. You tell me what you want, well do you know what I want? Do you, Samantha?"

She shook her head and began to tremble as Lucifer closed on her, his face scant inches from hers. "I want my servant back. I want Asmodeus. I want him to have been less implacable, to have evolved with the millennia. I want him not to have gotten himself destroyed. Do you know what that feels like? To lose someone who you've been with since time began? No. No you do not, Samantha. Oh, and he isn't just dead. Dead I could do something with. He's gone! Obliterated. His very essence converted to something new and used up." The fallen angel could feel the anger welling up, ribbons of red chaotic energy playing about his body.

"So, leave me Samantha Trelane! Go marry David and become David and Samantha Griswold. Have your three children. Live your lives and then watch David die at 76, but don't worry, you will live to the ripe old age of 94 before your end comes. From this day to that remember one thing. Every day you live is because I suffered it to be so. I restrained myself from snuffing you out like the guttering candles you humans are."

The woman stood paralyzed, eyes wild with fear. Lucifer gave an exasperated growl turned and gestured. A thin line of light appeared in the air, inches above the sand and revolved into a glowing blood red portal through which could be seen an elegantly appointed room with paneled walls and richly carpeted floors.

Lucifer stepped though and turned back to Samantha, his voice more measured but hard as ice. "Unless, you'd still like to be with me? Care to join me here, Samantha?"

She was reflexively shaking her head in negation, but managed to stammer, "W-Where?"

"Where am I? Come and find out."

"No!"

"See, you ARE capable of making good decisions. You decided not to join Satan in hell."

The portal closed and Samantha Trelane fell to her knees, wrapping her arms about herself and rocking as she heard the distant sound of people calling her name.

Chapter 2

DRAGON CON

A woman's voice cut through the din like a knife. She yelled, "Kellan! Sentinel. Kellan! Shannon! Look over here."

Kellan Thorne turned toward the sound of his name and squinted at the plump woman standing near the hotel entrance. He turned to Juliet in confusion and asked, "Who's that and why is she calling my name."

The young woman grinned at him mischievously and said, "She's not even looking at you, maybe she's calling to another Kellan."

The woman continued facing away from Kellan and Juliet, but waved her hands frantically and called again, "Kellan! Shannon! I want a picture."

A tall man with tousled brown hair, black pentagram t-shirt, and faded jeans turned to the woman and smiled. He reached out for the hand of his flame haired companion and both looked toward the woman who raised her camera. His eyes were bright green and enochian runes ran down his arms as he extended both hands in an exaggerated aggressive stance. The woman, likewise, struck a pose, freezing for a moment after filling each hand with a dagger from one of the many sheaths strapped across her hips and legs.

Kellan stood still, mouth open in a slack jawed expression that somehow managed to convey both shock and dread. He pointed mutely as the camera flashed several times after which the duo smiled again in response to the thanks offered by their admirer. Juliet turned to him, laughing, and said, "I told you she was calling to another Kellan. C'mon, let's go talk to them. This is so cool!"

He seemed far less excited. "Juliet, no. This is decidedly not cool and we should—" He trailed off as she stopped for a moment, spun around, and grabbed him tightly on the arms.

"Listen very carefully, Kellan. This is important. For the next ten minutes you are not Kellan."

"I'm not?" He said questioningly.

She shook her head. "No, for the next ten minutes you are Kevin. Got it. *Kevin.*" Juliet then spun her her heels and scampered toward the two departing figures shouting, "Kellan. Shannon. Hold up a sec."

"No it's a wig. I got it from Arda so it's pretty nice. I wish I had hair like this. Mine's a lot thinner and brown." Juliet nodded understandingly as Shannon looked past her.

"Oh," Juliet began, "this is my friend, Kevin. Really kind of a wonky uncle, but none of my friends wanted to come to Dragon Con this year so Kevin's the closest thing I could find." She smiled and gave Kevin a playful punch on the arm. "Isn't that right, Kevin?"

He grunted something that couldn't be understood.

Juliet ignored him and turned to Kellan. "Tell me about your eyes, they look so cool?"

Kellan, who had been quietly allowing the girls to chat suddenly became animated. "I know, right? I found them online and they actually have some iridescent flakes in them that gives this glowing effect. They hurt like a son-of-a-bitch though after a couple hours and I have to take them out. Oh, hey. Do you see the flecks?"

"Not really?" said Juliet.

"Look closer," he said insistently.

"Why?"

Shannon gave a small sigh, "Just humor him, Juliet. He wants you too look at them and see each tiny fleck of green. He's very proud of them."

Kellan leaned down and Juliet peered closely into his eyes. Sure enough, she could just make out tiny specks of green that seemed to catch the light and reflect it outward. "Wow, that's impressive. Did they come that way or did you modify them yourself?"

Kellan straightened and smiled. "Modified. I had to use watchmaker's opticals to see close enough and embedded crushed synthetic emerald. That's why they hurt. But sometimes you have to suffer for cosplay, right?"

"So true." agreed Juliet.

"Hey, we're about to head to the Con-Suite and grab a drink, you guys want to come with?" asked Shannon.

"Hells yeah," shouted Juliet.

"No!" growled Kevin. It's almost 10:30 and I really want to get back to my room and chill a bit before Dragon Con strikes crazy time. You guys obviously know about *Dragon Con After Dark?*"

Kellan and Shannon both absently glanced at smartphones to confirm the time then nodded gravely. Shannon brightened. "You know what they say, 'what happens at Dragon Con after 10:30 stays at Dragon Con.'"

Kevin smirked. "Do they really say that? Well, nice meeting you guys. We gotta go. Juliet...please."

"Hey," *shouted* Kellan as if having just having made a critical realization "Juliet...your name is Juliet and you kinda look like her."

"You think," asked Juliet, "Really?"

Shannon's eyes widened, "Oh my god, You do, Juliet, you really do. I mean you have the same kind of buttony nose. You even have freckles like she does."

"Same blue eyes too," added Kellan, "You could totally cosplay as Juliet and hang out with us."

Juliet glanced up at Kevin, face splitting into a fierce grin, "Wow, that sounds like a great suggestion. Should I do that? Should I Uncle Kevin?"

"No, Juliet. No you should not. Besides, I doubt anyone would recognize you. I have no idea who these folks are cosplaying." He paused. "No offense."

"Oh, none taken, dude," responded Kellan slipping into a millennial bro accent. "It's a pretty new graphic novel and not many people have read it yet, but they will. You see, we're on the leading edge of cosplay here."

"We've had about five people stop us," offered Shannon. "That's pretty good since this is the first *Con since the book came out."

Kevin narrowed his eyes and felt his molars grind. "Book?"

Kellan and Shannon exchanged a glance, "Well, not a book—book. You know a graphic novel, like Doctor Strange, but darker."

Kevin looked stunned but managed, "What's this thing called?"

"*Sentinels and Demons,*" they responded together and Shannon continued, "It's written and inked by a guy named Richard Rumpkins."

"Who?" asked Kevin.

"Richard Rumpkins. It came out last March. I downloaded it from ComicFire for free."

"For free, huh? Must not have been very good if he had to give it away."

"That's a really cynical way to live your life, man. It was a limited special. Rumpkins does that from time to time. There's also a printed version, but that's nine bucks."

"Merciful Tehlu!!" exclaimed Kevin and glared at Juliet then back to Kellan and Shannon. "Nine whole dollars. That's just way too much. Anyway, nice to meet you two. We gotta go. Any minute now Leeloo Multi-Pass wearing orange electrical tape or Sulu with an Enterprise shaped codpiece will be jaunting about and I'm not ready for that."

Kevin turned to leave and caught Juliet waving goodbye out of his peripheral vision as she joined him walking down the hotel hallway which was festooned with all manner of British Scifi geekery. The placards outlined the events which were scheduled for each conference room. They all currently displayed, *11:00pm - 2:00am, Doctor Who Ball. Be sure to bring your banana to the party, Rose.*

Kevin paused reading the placard. Juliet nudged him with her shoulder. "You totally want to go to that don't you?" She paused and added, "Kevin."

He turned and glared at her. "Elevators, now."

She snickered but kept quiet until a few minutes later when door to the little two room suite clicked shut behind them.

"You seem stressed, Kevin." She lowered her voice to a rasp. "Why so serious."

He rounded on her, "What the Fu—Frak was that? And stop calling me Kevin!"

Juliet collapsed into one of the sitting room chairs, kicked off her shoes and pulled her feet into the chair with her, peering at him over her knees.

"What was what? Kellan?" she asked innocently.

"You're gonna do it aren't you. You are going to make me unleash a torrent of profanity and then rub my nose in it. You will then threaten to share my tirade with your mother which will, of course, result in one of her famous lectures on how profanity is the last bastion of those with limited vocabulary. You know how much I hate her lectures so will use that as leverage convince me to go to the Doctor Who Ball instead of the Heroes and Villains Ball. I know exactly what you are trying to do and it's not going to work, little miss thang. Like I told you last week, just go by yourself and when it turns out to be lame, you can come to the Heroes Ball later. I'm not gonna budge on this. I'm in complete control of my night."

"Yeah, you look it," She said with a giggle and then Kellan saw an impish expression cross her face. "I can't believe you haven't read that comic."

His eyes widened. "What? You've read it and you didn't tell me about it. How the hell did this Rumpkin jackass find out about me?"

"Someone talked?" offered Juliet.

"Well no shit, Sherlock. Someone talked. And you are supposed to be the smart Herrick. I cannot believe this! And you have no idea who it was that blabbed. I mean not that many people know."

"I didn't say I didn't know."

"Huh? Wait, but you said—"

"I said, 'someone.' You just assumed I didn't know who the someone was. Why would I disclose such valuable information for free?"

Kellan squinted at her. "Free?"

"Remember, I'm the smart Herrick."

Kellan's voice took on the flat tone that Juliet knew meant he was both pissed and resigned in equal measure. "What do you want?"

She smiled, held up two fingers and pointed to a fruit bowl that rested on the counter of the small kitchenette.

"You want a bowl of fruit?"

She pointed again.

"You want an apple? Two apples?"

She shook her head and pointed.

"Jesus, Juliet, do we have to play this game?"

A nod.

"Damnit to hell. You want two oranges?"

Headshake. Point.

"You want two—" Kellan paused and stared from the bowl and back to the young woman. "No way."

She smiled and Kellan sagged onto the barstool while reaching into the fruit bowl. He tossed her the banana which she deftly caught and raised to her cheek with a grin as she saw Kellan take the second one for himself. "Now we have bananas to take to the Doctor Who ball."

"You are an evil genius, Ms. Herrick. How long were you planning this?"

The young woman affected a seated curtsey. "Why thank you good sir. As for how long, I saw those cosplayers in the Urban Fantasy panel earlier today. I couldn't believe you didn't notice them, but you are mostly oblivious so I guess it makes sense. Anyway, I almost pointed them out when I thought up this little plan. Just had to find the right time and place, then whammo!"

"I hate you," Kellan said with a sigh.

"No you don't. You love me and you wish you were as smart as me, but seeing as how we are now in complete agreement about which ball we'll be attending tonight, I am perfectly happy to answer all your questions."

"Whatever. I'm just happy that you put those guys up to it and that there isn't some dumb comic out there about me."

Juliet broke into a hearty laugh. "Oh, there's a genuine graphic novel out there, Kel. And, those folks were totally cosplaying you and Shannon because they read it"

Kellan closed his eyes and slowly shook his head. "You are shitting me, right?"

"No shit, sir. Girl Scouts honor."

"You were never in the Girl Scouts."

"Geek Scouts honor," she corrected, holding up three fingers solemnly, then added. "You know, Geek Scouts, would be an awesome thing for kids."

"Really? And just what would one do in the Geek Scouts? Not go outside and not camp?"

"Yes!" yelled Juliet, pointing.

"Argh," yelled Kellan. "I swear, tell me what's up with this book thing right now or you can find another unwilling escort, missy."

"Oh stop. You love Doctor Who and are going to love the ball. Anyway, Meghan did it."

"Fucking Meghan," yelled Kellan.

"I have a feeling," snickered Juliet, "*that* happened after she told her boy-friend about you; they were dating at the time. It was pretty serious. You knew that didn't you?"

Kellan cringed. "That's not what I meant and why on earth would you have any insights into Meghan's sex life. No, don't answer that and no I didn't know she was dating someone. Sheesh, and your folks were worried about you being corrupted at Dragon Con. They should be worried when Megan Daugherty takes you to dinner."

Kellan got up and pulled a beer from the mini fridge and frowned, "Bloody thing is barely cold. $300 a night and is it too much to ask for a cold fridge." Juliet watched as Kellan's eyes burst to life, glowing with their bright green fire. He held his beer in one hand staring at it as misty ice began to condense along the glass. His eyes returned to normal and he took a long drink from the bottle. "Ahhh, that's what I'm talking about."

He looked back at Juliet, "What's with the disapproving mother face?"

"Oh nothing, I'm sure your sliver of godliness and insights into creation were granted so you could chill beer to optimal temperatures." She paused, a thought-ful expression crossing her face. "You know, I think men are, collectively, just too stupid to have powers. Raphael should have picked a woman Sentinel."

"Whatever, so Meghan was dating this Rumpkin guy?"

"Hmm, oh no. Kyle. She has a thing for K-named guys apparently. Kyle Reese"

"Kyle Reese? Like the dude from *Terminator?*"

"Well, yeah, but I doubt it's really the character from *Terminator* come to life, Kel."

"Who the hell knows now. Remember what Micah told me about works of fiction being distorted reflections of alternate realities?"

"Yes, I remember but still don't understand it. Anyway, this Kyle Reese raced motorcycles and didn't fight intelligent machines from the future."

"Raced motorcycles?"

Juliet nodded.

"Of course he did and I'm sure that relationship went swimmingly."

Juliet rolled her eyes and continued. "Anyho…Meghan will have to give you all the details because I didn't want to press her. Apparently she slipped up somehow and part of your story came out then she decided to try and cover it up by telling Kyle that it was part of a dream she'd just had. Kyle knows the Richard Rumpkin guy, who is an graphic novelist, tells him Meghan's—your—story and bing-bang-boom, you're in a book. Congrats Kel."

"Thanks. Just what I wanted, to be written about by some unknown author who gives my story away on ComicFire."

"Yeah, but Rumpkin is a great artist and could make you look pretty dashing. Try focusing on that."

Kellan took another long drink from his beer and pointed the bottle at Juliet, "That's a very good point. I wonder how cool I looked?"

"Well, other than your hair, you really didn't look like you. He gave you brown eyes and made you taller. Basically, graphic novel you is much better than real you."

"Wonderful. Well that's not—wait, what? You've seen this thing? When you were talking to those cosplayers, you acted all excited like you just found out."

"I was in character, Kel"

Kellan took a deep breath. "So, you read this graphic novel but didn't tell me?"

"I thought it would upset you and make you mad at Meghan."

"Right on both flipping counts, Juliet. Jesus, Mary and Joseph!"

"Meghan broke up with the guy over it. She was really pissed. I think she may have pulled a gun on him."

Kellan waved a hand dismissively, "Big deal. That's practically how Meghan orders fast food and certainly how she expresses displeasure with referee calls at sporting events."

Juliet snorted, "Ha, that's true, but I think she really liked this one and felt betrayed. She's also totally freaked out what you are going to do when you find out. You mean a lot to her Kel and you know how she is about loyalty."

Kellan sighed, "I know, and truth be told, it is actually kinda cool."

Juliet brightened, "It is absolutely cool! You are a published super hero. We should go see the author at his signing."

"He's here?"

"Yeah he's part of the urban fantasy track this year. Just a fan run panel, nothing fancy."

"Nah, I don't want to see him. He needs to figure some way of getting content for his next book without any help from me. How much did he get right?"

"Not much, really. He's got the whole Sentinel thing with the abilities mostly right. Shannon is Scottish but not from the past. No Micah or Meghan. I'm in there, but as a two dimensional plot device rather than critical to your very life, which I am. Oh, and he got the snuffing of Asmodeus right. That's about it."

Kellan just shook his head and grumbled, "Well, I suppose it could be worse and what kind of bullshit pen name is Richard Rumpkin? It's clearly too alliterative to be real."

"Richard W. Rumpkin actually"

"W, huh. What's that stand for"

"No idea, boss, but let's pretend it stands for, *w*hen are we heading down to the Doctor Who Ball? I've got my banana and brought my *Rose* outfit so will be ready in a tick. I also brought a Doctor 12 outfit for you."

"Doctor 12? What? Why? I wasn't ever going to the—" Kellan paused as he watched the knowing smile spread across Juliet's face and simply shook his head in resignation.

"I picked Doctor 12 because he has very severe eyes coupled with a grouchy personality and I knew you'd be displaying both at some point this weekend."

With that, Juliet unfolded her legs from the chair, stood, and bounced once on the balls of her feet. "Now shoo, go get ready, I don't want to miss anything."

Kellan slowly got up from the stool, still shaking his head as he heard the door to her room click shut.

Chapter 3

THE HERRICKS

Kellan swung his Impala into the Herrick's driveway and slid to a jarring stop with a slight screech of tires that he knew would announce his arrival better than any doorbell. He sat silently for a moment, took a deep breath, and reached over to pick up the large manilla folder that rested on the passenger seat.

"Time to change your life again, Kellan," he said as he glanced in the rear-view mirror.

The door creaked and groaned slightly as he exited the car. He glanced up taking in the small home. On the outside, it seemed fairly ordinary, a house that real estate pros referred to as "5-4 and a door," referring to the five windows up, and two pairs of windows down, separated by a door. Kellan knew better as this house held all manner of tiny changes that all added up to turn a sterile dwelling into the cottagesqe home of Juliet and her family. He gave the car door a solid hip-butt and it swung closed with a satisfying cerklunk then turned to the flagstone path that led to the front door. It stood open with warm yellow light spilling out, silhouetting the figure standing there.

Rachel Herrick regarded him with an inscrutable half-smile and Kellan paused, unsure if he was in trouble—again. Then he saw her eyes narrow slightly as his mind raced to discover what mischief he had recently brought to the Herricks in general or Juliet specifically.

"Hey, Rach!" he began putting on the most genuine smile he could manufacture, "What's up?"

He saw the eyes narrow further and his stomach sank. *Oh shit, what did I do this time?* Kellan thought as he, again, walked toward the door, stopping right before her in the threshold.

Rachel Herrick was a beautiful woman in her own right. She was slender with chestnut hair that tumbled down carelessly to just touch her shoulders. Kellan knew she had just turned 50, but easily looked ten years younger. Her eyes, a mossy brown were alight with their own mischief as she leaned against the door frame, blocking his entrance. She wore what he had described many times as Rachel's uniform, a graphic tee, jeans, and Bass Weejuns.

Kellan looked up at her from the stoop, "Yesss," he said with a sigh. "What did I do this time?"

"You know very well," she responded.

Kellan's mind clicked through thousands of possibilities, discounting each one in turn as either being trivial or impossible for her to know about. Finally, he narrowed his own eyes, locking with hers. "You got nothing. Because," he paused for effect, "I've done nothing."

Rachel sighed, turning to allow him entry. "Well, you are half right. I don't *know* what you've done this time or what you have up your sleeve, but I also *know* you have done something, or you are about to. What's in the folder?"

"Something for Juliet, not you," he said with a smirk. *She's a grown woman and doesn't need to show you it if she doesn't want to.*

"Then why bring it here? Why not just give it to her at your store? You clearly wanted us to be part of this, whatever it is."

Insufferable woman thought Kellan as he walked into the foyer. *How does she know these things; she's probably a witch. That actually would explain a lot—*

"Ow," exclaimed Kellan after Rachel flicked his ear. "Why'd you do that?"

"You were spacing out again—that thing you do when you chatter with yourself in your head. Do you not think I notice it?"

"I do not, 'space out,' Rachel. I was just—"

"Yeah you were," came a voice from Kellan's left where Rachel's husband, Thomas, had emerged from the little office located off the foyer to stand in its doorway regarding them both.

"Et tu, Thomas?" said Kellan with a defeated sigh.

"Hey, dude, I call 'em as I see 'em. She's got your number and you'd do well to just accept it. I've had over twenty years to learn this important lesson, accept my hard won knowledge with grace and humility, mah Brotha."

Kellan snorted, "I bow to your wisdom and advanced age, Mr. Herrick."

Rachel laughed as she closed the door and headed into the house, "Now you managed to piss off both of us. Well done, Kel. You truly have a gift."

"What? What did I do to piss of either of you?"

She grinned at him. "I try to stay perpetually pissed at you. It saves me time,"

Rachel disappeared into the kitchen and Kellan turned to Thomas who was slowly shaking his head. "You really are the most stupid genius I've ever met."

"Holy shit, you both are nuts. You know that. I haven't even done anything yet."

Thomas smiled and it lit up his face. It was what Rachel called his "evil" smile, infectious and filled with guile. Kellan found himself grinning like an idiot. "What?"

Thomas held up one finger. "Advanced age." He uncurled a second finger, "Mr. Herrick."

"Oh."

"Yeah," said Thomas with a low chuckle.

Thomas Herrick was the yin to Rachel's yang. Where she was fiery, impulsive, extroversion, he was cool, deliberative, introversion. He was the saucer that cooled the cup of her passions and Rachel's personality served as a contrasting mirror to his own, in many ways, just as her eyes contrasted with the blue of his. Thomas' easy going manner hid a keen intellect and biting wit that Kellan knew he didn't want working against him, especially this night so he raised his hands in submission. "Ok, so advanced age might be a bit much and the Mr. Herrick was completely uncalled for."

Thomas laughed, "Indeed, especially when we don't even let the kids' friends call us Mr. and Mrs. Herrick."

Thomas and Rachel were a bit of an enigma, children of the 80s, steeped in the music of the era and the politics of Reagan, but lived their lives with the egalitarian zeal of 60s flower children. Kellan loved them both fiercely and despite their outward jabs, he knew they loved him as well. There was no more evidence of their affection and trust than in how they supported his friendship with Juliet. This was certainly true for Rachel, but even more so for Thomas. Kellan knew Thomas loved all his kids, but Juliet being both the youngest sibling and only girl, held a special place in her father's heart.

"Beer?" Thomas asked.

Kellan grinned, "Need you ask, good sir?"

"How silly of me," Thomas replied as he headed to the kitchen with Kellan in tow. "What do you want?" he added.

"Dunno, whatcha got?"

"Beer fridge?" Thomas asked?

"Beer fridge!" Kellan agreed enthusiastically while seeing the not so subtle shake of Rachel's head as she puttered about by the sink.

Thomas opened the back kitchen door that led into the garage and went to a large refrigerator against one wall. He opened the double doors and bright LED light spilled out, brightening the immediate area. Kellan stood next to him taking in the choices, then reached for a lone Rum Cask Innis & Gunn.

Thomas grunted and Kellan pulled back.

"What?"

"Nothing, you are just so predictable."

"I am not."

"Then try something different, prove me wrong."

"Fine, I will," said an indignant Kellan as he pulled a St. Barnabus Belgian Ale from the fridge, "See—not predictable."

Thomas smiled as he retrieved the Innis & Gunn that Kellan had put back. "Nope, you showed me. Then again, this was my last Rum Cask, and it would have been rude of me to not let you have it. Good thing you decided it wasn't what you really wanted."

Kellan ground his teeth as Thomas closed the fridge and headed back toward the kitchen. "That was some psychological bullshit right there, dude. You know your daughter has picked up that trait of yours and it's not cool. Not cool at all"

"Yeah, well, her language seems to be something she's picked up from you so payback's a bitch."

"What?" said Kellan following Thomas back into the kitchen and absently slamming the door behind him, "You're blaming me for Juliet's salty tongue? Seriously? Have you ever met your wife? Allow me to introduce you. Thomas, this is Rachel, who, for the record, is where I got MY salty tongue."

Rachel glance over her shoulder, "Damned straight but if you weren't always over here during your formative years, you would've been spared my corrupting influence."

"You guys were the only ones with Laser Disks and Internet, where else was I going to go?"

She smirked at him, "Whatever. Are you staying for dinner? I need to know how much chopping *Mr. Herrick* there needs to do. We're having Carnitas."

Thomas rolled his eyes at his wife as he slid next to her picking up a knife to begin chopping that assembled onions and peppers.

"No, I was really just here to talk with Juliet about something and thought you guys would be interested in, wait, what? Carnitas?" Kellan looked around and quickly spied a pressure cooker on the kitchen island. It was counting down with a bright 12 on its screen. "Twelve minutes to go? Hell, yeah, I'm staying."

Rachel laughed, "Well then put that mystery envelope in the mail cozy and make yourself useful by clearing the crap off the table so we can eat."

"Yes ma'am *Mrs. Herrick*." Kellan said with a chuckle in his voice.

She gave him a sidewise glance. "Shut the fuck up Kellan."

"See!" Kellan yelled triumphantly, "It's all her fault."

"It always is," replied Thomas, "but not at all wise to point it out. Remember, don't taunt happy fun-ball."

Rachel glanced to Kellan, her face serious, as she nodded in agreement. "Table. Now."

Kellan Thorne, second Sentinel of Creation, swallowed hard, deposited his folder on the counter and proceeded to clear the table.

⌒⫸⫷⌒

Juliet slid to a stop, her sock covered feet scooting across the tile. Her eyes washed over the room. "Kel? What are you doing here?"

"Nice to see you, too, Juliet," responded Kellan as he set the last plate down on the dark walnut trestle table. "I see you've taken to heart Lady Granthum's guide for dinner dress: Meals taken between six and eight require XL Minnie Mouse t-shirts with matching pajama pants and socks."

Juliet glanced down and her face reddened. "Kellan Thorne, you can just F—"

"Juliet—" said Thomas and Rachel simultaneously, their voice steeped in mock seriousness.

"Frak off," continued Juliet. Her parents nodded appreciatively.

"I will happily frak off after dinner, Miss Herrick, but right now I am about to enjoy your mother's amazing carnitas. As for why I am here, that can wait a second, but I wager you are gonna feel really guilty for being mean to me once you find out."

"No I won't," she responded petulantly.

"Harrumph," said Thomas.

"Well, I won't," said Juliet again, her hands going unconsciously to her hips.

"You probably will," began Thomas, "but that's not why I 'harrumphed,'" He stared and his daughter locking his eyes with hers. "Ha—rumph,"

"Oh," Juliet said, her face breaking into a grin. "Sorry, Daddy, I didn't hear you come home earlier." Then she pranced over and placed a kiss on his cheek. "Better?"

"Yep. All's right with the world."

"Ok, everyone!" Rachel called out. "Grab a plate and have at it."

"Woot!" yelled Kellan grabbing his plate and dashing to the counter where he slathered a tortilla with guacamole, pico de gallo, jalapeño, and a pile of shredded pork.

"Someone's hungry," laughed Rachel.

"Yeah and polite guests wait their turn," chided Juliet.

"Pfft…I've known your parents longer than you have and I'm not a guest, am I Rach?"

"No, you are not a guest, Kellan."

"See. The matriarch hath spoken."

"If I had wanted a stupid older brother, I would have asked Mom and Dad to adopt someone," Juliet grumbled. "You are as bad as Jonny and he's half your age."

"He's no way as bad as Jonny," answered Rachel and Thomas.

"Stop doing that!" yelled Juliet.

"What?" they said in unison looking innocent.

"God! I hate you all."

Thomas laughed, "Ok, Julie-boo-bear, but Kellan really would have to be kind of a stupid Uncle. Since we were only around sixteen or seventeen when he was born. That about right Kellan?"

Kellan had already seated himself at the table and taken a huge bite of his carnitas wrap. "Yup," he managed around the mouthful.

"And," Rachel began, "I was pure as the driven snow at sixteen while your father was far too much of a nerd to even have touched a girl outside of his dad's Playboys."

Thomas feigned sadness and slowly nodded.

"Gross, Mom," said Juliet as she filled her plate.

"But, five years later," Rachel continued, "boy he sure knew his way around the ol' TARDIS. Right, hunny-bunny?" she asked going up on her toes to give Thomas a quick peck on the lips.

"If you say so, babe."

"Bigger on the inside," said Kellan around another bite of food.

"Oh, shut up, Kel," sail Juliet with a glare, "You are just trying to upset my stomach so you can have seconds."

He grinned.

Moments later everyone was contentedly eating, the lively banter having given way to the easy small talk common to families and intimate friends. To his joy, there ended up being enough extra for Kellan to have the seconds he wanted so desperately.

"Babe, that was the bomb," said Thomas sliding his end of the bench seat back from the table and standing up. Juliet and Kellan murmured words of agreement as they, too, moved to stand.

"Kel, you mind hanging out and helping me clean up so Rach can chill out on the porch?"

Kellan flashed a smile, "Sure thing. Small price to pay for such awesomeness."

Juliet peered over her half-full wine glass at her mother. She had her legs folded under her in the chair and rocked back slightly.

Rachel snickered. "Why do you look so anxious?"

"Mom, have you met me? Anxious is my middle name. Juliet Anxious Herrick. Now what do you think he has up his sleeve?"

"I've really no idea." Rachel said and Juliet stared at her in clear disbelief. "Honestly, I have no earthly idea what he wanted to talk to you about. I bet it has something to do with that folder he brought."

"You didn't tell him about Glenn, did you? Oh my god, Mom, tell me you didn't. He's going to make my life a living hell." Juliet took a gulp of wine and reached for the bottle.

Rachel laughed again. "Relax, you asked me to keep it to myself so I have, but I really don't see what the big deal is. You're nineteen and nineteen year old women date men. I mean if your *father* is ok with Glenn that why are you nervous about Kellan?"

"Because Daddy is all smoke and no fire." Rachel raised an eyebrow. "Ok, yes, if Glenn were to actually hurt me, Dad would dig a hole, fill it with lye and we'd never see Glenn again, but barring that..."

"And what do you think Kellan will do, exactly?"

"He's going to tease me mercilessly, for one."

"He does that already."

"I just don't want him doing something stupid."

"Like what," asked Rachel smiling.

"I dunno," began Juliet as she drained her second glass, "light him on fire, pepper him with icicle daggers, send him back in time to live to death."

"What?"

Juliet froze, her hand on the wine bottle and forced out a laugh.

"Nothing, just kidding, Mom. I don't know what he'll do but it will be something stupid and embarrassing."

Rachel narrowed her eyes and took the bottle from her daughter. "I think you've had enough, lightweight."

"Who's a lightweight," asked Thomas as he and Kellan strolled onto the porch, "Certainly not you, my love." He bent down and kissed Rachel. "Kitchen is all spic and span!"

She smiled up at him. "Thanks babe. Your daughter is the lightweight."

"Oh, well, I should hope so since she's only 19 and wouldn't be drinking at all if not for your corruptive influence."

Both Herrick women rolled their eyes in unison.

"How do they coordinate it like that," asked Kellan?

"It's just one of their many super powers, Kel. They also get their periods at the same time which is all sorts of fun."

Rachel and Juliet shook their head while staring daggers at Thomas.

"Yeah, that one should be filed under TMI," said Kellan as he sat down placing the folder on the table before him.

Juliet reached for it, saw his eyes flash green for the barest of seconds, and felt the folder adhere to the table as if weighted down. Kellan gave her a subtle shake of the head and his mouth curved up slightly.

She glanced at her parents, but Rachel had turned to give Thomas room to sit down. Juliet sighed in relief. She looked back to Kellan who wore a smug expression that made her want to smack him, mouthed the word, "Idiot," then crossed her arms and glowered at him.

"Ok Kellan," began Rachel. "You've been fed and you've tortured our daughter with your mysterious folder."

"You know she has anxiety issues, right?" asked Thomas with a smirk.

"Really?" asked Kellan, "Well if only I had known..."

"Have I mentioned that I hate you all," growled Juliet. "Hate, hate, hate—"

"Loathe entirely!" all four said in unison with a laugh.

As the laughter faded, Kellan said, "Well, you know how Juliet has been getting her degree in American Sign Language, right?"

"Really?" began Thomas, "Is that what all that finger waving is about? I thought she was developing a tick."

Rachel punched him then said, "Go on, Kellan. My ex-husband knew that was rhetorical and is just being an ass."

Kellan nodded, nonplussed, and continued, "Well, I'm going to have to be traveling a lot more over the next year or so because I've been asked to accept a fellowship at Emory in their Humanities department. I'll be seeking out rare books and helping the University curate them."

"Wow, that's great, Kellan," said Rachel. "You must be very excited. Sounds like it's right up your alley."

"Yeah it is pretty cool, but that means I'm going to be away from the shop for long periods of time."

"I can manage the store, Kel. You know that," said Juliet warily, unsure where he was going.

"I know you can. I know that. But it may be hard with your studies and just normal life stuff to cover all the times I will be gone. And, there may be decisions to make while I am," he paused, "um, unavailable."

"Unavailable?" asked Thomas. "Kel, there are these amazing devices called mobile phones. You carry them with you and people can reach you anytime they want."

"Not any time, Dad," Juliet said as she locked her eyes on Kellan's, worry entering her voice. "How long would you be unavailable Kellan?"

"Well, there's really no telling. Just depends on where I have to go. You know, for the books."

"Right, for the books," she echoed.

"Anyway, here's the deal. I'd be asking a lot of you Juliet and I don't want to unduly distract you from your studies, especially since your parents are paying for your tuition. So, I want to make some changes at the shop." Kellan opened the folder and took out a sheaf of papers, placing them in front of Juliet. "I want to give you half ownership of my bookshop. We'd be partners not employer and employee anymore."

Juliet raised her hand to her mouth and her parents both glanced at each other. They all knew how much the bookshop meant to Kellan and how hard he had worked to make it successful.

"Kel," said Juliet, "No, Kel, that is crazy talk."

"It's not crazy talk at all. You will be running the place when I'm not around and I've thought this through. I know you. You will drive yourself crazy wondering what I would do if I were there because you wouldn't want to screw up *my* bookstore. This way when you screw up, you'll be screwing up *our* bookstore."

Juliet became noticeably pale and Kellan caught himself and said, "That sounded better in my head."

Rachel reached over and patted Juliet's hand, "Breathe girlie, it's gonna be fine."

Juliet looked down, eyes running over the partnership papers in front of her:

Belove'ed Books LLC
Kellan Thorne, Proprietor — 49%
Juliet Herrick, Proprietor — 49%
Thomas & Rachel Herrick, Tiebreaker's N Chief — 2%

She snorted despite herself and spun the papers so her parents could read.

"Ha, Tiebreakers N' Chief," said Thomas. "I like the sound of that. Sounds important. Then again, I have no idea why it would be needed. I mean you two always agree on everything and never fight." Rachel nudged him and he fell silent.

Juliet had turned the papers back around and they saw her trace her fingers along her name, eyes welling up as she turned to Kellan. "For true, Kel?"

He smiled at her and reached over to set a pen on the papers, "For true and always, Juliet."

She looked up at her parents who both smiled and nodded then took up the pen and signed, *Juliet Herrick, Proprietor.*

"Congratulations," said Kellan clapping his hands, "You own a bookshop!"

Juliet slid out her chair and wrapped her arms around Kellan's shoulders giving him a kiss on the cheek while whispering directly in his ear, "Mr. Sentinel, if you get yourself killed while I'm tending this shop, I'm going to burn it to the fucking ground."

She felt him tense and smiled beatifically as she returned to her seat then pointed at the bottle. "This calls for a toast dontcha think?"

Kellan jogged up the alley stairs that led to the back of the bookshop, unlocked the door and slipped silently inside as an evil grin spread across his face.

"Just because she's my partner now doesn't mean I can't scare the shit out of her, now does it?" he whispered to himself. Kellan paused for a few heartbeats with his left hand on the knob to his small back office, reconsidering. Then he shook his head slightly, "Of course it doesn't."

Twisting the knob, he rushed into the room, eyes blazing and a ball of sparking energy rotating in his outstretched right hand. "Arrrahhhh wha?" His primal yell cut off before it he could really get it going as Kellan's eyes took in the scene and he instinctually bent time to a crawl.

Juliet sat on the desk, facing the door, her eyes locked on Kellan's. Her head was tilted as she was clearly engaged in kissing the person in front of her. Her ankles were crossed behind his calves as he stood between them. One of her hands gently cradled the back of his neck while the other held a handful of short black hair.

Kellan cocked his head. *She clearly likes him,* he thought. Then, glancing down at the still rotating ball of pure electrical power he held, *I'm gonna kill him.*

Time was slowed, but not stopped, and Kellan saw Juliet's eyes slowly widen as the young man's head tried to turn, reacting to the sound of Kellan's noisy entry. She increased her grip, keeping him facing forward as Kellan strained to slow time further.

He walked into the room and circled around the two, careful to keep enough distance between himself and the unknown man to prevent him from being caught in Kellan's time distortion bubble.

He looked to be in his early twenties, was wearing jeans, some kind of imprinted t-shirt, a hoodie, and red converse high tops.

Props for that Kellan thought, then added, *Don't get attached to the boy you are about to vaporize. Be analytical.*

Kellan knew that even with time slowed to a trickle, he could be seen if he stood still for too long so continued circling while taking a few unnecessary back and forth steps. He would just appear like a blurring outline to them both, but Kellan saw how Juliet's eyes tracked him.

Uh oh, those eyes are starting to look mad, he thought as he moved past the boy's line of sight once again standing behind them.

"Careful Kellan," he said softly. "Focus and be very careful or this could go very wrong." With that self admonition, Kellan dismissed the energy ball and tightened his time distortion so it felt almost like a second skin with even some of the hairs on his arms extending past it causing a tingle up and down. Kellan reached out and gently touched the back of Juliet's hand bringing her into his frame of reference. Instantly her face slid to his left just enough to she could see him fully.

"Hi Juliet!" Kellan began brightly. "I see you are working hard to keep our business humming along. As you may recall, we were going to review Quickbooks this morning and I was going to give you all the various account codes n' such."

"Well," she began, but he interrupted.

"Oh, yeah, by-the-by, who is the Korean boy that you've attached yourself to like the Kraken pulling down a ship."

"He's Glenn. Glenn is my boyfriend."

"Oh, great. He seems nice." Kellan gestured with his right hand and a portal rotated into view through which could be seen deep alien looking forrest of huge trees and twisted ferns. "I'm gonna send him back in time to live to death."

"No, you are not going to Weeping Angel my boyfriend, Kellan Thorne! I'm a grown woman not some adolescent. Stop being an asshole before he picks up on something. If you screw this up because of your Sentinel'ness, I'm never going to forgive you."

"Pffft, you totally would forgive me."

Her face went hard. "Not for a very very long time. I'm serious. I really like him and you will too."

Kellan stomped his foot. "Fine, but why couldn't you just stay fourteen?" With that he returned to the door and turned, keeping an thin tendril of power connected to Juliet like the finest spider silk. "Get ready and, for the record, I hate you being 19."

"I am ready," she growled.

Kellan smiled tilting his head, "Really, you want our asian Romeo there to wonder why he's been kissing your chin? Put your lips back."

"Oh, crap." Her face disappeared from view until only the eyes were visible again. She winked at him and Kellan snapped back into normal time.

Glenn spun around, alarmed at Kellan's yell and Juliet didn't have time to untangle her legs. She fell backwards across the desk, and would have slid into the chair headfirst had she not clamped on more tightly with her crossed ankles.

Glenn seemed to have completely forgotten about her as he faced Kellan who couldn't suppress the chuckle at both the boy's panicked expression and Juliet's struggles to regain her seated position.

"M-Mister Thorne," the boy stammered, "Hi, Mister Thorne. I've heard a lot about you. I'm Glenn. Glenn Yeung." He extended his hand and tried to step forward, but Juliet was still using him as leverage to sit up.

"Hi Glenn. You seem like you might be caught on something there." Silently, Juliet's ankles parted slightly, releasing him and the two men grasped hands. Kellan smiled. "Mister Thorne, huh? Did my dad walk in the room when I wasn't looking. Please, I don't even let toddlers call me Mister Thorne. It's Kellan."

Glenn brightened as he continued to pump his hand, "Kellan. Great. Yeah. Kellan."

"Yup. That's me. And, that's my hand, which, I'll be wanting back," Kellan said as he glanced past Glenn to a now upright Juliet who slowly shook her head completely unaware that she'd covered her face and was peering through fingers at them both.

"Right. Right," said Glenn releasing Kellan and absently rubbing his hands on his jeans.

The two men stood silently, staring at each other, as Juliet scrambled off the desk to stand next to Glenn, her hand intwining in his.

"Why do you have that stupid grin on your face, Kel," she asked.

"Huh? I do?"

"You do."

"Well, you two are adorable. That must be it. She seems pretty happy with you, Glenn."

"I hope she is," he answered nervously.

"Of course I am," she said tugging on his hand and going on toes to place a kiss on his cheek. "Silly boy."

Before another awkward silence could develop, a loud pounding could be heard coming from the front of the shop. Kellan looked down at his watch: 10:00 am. He looked up with a sigh and he and Juliet said in unison, "Hamish!!"

Juliet breezed past Kellan and out the office door as Glenn called after her.

"Hey Jules, I really need to get to class. If I don't leave now I'm gonna be late. I'll come by after."

Her voice drifted back mixed with the tinkling of bells as Juliet opened the front door. "Ok, babe, I'll see you then."

Glenn started toward the office door. "It was really nice to meet you, Kel. I'm just going to slip out the side since my car's parked out back."

Kellan extended his hand again as the young man moved past him. Glenn accepted it and Kellan held it tight pulling him close. "It's Kellan, not Kel, and just a tiny bit of advice for ya, Glenn. Juliet is one of my four most favorite people in the whole world. Like I said, she seems very happy with you and that's good because if she were to become very unhappy with you, that would be bad—for you." Kellan released Glenn's hand and the young man stared up at him with a mix of shock and discomfort as Kellan wiped non-existent dust from Glenn's shoulder then gripped him there, smiling warmly. "Remember that, OK? Now get going, dude, you don't want to be late."

"Uh, yeah. Sure. Thanks. And I'll remember. I will"

"Oh, I know you will, Glenn. Juliet only likes smart boys."

With that the young man quickly turned the corner and Kellan heard the side door slam a moment later.

"Operation 'Scare the shit out of boyfriend," complete," Kellan said to the air as he slid around the desk and plopped into the chair. He looked up as Juliet whirled in.

"What did you do?"

"What?"

"What did you do, Kel?"

"Nothing."

"Don't try to look innocent."

"I'm not."

"I know your innocent look and that's it, which means you did something."

"I didn't *do* anything, Juliet. I just *suggested* that your boyfriend be good to you."

Juliet groaned. "You are worse than Dad. I already had Glenn run the Thomas gauntlet, you know and Dad was perfectly nice."

"No he wasn't. He threatened him worse that I did."

Juliet froze. "Wait? What? You knew about Glenn?"

"Of course."

"What do you mean, 'of course,'?"

"I mean that I knew. Your dad told me weeks ago and I promised him I would threaten the kid the same way he did. Well, not exactly the same way. I love the way Thomas throws in the shovel and lye thing. It's a classic."

"I'm going to die alone," said Juliet groaning again.

"Nah, he seems like a stalwart lad. He made it through both of us and if he comes back tonight, I think he'll hang around."

"If?"

"Well, I kinda threw a tiny lightning bolt at him, by accident."

"Kellan! Oh my God. You did not go all green eyes on him. Tell me you didn't do that. Oh no. Oh no." Tears started flowing as Juliet whirled around and ran into the bathroom, slamming the door.

Kellan got up and went to the door, knocking softly. "Juliet, hey, I was just kidding. I didn't do anything. I didn't shock him or even singe him. I just told him he better treat you right."

Through the door he heard more sobs, "I really like him, Kellan, and I don't need you interfering. I am not a child. I'm an adult and I know my own mind.

I also know how to protect myself without some man with delusions of chivalry protecting me."

"I know, Juliet. I know you don't. I'm really sorry. Look. I promise I will never interfere again. You are right. Your life is your own and you can certainly take care of yourself."

There was a long pause and then through the door, "Promise again."

"I promise," he said and the door flew open revealing a smiling Juliet and no tears to be found.

"Excellent! Now, don't we have some quickbooks to do?" she asked, breezing past him and back into the office.

"Holy shit, Juliet, you totally faked me out. You weren't upset at all."

She settled into the desk chair and looked at Kellan. "Oh, I was upset alright. I was super pissed at both you and Dad for being such idiots. But what's the best way to make two overprotective testosterone laden idiots realize they are idiots?" She paused meaningfully, raising her eyebrows at Kellan.

"Um...by pretending to cry and making us feel horrible?"

"For—"

"For treating you like a fragile girl in need of saving?"

Juliet slammed both hands palm down on the table making Kellan jump, "Yes!"

Kellan slumped into the side chair and looked over to her. "You did this to your dad too?"

"Oh, I did worse to him. I anticipated his reaction and also got Mom into the act. She had him convinced I would elope with Glenn, have six kids and never let him see them. Mom's awesome!"

"Bastard didn't even warn me," Kellan mumbled almost to himself.

"What was that?"

"Nothing," he said sullenly, but she had heard him just fine.

"Don't blame Dad. He was threatened with horrible things if he breathed a word of this to you. Now don't look so crestfallen. You know you can always protect me from skin walkers, demons, and such."

"And zombies?" asked Kellan brightening?

Juliet sighed, "And Zombies. I see where this is headed. Go ahead, get it out of your system. Mom and Dad had to, so I knew you would too."

"Juliet, you are totally dating a Korean boy named Glenn. Did you guys meet at *Walker Stalker* or something?"

She stared back at him with a flat expression. "Done?"

"Yeah, I guess."

"That joke wasn't as satisfying as it was in your head, huh?"

"No, not even close," said Kellan sullenly.

Juliet gave him a consoling pat on the arm, "Don't feel too bad Kel, yours was better than Dad's Neegan reference." Kellan winced and Juliet nodded as she continued, "Yeah, too dark Dad, just too dark."

Kellan glanced up meeting the young woman's eyes and gave her his best serious look, "But listen, Juliet, there is just one thing I have to ask you about him. I mean there's one thing I think he really has to change."

Juliet arched an eyebrow, "And that is?"

"Jules? He called you 'Jules.' That shit just has to stop."

She burst out laughing, "I know, right. Maybe you could just zap him a tiny bit anytime you hear him say it? You know, like a mild but corrective shock."

"Really? Can I?" asked Kellan looking hopeful.

"No, now show me the Quickbooks."

Chapter 4

THE GIFT

"So, that would be classified as Cost of Goods sold and not office expense, right? Because it is part of the refurbishment process?"

"Yep," answered Kellan with a grin. "By George, I think she's got it. We should go get lunch. And by 'we,' I mean you should go get us sammiches from Roswell Provisions while I keep an eye on things."

Juliet looked up from the glowing MacBook Pro where the they'd spent the last two hours working though how to use Quickbooks to keep track of the bookshop's finances. "Sandwich? I need a beer."

"It's not even 1pm," replied Kellan, shaking his head.

"Scotch?" she asked with a grin.

Kellan pointed at her. "Nice Mr. Mom reference."

"Especially since I wasn't even born when that one came out."

Kellan frowned, "Well, neither was I."

Juliet narrowed her eyes and pursed her lips the way she did when suspecting Kellan of lying to her.

"Don't give me that face. Mr. Mom came out July 22, 1983. Kellan Thorne came out December 5th, 1983." He gave her a self-satisfied look.

She waved it away, "Whatever. Fine, I'll go get us sandwiches, but you are paying."

"Pfft, have you learned nothing, young padawan," said Kellan tapping the lid of the computer.

"What?" He tapped again, this time pointing to a specific location on the Quickbooks screen. "Ahh," she said, smiling with recognition. "Business lunch, classified as 'meals and entertainment,'" Then slid out of her chair and out the office door.

Kellan called after her. "Don't go crazy, remember it is still real money and now you are spending half of your own." There was no response, but Kellan hadn't heard the front door's bell jingle to indicate Juliet had left that way nor the tell tale slam of the side door. "Juliet? I know you are there. I'm serious don't come back with a $50 lunch tab."

Still nothing.

Grumbling, Kellan heaved himself out of the side office chair and headed to the front of the shop. As he approached the front desk, Kellan saw Juliet standing there, unmoving and he felt the hair on his neck start to stand up. Beyond her, stood a tall, lean, man only a few paces inside the front doorway. He held a large, leather bound, book under one arm and shifted his gaze warily from Juliet to Kellan. As he did so, Juliet took half a step as if her forward momentum had been restored.

"What?" she began, confused. "What just happened?" Looking back to the man, she added, "Who are you and how the heck did you get in here without jingling the bell?"

The man turned back to Juliet and she felt her face flush. She felt her whole body tingle, and suddenly thought it didn't much matter who this man was or how he had entered so silently. She took a step toward him, looking up as he was nearly a foot taller than she. He wore an impeccably tailored blue suit that seemed to almost shimmer as it moved against his athletic frame. He had dark brown hair that cascaded down nearly touching his shoulders. As the light hit it, she could see endless blonde highlights throughout. His skin was the color of heavily creamed coffee and appeared completely flawless. Sharp brows framed almond shaped eyes that were so pale blue as to almost appear white. He had full lips that were parted slightly in a half smile of greeting as he allowed the large book to slide down his arm to rest momentarily in his outstretched hand before deftly setting it on the counter in a motion so fluid as to appear magical.

"Miss Herrick, I presume," the man said reaching out a thinly gloved hand.

"Stop!" growled Kellan as he tried to fill the one word with as much menace as possible. The man paused, lowered his hand and, again, turned to regard Kellan. It his peripheral vision he saw Juliet's posture loosen again as she shook her head, appearing to try and clear of an unwelcome thought. The man cocked his head slightly and smiled more broadly at Kellan.

"And you must be Kellan Thorne. It is my distinct honor to meet you." He clicked his heels slightly and affected a small bow, as Kellan suddenly felt a warmth flow throw him and then twist about like butterflies in his stomach. He started to feel himself leaning forward a smile forming, unbidden, on his face. A distant voice within him nudged, gently at first, and then more urgently demanding his attention. Kellan reached into the emerald river that raged within and called to it. Instantly, it flowed, coursing through him eyes coming alight, glowing their fierce green and the man's image shattered like a mirrored reflection struck with a stone.

The man's entire frame began to pulse with a glowing red aura. His hair lost its sheen. His skin became grey and lifeless and his lips paled from red to the lightest pink with two sharp teeth visible in the slightly parted mouth. Only his eyes remained as they were. Bright and clear and beautiful, appearing almost like small portals into this creature's soul.

"Vampire!" yelled Kellan.

"Oh, shit," cried Juliet, stepping back from the counter as her words misted in the air. The room became cold as Kellan drew the ambient heat from himself and his surrounding forming a blazing sphere that rotated in his right hand.

The man took a step back in alarm, bumping into the front door and causing the bell to chime. "Peace, Sentinel of Order. Peace! I mean you no harm."

"Bullshit!" responded Kellan as he drew back to throw the flaming sphere.

"No!" the vampire yelled. "No! Lamia sent me."

"Bullshit!" yelled Kellan again, but he did not throw.

"I have proof. I have proof. Allow me but a moment to show you. Please. I have risked everything to speak with you. They told me I was foolish to do so.

Micah would have attacked me on the spot, but Lamia said you were different and these are perilous times."

"What proof?" asked Kellan warily.

"A gift from Lamia. From Amy and her children. I will put in here on the counter."

"Slowly. You are right, vampire, I was well trained to snuff your kind on sight."

"I know, but you were also trained to kill demons and yet, Lamia lives." The vampire reached into the suit's breast pocket and slowly withdrew what looked like a pale piece of folded cloth. He gestured and it lifted from his hand to float over the counter where it gently came to rest.

Juliet picked it up and Kellen heard her quick intake of breath. "What is it Juliet?"

"Proof." She said holding it up for Kellan to see. The young Sentinel felt an immediate wave of emotions crash over him as his eyes misted. Delicate stitching covered the cloth with fine threads of many colors used to depict a scene where three children and two adults were gathered about a large tree with violet leaves shaped like pentagrams. Such was the artistry that Kellan immediately recognized Lamia and her three children as well as himself. He dismissed the fire with a sigh but retained a trickle of power to avoid the glamor which he could see coming off the vampire in waves.

"Perhaps it would have been wiser to call ahead. And how do you move things with your mind?" Kellan asked, then thought glumly, *I've never been able to make any form of telekinesis work.*

The vampire lifted his hands in both acquiescence and confusion, "It retrospect, you are correct, it would have undoubtedly been wiser to give you notice. A mistake I shall not make again, I assure you. Forgive me. This is my first encounter with a Sentinel of Order. My name is Ah'Anon and I bear tidings of grave import." He gestured to the book and caught Juliet's eye.

"I'm sure you and Ah'Anon will sort it all out," began Juliet in an almost lilting tone.

"Huh?" asked Kellan as he turned to find Juliet gazing, again, at the vampire, entranced.

"Hey, Amenhotep, knock off the glamor!"

"Ah'Anon," the vampire corrected, "And I'm sorry, it is not within my control. I'm one of the eldest of my kind, Sentinel of Order, and our abilities grow stronger as we grow longer."

Kellan gestured to Juliet and willed a tiny strand of green energy to extend outward. As it intwined itself around her wrist, Juliet gasped slightly and grimaced, then looked chagrined.

Ah'Anon nodded to her and smiled, "Do not be embarrassed, Lady Juliet, my true appearance is a far cry from that which is perceived by mortals."

"Oh, it's not that different," she answered weakly.

"Are you kidding me, Juliet?" exclaimed Kellan. "I mean he was super hot before as in, 'I'm gonna change teams,' kinda hot. Now look at him."

"I know, Kellan," growled Juliet, "I'm very aware of how, *hot*, he was and am trying to be polite. Something you are obviously incapable of being."

"Oh pish posh, Antium here is old as dirt and I'm sure is quite aware of what he really looks like. How old are you?"

"My name is Ah'Anon," said the vampire, annoyance creeping into his voice.

"He know's that, Ah'Anon. This is just one of Kellan's things when he's mildly pissed off. It is pretty juvenile, but is also mostly harmless. Once you point out that he's doing it on purpose, he usually stops because it's not fun anymore."

Kellan frowned. "You know I hate it when you refer to me in the—"

"—Third person," Juliet completed, "Yes, I know. But just because someone is a vampire doesn't mean you need to be a dick."

They both turned back to Ah'Anon who was silently taking in the exchange.

"Oh," he continue. "I was born in the Old Kingdom, during the reign of Djoser which would be—"

"About 4700 years ago 2660 BC," said Kellan slowly, voice filled with awe and then added, "You actually look pretty damn good for 4,700."

Ah'Anon gave a short laugh and nodded to Kellan. "Very gracious of you to say."

"Wait, seriously," said Juliet her mind refusing the information she'd just heard. "You are *that* old? That's amazing! Where you like a Pharaoh of something?"

Ah'Anon chuckled again, "Hardly. I am the bastard child of Djoser's Vizier, Imhotep. However, they are all dust and I remain, so after nearly five millennia my birth status does not seem to matter as much as it once did."

"Yeah, I imagine not," she said absently.

"Um, so, Ah'Anon," began Kellan.

"Yes, Sentinel of Order?"

"You travel all the way here, without notice and risk being obliterated by a somewhat inexperienced Sentinel, putting 4,700 years of existence at risk. Do I have that right?"

"You do," Ah'Anon replied gravely.

"Yeah, well, I take two things from that. First, I don't think you simply forgot to call ahead. I doubt someone gets to become a 4,700 year old anything by forgetting to take precautions around people or things that could destroy them."

"True enough," Ah'Anon allowed.

Kellan nodded and continued, "So, number two. I'm thinking that whatever brought you here must be really fucking important, and," Kellan raised a finger for emphasis, "Is likely going to ruin my whole day."

"Sadly, Kellan Thorne, I fear you are correct on that point as well."

"To the Council of Havilah," said Kellan as he poured straight bourbon in the glass Juliet held toward him.

"The Council of Havilah," she echoed and they clinked glasses then drained the contents in a single swallow. Juliet shuddered a bit and then added, "And you were complaining about beer in the afternoon."

"That was before a five thousand year old bastard vampire wandered into my shop bearing proclamations of doom."

"Our shop."

"Huh? Oh, quite right, Miss Herrick. Before a five thousand year old bastard vampire wandered into *our* shop bearing proclamations of doom."

They both looked at Ah'Anon who sat still as stone in one of the overstuffed chairs located in Beloved Books' central reading nook Only his eyes moved, taking in first Kellan and then Juliet.

"Want one?" asked Kellan.

"I do not drink—alcohol," answered Ah'Anon emphasizing the the pause with a smile.

"Ha! Nice one," laughed Kellan. "You've read Stoker?"

"Of course."

"Hey," interjected Juliet, "Did you meet Dracula?"

"Twice, but he is far different than the accounts would have you believe. I always found him to be—"

Ah'Anon fell silent as the door to the shop rang out to indicate someone entering. No one moved but moments later a sharp voice called out with a thick Scottish accent. "Kellan! Juliet? Where are you? I've brought your damned sandwiches. Why is no one up front?" Her voice grew closer as she wandered deeper into the shop. "I'm not your house maid, Kellan Thorne, and Benjamin at Roswell Provisions says you owe him thirty five dollars for the three sand—"

Shannon broke off as she entered the nook, her eyes locking on Ah'Anon's. "Well, hello there?" she said, her voice lowering and becoming throaty. "Who might you be?"

"Um, Shannon," began Kellan.

"Here." She said absently tossing the bag of sandwiches to Kellan and sliding into a chair next to the vampire. Kellan rummaged through the brown bag and pulled out two sandwiches, Mexican Cokes, and a couple bags of chips. "Turkey and Swiss with extra pickles?"

"Yay!" cried Juliet reaching for it. Kellan placed her Coke and chips on the side table between them along with his own and took a big bite of his chicken salad sandwich.

"Shannon," Kellan tried again around his mouth full of sandwich.

The Scottish woman simply held up her right hand, palm facing him as she leaned against the side of her chair and toward Ah'Anon. Kellan looked at Juliet and they both shrugged, attention returning to their lunch.

"I am Ah'Anon," said the vampire.

"Well now, that sounds exotic and where are you from?"

"Egypt originally, but I spend most of my time in Havilah now, what you call Ethiopia."

"Fascinating," Shannon purred, "Please tell me more."

"Oh for God's sake," exclaimed Kellan. "Anon, Shannon here is from thirteenth century Scotland and unless she's developed a cartographic hobby about which I'm unaware, she's just trying to seduce you with her wily Scottish-Ginger ways." With that Kellan extended another fine tendril of power and as it wrapped around Shannon's wrist, she almost managed to mask her emotions."

Ah'Anon smiled broadly, "She's quite disciplined isn't she. Only micro-expressional changes."

"Yep, she's a pro, my Shannon," said Kellan taking another bite of his sandwich.

"Well, she certainly did better than you and me," defended Juliet.

"I know. I wasn't being sarcastic. She *is* a pro."

Shannon let out a long breath. "What exactly are you?" she asked.

Ah'Anon made to respond but Kellan jumped in, "5,000 year old bastard son to an Egyptian Pharaoh's advisor."

Juliet and Ah'Anon both stared at him. "What? We've already covered all this. I gave her the Cliff's Notes version.

"And you look like that because—"

"I am a vampire, yes." Answered Ah'Anon.

Shannon looked back to Kellan. "We're friends with vampires now are we, sweetie?"

"This one," Kellan said. "So far. And don't sweetie me after you tried to seduce him right in front of me."

"I did not!" yelled Shannon.

"You did," responded all three in unison.

Shannon leaned back in her chair and folded her legs crosswise beneath her. "Well, I don't remember doing so and he clearly had me in thrall."

"Clearly," said Juliet flatly.

"Well, thank you for the support, Juliet Herrick. Remind me to keep secret all your dalliances with a certain Korean boy."

Juliet raised her chin. "Kellan already knows about Glenn. He's fine with it and it wouldn't matter anyway. I am a woman, not some tween with a crush."

"A woman are you now," laughed Shannon. "I guess there was more going on in that store room than even I knew about."

"Stop stop stop," said Kellan holding his hands up. "First, I don't want any stray images in my head and second, I never said I was 'fine,' with anything. I just said I wouldn't light him on fire and put him in hole filled with lye. That's hardly a testimonial, Juliet."

"Excuse me," said Ah'Anon quietly, "I have a great deal more to impart and must gain your support then return to the Council before my protection spell wanes. I do not want to be caught in daylight without it."

"I hadn't even thought about that," said Shannon. "What protection spell? I assume without it you would, what, burst into flames?"

"One of the Council anointed me with an oil that grants protection from the sun, but only for a short duration. Without it, my travel here would have been uncomfortable but, no, I would not burst into flames as you put it. I am far too old for that."

"Magic suntan lotion." said Kellan.

The vampire smiled. "Something like that, if suntan lotion were available in SPF 1,000. Now, please let me continue. The Council of Havilah is currently trying to retrieve the five artifacts of power that have been stolen, but, given our past failures, is seeking your assistance to prevent the remaining two from being obtained by the Cabal."

"SPF 1,000," repeated Juliet with a whistle, "That is a surprisingly modern reference."

Ah'Anon inclined his head, "Those of us who survive the passing of centuries, must embrace each new age." He shrugged, "Those that do not, usually kill themselves or or killed by others."

"Wait!" shouted Shannon. "Back up. I am completely lost here."

"Shannon," responded Kellan, "We've already—"

"No, Kellan, just because you asked me to be sandwich girl, doesn't mean I'm going to try and piece all these parts together like some kind of Disney princess." She looked at Juliet. "Disney princess?" The younger woman nodded in solidarity.

"Well, I'm not sitting through it again, and have to take a piss anyway. You and the vampire have fun." Kellan got up and walked toward the back-office bathroom.

"Sentinel, it would not hurt for you to hear me repeat—"

Kellan waved a hand without turning, "I remember, Anon. Havilah. Eden. A Cabal of evil that wants to destroy the world using artifacts and a Council of Immortals who want to stop them. When you get back to exactly how any of that works, give me a holler."

As Kellan disappeared from view Shannon huffed, "I have to take a piss? Really?"

Juliet shrugged. "Honeymoon's over. He's a man."

"I suppose he is at that," said Shannon. "Well, vampire, start talking."

Ah'Anon turned toward the scotswoman and she continued. "Let's take each in turn shall we: Havilah, Eden, Cabal, Artifacts, and Council."

"Very well," he began, "But let me leave the artifacts until the end, we hadn't discussed them in any detail and Kellan can return to hear that part." Shannon nodded and he continued. "First, Havilah and Eden are, for the most part, the same thing. Havilah is the region in which Eden resides; it lies within what you now call Ethiopia. The garden itself is not far from the sea and comprises about twelve square miles."

"Wait," said Juliet. "I didn't think about this when you talked about it before, but how come I've never read anything about this. I mean, you can't very well hide a giant biblical garden from satellites."

Ah'Anon chuckled softly. "Of course you can. So much in this world is hidden from mortal eyes. If you knew even a fraction of what has been obscured throughout the millennia, it could very well drive you mad."

"Awesome," replied the young woman, "But that really doesn't explain why no one has seen this place, especially since biblical scholars have been crawling over the region since, well, since forever."

"I don't have a scientific explanation for you. I'm sorry. A number of us have explored it off and on over the centuries, but now everyone simply accepts the garden's hidden nature as an act of the Creator."

"Act of God? That's the best you got?" Juliet asked. "Very unsatisfying."

"I agree, but there you have it. I'm confident there is a scientific explanation. God rarely violates his own physical laws. However, as you might imagine, the Creator's understanding and command of those laws far exceeds our own. That said, as best we've figured, there is both a visual cloak attached to the garden as well as a psychological repulser field involved. Oh, and the guards of course. So I suppose it's possible mortals *have* found the garden before and simply been slain by the angel guarding it. I have heard of other places with psychological warding but never a place with so many protections around it. Clearly, someone, doesn't want mortals going in the garden. If not the Creator, who?"

"You keep saying *creator*. You mean God, right? The one who Kellan kind of works for?"

The vampire smiled and shook his head slightly. "Please don't take this as patronizing for it is not my intent, but I could spend decades discussing this with you."

Juliet frowned and opened her mouth to speak, but Ah'Anon raised a hand. "No. There isn't time, but let me say these few things. Ask yourself what makes someone or something a god. I will tell you that there are many creatures that are believed to be, or believe themselves to be, gods. One thing they all agree on, albeit begrudgingly, is that there is only one Creator. As for Kellan working for him. No, the Sentinel of Order does not work for the Creator. The Sentinel of Order works on behalf of creation itself. There is a difference."

"Uh, I think we need to unpack that a bit, don't you Shannon?"

The older woman nodded, "A bit, yes. I'm less interested in gods. Let's start with *repulser field*. What is that?"

"And the garden itself added Juliet. You aren't telling me that this really is the place Adam and Eve hung out eating apples and playing with snakes."

Ah'Anon sighed. "You are referring to the Biblical book of Genesis. Those books are, in many ways, metaphorical, but some components are accurate as well. Did the entire human race grow out from two people named Adam and Eve? Of course not. They couldn't provide a genetic pool large enough to result in such a diaspora of humanity. That said, there is a garden. It is guarded by an angel and we are fairly certain that in the distant past a man and woman named Adam and Eve both lived there."

"Fairly certain, how?" Asked Shannon, dubious.

"The angel told us."

"The guardian angels?" Asked Juliet.

"He isn't a guardian angel," answered the vampire. "He is an angel that guards something. There really is a big difference. But, yes, that angel told us and we couldn't get much more from him because his is, well, he is just not very talkative."

"What is he guarding Eden from?"

Ah'Anon sighed. "This really is beside the the point. I was just trying to give you context not a history lesson on Eden."

Both women just stared at the vampire with flat expressions.

"Very well," he said, "He is guarding it from mortals. None of your kind is allowed within the garden. I suspect, the angel was intended to guard it from anyone entering, however, his instructions may not have been precise and this angel is rather literal."

"Got it, so no mortal humans can get in, just vampires."

"Not just vampires, anything other than mortal humans may enter. vampires, werewolves, demons, djinn, kobolds." He paused, gesturing with one hand. "Really, too many to mention them all. We have a very diverse community. It is largely self-policing and we do not have truly evil residents, perhaps Chaotic Neutral.

Juliet laughed and said, "You really do keep up on things, Ah'Anon." Shannon looked perplexed so the young woman explained. "Chaotic Neutral is a descriptive alignment in Dungeons & Dragons. It basically is a person who does whatever the frack she wants but isn't out to specifically hurt anyone." Juliet turned to Ah'Anon. "And good on you, Mr. 4,000 year old vampire, for getting your geek on and knowing the D&D lingo."

"That is a bit condescending, Juliet," replied Ah'Anon. "I'll have you know that we have a thriving D&D community. As for *knowing the lingo* it was a Council Demon who originally gave Gary Gygax the idea for Dungeons and Dragons, so consider that for a moment."

Shannon sighed, looking confused and disgruntled, but said nothing.

"Oh sorry Shan," said Juliet quickly, "D&D is a game where you pretend to be an adventurer, fighting and exploring. Gary Gygax created it a long time ago, maybe the 70s or something. And I cannot even begin to believe that someone in this Council of Ah'Anon's was the father of the coolest game in the world."

"Sooo," Shannon began drawing out the word, "Dungeons and Dragons, the coolest game in the world, is where you basically pretend to be me?"

Juliet had gotten up, walking behind her chair and looking at one of the book shelves. She turned to Shannon, "Well, when you put it that way it either makes the game sound less cool or you amazingly cool."

"I am amazingly cool," said Shannon dryly

"May I continue?" Asked Ah'Anon but didn't wait for a reply. "The Council of Havilah established itself in the Garden of Eden because it is, quite frankly, the safest place in the world from human interference. Humans can't see it. If a human gets too close to it, they start to feel anxious and tend to turn away. If some stalwart human persists and makes it to the gate, they are confronted by an angel guard who prevents their entry. Finally, if they try to get past that angel, well, let's just say that angel doesn't talk much, but he is quite insistent."

"So you established this Council to defend against this Cabal which we haven't gotten to yet?"

"Not at all," answered Ah'Anon. "The Council predates the Cabal by centuries. I first heard of the Cabal shortly after the fall of Rome, which they facilitated."

Juliet looked excited and twirled around her chair sitting abruptly and leaning in. I love Roman history. How—"

"No. No. No." Cried Ah'Anon, that is completely unrelated to our task here."

Juliet looked crestfallen and slumped back, pouting.

"Perhaps," continued the vampire, "assuming the Cabal doesn't succeed in ending the world, I can offer you a private discussion on Roman history. Fair?"

"I suppose," said Juliet, "it just depends on how likely it is that the world's gonna end."

Shanon unfolded her legs and stretched them over the arm of the chair, "That's our Juliet. She always has her priorities straight. Never mind the world ending. She likes Roman history so give her some." Juliet stuck out her tongue.

"The Council," said Ah'Anon raising his voice to take command of the room again, "was conceived simply as a loose confederation of beings who were widely regarded by humanity as evil. By our very natures we lived outside the natural order of things, but still thought there was a spark of good inside each of us.

"But you are a vampire, right?"

"I am, indeed."

"And you feed on human blood?"

"Sometimes, but only if the host is willing and never enough to harm them. I more routinely drink the blood of animals we keep for such purposes."

"That sounds cruel," chided Juliet.

"Oh?" Said the vampire with a smile. "Just where do you think the turkey and ham on your sandwich came from?"

Juliet opened her mouth to protest, then closed it. "I'll give you that one. I'm not vegan and I guess if we can raise animals to eat you can raise 'em to drink."

Ah'Anon sniffed. "I'm so glad that you are validating my life choices."

Shannon laughed and pointed at Juliet. "Ha!"

"Shut up, highlander."

"In any event," continued Ah'Anon, "after Rome fell we became aware of the Cabal but didn't know much about it. It was small at the time, perhaps less than ten in total, but it was the membership that struck us as dangerous."

"Membership?" Asked Shannon.

"Yes, only two beings were members of the Cabal and those two should never be members of anything together." He paused as both women looked at him without recognition. "Two beings that should never join anything together?" They each shook their heads. "Angels and demons," the vampire exclaimed. "Angels and demons should never work together on anything and yet, they were exclusively part of the Cabal."

"Yeah, that's probably a warning sign," said Juliet. Shannon nodded.

"Indeed," agreed Ah'Anon. "Yet, while we were alarmed by this alliance, we had no insight into what their goals might be. It was impossible to infiltrate because in those days we had no angelic or demonic members within the Council. All we knew was that they seemed destructive and chaotic. We even thought they might have been aligned with the Sentinel of Chaos, but that was proven false."

"Cut to the chase, Ah'Anon," said Juliet. "You clearly know what they are up to now or you wouldn't be here looking for Kellan's help."

"Yes, we have uncovered their end-game as it were. The information we gained was obtained at quite a cost, but it may be the most important thing the Council has ever done because now, at least, we are in a position to resist their plan."

"Which is?" Asked Shannon.

Ah'Anon stared at each woman in turn, "The Cabal is a group of angels and demons who reject the antipathy between God and Satan. They seek to undo it. Undo the original war in heaven."

"Well," began Juliet, "That doesn't sound so bad. Maybe it's time the big guys got along a bit better?"

"You weren't listening. I didn't say that the Cabal sought to bring about an armistice between God and Lucifer. I said that they wanted to undo the original source of their antipathy."

"Which was?" Asked Shannon

"Creation." Answered the vampire. "Creation was the spark that lit the flames of war. The Cabal seeks nothing less than to breach time and undo Creation itself."

"Done! Done! Done!" Came a booming voice causing them all to jump in alarm and then glare at Kellan who grinned at them all.

"You are an ass, Kellan Thorne," yelled Shannon, "and I hope you enjoyed your piss."

Juliet walked back from the front counter as they all heard the door jangle with the departing customer. She grinned broadly at Kellan.

"That was over $1,000 of first additions I just sold, boss. And she's looking for the original *World of Tiers* novellas as well."

Kellan glanced up from the floor where he, Shannon, and Ah'Anon had been sprawled as they poured over the large tome the vampire had been reviewing with them.

"I'm not your boss anymore, Juliet." He saw her expression start to sour and quickly added, "But great job on that sale, seriously. I heard you discussing both the Asimov and the Emerson with her. That's quite the eclectic taste she has. Add to that Farmer's novellas and we may just have a customer for life."

"I know, right?" Said Juliet becoming even more animated as she walked over and sat in one of the chairs. "Do you have any idea where we could get our hands on the original *Tiers* novellas? She already has the bound anthology, which is also out of print."

Kellan had turned his attention back to the illuminated pages before him, but answered, "I might have a few ideas where you could start, assuming these Cabal guys don't end the universe before then."

Juliet sobered, "Uh, yeah. Sorry, I guess my priorities are a bit wacked, again."

Kellan looked up again. "Not at all, Juliet. This is exactly why I wanted you to own the shop with me. You should focus on this. You should assume the world *isn't* going to end. I've got this. You focus on finding *The World of Tiers*. For our newest wealthy patron."

"*We've* got this, Kellan Thorne." Said Shannon. "If you think you are going to head off on an adventure such as this without me, you have another think coming."

"The thought never crossed my mind, you ginger minx," he said and leaned forward to give her a kiss which she accepted for the barest of moments before forcefully pushing him back.

"Well, good, because this seem like it is going to be tremendous fun," she said as Kellan rocked back.

"You certainly have a strange definition for fun, Miss McLeod," said Ah'Anon. "Extremely powerful celestial beings are bent on destroying reality itself and, I might add, have a very real chance of success. As I just pointed out, they have already acquired five of the seven artifacts we think they need."

Shannon simply shrugged, but Juliet asked, "Did I miss something while I was selling those books to Rebecca? How do you know the seven artifacts they need. I thought you didn't even know how they would use them."

Ah'Anon stood and stretched in a very un-vampire like fashion and sighed, "We don't know how they will be used and only know the seven because of an infiltrator who passed along the information before he was discovered and killed."

"Well, you know that they will be used for some kind of temporal event," said Kellan.

"Yes, but that could be almost anything."

"Go over them again," said Shannon. I want to make sure I have them clear in my head.

"Very well, but then I must leave. I have barely enough time to return to Havilah before my protection fails me."

"Wait," said Shannon raising a hand, "before you get back into the artifacts, I have a question about the Gospel itself. You said it was from the Gospel of Judas, right?"

"Yes? And?" Said the vampire.

"Well, I mean it is Judas. Not the most trustworthy of people, right?"

"That, Miss McLeod, is another whole kettle of fish. We could spend a fortnight debating the character of Judas, his actions, and motivations. Suffice it to say that while there is no debate about what he actually did in Gethsemane, there remains much that we do not know about why. What is relevant is that he claims to have acted in defense of creation and outlines how at some future date creation will once again be at risk by the assembly and usage of seven powerful artifacts. It wasn't until three of them went missing that anyone began to take this Gospel seriously. Now that five are gone, there can be no debate that someone believes them to be the key to undoing God's creative act."

"Whatever, Judas was a traitor and I don't trust him," said Shannon as she leaned back against one of the chairs arms crossed.

Ah'Anon was about to respond when Kellan intervened. "Don't waste your breath, Anon. When she has that look on her face and her arms crossed, nothing you can say will make a bit of difference. It'll be like yelling at the wind for messing your hair." She raised an eyebrow at Kellan and he hastily added, "That's not to say she's isn't entirely justified in her opinion, mind you." She smiled at him and winked.

The vampire merely gestured to his book, "May I?" He asked.

"Go ahead," answered Shannon.

"The first item to go missing was the Ring of Gyges and that was almost a year ago. It was stolen from a Council member in France. A vampire who was found immolated but not from sunlight. We suspect angelic interference as they are capable of such things depending on the relative strength of both angel and vampire. The ring belonged to Gyges of Lydia who founded the third Mermnad dynasty of Lydian kings and reigned from about 716 BC to 678 BC. His ring had the ability to make the wearer invisible."

"Like Bilbo's ring," added Kellan helpfully, "but without the whole consuming your soul side effect."

The vampire eyed him, "Yes, like Bilbo's ring. Thank you Sentinel."

Shannon snickered.

"Shut up, you!" grumbled Kellan.

"The second item was Lævateinn a norse sword that had the ability to wield itself once bonded to its owner. It was unclear to us how such bonding occurs since it never had done so once the sword came into our possession nearly five hundred years ago. We suspect that the sword has some base level awareness and chooses its bonded partners, but only does so with mortals. Since it has had no contact with mortals since our acquisition that would explain its inert nature."

"Where was that one kept," asked Juliet.

"Syria."

"Well, that was a shitty place to put it," said Kellan absently. "You know there's been a war there for several years, right?"

Ah'Anon stared at Kellan, "Thank you again. We hadn't noticed," then turned back to Juliet. "We do not partake in mortal wars or conflicts. Both the sword and its guardian were far away from any populated targets, but a drone strike destroyed the facility. When we arrived to examine it, both the guardian and the sword were missing."

"The third item is another sword, this one called Nandaka."

"That one is my favorite," chimed in Kellan as he started to eat from a can of peanuts.

"I want some," said Shannon reaching.

"These are Hubbs, you crazy highlander. Ask nicely."

"Please may I have some peanuts—before I stab you with a knife."

"That's better, babe." He handed the can over after grabbing a fistful, then looked back at the vampire. "Go ahead. Nandaka. The sword of Vishnu, who I totally thought wasn't a real person."

"Vishnu is not a person. He is a god."

"There's only one God, Ah'Anon," said Kellan incredulously.

"As I have already mentioned to your friends, there is only one Creator, young Sentinel. There are many gods who are capable of manipulating creation. Some might call you a god"

Shannon spat, shooting a peanut across the room. "What fool would call him a god?"

"Hey!" Said Kellan, "I could see someone thinking I was kind of godly or at least demi-godly."

"No, Kel. Just, no." Said Juliet shaking her head. "Maybe from a very far distance, but as soon as they actually met you, no."

"You both really suck, you know that?"

The two women shrugged in a fashion that clearly indicated that they had no concern for how Kellan took their comments.

Ah'Anon shook his head slightly in agitation. "Godhood has far less to do with personality and much more to do with the ability to bend or break natural laws. Vishnu can do that rather effectively, not to mention that he is blue with four arms and that makes an impression, I assure you."

"That's a fair point," said Kellan, "What does Vishnu say about the sword being stolen?"

"Vishnu is not happy about it," that much I can tell you for certain. "However, his sword was the first irrefutable evidence we had that the Cabal was behind these thefts. Vishnu told us his palace was attacked by a small force of both angels and demons who clearly were working together. He refused to give us any details around the attack and I suspect that is because it would demonstrate weaknesses in himself, his palace, or both."

Juliet raised her hand, then lowered it, looking sheepish. "Uh, just out of curiosity, where exactly is Vishnu's palace?"

"India of course," said the vampire.

"Ok, where in India. I mean, does it have the repulser thingy that Eden has? Why don't we hear about this palace of the four armed blue god-man?"

Ah'Anon sighed, "As I said before, several times, there are many things about which mortals are unaware. No, what protects Eden is of creation itself. Vishnu's palace is much more simple to understand. It exists in a shadow dimension slightly out of phase with our own."

Kellan stared at the young woman, "Yeah, Juliet, a shadow dimension. That's much easier to grok than a psychological repulser field. Please try to keep up." Kellan deftly caught the empty can of peanuts that she threw at his head. "Hey, you two ate all my peanuts!"

Shannon said, "Please ignore them, Ah'Anon. I'm listening, but am unclear about this shadow dimension."

"It's not really relevant—"

Shannon smiled and raised a hand waving it slightly, "Indulge me—"

Kellan fake whispered, "She just did an Eldon Tyrell, from *Bladerunner*. I taught her that!"

The vampire ground his teeth slightly trying to ignore the Sentinel. "Very well, a shadow dimension is simply this world but," he paused as if trying to find the right words. "Hmm, maybe it's not as easy as I thought. Let me put it this way. You know how radios work?"

Both women shook their head.

"What's a radio," asked Shannon.

"It's how people used to listen to music before iPods," answered Juliet and then added, "But I don't remember actually seeing one. Oh, but XM is a radio, right?"

Kellan snorted but said nothing.

"No, XM is not that kind of radio," said Ah'Anon, "It is digital from a satellite. I'm speaking of original radio. AM and FM."

Shannon and Juliet started back blankly.

"Try WiFi," offered Kellan, "May I?"

"Please," said a clearly exasperated Ah'Anon

"You know how WiFi comes in 2.4 GHz and 5GHz?"

"I love WiFi," said Shannon. "Meghan's told me all about it."

"I know you do," said Kellan with a smile, "So, remember how each of those frequencies can be used by different devices but not all devices can see both?"

"Right," said Juliet, "Like that stupid Samsung phone that could only use the 2.4 GHz"

"Exactly," said Kellan. "If I'm right in where Anon here is going, our buddy Vishnu has his palace living in the equivalent of a 5GHz plane while we are all living in 2.4. Apparently Vishnu is able to do both."

Shannon's and Juliet's eyes grew wide at the implication as they turned to Ah'Anon who nodded. "What Kellan describes is essentially correct."

"So how many of these shadow dimensions are there?" Asked Juliet.

"Countless, I assume," answered the vampire, nonplussed, but I am only aware of a few and each were created by one of the gods. This seems to be an ability they each share. This ability to shift their frequency as it were."

"Gods?" Asked Juliet and Shannon simultaneously

"No," said Ah'Anon sternly. "The only god we are discussing is Vishnu, and I would rather not have even had to discuss him."

"Well that's three of seven. How much more time you got before turning into a pillar of flame."

"Not enough to go through the remaining ones in this much detail. If you have more questions, I suggest you research them yourself."

"No problem; I'm familiar with them anyway," said Kellan. "Tarnhelm, an ancient Teutonic helm that grants either invisibility or polymorph and Fafnir the Icelandic dragon's Golden Coat of Chainmail, supposedly impenetrable to even god-forged weapons. I assume they both disappeared under circumstances similar to the first three."

The vampire nodded.

"Any relevance to Tarnhelm also being invisibility based."

"We think not, likely more the polymorph."

"Ok, got it. And the remaining two artifacts that are still safe."

"I wouldn't describe them as safe, Sentinel. I would simply say they are well guarded. The Spear of Destiny and the Seal of Solomon remain outside the control of the Cabal."

"Wait, Ah'Anon, don't play semantics with me. Do you have those artifacts in hand or not."

The vampire looked down. "We do not, nor have we ever. The Spear of Destiny lies in a vault beneath the Vatican and the Seal of Solomon in a North American crypt where nine ley lines meet to form a mystic prison of sorts."

"Those sound rather, Biblical," said Juliet.

"And dangerous," added Shannon. "What do they do?"

Ah'Anon stood and picked up his book. "They are the two most powerful artifacts we've ever encountered. The seal of Solomon is actually an intricately embossed amulet, but any seal made with its engraving is empowered by the amulet itself. The seals take the form of a pentagram surrounded by a circle, although many would have you believe it a star of David surrounded by the circle. Such is not the case. The wearer of the amulet or possessor of a seal has the power to command demons and djinn once it has been imbued with Chaotic energy released by destroying such a demon. The wearer may do this without limit, but those who hold a seal can only do so until the seal breaks. Such a seal is only as strong as the material on which it is pressed. For example, paper and wax will fail long before wood, which will fail before iron or steel. As for the Spear of Destiny, well, that is the weapon Longinus used to pierce the chest of Jesus of Nazareth while on the cross. I'm not sure whether the spear itself can grant immortality or if it was a one time event, but Longinus would be the best one to ask"

"What?" All three asked in unison as they followed Ah'Anon toward the side door of the shop.

The vampire turned, confused, "Longinus. He is obviously the foremost expert on the Spear."

"Yeah, I think we get that part," began Kellan, "I think what caught us a bit off guard is the fact that a 2,000 year old Roman centurion is wandering around. What's his deal?"

"Well, he wasn't a centurion, just an unlucky soldier, who happened to pull the wrong duty shift and shoved his spear into the mortal incarnation of the Creator. Remember how the story has it that blood and water streamed out?"

"I remember that," said Juliet.

"Well, that's pretty forensically accurate," said Ah'Anon. "The spear pierced the peritoneal sack surrounding the heart which had filled with fluid from the flogging. Because Jesus was already dead, more water than blood came out and some sprayed on Longinus, including some entering his mouth, or so he says. As that occurred, he says he heard a voice that said, 'If you are so content with what you are soldier, so shall you remain until we meet again,'"

"Woah," said Kellan. "That would freak the shit out of me."

Ah'Anon chuckled softly, "A bit more colorful that how Longinus describes his reaction, but essentially the same. Regardless, he's immortal. Very immortal. Probably the most immortal of anyone. He's been burned, beheaded, drowned, and crushed. Nothing sticks. He's really, quite—"

"Fucked," said Shannon sadly.

"In a word," said Ah'Anon, "Yes, especially because he is continually drawn to a life of a soldier as well. I will get a message to him and ask that he speak with you about the spear. I'm sure he will do it, although he will, no-doubt, extract something for the favor."

"Great," said Kellan, "something to look forward to."

The four of them were now standing in the alley and Ah'Anon embraced each in turn. "Farewell Sentinel of Order, Soulborn, and Juliet. Do not fail in your task. I am sure we will meet again soon."

With that, the ancient vampire tilted his head staring up at the late afternoon sky, closed his eyes, and shot skyward.

"Holy shit!" Yelled Kellan. "He can fly? He can use telekinesis? I can't do either one. This is total bullshit. I'm a god and I can't fly."

Shannon punched him on the arm. "You are NOT a god, Kellan Thorne. You are not even a demigod. Trust me on that."

"Juliet," said Juliet sadly.

Shannon and Kellan turned to her questioningly.

The young woman tried to mimic Ah'Anon's clipped accent, "Farewell, *Sentinel of Order*. Farewell, *Soulborn*. Farewell, *Juliet*. Just Juliet. You have to admit, that's a little demoralizing."

The Sentinel and his Soulborn stared at her dumfounded, then all three started laughing.

Chapter 5

OUT OF TIME

The front door to Kellan's home banged open, causing him to jump and spill the bourbon he had been pouring. The young Sentinel closed his eyes and mentally counted to three, then spoke with a slight lilt, "Shannon, babe, can you please, please, for the love of all that is holy, stop kicking that door open. It's nearly two hundred and fifty years old from colonial Pennsylvania." He turned to find her glaring at him, two pizza boxes in her hands.

"And I am almost 750 years old, Kellan Thorne, and hungry. How else am I supposed to get the bloody door open? Bump it with my arse?"

"I'm sure the door would appreciate your lovely bum as much as I do. You also caused me to spill my bourbon."

She set the pizza boxes down on the rough hewn trestle table and walked over to Kellan as he held up the glass. Shannon leaned in and he brought it to her lips and tilted. "Mmmm, that is good. Is that the product of another one of your inappropriate time travels."

"No!" replied Kellan indignantly, "I only did that once and that was over a year ago, for the Scotch."

She snatched the glass from his hand. "Hey, that's mine." Shannon ignored him and moved to a small painting in the corner of the living room. She leaned against the wall, tilted her head toward the painting and said, "What about that?"

"What about that?" Kellan replied innocently.

"Meghan told me."

"God damn it! You two need to stop talking about me."

"That's just not going to happen, sweetie, so you best learn to keep your lies straight. Soooooo?"

"Ok, fine, but it's just one painting. And I paid for it."

"Where did you get it, Kellan?"

"France."

"When in France, Kellan?"

"I don't remember."

Shannon took a long pull from her glass and started to walk back toward Kellan, a wolfish smile spreading across her face. "Oh, Kellan, you remember everything, but let me help you. Was it perhaps 1888 or 1889?"

"Maybe."

"Let's just say it was. And from whom did you get in France, Kellan?" Kellan mumbled something. "What was that?" She asked softly, having crossed the distance between them, and purred into his ear. "I didn't quite catch the name. Here, if you are shy about it, just whisper to me." She pulled back a lock of flaming red hair and tilted her head toward Kellan placing her ear next to his lips. He bit her. "Ow," she cried but Kellan immediately knew he was in trouble as she whipped her head around, eyes blazing bright green.

"Shannon," he said holding up his hands, "Shannon, wait." Moving faster the he could track, she swept her foot outward knocking Kellan's legs from beneath him and causing him to fly backward. He could feel her bending time has her hand caught him behind the head a fraction before it would have crashed to floor. She straddled him, her left hand flat against his chest, pressing him to the floor even as her right hand lanced outward to deftly catch the falling glass of bourbon she had thrown in the air. She leaned down and kissed him for what felt like years, then slowly pulled back and drained the rest of the bourbon. "Who's painting, Kellan, she asked with a smile?"

Kellan sighed with equal parts contentment and resignation, "Van Gogh. I bought if from Van Gogh."

She patted his cheek, swiveled her legs and hopped up. "See, was that so hard. I'm hungry. I brought Fix pizza. Oh, Jacamo says you owe him $200."

"What? $200? How much pizza have you been buying and why does he give you pizza without paying?"

Shannon had opened a box and pulled out a slice. She glanced at Kellan and tossed her hair, "Oh, I have no idea why he might do that, Kellan." Then took a bite.

"You are incorrigible!" The soulborn simply smiled as she leaned her chair back and watched Kellan scramble to his feet.

"Did you at least get me one with sausage?" Kellan watched the green fade from her eyes as she gestured to one of the boxes causing the lid to fly upward revealing a sausage and mushroom pizza. She grinned at him. "How the hell do you do that?" he yelled grabbing a slice for himself.

"What?"

"You know very well, what. That telekinesis. I'm the Sentinel here. You just use stolen power."

"Borrowed."

"Fine, borrowed. But still, I'm the Sentinel."

She patted his hand reassuringly. "You are, sweetie. You are the Sentinel."

"Oh shut up!"

She smiled at him. "I love you."

Kellan narrowed his eyes at her then sighed again, "I love you too, but you drive me fucking nuts!"

"That's what love is, Kellan. It's spending your life with someone you want to kill but not doing so because you'd miss them."

Kellan laughed. "I would miss you."

"I know. Now, what have you decided to do about these Havilah folks?"

Kellan walked over to the the fridge and pulled out an Innis & Gunn beer. He glanced over his shoulder at Shannon questioningly. She nodded and he grabbed a second one, opened both and reseated himself at the table, sliding hers over. "I was going to ask Micah what he thought."

Shannon shivered a little and Kellan knew she didn't like seeing the old Sentinel's avatar, but she nodded in agreement nonetheless. "Let's finish dinner first ok?" she asked.

"Sure thing, Ginge, never interrupt a good meal by summoning your dead master, I always say."

A half hour or so later Kellan walked back into the living room from his home office to find Shannon seated crosslegged in the large leather chair, bare feet pulled beneath her. He smiled at her reassuringly knowing that she always sat that way when she was nervous. He sank into the couch facing her and pulled out the warmly pulsing hexagonal crystal that served as Micah's fetish stone.

"Ready?" he asked.

"No, but go ahead. I'm never ready"

Kellan took a deep breath and he's eyes burst to light as he stared deep into the crystal. "Micah Ben Judah, first Sentinel of Creation, I summon you!" Almost instantly Micah appeared before them and Kellan saw Shannon flinch. He looked just as he had when they both last saw him: tall and strong, his wavy salt and pepper hair and full beard framing a face deeply lined with age. He wore the simple homespun robes that Kellan and Shannon both knew from Micah's time in Glenn Ferry. Kellan was taken aback as he always was, by how lifelike he seemed, but this was just an artificial construct embedded in a crystal that Micah had fashioned to look like the one used by young Kal'El in the Superman movies of Kellan's youth.

"Please state the nature of your medical emergency," the avatar said with a deadpan expression, and Kellan burst out laughing. The avatar smiled and its eyes locked with Kellan's. "I figured you would like that one," it said.

"That was Awesome!" cried Kellan as he glanced over to Shannon who stared back blankly. "Oh, Shannon, see there was this hologram doctor in Star Trek Voyager and I told Micah about it when we were in the Workroom. Anyway, whenever the hologram doctor appeared he always said the same thing." Kellan paused and pointed to Micah.

"Please state the nature of your medical emergency," said the avatar again.

"See," said Kellan, "Isn't that awesome!"

Shannon looked unimpressed. "That's not what it said the last time you summoned it."

"No, he says something different each time. It's like an Easter egg from Micah. Do the one you did last time. That was great too."

The avatar vanished and immediately reappeared. Micah stared at Kellan with heavy lidded eyes and said "All I need are some tasty waves, a cool buzz and I'm fine."

"Spicoli!" Yelled Kellan at the avatar which smiled as his countenance returned to its normal state.

Shannon just shook her head. "How many of those sayings do you have in there," she asked the avatar.

It turned to her but she would not meet its gaze. "Micah has embedded 624 unique greetings for Kellan, each designed to lift his spirits and remind him of their time together."

"Something to look forward to," said Kellan, rubbing his hands together. "Now, Micah, I have some questions. A vampire came into the book shop today."

"That is not a question."

"I know. I was getting to the question."

"Did you destroy it?"

"What?"

"The vampire. Did you destroy it?"

"No, he was quite nice and polite. I don't destroy people who are quite nice and polite."

"He is not a person. He is a vampire. You should destroy him."

"Stop." The avatar normally performed micro-moments that gave the illusion of life. It would occasionally shift its apparent weight from foot to foot or scratch its beard and Kellan had even seen it yawn a few times. Now, it stood perfectly motionless, appearing all the world like a full color statue.

Shannon shook her head. "That thing creeps me out."

Kellan sighed, "Creeps you out, huh? You've been spending too much time with Juliet. You are starting to sound like a GenZed'er." He turned back to the avatar. "Resume." The avatar locked eyes with Kellan and smiled. "Now focus, Micah. I don't want lectures on why I need to destroy vampires. I told you that before."

"No, you told me you didn't want lectures on why you needed to destroy demons."

"Same thing."

"No, demons are—"

"Stop."

Shannon looked over at Kellan. "Do you really think this thing is worth it?"

"It's not a thing, it's Micah. Well, kind of, and we're still getting the hang of each other. He is getting better."

She sniffed and mumbled something barely intelligible, "...nothing like Micah."

"Resume. Micah, do not lecture me on things I should kill. vampires, djinn, demons, etc. Ok?"

"Ok."

"Now, this vampire was named Ah'Anon and said he was from someplace called Havilah. Do you have any information on that him or that?"

The avatar furrowed its brow and rubbed its chin with one hand as it appeared to consider the question. "Only rumor, Kellan, no direct information or interaction. Would you like to hear about rumors and innuendo?"

"Yes."

"The Council of Havilah is a loose confederation of unnatural creatures who appear to have benign intent. Few members have ever been involved in acts normally associated with their species. No exsanguination, possession, infection with lycanthropic virus, etc. It is really quite strange. What few examples there were of members committing such acts have resulted in the perpetrators being executed by the Council itself. Micah suspected this to be subterfuge of some kind, but never uncovered evidence to support his suspicion. "

"What about Ah'Anon?" Asked Kellan.

"Micah never met him. However, about two hundred years ago, he did receive a letter from the vampire asking to meet."

"Really?" said Kellan raising his eyebrows and glancing over to Shannon. "See. He's very helpful." She simply frowned and stood up, heading back toward the kitchen to get another beer from the fridge.

"So, what happened at the meeting?"

The avatar looked surprised. "There was no meeting, Kellan. Micah did not meet with vampires. He destroyed vampires."

Kellan groaned. "Fine, what did the letter say."

"I can only impart information that Micah imparted to me. He did not provide the full text of the letter, likely because he didn't recall it."

"Whatever, just give me the highlights."

"Very well. Ah'Anon believed there was a group forming with the intent to destroy creation by shattering a foundational pillar."

"What is a foundational pillar?"

"The vampire did not include that information in the letter."

Kellan sighed deeply, "Which is why it's always good to meet people."

The avatar cocked its head slightly. "Vampires are not people. They are sentient human corpses animated by the fragmented spiritual essence of—"

Kellan interrupted. "Micah, what are examples of foundational pillars?"

"Time, Matter, Energy Conservation, and Light-speed."

Kellan heard the pop, hiss, click, of Shannon's beer opening and the cap being caught by the a magnet attached to the opener, but didn't spare her a glance. He leaned forward.

"Now, that's interesting," he said to the avatar. "How do you even know about those things? Micah couldn't rip time and I doubt he had any concept of the theory of relativity."

"Raphael joined Micah briefly when this avatar was being created. Micah thought you might have need of this information and knew his understanding was lacking."

"Hmmm, well, I've already mucked around with Time and Matter without destroying all of creation."

The avatar laughed and it seemed so natural and lifelike that Kellan was taken aback. "Creation is not so fragile as to be undone by a young, half-trained, Sentinel bumping into principles he barely understands."

Kellan narrowed his eyes. "Hey, that sounds a lot more like Raphael or Michael than you."

The avatar smirked, "You caught me. But to your underlying question, the foundational pillars are quite resilient. It would take specific intent, incredible power, and artifacts of focus to even begin to crack, let alone, shatter a foundational pillar."

"Artifacts?" Asked Shannon from behind Kellan, as he felt her fingers begin to comb through his hair in an absently intimate way. "Artifacts like the Spear of Destiny or Seal of Solomon?"

"Yes, exactly like that," said the avatar, its gaze shifting to Shannon. It paused, staring at her then seemed to shimmer, judder, and shake, stabilizing a moment later.

"What's it doing? Is it broken?" Asked Shannon.

"No," Kellan began glancing back at Shannon, "He does that sometimes when the conversation takes an unexpected turn. Give him a second." The young Sentinel turned fully around. "Shannon, your nose is bleeding again."

She reached up, fingers coming back stained bright red and she tasted blood as she felt it trickle down to the corner of her mouth.

The avatar's eyes focused on Shannon and it looked concerned. "Shannon McLeod, how long have you been outside your native timeline?"

Kellan felt his stomach twist as he pulled a tissue from the small box that was sitting on the end-table and handed it to Shannon. She dabbed her nose in annoyance. "My native time-what?"

"She's been absent from the Glenn Ferry timeline for about a year and a half," said Kellan anxiously.

The avatars face registered alarm. "Kellan, she must return home immediately!"

"Home?" Said Shannon angrily, "I am home, you stupid doll. *This* is my home. Tell him Kellan. Tell him this is my home."

Kellan looked into her pale brown eyes, reached up and she grabbed hold of his offered hand. He knew that look. She was scared to the point of anger. He pulled her hand leading her around the couch as he stood to hug her. "It'll be ok Shannon. We'll figure this out."

"No Kellan, it will not be ok," said the avatar. "If she does not return to her native timeline immediately, she will die."

The young Sentinel felt her tense in his embrace and begin to tremble. He pulled back and lifted her chin up with a finger, placing a soft kiss on her lips. Very few things scared Shannon McLeod and this was one of them. He locked his gaze with hers while holding up a hand, index finger extended toward the avatar. "Shannon. I tell you three times. It will be ok. We will figure this out."

She barked a frantic half laugh. "Ok, my Kvothe. I tell *you* three times. We damn well better figure it out. I told you that I didn't give my heart easily and you accepted it."

"I did and I do, Shannon," then helping her sit back down he turned his attention back to the avatar which appeared to be anxiously shifting its weight back and forth. "Explain."

"Time is a foundational principle of creation. It is linear. Mortals exist within creation, their souls tethered to the moment of conception. To travel through time is to extend that tether into the future beyond what is natural or, worse, into the past before the soul existed. Creation is self correcting. That anomaly cannot exist. She—cannot exist."

"Why the hell didn't you tell us,"yelled Shannon.

"Easy Shannon," Kellan said, "This sounds like more Raphael insights than Micah." He looked back to the avatar.

"Explain the limits."

The avatar shimmered again, then nodded. "A typical mortal can travel backward or forward in time without danger so long as he or she traverses no more distance than the duration of their natural life. In such circumstances, the tether is not stretched. If one travels beyond what would have been the beginning or end of their natural life, the length of time they may remain in the future without repercussions is directly related to the distance beyond the relative point of birth or death they have traversed.

"But, I was born in 1261 and it's 2017," said Shannon in a small voice.

"Yes, and because you traversed some 750 years, were you other than Micah's soulborn your spiritual tether to creation would have snapped immediately as you passed into this timeline, causing your death. Sentinel souls have been untethered to both fixed and relativistic points in creation which enables them to traverse time without ramification. You have a fragment of that power within you which has sustained you to this point, but your tether is fraying and could break at any moment.

"The nose bleeds," said Kellan in alarm. "Those have been going on for how long, Shannon?"

"A couple weeks I think?"

"Micah," yelled Kellan, "How long does she have? What do we do?"

"Physical symptoms are the last stage of a temporal cascade, Kellan. If Shannon has been experiencing this for weeks, I am surprised she is still alive right now. She must return to Glenn Ferry immediately."

Kellan leaped to his feet eyes ablaze and turned to Shannon who stared at him face pale as she shuddered and coughed, spraying him with blood. She teetered, then slumped into Kellan, his left arm encircling her waist even as he whipped out his right hand tearing open a portal in both time and space. The oval rotated into view and he jumped though without a second thought, tripped and fell backward onto lush grass with Shannon landing motionless on top of him.

Kellan rolled Shannon's still form off him and on to her back. She wasn't breathing and her face appeared ashen, drained of all color. He whipped his head around, quickly taking in the surroundings, spied a large boulder by the nearby stream and mentally checked off one of the many worries now cascading through his mind.

The portal remained opened and Kellan felt the power rushing out from him in a torrent. He leaped back through, snatched up the fetish stone and tossed it though the portal to land next to Shannon. "Go there!" he yelled at the avatar and raced toward his bedroom without a backward glance to confirm it had obeyed. "Where the fuck is it?" he screamed to the open air as the young Sentinel frantically searched his closet. Then he saw it, a rustic leather backpack, perched in the back corner of a top shelf in the closet. He grabbed it while growling to himself that once he got Shannon alive and kicking, he was going to kill her for moving his bug-out bag.

Scant moments later Kellan was kneeling next to her trying to concentrate through the wooziness caused by keeping his temporal portal open so long. He had nearly exhausted his entire power reserve in a span of minutes and serving as the conduit for so much energy had taken its toll. He tried a calming breath and took stock of the situation as he pressed two fingers to Shannon's neck.

No pulse. No breath. No wound. This was bad.

He glanced at the avatar which was staring down calmly but with concern on its aged face. "How long since she collapsed, Micah?" The avatar shimmered and responded.

"Three minutes, forty-five seconds."

Kellan's mind clicked through medical facts and, as he often experienced in stressful situations, he heard a calm, dispassionate inner voice, that he had come to affectionately call, Vulcan-Kellan, *Anoxic brain damage can occur after as little as four minutes. Begin immediate CPR.*

Kellan placed the heel of his left hand in the center of Shannon's chest with his right hand over the other and compressed her chest quickly as Vulcan-Kellan counted to thirty in his head.

Breathe

Kellan tilted her head back, brushing locks of fiery red hair from her face and sealed his lips to hers while pinching her nose. He gave a long breath and felt her chest rise.

That is a good sign. One more now.

Kellan leaned back and touched her neck again. Still nothing. He gave her another 30 compressions and two breaths.

"Damn it, Shannon, this is not cool. Why the hell didn't you tell me about those stupid nose bleeds!"

Kellan reached into his bag and quickly withdrew an adrenaline needle, preparing to inject her heart as a drastic step.

Adrenaline shots, while effective at restoring heart function, result in brain damage 75% of the time as compared to defibrillation.

Kellan paused, unsure. Then yelled in frustration, "I don't have a fucking defibrillator, you stupid stupid Vulcan."

It is a shame no-one present has the ability to harness natural energies and channel them into charged electron pulses, like lightning.

Kellan's eyes widen as the realization dawned on him and he cursed himself a fool. His eyes blazed to life and he opened himself to the world around him. He bent time, slowing it as his mind drank in all the available information. Ever since Kellan's near disastrous attempt to channel his own body heat he had practiced gathering environmental sources when possible. The year of endless practice paid off as he looked around seeing countless eddies of heat rising from warmed stone and bio-electricity from plants and animals. Photonic energy played about him in waves even as he could feel bands of charged electrons dancing in clouds above. He focused on the clouds and plants and, with the intention firmly fixed in his mind, willed the forces to him.

The air warped moving inward toward him and grass withered. Above him, a dark cloud split apart and vanished as unseen energies flowed into the Sentinel and bright runes ran down his arms. He opened his eyes, allowing time to snap back and quickly ripped open Shannon's shirt exposing her bare chest. Kellan focused his mind on both hands. About them played tiny sparking lighting bolts that sent tingles up his arm.

Position your left hand on her right chest by the collar bone and your right hand on her side just below the left breast. Clear!

Kellan lowered his hands and Shannon's whole body arched and settled back. He willed the electrical energy away from his right hand and checked for a pulse. Nothing.

Again!

Kellan lowered his hands and Shannon bucked wildly her head flying to one side. Still no pulse.

"No, no, no!" yelled Kellan.

She is Soulborn, Kellan Thorne. Her body is accustomed to channeling your energies as if they were her own. Now is not the time for half measures.

Kellan reached upward, eyes blazing, and pulled bands of energy to himself. More grass withered, several birds fell from the sky, and an angry thunderhead formed only to have its energy released not as lightning, but as fuel for the near frantic Sentinel below.

Kellan slammed his hands back down on Shannon weaving ribbons of blue electricity with the green of his own power and forced them into her body. It bucked so violently that Kellan feared her back would break, but has he reached down, he could feel a slow, but steady pulse in her neck. He watched dumbly as tears dripped onto her bare chest unaware he'd been crying. Kellan rocked back with his legs folded beneath him and gave a ragged sigh.

She is not breathing.

"What!"

You have restarted her heart, but spontaneous breathing has not resumed.

Kellan quickly leaned forward again sealing her nose and give two quick breaths. He paused a moment, then leaned down again, but as the breath left him, he felt a hand on the back of his head, pulling him toward her. He felt her mouth move beneath his and the softest nip at his lower lip.

Kellan pulled back, tears flowing down his face and looked at her.

She smiled up at him and said in a faint voice, "Hello Sweetie…"

Chapter 6

A RETURN TO GLENN FERRY

S hannon leaned against the leather backpack drinking from a pouch labeled *Balanced Electrolyte Hydration Drink.*

"This tastes horrible," said Shannon with a grimace.

Kellan sat half sprawled on the grass, leaning on one arm while he kept running the other through his hair. "Shut up. Drink it."

"Why, what is it good for?"

"It's good for dead people. Drink it!"

"I am not dead, Kellan Thorne."

"You were dead for five minutes and twenty-nine seconds," said the avatar.

Shannon glared at him. "No one asked you!"

Kellan retrieved the fetish stone from the grass, concentrated on it and said, "Release." The avatar vanished without a word.

"Thank you," said Shannon. "I really don't like having that around unless we have to."

"Oh don't thank me highlander. I just didn't want even the avatar of my old master seeing me beat you senseless for being so stupid and scaring the living shit out of me."

Shannon peered over her pouch, brown eyes locking with Kellan's. He stared back at her, suddenly wary.

"What are you doing?"

"Nothing," she said innocently as she set the pouch aside.

"No, you are doing something. I know you Shannon McLeod and your are definitely doing some—"

She stretched like a cat and her torn shirt, which Kellan had folded over to cover her, fell away exposing her breasts. "Oops," she said following his gaze. "Seems I'm just falling out all over. Could you come help me. Please, Mr. Sentinel."

Kellan narrowed his eyes. "No way, missy. That is not gonna work with me. You were reckless and stupid. You should have told me about the nose bleeds."

"Oh, I know and I'm sorry. I should have told you about the headaches and blurry vision as well, but I'm not the kind of lass that complains."

"Headaches? Burry—what? God damn it, Shannon. Now I'm really really pissed."

By this point Shannon had nearly reached him, slowly crawling on hands and knees. "Yes," she said, reaching up to cup his face with both hands, "Yes, I can see you are." She pulled him in for a kiss and he resisted, but her grip was insistent and he melted into it.

Finally, she broke the kiss and pulled back. "Still angry with me."

"Yes," he said, but there was no fire behind the word.

"You aren't truly angry, you know?"

Kellan smirked, "Really? I can tell you with one hundred percent certainty that I am."

"Well maybe you are mad, but behind the anger is fear. You were just scared and that's what made you mad. So, it's the scared part you should pay attention to."

"What are you talking about, Shannon," asked Kellan becoming frustrated. "It's a distinction without a difference." He stood up and walked to the backpack, absently picking up some items that were scattered on the ground.

"No, it is a very important distinction," she said, standing to join him. "Kellan." He turned to her. "You love me." It wasn't a question.

"Of course I love you."

"Well, I love you, too. I have since we first met." She looked around and pointed to the boulder. "Right there."

"Great, so we've established that we love each other, which I'll stipulate is awesome, but also irrelevant to whatever the hell you are going on about right now."

"It's not, you stupid, stupid man."

Kellan frowned again, and crossed his arms. "Ok, you brilliant, brilliant woman. Why don't you educate me."

She smiled. "If you insist, my love. So, I was dead for a couple minutes, right"

"No, you were dead for almost six minutes." Kellan corrected.

"Fine, six minutes. And how did that make you feel?"

"How did it make me feel?" he yelled, "It made me feel completely panicked, freaked out, and my stomach wanted to leap out my mouth."

Shannon smiled sadly at him, leaned over and gave him a soft, quick, kiss. "And that, my dearest Kellan, is how I feel every time you battle darkness. That feeling which you never appreciate because you are so damnably flippant about everything. You risk your life and I understand. You have accepted the Sentinel's mantel and that was your choice to make. I am even glad you made it because had you not, we never would have met. But," she held up a finger, "You are casually stupid about your life because you never consider those of us who love you with the same fire you do us. Maybe next time, you'll think about me, about Meghan, about Juliet and even your idiot friend James who has no idea who you really are."

Kellan stood dumbfounded and then lowered his head. "Wow, that was quite the torrent. Tried and convicted in the blink of an eye."

She arched an eyebrow, "Tell me I'm wrong."

He stared at her for a long moment. "I can't tell you that, because you are right. I have been cavalier with the feelings of those who love me most, and really have no excuse."

Shannon reached out taking his hand in hers. "Sure you do, it's just not a good excuse. You act as you do because to do otherwise would make it real for you. The danger. The risk of death. I understand that, Kellan. I'm the soulborn after all. I exist so that I can understand you and you me. I had years to learn how to live this life before you and I met again as adults. I had a family who loved me and responsibilities as the soulborn that I couldn't fulfill if I didn't take risks. I had to learn to take the risks I needed to and avoid others. I had to learn to put that fear in a box when I needed to but never to ignore it. Fear will keep you alive, my love and I need you alive."

Kellan just stared at her as his anger faded to admiration. "When did you get so smart, highlander?"

She smiled. "I am a woman, Kellan Thorne. We are born smart. You are a man so you are born stupid. It's just the way of things."

He laughed and pulled her in to a deep hug, then leaned back eyebrows knitted, "You aren't going to try and tell me that you planned all this just to teach me a lesson are you?"

It was Shannon's turn to laugh. "No, I am neither that smart nor that cruel. My only excuse is that given my close proximity to you, some of your stupid may have worn off." She gave him an impish grin, released his hand and started walking up the hill away from the river.

Kellan watched as she turned to look at him over her shoulder, sunlight glinting off her loose red ringlets as she tossed her head. "What year is this? Is my house even up there?"

"Wow, the place looks a whole lot better than it did the last time I was here," said Kellan as he walked up beside Shannon where she stood several feet in front of a rustic but well constructed cottage.

She looked at him. "No, the last time you were here you helped Dad, the boys, and me rebuild it."

Kellan stared at her uncomprehendingly. She sighed.

"Future you, Kel."

"Oh, yeah. I keep forgetting about future me. Future me is pretty awesome." He paused a moment, questioningly, "When was future me here again?"

"The year Glenn Ferry was annexed, around 1280, about five years after we met the first time with Micah."

Kellan rubbed his temples feeling like he was developing a headache. "But, wait, you were around 19 in 1280 and you told Meghan we didn't," he paused gesturing randomly with his hands, *you know*, until you were 25."

Shannon laughed. "Yes, Kellan Thorne, you remember correctly, as you always do. We didn't *you know* until then because I got tired of waiting for you to try and *you know*, so took matters into my own hands." She lifted her chin slightly and stared at Kellan. "I'll tell you this for nothing, you certainly didn't object when I tripped you into my bed."

Kellan felt a fierce blush rise up his neck and looked away from her as she continued. "Anyway, it's best you keep these things straight in that clockwork brain of yours. Come inside, I'll make us some tea and explain this once and for all because you aren't going to find a nice neat timeline chart of our lives on The Google."

Kellan snickered as she opened the door. Shannon turned back mouth set in a line, "What?"

"The Google. It's just Google."

"Shut it, mister and come inside."

Kellan did.

A few minutes later, Shannon, handed Kellan a mug steaming with warm tea. He smiled at her. "Thank you, ma'am."

She gestured to the crackling fire over which simmered a pot of water. "Well, thank you, sir, for going all sparkly green eyes and making the fire. What do you think of the place."

Kellan let his gaze wash again over the small cottage. "It looks very much like I remember, but there are some differences too. Everything seems a bit better put together and it certainly is a whole lot cleaner than it was before—" he paused.

"Before you were seduced by a demon and burned it down?" asked Shannon with a wry smile.

Kellan held up a finger. "Almost seduced. Almost is very important here."

She waved him off and settled herself in one of the chairs by the kitchen table as Kellan leaned against the wall taking an exploratory sip of his tea.

"Well, much of the stonework from the original cottage remained after the fire, so we just rebuilt around it. You were very helpful. Saved us days by moving timber for us and doing all manner of Sentinel'y things."

"Wait, what? Who knows about me here?"

"Hmm, just Papa, Donal and Liam."

"Jesus, that's enough. What was I thinking?"

"Will you think," corrected Shannon.

"Huh? Oh, yeah, what will I think? Hold on. If that's future me, maybe I let them see me do those things because you told me now that I would."

Shannon just grinned at Kellan knowingly. "I know you hate time travel, sweetie, but it really is best to not worry about the paradox. They work themselves out." She paused thoughtfully and added, "for the most part."

Kellan plopped down into a chair facing Shannon.

"You're angry," she said.

"No, I'm not angry."

"Yes, you are."

"Ok, I am angry. I'm the Sentinel here and I feel like I'm just bumbling around being schooled by my sidekick."

Shannon took a deep, calming breath. "I promised future you I wouldn't get mad when you said that, and I'm trying, but Kellan, I am *not* your sidekick. I am many things. I am a woman. I am your lover. I am your friend. I am your tether to your humanity. One thing I am not, have never been, will never be, is your sidekick." She sighed then said softly, "That came out better than I expected."

Kellan stared at her. "So future me called you my sidekick before?" She nodded. "I'm guessing it didn't go so well?"

She shook her head. "Once you explained what a sidekick was? No, Kellan, it did not go well. However, it did move our relationship along in a quite enjoyable way once the fighting was over." She smiled at him wolfishly and he felt the heat rising again as she added, in a throaty voice, "I *you knowed* you the first time that very night and it was spectacular. I probably shouldn't have told you, but now that I think of it, you looked oddly happy when I started yelling at you, so you must have known how things would end up."

"Ug," Kellan said, "This makes my head hurt, can we please stop talking about future me."

"Timey Wimey. Wibbly Wobbly." Shannon said, tapping her mug to the table. "More tea?"

"Sure, so why did I let your dad and the boys know about me?"

Shannon turned from the kettle, glancing over her shoulder for a moment, "Oh, they saw you levitating a beam and moving rocks while your eyes were doing their sparkles. They thought you were a witch." She sighed. "That wasn't fun to straighten out. I'll tell you that for nothing."

Kellan leaned forward, "I was moving things? With my power?"

She looked back at him, brows furrowed with confusion and then frowned, shaking her head, "Yes, Kellan, you figure out teleki-whatsis at some point between now and when you go back."

"Telekinesis," Kellan corrected.

"Whatever."

"Did I fly too?"

"No, Kellan Thorne, you did not fly and I am done talking about your future self."

Kellan banged the table, grumbling, "That stupid vampire still has it over me." He felt her eyes on him and added with a grumble, "Fine, explain the rest of the timeline."

"There isn't much more to explain. As I've said, 1280 we rebuilt the cottage, and you returned many times between then and when I traveled to Atlanta."

"Which was when, for you?"

Shannon thought a moment, "That would have been around 1288 or 1289. I really don't pay much attention."

Kellan shook his head in confusion, "But when is now?"

Shannon raised her hands, "Why ask me? You brought us here. I thought you had to fix a time and location in your mind to open the portal.

"I do," said Kellan, frustrated, "So I must have, but you were kind of dead at the time so I wasn't completely in my right mind. It's all a jumble. I just wanted to make sure I got you back somewhere in your timeline to keep the tether from completely snapping."

Shannon leaned over the table and gave Kellan a soft kiss. "Thank you for that," then she stood and walked around the cottage examining things. "Well," she began. "We know it is some time after 1280 because the cottage is here and it's before 1288."

"How do we know that?" Kellan asked.

"Because something is missing that should be here if it is after 1288."

"What's that?"

Shannon smiled and placed a finger to her lips, "Spoilers..."

"Oh, for god's sake," said Kellan with a laugh, "I should never have told you about River Song."

"You haven't told me," Shannon said innocently then showed her teeth, "but you will."

Kellan awoke to the sounds of birds and gentle rain pattering against the thatched roof. He reached over to the other side of the bed but found nothing. Sitting up, Kellan glanced at his Apple Watch noting with some interest that it still displayed time: 6:20 am.

"Shannon..." he called into the early morning gloom. No response.

Kellan rolled out of the small bed, having fallen asleep in his clothes after he and Shannon decided to just 'rest their eyes' for a few minutes the evening before. Apparently the day's events had gotten the better of both of them since sleep came quickly and lasted until the morning, or had for Kellan at least.

He stumbled into the small kitchen area and found a plate with some salted meat and cheese sitting on the table with a Post-it note stuck beside it. Kellan chuckled as he tugged on the small piece of yellow paper feeling the adhesive release. Shannon loved many aspects of the 21 century, especially paper. Kellan remembered taking her to an Office Depot and how she marveled at the wealth of paper available for anyone to buy. Post-it notes where her favorite and it didn't surprise Kellan a bit that she might have a pad or two secreted away in some pocket. He glanced at her wavy writing and nodded as he grabbed a bite of cheese. Only two words were written on the paper: My Rock.

Kellan continued to gnaw on the bit of salted meat as he strode down the hill toward the stream. The morning mist hadn't even begun to lift and the air was sharp and cool. He paused as the grass changed from its verdant green to a dull brown. Kellan kicked at the ground with his foot and lifted his eyes to take in the large expanse of dead grass that spread outward from where he stood all the way to the stream. There he saw the large boulder on which sat Shannon, eyes closed, legs folded crosswise with her arms resting on knees.

The young Sentinel felt his heart quicken at the sight of her. "Stupid," he whispered aloud, "You are acting like a schoolboy with his first crush." Kellan cocked his head, still staring at her distant form, then decided he really didn't care how he was acting. Just the sight of her could make his stomach do flip flops and that was after a year together. He counted himself lucky, especially given the trauma of the day before.

Moments later he stood before her still form, staring up at her closed eyes then glanced away wondering what he should do next. He remembered the first time he'd seen her there, more girl than woman, barely into her teen years. How strange he found her, and then her completely unexpected declaration of love as he left her to return to Atlanta that first time. He shook his head clearing away the revelry.

"I remember that too," she said and he looked up to meet her now open eyes. "Truth be told, I replayed the moment a hundred times after you left, wondering why I said what I did. I didn't know what love was. I just knew it to be true. I do know now though."

Kellan just nodded. He knew too.

Shannon unfolded her legs and slid off her rock and into Kellan's arms, hugging him tightly then tilted up her face to accept his kiss.

"We're pretty well fucked, aren't we?" she said and Kellan barked a laugh at her unexpected outburst.

"Probably," he responded, "but in what way do you mean?"

"Time, stupid. I'm stuck in this timeline. I can travel, what, fifty or sixty years and then my soul starts to unravel."

Kellan leaned against the rock and nudged her with his shoulder, "We don't know that. All we know is that you can't travel 750 years into the future and spend eighteen months there."

She nodded, then said, "But I could be stuck here. We don't know whether my tether to this time has been fully restored or if it's still weak. We really don't know anything."

"I'll find out, Shannon. I will."

She nodded again, but didn't seem convinced. "You're leaving aren't you?"

Kellan sighed. "I don't want to. God knows I don't want to, but, I need to find this Council of Havilah and figure out what the hell is going on. When I first woke up, I decided I'd just stay here until we figured out your soul-tether problem and travel back to arrive the same time we left."

"So why don't you," she asked then answered her own question. "Fixed points in time?"

"Yeah. If this Cabal is planning to muck with time to the point where it unravels all of creation, you can pretty much bet they are doing it at a fixed point or in doing so they create one. I don't know which, but either way—"

"You have to leave," she answered for him.

"I have to leave," he repeated.

She laughed mirthlessly, "This sure does seem familiar. Same place. Same us. You leaving me."

"Sucks," Kellan said.

"When will you be back?"

The young Sentinel brightened, "Soon Shannon. Very soon. I'm planning to bring one of the artifacts to you for safe keeping."

She arched an eyebrow questioningly and Kellan continued. "Yeah, this Cabal is looking for the Spear and the Seal, but they wouldn't think to look here."

"Makes sense." She said.

"Yep. So I'm just going to head back, go to Havilah, find the Seal and Spear, then bring the Spear here, no problem."

"Well, I can't stay here, Kellan."

"Shannon, you know I'd want you to come back, but not if it means—"

"No, Kellan. I know I can't go with you, but I can't stay here either. It's somewhere before 1289."

"So?"

Shannons sighed, "You really have to get a handle on this time traveling. Now think. Why can't I stay here?"

Kellan looked blankly and shrugged. Shannon continued. "Who lives in the cottage up there?"

"You do?" Kellan asked slowly and his eyes grew wide, "You do."

She smiled. "Now, I don't ever remember meeting myself in my house so I'm pretty sure that's because you portal me to 1289 so my past and future selves don't bump into each other."

"You are very smart," Kellan said bumping her again with his shoulder.

"Yes, fortunately for both of us. Now, no long goodbyes my time challenged Sentinel. You will be collecting me very soon, right?"

"Promise." Kellan said moving his finger across his chest.

"Good, then portal me to 1289 and give me a kiss, but make it a good one."

Kellan did just that. Moments later he found himself standing beside Shannon's rock feeling more alone than ever he had before.

Chapter 7

EDEN

K ellan stepped out of the portal and immediately looked around. He sighed in relief. No one around. The young Sentinel recalled Micah explaining how, unless specifically directed otherwise, portals tended to open as close to the desired destination as possible but in a place that was also the most discrete available. He had traveled by portal hundreds of times at this point, but hadn't completely gotten over the fear of stepping into a throng of people.

Pulling his iPhone from the back pocket of his jeans, Kellan quickly tapped the Messages icon and scrolled down. He chuckled as he reread the conversation from several hours earlier, comprised of a dozen blue and gray bubbles.

Unknown sender:	Travel to this location at your earliest opportunity and let me know when you arrive.
Kellan:	Who is this?
Unknown:	Ah'Anon
Kellan:	WTF? Vampires use iPhones now?
Ah'Anon:	You expect us to use Android? ;-)
Kellan:	Cute. I don't know what I expected, but not to get a text.
Ah'Anon:	I told you. We must change with the times or be swallowed by it.

Kellan:	You read that on a bumper sticker? Send me your loc. I'll text you when close.
Ah'Anon:	Accept my friend request and I will track you.
Kellan:	NFW
Ah'Anon:	??
Kellan:	No. Fucking. Way!
Ah'Anon:	:-(
Ah'Anon:	Map Location Sent

Kellan tapped the map and waited as his phone calculated his current location and plotted the most direct route to the destination pin. As the activity indicator spun, he glanced around again, absently wondering what kind of roaming data charges he was racking up. Having never been to the indicated destination before, Kellan knew his portal would have gotten him reasonably close, within a few miles anyway. The terrain was much greener than he had expected, while still being far from lush. Thin grasses could be seen stretching into the distance with patches of much darker green that seemed to be low lying bushes. To the west, lay rolling hills and with even larger ones further on that seemed to be foothills to the most distant mountains. The low 70s, temperature was a pleasant surprise. Kellan had always thought of Africa as being unbearably hot and humid. He made a mental note to spend time reading global temperature and weather charts in the future.

Kellan felt his phone pulse, looked down, and frowned at the display. It indicated he was about three and a half miles from his destination. He sighed knowing that his portal accuracy to an unknown location couldn't be relied upon to get him any closer. Kellan spun around until he was facing the appropriate direction and identified a fixed object in the distance. The Sentinel took a calming breath and reached inward for the raging green river of power. He felt it course upward and through him. Kellan's eyes warmed as he channeled the power to his purpose. He began running westward, slowly at first and then with ever increasing speed feeding off his internal energy while slightly decreasing the gravity and fragmenting lightwaves around him. Should he be spied by a casual observer, Kellan would only appear as a fast moving shimmer across the landscape.

He continued to run for some fifteen minutes, occasionally pulling up to course correct with his phone. Kellan slowly jogged to a stop just as he heard the chime indicating that he had arrived at his destination. Before him stood an old rock-cut church, or, more accurately, the top of a rock-cut church. Kellan whistled softly at the enormity of it. He walked up to the deep gash cut in the ground and looked down. It had to be almost a hundred feet to the bottom. Kellan remembered reading about the rock-cut churches made in the 12th century as Ethiopian Orthodoxy spread throughout the country. The pictures flashing through his memory didn't do justice to what his eyes now saw directly.

Viewed from above, the church would have looked like a large cross carved into the earth surrounded by a deep pit. The cross itself was simply the top of a multi story structure carved directly into the bedrock. Seen from the side it rose up from a tiered pedestal with its first story entrance standing at least thirty five feet high and each of the subsequent three stories being around twenty feet. The stone had a faintly rust colored hue to it and the architecture was as plain as the effort to carve such a massive structure was impressive. Simple, horizontal bands marked where one story of the building led to the next with only the first and third stories having windows. The church maintained the cross shape throughout with each section of the structure having been carved at right angles to the other. Kellan found himself shaking his head in awe at the amount of effort required to carve the building out of solid bedrock.

"That thing is never going anywhere," Kellan said quietly as he looked around for a way down. There were no steps carved into the side of the rough bowl shaped hole in which sat the church proper. As Kellan walked around the edge he found iron rings attached at various intervals. "I bet they used some kind of pulley system to raise and lower a platform," Kellan mumbled.

"Quite right, Sentinel," came a voice from behind.

"Wha!" screamed Kellan whirling, eyes ablaze.

"Peace! I mean you no harm," said the creature before him, glancing upward as angry clouds formed in an otherwise blue sky.

She stood over six feet tall and wore tan boots, blue jeans, and a loose fitting olive green work shirt through which extended two massive black leathery wings. Her hair framed an angular face with a sharply pointed chin and cascaded down her shoulders in tight dreads. At first Kellan though her to be dark skinned but as he looked more carefully, he saw it was comprised of delicately interlocking scales colored a deep red.

"Uh," began Kellan, "So, you're a—"

"Demon," she said her eyes suddenly blazing with a brilliant red light causing Kellan to jump back in alarm. "Careful, young Sentinel, I wouldn't want you falling over the edge and cracking your pretty skull on the stone below. It took quite some doing to gain agreement among the council to involve you. After all that work, I'd prefer you not die." She smiled. "At least not yet."

"That's comforting," said Kellan with a snort, "Now why don't you stand down and turn off the juice."

She smirked at him and asked, "Which one of us killed the other's Prince? You first."

She has a point thought Kellan and then added to himself, *but Asmodeus was a douche. Maybe she's a douche too. I mean, she is a fracking demon and doesn't look—*

"Sentinel," the demon said, head cocked as if she could hear his inner monologue. "Did you hear me?"

"Yeah, I heard you, but you look a lot more like Asmodeus, than Lamia and she and I had a pretty rough start."

The demon laughed, "I imagine we do look differently. Lamia is a seductress. I am a soldier." She lifted one foot. "See, boots. Soldier."

Kellan stared at her. "Was that a joke?"

The demon inclined her head slightly and said, "Honestly, Kellan, would we have gone to all this trouble just to try and kill you? The council has great need of your assistance."

"Sorry, babe, I'm not unilaterally disarming."

Kellan could see the demon's jaw clench as her eyes glowed even more brightly than suddenly faded to a solid black. She spread her arms and unfurled her wings causing a dark shadow to fall over Kellan. "Very well, Sentinel of Order. I am in your power, but know this. I am the only key into Eden. No other will come if you harm me and without our cooperation, creation itself will likely fall."

Kellan released his power with a snort of derision, "Drama much. I'm not going to attack you. I rarely throw the first punch." He took a step forward extending his hand. "Nice to meet you, demon."

She accepted his hand in hers. "I have a name. It's Kali. Nice to meet you too."

"Kali, that's a pretty name isn't it…Hey, Kali, as in the Hindu Kali, source of all evil? Who named you after her?"

She gave a hearty laugh, "Named me after? Sentinel, I am she, but don't believe everything you read or hear. I don't. If I did, I might believe Lamia when she talks about how easy you are to seduce."

The demon smiled wickedly and leaped into the air wings flapping slowly. "Meet me below and I will take you to the gate."

"She didn't seduce me!" called Kellan after the demon who was sailing toward to the massive church entrance, "I was just luring her in with a false sense of security."

I can't believe Amy said that about me, thought Kellan as he stepped off the edge unconsciously wrapping himself in a gravity bubble to soften his fall. *I definitely need to make sure that version doesn't make it to Shannon. She'll bloody well kill me.*

Kellan touched down amidst his mental musings and found himself staring directly at a blue skinned man, heavily muscled with long white hair that appeared adorned with hundreds of feathers. His lower torso dissolved into a roiling cloud of smoke that appeared to have small lightning bolts continually coursing throughout.

"Holy shit!" exclaimed Kellan. "Who the hell are you and where is Kali?" He felt a tap on his shoulder and turned to see her massive form just behind him. "Oh, there you are."

She smiled evilly, "See, I could have killed you again."

"Ha! You could try."

"We both could try, Sentinel of Order," said the blue man "and we would have a good chance to succeed."

"And you are?" Asked Kellan trying to appear nonchalant.

The man bowed, an awkward moment given his lack of lower extremities. "I am Focalor, high Djinn of—"

"Water," finished Kellan.

Focalor inclined his head. "You honor me, Sentinel."

Kellan shrugged. "How much of what I've read is true…about the women I mean?"

The djinn smiled widely, "Some of it I'd assume."

"Most all of it," added Kali. "He is incorrigible. I suggest you keep him away from that soulborn of yours Kellan. He makes Lamia look like an amateur in the seduction game."

Focalor looked stricken. "Why Kali. You wound me. You wound me deeply. I would never interject myself into our dear Sentinel's one true love."

Kellan narrowed his eyes and stared at the djinn, "And why don't I believe that?"

"Because you are not a complete fool," answered Kali and then added, "Enough. Come inside. Both Focalor and I are needed to open the first gate.

As the three walked up the steps leading to the Church entrance, Kellan turned to Focalor, "Say, didn't you live at Alma Torran for a while?"

The djinn looked surprised but didn't pause as he gave his response, "You are remarkably well informed or is there truth to the tale of your perfect memory." Kellan just gave a non committal tilt of the head and Focalor, continued, "Yes, I lived in Alma Torran, why do you ask?"

"Well, Ah'Anon mentioned that the Seal of Solomon was one of the items I needed to keep safe and since you lived in Alma Torran with Solomon, I figured you might know about it."

The djinn nodded thoughtfully, "Well informed indeed. Yes, Kellan, I know much about the seal including where it is housed, but you get ahead of yourself. All this and more will be discussed with the broader Council, assuming you survive entering Eden of course."

"Focalor!" shouted Kali in annoyance.

Kellan stopped short. "What?"

The djinn spread his hands looking to Kali. "You didn't tell him? How was I supposed to know you didn't tell him about the guardian?"

"What guardian?" asked Kellan.

"Why would he need to know, Focalor," said Kali with a growl. "Either he would pass or he would be dead. In either case, knowing about the guardian would do him no good." She turned to Kellan looking down. "Don't pay him any mind, young Sentinel, I'm sure you will be fine."

Kellan laughed. "Yeah, bullshit. I'm not going anywhere until you tell me what's up with this guardian."

Kali ground her teeth and glared at Focalor, "See! See what you did now?"

The djinn simply smiled and opened his arms, "Can I help it that I am honest with our newest ally. I am just not built for deception."

Kellan heard a deep growl from within the demon but she turned to him and sighed. "This stupid djinn and I will open the first gate that separates the mortal plane from that of Eden, but after that comes the garden's gate itself. It is guarded by an angel set there ages ago with but one task."

Kellan took a deep breath and sighed. "And that would be?"

"To keep all humans from entering."

Kellan mused on that a moment. "Well, if it's on a different plane, how would humans get there in the first place?"

"You'd be surprised, Kellan," began Focalor, "Humans get into all sorts of places they aren't supposed to. They are like mice always sneaking in through little cracks you never knew were there."

Kali ignored the djinn. "Irrespective of how they arrive at the gate, the guardian is there to prevent their passing."

"Ok," said Kellan, "And how does he do that exactly? Does he ask nicely?"

The demon shook her head. "No."

"Does he just bar the way?" asked Kellan?

"No, he generally just cleaves them in two."

"Of course he does," said Kellan shaking his head. "So why am I going on this suicide mission? Why don't we just meet at a nice hotel somewhere?"

"That is impossible," answered Kali. "Much of your plane is toxic to members of the Council and it is our considered opinion that you are no longer human so it is unlikely the guardian will kill you."

"Unlikely?" asked Kellan. "Well, as long as it's unlikely, then let's head on in."

Kali smiled, "Really? Excellent and she turned back to the entrance."

"No, not really," yelled Kellan. "I'm the only Sentinel of Order there is and I can't just go sticking my head in someplace for a guardian angel to lop it off."

Kali stared at the djinn. "This is your fault. Fix it."

Focalor raised his hands in acquiesce, trying to cool the demon's rising ire. "Very well. This is not that difficult to navigate. Kellan, all you need do is ask the guardian if you may pass. If he says yes, then you are safe. As we all know, angels cannot lie."

Both Kali and Kellan nodded at this and the young Sentinel stepped into the church doorway before pausing again. "As long as I stay outside Eden's gate, I'm good, right?"

"Yes," said Kali in exasperation.

"Almost certainly," said Focalor, earning himself another glare from the demon.

Kellan shrugged, "Well, I suppose that's about as good as it's going to get. Let's go."

The three walked into the main floor and Kellan took in the expansive room. The ceiling disappeared into darkness with the gloom only partially dispelled by the several carved windows he had seen from atop the surrounding land. The walls and floor were made of that same rust colored stone with no masonry present or needed. Truly, the room was hollowed out from solid stone and completely stark without the slightest adornment. They walked to the back of the room where stood a massive stone altar raised on a dais. To either side, there were stairs heading up, presumably to the second floor. Kellan angled for one of the stairs but was stopped by a hand on his shoulder.

"Not that way," said Focalor with a mischievous grin. He pointed to Kali who stood behind the altar and just in front of a slightly recessed alcove that Kellan had dismissed as being the room's lone decorative element. He allowed himself to be led there and waited with Kali to his right and Focalor to his left. The demons eyes began to glow their ruby red but Focalor held up a hand.

"Wait, let him try to open it himself. If he can, then we know it will be safe for him to enter the garden." Kali nodded curtly and her eyes returned to their normal onyx color.

The djinn grinned widely and nudged Kellan with his shoulder. "Go on. Open it up."

Kellan drew on his power feeling his eyes warm and seeing the slight green aura reflect back from the polished stone. He concentrated on the alcove and, as he did so, a door resolved where there was only stone a moment before.

"Nicely done," said Focalor, "Now, trip the lock and open it."

Kellan reached out and grasped the large metal door handle while concentrating on the lock beneath it. He pressed the handle downward, then lifted it, then tried turning it. Nothing. The door did not budge.

"Just press the switch down with your thumb and push," offered Kali.

Kellan did. Still nothing. He tried channeling more power, to the point where ribbons of green energy starting rippling around him and both demon and djinn seemed to shrink away slightly. After another moment, Kellan let out an exasperated breath and released the power. "It's no use. It won't open for me. I suppose that means I'm human and the guardian is going to try and cut me in half."

"No, no," said Focalor quickly, "None of us were able to open the door the first time either. We each needed help, but once we'd been in the garden, we could then open the passage at will each time thereafter."

Kellan raised an eyebrow. "If none of you were able to open the door the first time, how did the first person get in there?"

Kali grinned at the djinn, "See, he's not as stupid as you thought. The truth, Kellan, is that we don't know. Ah'Anon believes it was Lucifer who first unlocked the door from within. He alone had remained in the garden when all were exiled and so was able to unlock it for the first who made it back. Whether those first were humans who Lucifer wanted to see destroyed by the guardian, or inhumans he wanted to assist for his own reasons, is unknown. In fact the whole story is just that, a story. All we know is that none have been able to open the first gate without having first been inside. Some few, like Ah'Anon can open it by themselves. For most of us, it requires two. One to trip the lock and the other to push open the door. That is why we two are here."

The djinn affected a yawn. "I'm bored, Kali. Let us be done with this. Unlock it," said Focalor. The demon nodded and reached out her hand as her eyes flashed. The door appeared again and Kellan could see the locking switch slide downward in response to her channel power. As it did, Focalor, reached out with both hands and wind rushed upward from his lower extremities revealing normal human legs. The power continued up and then down his arms, finally to fly out amidst a rush of wind and crackle of energy. The door swung open and bright sunlight bathed the three of them in its warmth. "Kellan, go," yelled the djinn, "I cannot hold it open long. Kali will be next and I will follow."

Kellan's stomach did summersaults as he took a breath, clenched his teeth, and leaped through the open door. Nothing happened. A heartbeat later he was slammed from behind, lost his footing and sprawled on the soft, lush, grass. He rolled onto his side, looking backward to see Kali struggling to keep her feet and looking frustrated.

"Why did you stand there like a fool?" she growled stepping to one side.

Another second passed and Focalor deftly jumped through with the door slamming shut behind him. The djinn looked down at Kellan. "You stood in the doorway?"

"Yeah," said Kellan.

"Pretty stupid," said the djinn reaching down to offer Kellan his hand and hoisted him back to his feet.

"Sorry, it was my first time through the magic door," Kellan replied then motioned to the door. "Does it just stay like that, a disembodied door floating an inch off the grass?"

Both demon and djinn just nodded and then Kali shrugged. "To be honest, I never really thought about it. The door has always been thus so it does not seem strange to me."

Kellan just shook his head a took in the rest of the visible area. It clearly didn't look anything like Ethiopia. The grass was a deep verdant green and so thick as to feel like the richest carpet. Looking back the way they came and past the portal door everything seemed to grow dark and indistinct. Turning, Kellan's eyes followed a barely visible path stretching from the portal door and leading a couple thousand feet where it ended at a giant gated archway made of some shining metal.

Kellan took a few steps in that direction and paused, looking over his shoulder at his companions, then back to the gate. Standing to its left and rising at least twelve feet tall was a massive, unmoving angel, a giant sheathed sword lashed to its back. "The guardian, I presume," asked Kellan.

"That's him," answered Focalor walking up beside the Sentinel.

"He looks like a statue," said Kellan.

"He mostly is a statue," said Kali.

"Right, he only moves when he kills humans," offered Focalor, then added, "What?" as Kali glared daggers at him.

Kellan was already walking along the path toward the silver gate. He was within maybe a hundred feet when the angel's head swiveled and it stared at him. Kellan immediately stopped.

"Is that bad?" he asked.

"Well, it's not as good as if he hadn't moved," replied Focalor hesitantly looking askance to Kali who this time seemed to agree with the djinn.

Kellan took another few steps and the angel reached across its back, withdrawing the massive sword from its sheath. "Stop!" it commanded in a voice so loud that Kellan felt himself rock backwards from the force of it.

"Ok," said the young Sentinel, "This is definitely not good."

"Try talking to him," offered Focalor. "He never will talk to us, but I've heard he will talk to humans. You know, before he kills them."

Kellan took a deep breath and tried to ignore the djinn, but locked his eyes on that of the angel and said, "What is your name, angel. I am Kellan Thorne, Sentinel of Order and, I would like to pass through this gate."

"You shall not pass!" said the angel.

"What if I tell you my favorite color," offered Kellan and then looked to his companions with a grin. They stared back at him blankly. "Oh come on," he added, "that was classic Monte Python right there. You know," Kellan affected a a British accent, "What, is your favorite color?" More blank stares. "Never mind."

He turned back to the angel. "What is your name?"

"You shall not pass!"

"Do you know Raphael? He's a friend of mine."

"You shall not pass!"

"Do you know Michael? He's not a friend but he hasn't killed me."

"You shall not pass!"

"What if I do pass?"

"You shall not pass!"

"Why can't I pass?"

There was a pause, then the angel said, "No human may pass. You shall not pass."

"I am not human," said Kellan. "I am the Sentinel of Order. I am God's unchecked hand on the world."

"You are human. You shall not pass."

"No, I'm not human and I shall pass," said Kellan as he took a couple steps toward the gate.

The angel lifted the sword high in his right hand, while reaching upward and to the left with his other, striking an attack posture.

"Um, Kellan," began Focalor, "I think the next move is going to result in you losing about a head's worth of height."

Kellan opened himself up to the power and felt the emerald energy fill him. He called to it again and again, until his body radiated with its heat desperately seeking release.

"I'm going through the gate now," said Kellan.

No response.

Kellan took another step but the angel did not move. The Sentinel smiled and looked back to Kali and Focalor. "See nothing to it, just had to channel the power so he could see I wasn't human." Kellan turned and closed the last few feet to the gate then reached for its handle.

Kali yelled a warning and Kellan looked up just in time to see the massive sword arcing down toward him. He hastily erected a shield, involuntarily closed his eyes, and braced for impact. It didn't come. Kellan sheepishly cracked open one eye and saw the massive sword buried in the ground half way to its hilt. The angel's right hand remained on its pommel with his left crossing his waist as he knelt before Kellan, head bowed.

"Uh, hello?" said Kellan hesitantly, "As you were?"

The angel looked up. "Sentinel of Order, Eden greets you. Enter and be welcome."

Kellan brightened, "Well, that's more like it. You may call me Kellan. No need to be that formal. You have done well, guardian of Eden. What is your name."

The angel continued to stare at Kellan, then said, "Sentinel of Order, Eden greets you. Enter and be welcome."

The young Sentinel glanced to his companions who just shook their heads in answer to his unvoiced question.

Kellan looked back to the angel tried to affect his best formal tone, "Thank you, guardian of Eden. Return to your post."

The angel immediately stood, replaced the sword in its sheath across his back and became still.

"Well come on then," said Kellan and opened the gate to Eden.

Eden exceeded all of Kellan's expectations, a perfectly beautiful and expansive garden. He had thought the area beyond the first gate wonderful, but this, was something beyond imagining. The air seemed to shimmer and light played off leaves, grass, rocks, and wood as if they all were slightly reflective. He knelt down and ran his fingers through the grass, then looked up at Kali and Focalor.

"It's so soft and fine." Kellan said as he continued to trace his fingers through the lush green blades, "Almost. Almost as if it were made of silk." His companions shared a knowing look but said nothing and Kellan regained his feet then headed away from the second gate.

The grassy entrance to Eden quickly gave way to groves of fruited trees that spread out before him to either side as he continued deeper into the garden. It was unlike anything the young Sentinel had ever seen. There seemed no organization to the trees in that they neither clustered together by kind, nor were each distinctly different. Rather, each tree's placement seemed random, yet in some way, purposeful. Kellan pondered the seeming inconsistency of his perception as he plucked a perfectly ripe apple from the nearest tree. He rubbed it absently on his shirt and brought it to his mouth, then paused, peering over it at Focalor who watched him smiling.

"What?" began Kellan pulling down the apple and staring at the fruit intently. He looked to Kali and the demon smirked at him. "Well screw both of you," said Kellan taking a forceful bite. "It's just an apple."

"Is it now," asked Focalor with a chuckle in his voice.

"Yes, and it's delicious," mumbled Kellan around one mouthful before swallowing and taking another. He pushed further into the garden looking over his shoulder and asking, "I assume I'm headed in the right direction?"

"The others are not far ahead," answered Kali. "They are waiting for us in Eve's bosom."

Kellan stopped and turned. "Eve's bosom? Really? What is that?"

Kali spread her hands, "Just a name, Sentinel. At the center of the garden is a spring fed glade that spreads out into several small streams. The trees there form a natural canopy over a broad circular area. Legend had it that it was there that Eve and Adam lived until their expulsion."

"Uh huh," said Kellan resuming his slow progress forward, weaving in and out among the trees while taking note of the various fruits and nuts belonging to each. He added, "You realize that two people wouldn't be able to populate the earth simply because genetic abnormalities would cause a deformation cascade within three or four generations."

The demon increased her pace coming along side Kellan and glanced over to him, "I am not here to debate theology or biblical history with you, Sentinel of Order. Believe as you wish. I was not there and was simply providing the background for its name. That said, I warn you not to rely overmuch on your human science especially given that your mere existence is a violation of natural laws."

"I always found Genesis to be more metaphorical," offered Focalor helpfully. "Although, I must admit, the thought of having a garden full of naked women does sound appealing."

Kali gave a snort of derision. "Your reputation precedes you, djinn, and clearly you did not read very carefully. The garden had but one woman in it."

"One?" cried Focalor in mock horror, "Well, no wonder the poor chap got himself expelled; the sheer monotony of it all."

Kellan simply shook his head, "Don't the two of you have something better to do than shadow me. How much trouble could I get into? It's Eden. I don't think I'm likely to get eaten by lions or—"

Kellan paused and Focalor bumped into him, not paying attention, then backed up staring at the Sentinel quizzically as the young Sentinel looked around, then said, "Where are the animals?"

Kali laughed, "You are as unobservant as our research has led us to believe. You just now have noticed that?"

Kellan scowled, "I have other things on my mind. So?"

"So? What?" asked Focalor.

"The animals? What happened to them. Are they hiding or are they gone?"

"Oh, they've been gone almost forever. At least as long as I've been coming here. I suspect they left when the guardian arrived and erected the second gate. Native animals couldn't survive the garden's stasis, so either they left or they died at the end of its first cycle."

Kellan stared blankly at the djinn. "What the hell are you talking about, Genie. Stasis? Cycles?"

"No," interjected Kali. "We are not going to get into that now. Focalor, try not to talk. Kellan, the council will answer all your questions. I promise that the characteristics of this place, its static nature, and the cycles with which it operates present no danger to you. However, we have been charged with conveying you directly to the Council itself and that is exactly what I intend to do." She then extended an arm in the direction they had been heading. "Please, we are almost there."

Kellan sighed, "Fine, but I'm not going to forget to ask about this."

"I'm sure you won't she grumbled softly as they began walking again."

True to her word the trees began to thin a few minutes later and opened up to a broad circular glade. In its center was a large placid lake from which several small streams flowed. Just in front of them bubbled a spring that seemed to feed directly into the lake. Kellan knelt down and placed his lips to the gurgling fountain and drank deeply. It was ice cold and sweet like he imagined the purest mountain water must taste. He stood up and smiled at both Kali and Focalor. "Have you guys tried this? It's amazing. I wish I could take some of that with me."

The djinn's face registered immediate shock and distress, "Of course, I've never tried that. It's poison!"

"What!" cried Kellan, his mind immediately starting to run though hundreds of remedies, then he spied Kali slowly shaking her head as she stared at Focalor with a disapproving look. The Sentinel narrowed his eyes at the djinn, "You are an asshole," at which point Focalor burst out laughing and pointed to Kellan.

"Have you guys tried this?" he asked mocking Kellan's earlier question. "Ha! You should have seen the expression on your face."

Kellan gave the djinn his best death look and and mumbled something unintelligible about finding a bottle and corking him. The Sentinel stood and peered into the distance, scanning the fullness of the glade, then turned to Kali. "You said the Council would be here to meet me. I don't see anyone, or is this not the place?"

The demon nodded toward a specific area of the glade and said, "No, we will be meeting over there. You can't see it from here, but there's a small outcropping to our right where the stream branches off from the lake. We'll go there and once you complete the binding ritual, they will come."

Kellan sighed, "Binding ritual?"

"Oh, did we forget to mention that," said Focalor with feigned innocence. Kellan glared at him and was about to respond when Kali stepped between them.

"It is a minor thing, Sentinel of Order, but none will come without it having been done. All of us have done it. There is an artifact preserved in a reliquary. You place your hand within and repeat an oath of non-aggression toward members of the Council. The combined words and action binds the artifact to you and restrains all overtly aggressive acts."

"I'm not doing that," snorted Kellan, "Leave myself defenseless around a group of powerful unnatural creatures including demons. He looked to Kali, "No offense."

Kali showed her teeth, "Non taken, young Sentinel. However you were not listening. I said it restrains aggressive action, not defensive. Should you be in danger from any within the Council you would be free to protect yourself."

Kellan wasn't convinced but started walking to the area Kali indicated, glancing at her as he passed, "I'll think about it."

〜〈⋀〉〜

A few minutes later, Kellan found himself staring at an ornate wooden box with numerous enochian runes carved into its surface. Interestingly, the box was levitating several feet above the ground, coming up to Kellan's chest as he stood before it. On the side facing them, there seemed a recessed panel, but Kellan couldn't tell if was a means to open the box or simply decorative. He turned to his two companions. "Now what?"

Focalor opened his mouth to respond, but Kellan held up a hand. "Not you. I can't believe I'm saying this, but I don't believe you and think Kali here, the embodiment of all that is evil, is far more trustworthy." He locked eyes with the demon who simply stared back at Kellan, dark eyes revealing nothing. "What do I need to do, exactly."

Kali smiled, "It is really quite simple. Just reach into the box, rest your hand on what's within, and say, 'I bind my soul to the purpose of peace and will take no aggressive action against the Council of Havilah.'"

Kellan nodded. "Seems simple enough."

Both demon and djinn nodded, then looked anxious as Kellan stepped aside. He smiled and said, "You guys go first."

They exchanged glances and Kali said, "We have both performed the binding ritual centuries ago."

"Well," Kellan began, "then it shouldn't be a big deal to do it again, right?"

Kali growled menacingly but shouldered Kellan farther out of the way, then moved her right hand toward the recessed panel. Kellan noted with intense curiosity that the wood seemed to fuzz and mist as her hand appeared to pass through it until she had buried her hand up to its wrist. She glared at Kellan and but repeated the phrase.

Nothing happened and she removed her hand then rounded on the Sentinel, eyes beginning to glow red, "You see, I told you. I have already done this thing."

For his part Kellan simply turned to Focalor and made an exaggerated sweeping gesture toward the box. The djinn snickered, but immediately strode forward, placed his hand in the box and repeated the same oath with an identical result. "Disappointed?" Focalor asked with a grin. "You really aren't very trusting?"

Kellan squinted at him, "Yeah, I wonder why that is?"

"Well?" asked Kali.

"I'm going," said Kellan as he moved to again stand before the levitating box. He stretched out his right arm making a windmilling motion and then jiggled it rapidly by his side. With a final distrustful glance to his two companions Kellan slowly reached into the box. It seemed lined with a quilted fabric of some kind and was exceptional soft. In its center, Kellan could feel a slight hollow on which rested an object of some kind. He couldn't quite make it out, but it, too, was soft and felt like a small animal or bird. With his hand loosely grasping the object, Kellan repeated the words. "I bind my soul to the purpose of peace and will take no aggressive action against the Council of Havilah." As the last word faded, Kellan began to pull his hand free but found he could not. He tugged a bit harder but his hand remained firmly captured by the box that, itself, did not move even though nothing anchored it to the ground. Anger filled the young Sentinel and he began to call to his power. Before it could answer, his world seemed to splinter like a mirror being shattered from behind. Shards of his reality spun about like reflective motes to finally puff away entirely and Kellan's new reality exerted itself.

He immediately recognized where he was even though it was much different than it had been when he was there. Before him, and to his left, a rough hewn throne grew from the stony earth. Kellan could see that someone lounged upon it but standing behind it as he was, the Sentinel could only see loosely curling dirty blonde hair that framed a man's head. Beyond him, and facing slightly away from Kellan, stood a tall figure who seemed to glow with an inner light. He wore a loose fitting robe that likewise seemed to sparkle in its own iridescent fashion. Shoulder length brown hair framed a somewhat long face that seemed incredibly gentle and loving to Kellan. The man held something in his outstretched hands but the Sentinel was fixed on this man's eyes. They glowed brilliantly but not with either the green of Order nor with the Red of Chaos, but rather with an intense violet that seemed to pulse with life. The man lifted his hands, gently releasing a small figure that immediately spread white wings which beat against the still air. It rose as all three stared after it.

"What was that?" asked the man on the throne, his voice betraying a sense of awe.

"A dove," began the second, "It will come to represent peace, love, tranquility, and many such things. I felt it right to create such a thing here, in the shadow of our enmity."

Kellan cried out in surprise and recognition. Instantly, the violet eyes locked on to his and a knowing smile tugged at the Creator's lips then the scene shattered bringing Kellan back to glade.

The young Sentinel found himself kneeling on the soft grass with the box hovering slightly above him. Focalor reached out to help him up, but Kellan shrugged him off.

"We each have seen and experienced what now you have as well, Sentinel of Order," the djinn began sounding serious for the first time since Kellan met him. "The binding shows all of us the same illusion at the moment our oath takes hold."

Kellan was shaking slightly as he reached out to touch the box, running his finger along the place where its lid should be. There were no seams. No hinges. Focalor continued as he watched Kellan, "It cannot be opened, Sentinel of Order, that is not its nature. It exists to—" The djinn broke off as Kellan's eyes flared to life and he gently lifted the lid with both hands causing both Kali and Focalor to gasp as it slid upward on nonexistent hinges. A golden glow bathed Kellan's face as he smiled, looking into the box and feeling his companions curiosity as they gathered close.

Three pairs of eyes washed over the quilted interior of the box where rested a beautifully preserved white dove, its feet curled beneath and eyes closed as if asleep. Kellan whispered, "This was the first. I saw him. I saw God create this Dove and He looked at me when He released it."

"Ridiculous," said Focalor, but he sounded shaken.

"Not so," said Kali who, for herself, sounded deeply sad, "Not so at all. The Creator exists outside time and can be where he wills. Perhaps he sees us all when we bind ourselves to His peace, but simply does not acknowledge us. Were I he and I knew all we have done, I know I would not." The demon glanced up to Kellan as he gently closed the box, his eyes losing their heat. "Did he say anything to you, Kellan? Anything at all?"

The young Sentinel shook his head. "No and I could have imagined the whole thing, Kali. It just seemed like he turned to me when I cried out in surprise. He looked right at me and I felt—" Kellan paused not know exactly what to say, "—Felt something when our eyes met."

"You cried out?" Asked Kali. "Perhaps it was what you said. We each only get the vision once when we first bind ourselves to the Peace of Havilah, but we could share your words with the next who does so. What did you say, Sentinel of Order to gain the attention of the Creator."

Kellan looked away and shuffled his feet.

"He won't tell us, Kali," said Focalor sounding bitter. "The Sentinel wishes to keep his secrets."

"No," said Kellan looking back to them both, "It's not that, honestly, it really isn't. It's just that I'm pretty sure my words were not the key."

"Then you should have no issue sharing them with us," said Kali as she crossed her arms defiantly.

Kellan sighed, "Ok, if you insist. When He released the dove and I realized who He was and that it was Lucifer on the throne, I said," Kellan paused again.

"Yes…" asked both demon and djinn, leaning in.

"Holy Shit!" Completed Kellan looking sheepish.

The two stared at him dumfounded for a moment and then Focalor tilted his head back and laughed uncontrollably.

Chapter 8

THE COUNCIL OF HAVILAH

M ovement caught Kellan's attention and he turned towards it. Figures began to emerge from the closest tree line and the Sentinel felt their eyes upon him. He saw Ah'Anon among them and raised a hand in greeting then opened his mouth to call out. The ancient vampire shook his head in a barely perceptible fashion. Kellan took his meaning, lowering his hand and affected a more sober demeanor. Moments later, seven of them were gathered around him while both Kali and Focalor left Kellan's side to join their fellows.

"Welcome, Sentinel of Order," began one of the newcomers, a tall woman with skin as pale as milk. She wore a tight fitted bodice colored a dark garnet red and trimmed in gold. Long loose black curls spilled out of a hooded cape that gracefully draped her shoulders and ran down her amply curved body to where it nearly brushed the ground. "He has completed the binding," she stated more than asked, but both Kali and Focalor nodded. "Excellent," she continued, shifting her gaze to the young Sentinel and causing butterflies to dance in Kellan's stomach. Sharp eyebrows framed almond shaped eyes of a deep, almost iridescent, brown. Her lips were full and almost as red as her cloak and Kellan noted how it quirked up in a sardonic smile. She took a deep breath and Kellan's eyes were drawn to the pale half moons of her breasts as they rose from her bodice.

Ah'Anon cleared his throat and Kellan started, shaking his head to clear the glamor, his eyes again meeting hers, but this time with suspicion.

The woman chuckled, "Do not blame me, Sentinel of Order, for being as I am. Had you held your power, my glamor would not have touched you. It is fortunate for you that we all have bound ourselves to peace even as you have."

Kellan reached inward and felt his power flow, but the woman reached out imploringly, "Wait, please." Kellan did, looking at her questioningly as she continued, "Before we part, you may view us with the eyes of a Sentinel, but for now, I ask that you simply see us as we are." She paused again, "As we see ourselves."

Kellan understood and nodded garnering him another smile. "Excellent," she said, "My thanks for that. And now, introductions are in order." She gave a half curtsey and said, "I am Countess Mircalla Karnstein and it is my very great pleasure to make your acquaintance Kellan Thorne."

Kellan inclined his head. "Countess Karnstein. Might you also be known by another name?" asked Kellan while trying to infuse his tone with as much diplomacy as he could manage.

She smiled and he noted its genuine warmth as it clearly touched her eyes, "I see at least some of the tales told of you to be true. Yes, there is another name by which I am also know, my young Sentinel, but I think you already know that, don't you."

"Carmilla," answered Kellan immediately affecting a more formal bow and spreading out his arms in a flourish. "Mother of all Vampires, if I recall my lore correctly."

"Your recollection is correct even if that title is both undeserved and unwanted. I prefer Mircalla."

"Mircalla then," said Kellan with a smile.

She continued, "To my right is General Seramai, our warrior, and stalwart protector."

The man stepped forward and extended his hand. Kellan reached out and Seramai grasped him by the wrist then the two men locked eyes. "Sentinel," said Seramai by way of acknowledgement then released Kellan's wrist and stepped back. He was the tallest among the assembled inhumans and the most well muscled. He had a beautifully masculine face with a strong chiseled jaw and an unruly mane of sandy brown hair that flowed to his shoulders where it met what looked like bronze and gold inlays. His leather chest plate was likewise adorned with two golden rams heads on either side, facing each other, as if to attack. The chest plate gave way to similarly adorned leather greaves and boots. Seramai crossed his arms a wry smile playing across his face. "Like what you see?" he said to Kellan who felt himself flush.

"Enough Sera," said Mircalla, "We have important matters to discuss and no time for your endless flirtations." The general seemed unconvinced and gave Kellan a wink but Mircalla moved on.

"Ah'Anon, you know. He is the saucer that cools the cup of our passions and my most trusted advisor."

"You are too kind, Mircalla. I merely serve with what talents I have."

She smiled at him warmly and Kellan thought he caught an unspoken understanding pass between them.

"I believe you also know the next member of our Council."

Kellan grinned. "I sure do. Permission to hug?"

Without a word the woman standing beside Seramai dashed forward covering the space between her and Kellan in an eye blink. He opened his arms and felt her fill them, hugging him tightly. Suddenly warmth filled him and he was awash with sexual arousal. Kellan pushed back as he fought for control. "Lamia! My favorite demon, tone it down girlfriend. You are getting me all hot and bothered."

"Sorry," she said looking embarrassed and kissed Kellan chastely on the cheek as he felt the warmth fade. "Am I still your favorite demon," she asked giving Kali a pointed glance.

Kellan laughed, "Always and forever, Amy. After all, you never forget the first demon who tries to seduce you, then crush the life out of you in snake form, then seduce you again."

"Fair point," she said still smiling.

"How are the kids," asked Kellan.

She broke his gaze and looked down for a moment before answering. "Kellan, that was almost 750 years ago and they were not immortals."

Kellan felt stricken and pulled her back into his embrace whispering in her ear, "Oh, Amy, I'm so sorry. For me it has been but a year. I'm so so sorry." He felt her sigh within his arms and push back, eyes glistening.

"It is alright, Kellan. They all had long and full lives filled with love, marriage, children, and grandchildren. My offspring are legion and I keep my eyes on them."

Kellan nodded as Mircalla gestured to her left. "This is Ariel who—"

"Greetings Kellan Thorne. I am not as enthused by this meeting as my fellows," she said interrupting Mircalla. "I have been warned of you and will be watching intently."

"Huh," said Kellan. "Let me guess. You are an angel."

"Archangel."

"What's the difference? Angel? Archangel. What's in a title?"

"Much."

"I dunno," intoned Kellan, "Seems pretty," he paused for affect, "prideful to me." He saw the Archangel tense, eyes narrowing at Kellan, her face becoming a mask of anger.

"Uh oh," said Kali as Lamia jabbed Kellan in the ribs.

"Ow, what? She started it. I bet Michael's been whispering in her ear. He's such a dick."

"Michael," the angel roared, "Is one of the finest among us. He,"

"Is not here," interrupted Kellan. "Why is he not here, but you are. Why is he not a member of your Council?"

"Peace," said Mircalla before Ariel could respond. "There will be time for that later. Now I need both of you to stand down. We are allies in this endeavor. Behave like it."

"She started it," mumbled Kellan.

Mircalla let out an exasperated breath, "Sentinel of Order, please. Behave in a way commensurate with your station." Ariel smirked, but the vampire rounded on her, "And you, do not provoke him. Your relationship with Michael is well known. Do not try to deny it Ariel, we all know of it. I will thank you to leave Michael's prejudices toward our ally, Kellan, where they belong, with Michael."

"That was entertaining," said the man to Ariel's left and stepped forward before Mircalla spoke. "I am Samael and anyone who pisses off Michael the way you do, is just fine in my book." Kellan accepted the extended hand and Samael pulled him forward giving the Sentinel three quick slaps on the back before releasing him.

"Samael," began Kellan, "As in the Angel of——"

"Death. Yes. That is me.

"Wow, you really aren't anything like I expected."

"I get that a lot," said the angel. "I suspect it is the hair and, well, the complete lack of being a skeleton with a scythe."

"You actually look a bit like Raphael."

Samael smiled broadly, "Do you think so? Why thank you, Kellan Thorne, that is quite nice of you to say."

Kellan shrugged. "I think it's the shape of the face, but Raphael would never wear his hair that long."

Samael laughed, "He has little choice in that matter. We remain as made, Sentinel. My hair is long and white even as his is short and brown. Any alterations we might make are undone and we revert to our original state with each dawn."

Kellan glanced at Amy questioningly. "The fallen have more freedom." She said matter of factly.

"Indeed you do, sister," said Samael without the slightest hint of envy or reproach.

"Finally," broke in Mircalla, "There is Dragluin."

"The Dragluin, I presume," said Kellan slowly, "I mean why not, given the rest of your pedigrees."

"Pedigree?" said Dragluin in a thickly accented voice whose origin Kellan couldn't place. "Are you sure that is the word you meant to choose."

"Uh, no, I mean, I didn't intend any insult. It's just that——"

Kellan paused as he saw everyone but Ariel trying to suppress laughter then looked back to Dragluin whose massive full beard concealed his expression so completely that the Sentinel could not be sure what lay beneath.

"You are messing with me?" Kellan finally said with a nervous laugh. "Great, the father of werwolves is giving me shit for referring to his pedigree. Nicely done."

Dragluin inclined his head. "It is a pleasure to meet you Kellan. You do not know this, but I am in your debt."

Kellan cocked his head, "Really, I love it when people are in my debt, but, uh, why exactly?"

"Sargon."

"Oh," said Kellan, "I'm guessing you didn't like him much, since I kind of killed him and all. Well, technically a friend of mine killed him, but I almost killed him."

Dragluin barked a short laugh. "No, I didn't like him. I loathed him. I am glad he is dead. Thank you, Sentinel of Order."

"Ah, sure thing, don't mention it,"

Mircalla clapped her hands drawing all eyes to her. "Very good. Time grows short and we have much to discuss and do. Seramai, if you please?"

As if in answer, the general drew in a deep breath and Kellan felt power gathering. It was unlike anything he'd experienced. It was not the calming, Ordered power he commanded nor the raw untempered Chaotic energies he grappled with after Asmodeus's death. It was primal and seemed somehow more natural than either Order or Chaos. Before he could explore it further, Seramai swept out his hands, the power vanished, and before them formed a massive wooden table with ten accompanying chairs. Mircalla sat at one end, gestured for Kellan to take the other, while the eight other members settled themselves to either side.

The Countess slid back the hood of her cloak in a fluid motion and her dark eyes swept along the table, momentarily locking with each of those assembled. Kellan felt himself leaning forward as she placed both hands on the table and said, "Let us begin."

Kali slammed her fist on the table causing it to jump despite its mass. She glared at Kellan, eyes glowing red. "As we have all told you over and over, the Micah you knew is not the same as the one we've encountered. We *did* try to to involve him and each envoy we sent was either killed or barely escaped with their life."

Ah'Anon placed a calming hand on her arm, but she shook it free and stood up. "I will listen to no more of this drivel. It is pointless. We have merely traded a murderous Sentinel for a pathetic whelp incapable of seeing his Master for what he was. A dispassionate killer."

Kellan felt his blood heat and rose, leaning forward with his hands braced on the table, knuckles white and eyes aflame. "Fuck you, Kali," he growled. "Don't let the door hit you in the scaly ass on your way out." The demon lifted one clawed hand and red energy began to play along its length.

"Sit down," came a soft and measured voice from the end of the table. The demon remained standing but didn't release the gathered energy. "Kali? Do you wish me to ask a second time?"

Kellan didn't think it was possible, but the demon actually seemed to pale. She let out a breath through clenched teeth and growled, "No, Countess, that will not be necessary. Forgive me."

The Sentinel watched as Kali lowered herself into the chair silently and smiled. "That's better," he said and noticed both Lamia and Ah'Anon wince at his words.

"Kellan Thorne," came the soft, almost lilting voice and he turned to Mircalla. "The Council of Havilah has existed for over two thousand years. Do you think our number is limited to these few before you?" The Countess didn't wait for an answer. "It does not, Sentinel of Order. The Council as of this day, numbers nearly a thousand world wide. Now I ask you, could you stand against the combined might of one thousand inhumans dedicated to your death? Could you stand even against we who are assembled today?"

Kellan said nothing, but felt the chill as all eyes were upon him.

"Ahh, recognition dawns," Mircalla intoned, "but not complete understanding. Allow me to to help my very young Sentinel. Why, do you think, would a legion of neigh immortal beings have suffered Micah Ben Judah to continue drawing breath when he so frequently spread death among our numbers?"

Kellan opened his mouth to object, but Mircalla cut him off with a voice so sharp it severed his words before he could form them, "No! Best you remain silent." She smiled at him but it did not touch her eyes as her voice again took on the softness from before. "It was a rhetorical question, Kellan. I will provide you the answer that you could not possibly have provided yourself. We let your master live because it was in Creation's interest that he do so. That is the only reason. Were it not so, I or those who headed this Council before me, would have focused the fullness of our power on him. But," she held up a finger, "It is so, thus we sent emissaries and never raised a hand in anger despite his violence toward us. Kellan Thorne, you have toddled around as a child this last year, but we can no longer suffer you to be so. You must grow up and put away childish things. Micah Ben Judah was a killer. You must accept this for us to move on and we must move on for all of Creation lies in the balance." She paused again her eyes locked on Kellan's, then spoke so softly that the slightest breeze would have carried away her words, "Now, sit. Down."

Kellan sat, glancing over as Lamia placed her hand on his and mouthed, "I'm sorry."

Silence stretched over a long minute and Kellan finally broke it by inhaling deeply and said with a sigh, "Very well, I will listen with an open mind."

Ah'Anon smiled and leaned back in his chair. "My young friend, no one ever said Micah was evil. What we've been endeavoring to explain for the past hour is that we are all shaped by our environ even as we are by our nature. Micah had a binary view of the world because both his training and power left him with no other perspective." The vampire held up a hand in admonishment, "That does not excuse his behavior, but it does explain it. The Council is comparatively small and those not in its membership do act as their nature dictates. It is understandable why he would distrust this tiny minority that claimed to act in a manner so different from his expectations and experience. Couple that with the bifurcation of creative energy into Order and Chaos, and it would be difficult for anyone to see past their preconceptions. While it is not popular to say around this table, the fault does not entirely rest with Micah."

Focalor stood up and stretched, "Yep," he began, "That is why we were both surprised and excited when Lamia told us of your first encounter. We knew her to be a thrall of Asmodeus," The djinn paused, looking across the table at the Succubus, "Sorry, Amy, but you were." She waved away his apology and he continued, "So, we weren't quite sure what to think, but then when you destroyed Asmodeus, returned Amy's children, and left her in peace, we began to hope."

"Why didn't you contact me before now," asked Kellan.

"That was my decision," answered Mircalla. "I wanted to be sure of your intentions before risking more lives. I was going to let you marinade for a century or so and see what kind of man you turned out to be, but circumstances being what they are, pressing matters forced my hand."

"The Cabal," said Kellan and the Council members all seemed to nod in unison, then Mircalla gestured to Samael who cleared his throat.

"I guess that is where I come in," he began. "I am the newest member to Havilah and am only on the high-council because of having been recruited by the Cabal. They assumed, as the Angel of Death, that I held a measure of antipathy toward humanity so asked me to join them."

Kellan smiled, "So you faked them out until you discovered what they were up to? Nice."

Samael looked perplexed for a moment then gave Kellan an icy smile, "Oh no, my dear Sentinel, I did not, as you say, fake them out. I detest humanity and revel in their deaths. I would love to see you dead too, but alas, other priorities take precedence." The angel said this so matter of factly that Kellan simply swallowed hard, but said nothing.

"Now where was I," continued Samael, "Oh yes, detesting humans and the Cabal. You see, I had assumed their goals were to merely destroy human civilization, thus spreading death and destruction. They correctly surmised that I would appreciate such an endeavor and so I joined them."

"Excuse me just a moment," said Kellan.

"Hmm," replied Samael, "You do look confused my young Sentinel, forgive me."

"Uh, yeah, well I don't mean to be insulting, really I don't, but shouldn't you be more of a demon. Detesting humanity, wanting to spread death and destruction, those all seem more demonic than angelic."

"A point I have made on several occasions," said Kali with Ariel nodding in reluctant agreement.

Samael sighed, "And as I have explained endlessly to both angels and demons alike, my delight in human deaths is not in conflict with my angelic charge. Rather it is in perfect consort. Must I fall from grace just because I enjoy my work. Ridiculous."

"You skirt the edges of perdition, Samael. God should cast you down," growled Ariel.

"Now, now, sister dear. Were you just suggesting what our Father should do? Careful. Sounds like pride to me."

Kellan could feel heat wafting from Ariel as the two angels stared at each other, but the tension was dispelled by Mircalla's soft voice.

"Enough. Samael, please continue."

He inclined his head, "Yes, well, unfortunately the Cabal did not, strictly speaking, have designs on humanity. I figured that out quickly once I noticed that there were both angels and demons working together and they were using Micah's blood to cloak their activities from God so the Cabalic angels would not be cast down. After that it was really just a matter of—"

"Wait, just wait," said Kellan, "Micahs's blood? Where on earth would they have gotten that and how the hell would that cloak them from God."

"Oh really, Countess, must I provide the child Sentinel a remediation? This is so tiresome. Just tell him what he must do and let us end this interminable meeting."

Kellan ground his teeth as his anger rose, but Mircalla gave him a placating gesture. "Samael, we seek to ally ourselves with the Sentinel and such alliances are strongest when formed between equals who all have a complete command of the facts. You will provide the requested explanation and will do so with the respect Kellan is due. Am I understood?" This last was phrased as a question, but her tone made it anything but and Samael blanched just as Kali had done before. Not for the first time Kellan wondered at the command Mircalla Karnstein exerted over the assembly, himself included.

"Of course," Samael replied, his manner differential, "Forgive me."

"You are forgiven, sir," said Kellan although he knew the angel's response had been directed to Mircalla. Samael stared at him flatly for a long moment, then laughed, shattering the tension that had, again, sprung up between them.

"I think," he began, "That I may actually end up liking you. That would be a first. I have never liked any human."

"I'm not human," said Kellan, "Just ask the autistic angel at Eden's gate, he'll tell ya."

"Ah, that must be it then. I must admit to a modicum of relief in that. My distain for humanity truly is a cornerstone of my existence to have it be otherwise would, I suspect, prove detrimental to my sanity. Now, to your question. As you are aware, the Sentinels for Order and Chaos exist outside divine providence. God cannot see what you do, hear what you think, or even know of your interactions with others. Lucifer is similarly bound by such a restriction, however, Kali assures me that he continually finds small and temporary ways around it. We have no proof, of course. Lucifer is far too crafty to disclose such a thing, but I have no doubt Kali is correct in her assessment. Be that as it may, agents of Order or Chaos are restricted from knowing most aspect of both you and your opposite. The Cabal has discovered a means to replicate this cloak by using blood from either Micah, now you, or Maurius."

Kellan grimaced, "What do they do, drink it? Smear it on themselves?"

Samael shook his head, "Nothing that mundane, Kellan. They use it to activate a runic charm they've developed. A single drop placed in the carving and any angel or demon wearing such a ring or pendant is obscured from our Father's sight."

"Really," asked Kellan, "That seems like a pretty big oversight for an omniscient being to make."

"Omniscient," snorted Kali, "Bah!"

"Do not!" growled Ariel rising and unfurling her massive wings, "Do not, denigrate my Father while I am present lest I breach this truce and—"

"Oh relax, Ariel," said Seramai, grinning through his beard. "Look at her," he continued, gesturing at Kali, "She's baiting you and you bit, again." The demon tried to look innocent, but simply wasn't built for it, finally giving up and showing her teeth to the angel. Ariel slammed her fist on the table and stalked away muttering.

"Sore subject?" Kellan asked.

"Pay it no mind," said Ah'Anon waving a hand dismissively, "Those two have been at each other since before I was born and I'm sure will still be long after I am dust."

Kellan nodded in understanding and turned his attention back to Samael, "And how do they acquire this blood. I doubt it was given freely, even by Maurius."

"Certainly not," the angel answered, "But Sentinels tend to leave blood all around them. From what I hear, you left pools of it across both Atlanta and Afghanistan."

"Fair point," Kellan conceded.

"Indeed," accepted Samael graciously, "So long as the blood has not dried, it can be used to this purpose. So," the angel clapped his hands together, "We have a group of angels and demons working together, but to what end? They have been acquiring artifacts of great power. Again, to what end?" He stared at Kellan expectantly.

"What? I have no idea. I didn't even know they existed a week ago."

"They seek to reconcile God and Satan," said Samael triumphantly. "That is the ends to which all their machinations strive."

Kellan's mouth turned down and he nodded slowly as the thought sunk in, "Well, that doesn't sound so bad. Maybe it would be a good thing."

Ah'Anon smiled and said, "That is almost exactly what young Juliet said while you were," he winked at Kellan, "indisposed."

Samael gave the vampire a sidelong glance then turned back to Kellan. "Well, there is a bit of a catch," said the angel.

"Of course there is," said Kellan, "What's the catch. Hit me."

Samael nodded toward the head of the table and Mircalla smiled mirthlessly, "The catch, my dear ally, is that for God and Satan to reconcile, Creation and all that came hence, must be undone."

"That's one big fraking catch," Kellan whispered, eyes growing wide, "How are they going to manage that?"

"We don't know," said Ah'Anon, "Samael, here, left the Cabal after he discovered their intent but before he could uncover the means."

"Well, that's less than ideal," mumbled Kellan, "Why didn't you stay and find that out, Samael?"

"There was a little matter of them deciding to kill me, Kellan. I am sorry that you are disappointed, but I rather enjoy the deaths of others a fair bit more than my own."

Kellan nodded mostly to himself, then glanced down the table to Mircalla, "I suppose this is where I come in? You need my help to find out exactly how they plan to unravel creation?"

"No, Kellan, we already have many who are focused on that very thing, although additional help is always welcome. What I need you to do is safeguard both Spear of Destiny and Seal of Solomon. We are convinced that whatever plans the Cabal has cannot be put in motion without the Spear and have divined that we cannot succeed without the Seal."

Kellan frowned. "You want me to babysit some old spear and a medallion? That doesn't seem to take full advantage of what I might offer, but never let it be said I turn down the easy stuff. Sure, hand 'em over and I'll keep your baubles safe." The Sentinel paused looking left at Seramai who was shaking, barely containing his laughter. "OooKayy," said Kellan, "Jokes on me again. What am I missing this time?"

Seramai slapped the table unable to contain his laughter any longer, "We don't have those artifacts, Kellan. As Ah'Anon told you, they are guarded elsewhere. Did you think we had suddenly acquired them in the span of the last few hours?" Kellan just shrugged and the general continued, "If we had, I assure you we would bury them in the deepest trench in the deepest ocean surrounded by a phalanx of inhumans to guard them. No, we need you to retrieve them before the Cabal discovers their location or, if they already know, figures a way to extract them."

Kellan looked thoughtful, "So why don't you go get them yourselves?"

"Ah, now you are asking the right questions, young Sentinel," said Seramai still chuckling. "The answer is these last two items rest in places exceptionally difficult for angels, demons, or inhumans to reach."

"Why does getting information from you feel like I'm pulling teeth," asked Kellan turning to Ah'anon. "Have they been moved or are they still where you described?"

"The spear," began Mircalla, "lies beneath the Vatican and is warded from all demonic presence, as you might expect. Even a Sentinel's blood medallion would not protect a Cabalic Angel from detection if they were to even touch the Spear of Longinus. They would immediately become fallen so, at present, we do not think they have means to extract the Spear."

"And the Seal?"

"Equally problematic, but for entirely different reasons. It can be found on a small island in Lake Michigan where several powerful ley lines meet. All attempts to venture inland have had," she paused as if seeking the right words, "unfortunate results. We suspect that you will have better results and so ask your assistance there as well. I will provide you the specific location, assuming you are willing of course."

Kellan didn't pause with his reply, "Of course I'm willing. Creation on the line and all that. Seems right up my alley." Kellan looked around the table noticing the distinct relief mingled with surprise among all those assembled accept Lamia. "What?" he asked as she touched his hand.

The succubus leaned over and kissed his cheek while whispering softly, "They didn't believe me when I told them you would help us." She pulled back but left her hand on his.

"We assumed you would be too fearful to aid those angelic among us and too idealistic to support the fallen or inhuman," said Ariel having returned to stand behind her chair. "I remain unconvinced that you will see this through to the finish."

Kellan waved a hand, "Whatever, Ariel. I swear, you and Michael should totally date." Then he pushed himself up from the table. "Ok gang, this has been fun, but I'm hungry and since no refreshments were provided for this little meeting, I'm going to head out and get a Po-Boy." Kellan turned to Mircalla. "Countess, thank you for trusting me with this. I won't let you down. Now, even I can find the Vatican, but do you have some kind of secret map that shows me where Michigan's mysterious island is?"

She smiled, stood and extended her hand. Kellan bent down and gave it a soft kiss, then looked up to see her suppressing a laugh. "Wrong move?" he asked embarrassed, "There are so many time lines. I can't keep my etiquette straight." Then she did laugh, but there was no mocking in it.

"Not at all, Kellan. It is refreshing that anyone even makes the attempt these days. As for the location," she smiled again, "I'll text you."

The young Sentinel stared at her a moment, then just shook his head and said, "Of course you will." He then made a quick round among the Council, receiving and offering both thanks and well wishes until he came to Seramai.

As the large man gripped his forearm again, he said, "You won't be getting rid of me that easily. Our Countess has asked me to accompany you to retrieve the Spear of Longinus. Let me know when you are ready, and I will come."

"Oh, well, sure, I guess," said Kellan confused, then turned to Mircalla. "I thought you said both artifacts were warded against all of you?"

The Countess had been talking softly with Ah'Anon but glanced over, "Hmm, oh, yes, but not him," she said indicating Seramai. "He's different. He'll be fine."

"Fine? But," Kellan stopped, noting that Mircalla was no longer paying him any attention. "Ok, big guy," he said, turning back to the general, "What makes you so special? If you are not demon, angel, werewolf, or vampire, what exactly are you?"

Seramai laughed, "Why, Kellan Thorne, I am a god."

Kellan stared at him flatly, "Fine, don't tell me. I've seen God and you are no God, but whatever. How do I reach you? Are you going to text me too?"

Seramai shook his head in disgust, "No, I never use the things of this age. They disgust me. Simply call my name three times and I will come. Such is the way of gods."

Kellan snorted, "Yeah, and Beetlejuice. I'll give ya a summons once I arrange for a bit more help on my end."

Seramai nodded while maintaining the enigmatic smile he wore most of the day. Kellan turned with a final wave to the remaining members of Havilah's high council and began walking back toward the second gate.

Chapter 9

VATICAN HEIST

Kellan waited for the elevator door to close then lifted both hands in an aggressive gesture toward the woman. The air shimmered as he became visible and he saw her eyes widen in alarm.

"Arrr…Ahhh!!" yelled Kellan, first as a battle cry, and then in pain as the woman smoothly tossed one of the two cups of coffee she was carrying into the air, backhanded him in the face, and then caught it again.

She smiled brightly at the Sentinel who rubbed his reddened cheek. "Hi Kellan, what brings you to New Orleans," then her face broke into mock sadness, "Oh, did I hurt the mighty Sentinel with my teeny tiny bitch slap?"

"What the fuck, Meghan? I was invisible. Invisible!"

"Not to me you weren't."

"Wha? How?"

The former Marine looked smug as the elevator chimed, doors opening, "I'm not telling."

Kellan followed her into the hallway, "Aw c'mon Meg, that's not cool. If I'm screwing something up it could get me killed and such. Then you'd really feel bad and—" He looked around, "Hey, this is a really nice hotel? What are you doing here?" He reached for one of the coffees. "Can I have one of those?"

"For God's sake Kellan, you are like a squirrel on meth and no, you may not have my coffee."

"But you have two."

Megan worked her jaw but kept her voice even, "One is mine and the other is—"

"Boyfriend?" interjected Kellan. "Are you on a little romantic excursion, Meghan? New Orleans is great for that. Have you had breakfast at Brennan's. They have these little rooster stickers that," he paused warily taking a half step back as Meghan narrowed her eyes at him, "Ok, shutting up now."

"Look at me, you unobservant geek-nerd hybrid. Do I look like I'm on a date."

Kellan took stock, eyes washing up and down her, instantly locking in details both large and small. "Nope, not a date."

"And why is that, Kellan," Meghan asked in a long suffering tone. Kellan's face broke into a fierce grin. "Fresh Demi Moore from *Ghost* haircut, impeccably tailored suit designed to obscure ballistic armor, a Glock 41 shoulder holster, Walther PPK ankle holster, and two tactical knives. Meghan. You are on a job, aren't you?"

"Three."

"You are on three jobs?"

"No, idiot. Three tactical knives."

"Really? Where's the third one?"

She smiled wickedly, "I could show you," her voice then changing to a singsong cadence, "but you—have—a girlfriend." Her smile vanished, mouth forming a line. "Now piss off, I'm working."

"What, as a waitress?"

"As a body guard, Kellan. And for what they are paying me, I'll bring them up coffee, croissants, and the NY Times."

"This place seems pretty nice," continued Kellan, "Don't they have room service."

Meghan sighed. "My client likes Cafe Au Lait from Cafe Du Monde, so that's what she gets."

With that Meghan turned the corner and headed toward two large double doors with a placard that read "Royal Orleans: French Quarter Suite," and spoke over her shoulder, "I'm going in now so my client can have her coffee hot.

There is another guard just inside the door and if he sees you, there's a reasonable chance he'll shoot you in the face."

"Ok, I'll wait for you by the elevator then."

"I'm not meeting you at the elevator. I'm on a job."

"I need your help—" began Kellan

"No. You have less than five seconds." She tapped the door with her shoe and felt a prickle on the back of her neck as the door began to open and Kellan whispered from behind her right ear.

"—to steal a magical spear from the Pope."

The door swung open to reveal a large man with distinctly slavic features standing well over six feet tall and nearly half as wide.

"God dammit," said Meghan shaking her head.

"What?" asked the guard in a thickly accented voice as he accepted the cup Meghan offered. His eyes took in the hallway, which appeared empty but for the two of them.

Meghan sighed, "Nothing Alexei, I just forgot the beignets."

"I call service for room," he said affecting a smile and winking at her. "You stay here." Another smile. "With me."

"No, Alexei," responded Meghan in a tone that clearly brooked no further debate. "Room service never delivers them hot enough. I will be right back."

The guard looked disappointed but nodded and Meghan turned, heading back down the hall. As soon as the door clicked behind her, she heard a disembodied voice speak from what seemed like empty air with a comically affected accent, "I call service for room. Maybe I service you too, girl with gun."

"Shut the fuck up, Kellan," lilted Meghan as she turned the corner and mashed the down button on the elevator bank.

The doors to the elevator closed and Kellan appeared next to Meghan. She rounded on him. "Ok, you've gotten my attention, you immature bastard." She glanced up to the floor indicators as they flashed by: *42, 41, 40...*

"You have until we get to the Lobby. Give me your best elevator pitch why in heaven or hell I should put my reputation at risk, let alone my client, to go off galavanting with you."

Kellan's eyes glowed brightly as he leaned casually against the inlayed wood of the elevator car.

"Better hurry, book boy," she said, "Tick tock."

He just nodded up and to the right. "What," Meghan asked? Another nod. She looked up and the floor indicator still showed 40. Meghan looked back to Kellan and then to the floor again as it lazily dimmed from 40 to 39.

She stared at him, "Jerk!"

He smiled, "Bitch! Now c'mere and give me a proper hug."

The elevator gave the deep moaning bong that they had come to expect as the floors changed with time being bent to a crawl: *29*

"So, let me get this straight," said Meghan, feet crossed at the ankles while she leaned into one corner, "How will this not put my client at risk? You know I'm horrible at this time stuff."

"No problem," began Kellan, "I'm not that great at it either, but this one is easy. However long it takes us at the Vatican, I'll just portal us back to this exact point and Bob's your uncle. Meghan Daugherty back with beignets."

"What if I get killed?" she asked calmly and Kellan looked horrified.

"Killed? Why would you get killed? It's the Pope were ripping off not the Cosa Nostra."

"I dunno, Kellan. I got killed last time, at least for a bit."

"Werewolves, Meghan and I was new at this. You are not gonna die."

She shrugged, "Maybe not, but I take my job seriously and have to make sure my client can't be hurt by my decisions."

Bong 28

Kellan shook his head, "I get that, but don't see how she could possibly be hurt if I bring you back to this exact time."

"Unless I'm dead and I can't be brought here. Or you are dead and I'm stuck in Rome with no way back to this point. Or we are both dead and—"

Kellan held up his hands in submission, "Ok, Ok, let me think a minute."

Bong 27

He glared at the floor indicator accusingly then snapped his fingers, "Wait, I think I've got it. What is today's date?"

"September 18th," she paused a moment and added, "2017."

Kellan rolled his eyes, "Duh, 2017."

"Well, you are you," Meghan said with a chuckle. Kellan ignored her.

"Ok, so we know your client is alive and well on September 10th. I will just portal us to Rome so we arrive on the evening of September 10th."

Meghan shrugged, "And that helps us how?"

"Wow, you weren't kidding. You really are bad at time travel." She just stared at him flatly and Kellan hastened on, "We leave now and go back a week, rip off the spear and I bring you back here. If things go casters up and I get snuffed, you have a whole week to get on a plane, fly back to New Orleans, wait until—" Kellan looked at his watch, "10:42 AM, Monday September 18th, and pick up where you left off, getting beignets."

Meghan nodded, "And what if I get taken out?"

"Well," began Kellan thoughtfully, "Pre-dead you would have kept your client safe until 10:42 today and then she, um, you, just wouldn't come back from getting beignets. But Ivan Ivanoff up there would figure something out, right?"

"I don't skip out on contracts, Kellan, ever."

"Dude, you're dead remember. That's like the best excuse ever." Kellan waved his hands. "Besides, that is just not going to happen, this time."

Bong 26 Bing

Kellan and Meghan both turned to see the elevator door slowly start to open. She put her hands on her hips and stared at Kellan intently. "No bullshit now, how important is this?"

The young Sentinel smiled wanly, "Oh, pretty important, kind of trying to help prevent the end of the universe."

Meghan cocked her head and smirked, "Really? And you are the best hope for that?"

Kellan just shrugged apologetically. She shook her head again, "Fine, I'll come, but portal us to my place, I need my gear.

Kellan opened the fridge and peered inside. "I'm gonna have one of your Innis and Gunns, ok?"

He heard the bang of a footlocker closing from within Meghan's bedroom along with sounds of various items being strewn about. "Is it my last one?" she asked in a voice muffled by walls.

Kellan stared at the lone bottle. "No," he said.

"You're lying and why do you need a beer now; it's the middle of the day."

"Not for me. I have time lag. I think it's night for me and I really want a beer."

Meghan walked into the kitchen wearing what Kellan called her "Black Widow" outfit of ballistic armor with lashings for twin Glocks and katanas on hip and back respectively along with at least six throwing and tactical knives strapped in various places. Kellan held the bottle up for her to see, his face hopeful.

She sighed, "Go ahead."

Kellan whooped, slid the bottle down into the opener and watched as its magnet captured it. He took a long pull from the bottle and gave a contented sigh. "I don't think you will need all that," he said gesturing to her gear with the bottle.

Meghan snorted, "Yeah, cause last time went so well."

"C'mon Meghan, as I said, that was Afghanistani werwolves. This is Vatican Catholics; how dangerous can they be? Ideally, we'll just sneak in, grab the spear and be off."

Meghan reached for the bottle which Kellan released with obvious reluctance. She took a drink and handed it back, "I'm sure absolutely nothing will go wrong, Kellan, because so many things go right around you."

He just shrugged noncommittally, "Hope springs eternal?"

Meghan shook her head, "Hope, Kellan, is not a strategy. Now what day is it?"

Kellan looked confused, "Huh, we just covered that in the elevator. Today is September 18th. What day did you think it was?"

She ignored him. "So now is still now and we haven't gone back to then, yet?"

Kellan winced slightly, "Man, you really butcher time language, but yeah. Making time portals is a big deal, takes lots of juice and concentration. I try to avoid doing that in elevators, while time is dilated and civilians are about to enter. Besides, I need to let the last member of our little band know we're ready to go. He was unaware of the whole time traveling bit, so need to fill him in on that too."

Megan blinked several times opening her arms in surprise, "What last member? Kellan, you know I hate surprises. You said 'he,' so I'm pretty sure it's not Shannon."

Kellan just waved a hand dismissing her concerns, "Pish posh, he's just one of the Council folks I was telling you about. You know for added muscle. No big deal."

Kellan raised his voice and said, "Seramai!"

"It is a big deal, Kellan. I do not like going into dangerous situations with people I don't know."

"Seramai!" Kellan said again.

"I especially don't like hooking up with monstrous creatures so you can bring whomever you like, but I'm going to tell the ugly bastard that—"

"Seramai!" Kellan said for the final time and instantly a circle of crackling blue energy formed in front of them causing the the wooden floor to smoke. A moment later the circle flashed so brightly that both Kellan and Meghan involuntarily blinked against the unexpected light. As their vision cleared, Seramai knelt on one knee within the circle, head bowed. He stood slowly to the soft creak of leather as his armor stretched around flexed muscles and he absently brushed flowing brown hair back from his face.

Meghan stared wide-eyed and Kellan nudged her, whispering, "...tell the ugly bastard that—?"

The former Marine stepped forward confidently, hand outstretched to Seramai, "—that I am looking forward to working with him on this mission."

Seramai accepted her hand and slid his up her wrist to grasp it there while locking eyes with hers. He smiled. "Kellan didn't mention bringing a valkyrie with him. What a nice surprise. I love surprises."

Meghan stared back into his brown eyes that seemed to pulse ever so slightly with amber iridescence and Kellan leaned in with a mischievous look on his face. "Yeah, about surprises. You see, Seramai, Meghan has this thing about surprises. She—"

"Loves them," Meghan interrupted as she covertly ground the heel of her boot onto Kellan's foot, "I just love a good surprise and you certainly seem like a good one."

Chapter 10

SPEAR OF LONGINUS

The portal winked out and with it, the glow that had illuminated the surrounding area. Meghan, Seramai, and Kellan were left in utter darkness. The Sentinel felt his eyes warm as he channeled the power and looked around while Meghan cursed, fumbling for her tactical light.

"This is so cool," began Kellan, "I can see different frequencies of light while I'm channeling. Who knew?" He then felt a strong hand rest on his shoulder and Seramai spoke in a feigned whisper that did nothing to diminish its resonate tones.

"Please, Sentinel of Order. Could you exercise a touch more decorum? Perhaps you could act a bit more like God's unchecked hand on the world, and a bit less like an adolescent slitting his first throat."

"Holy crap, Seramai, nice childhood you must have had," Kellan replied as he ran his fingers along cold stone.

"There," said Meghan giving a frustrated sigh. The room blazed with light causing Kellan to wince and squint as his eyes adjusted. The three were standing in a stone room that looked to be only about six feet by six feet. Looking up, Kellan was surprised to see that the room had no ceiling but just continued upward until it was lost in gloom. He looked down and found Meghan starting at him flatly, "What the hell, Kel? Nice portal job. Where are we? The smallest dungeon cell ever?"

Seramai chuckled and Meghan gave him a grin as Kellan frowned at them both. "I told you that it was hard to make a portal here. This was the only spot it would form within the whole of Vatican City. Last I recalled, we all agreed to risk this rather than trying to avoid being spotted walking in from Rome. I mean it's not like anyone would stop to ask why Black Widow and Spartacus were dropping in on the Pope."

Both Seramai and Meghan spoke over one another and Kellan raised his hands. "I don't care." He stared first at Meghan. "I don't care that Black Widow didn't have double kevlar woven battle armor with ceramic plates." Kellan turned Seramai. "I also don't care that Spartacus was a slave and only wished to have armor like yours. I was making an amusing commentary on your anachronistic garb."

"Amusing to whom?" Seramai asked. "Meghan, did you find it amusing?"

"I rarely find Kellan amusing. I think he confuses annoying with amusing. They both start and end with the same letters."

The Sentinel ground his teeth. "I'm already regretting having you two along. Now do something useful and see if there is a hidden door or something."

"Why don't you just fly straight up and see if there is an exit that way?" Asked Meghan.

Kellan had been squatting down pressing along one wall and spoke over his shoulder, "I can't fly, Meghan. You know I can't fly. I told you it's the vampire that can bloody well fly."

"Yeah, I know, but I just like reminding you from time to time."

Kellan was about to reply when a sharp grinding sound came from the wall nearest Seramai who immediately went into a crouch, short sword in hand. The three watched as a section of wall continued to rise in small increments as if being winched upward by some manual means. Light spilled through as the opening widened and Kellan snapped shields around the three of them. Moments later they found themselves facing a man in his late sixties or seventies who was dressed in formal Cardinal attire complete with red skullcap. To either side of the Cardinal stood two massive creatures measuring over eight feet high. They were humanoid but only in the most general sense and each seemed to be carved out of rough marble or granite. They wore no clothes, had no sex organs, and stared with a vacant expression except for deep-set eyes in which bright blue pinpricks of light burned. The creatures crouched as they entered the room causing Kellan and his friends to take several steps back until they bumped into the far wall.

The Cardinal smiled warmly as he walked directly to Kellan and extended his hand. The Sentinel shared a quick glance with his companions and reached out to take the Cardinal's hand, but instead the Catholic Prince deftly scooped up Kellan's hand bent over it and placed a kiss on the softly glowing green stone which flared at the touch of his lips.

"Greetings Sentinel of Order," said the Cardinal, "I am Cardinal Karras. On behalf of His Holiness, Pope Francis, I bid you welcome to Vatican City. Please follow me and I will lead you to someplace more fitting for discussion." With that he turned to leave, but Meghan stopped him.

"Hey, will the living statues be coming too? They don't seem very welcoming."

Karras glanced over his shoulder, "You have nothing to fear from our Golems, Ms. Daugherty. They exist to protect us from unnatural or Chaotic forces. You are neither."

Without another word, Karras passed through the doorway followed by the Golems. As he did so, the wall began to slowly grind downward causing Kellan and his companions to following quickly behind. For long minutes the small group walked in silence through winding, rough hewn, passages. LED lights illuminated the way at regular intervals but seemed far too modern for the ancient walls. Finally they came to a massive wooden door, wrapped in bands of iron that bore the patina of age. Karras reached to his neck and smoothly lifted a key which hung there by its attached leather strap. The lock released smoothly and the foremost Golem pushed it open.

The room beyond was as elegant as the passages were stark. Along the walls hung rich tapestries and ornately carved bookshelves. Thick area rugs with intricate patterns were placed beneath chairs, couches, and tables that were interspersed throughout the chamber. At one end of the room stood a large fireplace in which crackled several equally large logs. Doors stood to either side of the fireplace and each were attended by brightly colored Swiss Guards, hands gripping traditional halberts. The two golems retreated into massive alcoves which seemed carved for that very purpose. The blue fire faded from their eyes and the creatures appeared, for all the world, like simple, inanimate, statues.

"Please," said Cardinal Karras as he gestured to several chairs and a settee arrayed before the fire. Kellan shifted one chair slightly to give himself a better peripheral view of the room and settled in. Seramai reclined into the settee, leaning back into one corner and crossing his legs while giving Kellan an enigmatic smile. Meghan settled in next to the warrior and he gave her a quick grin. Kellan squinted at her. *What the hell is going on there* Kellan thought to himself. *Did she just blush? Meghan Daugherty does not blush.* The former marine caught Kellan's appraising gaze and glared at him. He smiled at her. *That's more like it* he thought.

Karras pulled a long golden rope that hung alongside the fireplace and rested himself on the large, high-backed chair, which was placed between Kellan's chair and the settee. "I've take the liberty of having some refreshments brought. We are quite a ways beneath the city so it might take a few minutes to arrive, but at least the fire has been prepared. It can get quite cold and damp this far down."

"You seem to have been expecting us," said Kellan.

Karras chucked warmly, "Well, we were expecting something. Wards throughout the city had gone off indicating multiple attempts to gain entrance. That is why we activated the Golems. There is, of course, no way to tell whether someone is friend or foe before they arrive."

"Of course," said Kellan confidently. Meghan smirked and gave him a subtle shake of her head.

"So you have warded the entire City except for that one room," Seramai said appreciatively. "Nicely done and I assume the lack of a ceiling is so you can pour all manner of things down on the unwary."

"Just so," said the Cardinal, "Depending on the need most anything can, and has, been used."

Seramai leaned forward, "Indulge me. What kind of things."

Karras steepled his hands, tapping fingers to lips absently. "Well, holy water of course. Holy oil, both burning and not. Molten metal. There are accounts, before my time, of other, more exotic, materials being used, but I cannot attest for the veracity of such accounts." Karras brighten as the door to Kellan's left creaked open and two young priests entered carrying trays. "Ah, the promised refreshments." The two priests silently placed the contents of their trays on the table and backed out of the room. Karras stood and looked to Meghan. "Tea?" She nodded, smiling and Karras poured her a cup.

"Coffee for me," said Seramai, "Black."

"And you, Sentinel," the Cardinal asked turning to Kellan who smiled mischievously.

"Well, do you have—" The Sentinel cut off as he could feel Meghan's eyes burrowing into him. "Coffee for me too, thank you Cardinal," his voice thick with resignation as Meghan gave him a self-satisfied nod.

"Excellent, the pastries are quite good as well. Please help yourself."

Seramai leaned forward, lifting the tray heavily laden with cookies and other items, then offered it to Meghan. Kellan watched as she held the warrior's gaze for a moment and took several items off the tray. *Oh for the love of god* thought Kellan. Seramai likewise took a couple items and glanced up, catching Kellan's eye long enough to see him shake his head, then placed the tray back on the table.

The Cardinal leaned further back into his chair and said, "There, now that everyone's settled and we've been appropriately hospitable, perhaps you could enlighten me as to the purpose of your," he paused for the barest of heartbeats, "visit."

Kellan was about to answer, when Seramai gestured with a cookie and said, "Kellan wanted to relieve you of the Spear of Destiny." He gestured to Meghan and back to himself. "We were backup in case of unforeseen resistance from, for example, Golems."

Kellan cringed as the older man looked to him, "I see. So you were going to break into our home and steal one of our most treasured relics. The very spear that pierced our Lord's heart."

Kellan smiled wanly. "Steal is such an awful term. We were just going to borrow it. You know, to keep it safe."

"Really," said the Cardinal, "To keep it safe? I think it is fairly safe right now. Nothing short of an Archangel or Sentinel could remove the Spear of Longinus from its reliquary."

"Which is exactly who's coming for it," said Seramai as he casually reached for another cookie, "These really are quite good."

Karras looked confused. "When you said *exactly,* who were you referring to, yourselves?"

Seramai laughed, "Oh no, Father. We're the good guys. The Cabal is going to send one of their unfallen Archangels to breach your walls and make off with that spear. I suspect the only reason they haven't so far is that it's pretty much a suicide mission for whatever Archangel tries it. No way a bit of Sentinel blood is going to hide them from Godly wrath after that theft."

Kellan was shaking his head in disbelief at Seramai's directness and leaned forward, "Cardinal, the Cabal is—"

"I know very well who they are, young Sentinel. Did the Council of Havilah send you?"

"Uh," said Kellan dumbfounded.

"Send us," laughed Seramai, "I am a High Counselor of Havilah."

Karras seemed shocked. "Are you? That changes much. I don't recognize you by name or face and believe I know all the High Councilors."

Seramai grinned broadly. "Oh you know me, Father Karras and I know you. Perhaps this will help." Seramai lifted his hand and traced the air. As he did so, trailers of red-orange light formed behind his moving finger. When he was done a complex glyph hung in the air for a moment and then broke apart with a shower of sparks. Seramai grinned again. "Does that help?"

Karras' eyes had grown wide with recognition. "I'd say it does, Lord—"

"Seramai," said the warrior, eyes locked with those of Karras.

"Seramai," the Cardinal repeated with a nod.

"So, the spear," said Seramai, "Would you mind fetching it for us, then we'll be on our way."

"Oh, I cannot remove it from the reliquary. I doubt even you could, Lord Seramai. The Sentinel should be able to, but even that is not certain. The best I will be able to do is take you to the reliquary but there I must leave you to succeed or fail."

Seramai slapped both hands to his thighs, "And that, dear priest, is all anyone can ever ask for—the chance to succeed or fail. Time to go then." Seramai stood, offered a hand to Meghan, who graciously accepted, and joined him beside the fire.

For his part, Kellan remained in his chair, bemused at the speed with which the conversation had turned, and wondering again about Seramai's enigmatic answers. When the Cardinal also took to his feet, Kellan simply shook his head in resignation, knocked back what little remained of his coffee, and joined them by the door.

Cardinal Karras placed a friendly hand on Kellan's shoulder and looked into the young Sentinel's eyes. "I will take you as far as the reliquary threshold. The spear, like a few other items of similar power, is stored alone. You will, of course, need to contend with it's immortal guardians, but I'm sure that was something for which you've already planned." With that he opened the door and gestured the small party through. "Make haste please, I'd rather the spear be gone before any of the Cabal come calling."

Kellan paused at the threshold grabbing hold of Seramai who turned back quizzically. "Wait, what immortal guardians? You guys never mentioned anything about—"

The large warrior laughed and clapped Kellan on the shoulder, "If you knew everything that was to transpire, from whence would excitement come, eh!"

Meghan pushed past the two men and jabbed Kellan in the ribs, "Yeah, *Sentinel*, don't wet yourself. How bad can a few immortal guardians be?" She looked up at Seramai and walked past him asking, "Am I right or what?"

"Indeed you are, my valkyrie. Indeed you are."

Kellan just looked at the Cardinal one last time before following and said, "I think I'm starting to hate both of them."

〜ᔓᓚ〜

The winding passages led generally downward with the air becoming ever more cool and damp. Moisture now clung to the rough walls as the four of them emerged into a large domed cavern. Doors were imbedded along its circular walls at regular intervals and in its center a massive inlayed cross broke up the otherwise plain polished stone floor.

Cardinal Karras angled to the right as they entered the cavern, walking deliberately to one of the twelve doors. He stopped and gestured. The door seemed to be made entirely of gold with numerous carvings that depicted aspects of Christ's passion. The upper third of the door was consumed by the carving of an intricate and stylized spear.

Kellan reached for the door's handle but Karras placed a hand gently on the Sentinel's outstretched arm, restraining him. The Cardinal looked at Kellan, his face grave, and said, "You may not leave without the spear."

Kellan cocked his head quizzically, "I don't intend to."

The Cardinal's lips turned upward slightly, "No, you misunderstand. The doors in this cavern," he began, gesturing, "are not simply physical doors, but rather threshold portals in their own right. They are constrained by wards even as your portals were when you tried to travel here. Once you pass over the threshold, its portal will vanish and only reappear for those who possess the relic within. If you fail to obtain the spear, you will be trapped like many before you were trapped. You will not be able to generate your own portal within the reliquary either. Be sure, young Sentinel, because time does not flow within these chambers. Close proximity to such power warps both body and spirit. The immortal guardians within were once simply human. They are now much more." The Cardinal paused, voice dropping to a sad whisper, "and much less."

"Wait," asked Meghan, "If the doors only allow someone to leave if they posses the relic, then how does the relic get returned." She paled in recognition. "Does anyone returning them have to stay?"

Cardinal Karras chuckled softly and turned to her, "Very perceptive, but no. Only a rare few ever notice that seeming contradiction. The door to these reliquaries are simply doors when no relic resides within. It is the relic's power that causes each threshold portal to manifest. When either returning a relic, or placing it initially, one has a short period of time before the companion portal activates."

She raised an arched eyebrow at the Cardinal. "How short a period of time?"

"Hmm, oh, I don't know exactly. Perhaps five minutes or so. Plenty of time if one does not dawdle."

Meghan looked dissatisfied with the answer, but Kellan turned the latch and pushed, causing the door to open inward without a sound. Beyond the doorway all appeared black as pitch as if nothing existed past the opening. "We'll be fine," Kellan said. He stepped through and vanished from sight.

Seramai rocked backward laughing as Meghan stared at the darkened doorway mouthing a silent curse, "Come, my beautiful valkyrie, let's do our best to keep your headstrong Sentinel alive."

She met his eyes and felt like she was being drawn into their strange amber glow. Her lips curled up with feral grin, anxiety suddenly replaced with a battle lust she hadn't felt since returning from her tours in the Middle East. "Hoo Rah," she yelled jumping through the doorway, "Who wants to live forever!"

Meghan felt her feet slide out from beneath her. She fell backwards, air escaping in a whoosh, while stars blossomed when her head hit the stone floor. Above her stood a giant of a man wearing animal furs and brandishing a massive double-bladed axe which was already arcing down. Meghan began to roll out of the way when the axe suddenly stopped with an ear wrenching clang. She looked up to see Seramai straining with his sword arm extended. The barbarian looked up and recognition seemed to dawn but before he could act further, Seramai reached out with his other hand and gripped the man's neck squeezing tightly. Meghan slid out from under the two and regained her feet as Seramai cast her a sideways glance. "I may want you to live forever, so do try to be more careful."

She smirked at him and slid the twin katana's from her back. "My lord," croaked the barbarian, "It is you my—" His words were cut off as Seramai twisted his grip violently causing a loud crack, then threw the man in a heap.

Megan gave him a quizzical look and said, "My lord?"

"Delusional. Come, let us find your Sentinel before he gets himself killed and strands us here."

As if on cue the whole chamber suddenly glowed with a brilliant white light as pillars of white hot plasmatic fire engulfed three shapes they could not quite make out. As the glow faded, Kellan came into their field of view. He was bleeding from several small wounds on his neck and face, but otherwise seemed in reasonably good shape.

"Why didn't you stay by the door, idiot," asked Meghan.

"What the hell are you talking about, I did stay by the door," he answered angrily then added, "What took you so long. I've been waiting at least an hour."

"Stop," said Seramai, "I suspect we were each brought to a slightly different place within this chamber and the priest did mention time flowing oddly within the chamber. " The general turned to Megan and continued, "Meghan, I was quite a distance from you when I entered, but closer than I think Kellan was, because we entered right behind one another. Even so, I was almost too late to reach you in time. Regardless, we are together now and that is what matters. So, Sentinel of Order, where is this spear that pierced the Creator's incarnate self."

Kellan concentrated and several balls of white light began to rotate between his hands. He hurled them upward and each rose about twenty feet into the air to hover, casting a warm glow all around them. Beyond the spheres could be seen the cavern roof maybe another ten feet further. In front of them the floor began to curve upward where it became a spiraling ramp. It seemed to curve around until reaching an apex where the three could barely see a glint of metal. Between where they stood and that apex, the ramp's spiral was interrupted several times by large platforms on which Kellan thought, but couldn't be sure, he saw movement.

"There," said Kellan pointing, "I can feel it. The power of this place emanates from above."

"Then up we will go, Kellan Thorne," said Seramai.

"I'll take point," Meghan said and started toward where the ramp met floor.

Seramai laughed, "Stand aside little valkyrie. I will lead."

Meghan took a deep breath and calmed herself. She had spent three tours of duty dealing with men who all thought they were more capable then she. Years of training had taught her both how to fight and how to manage those who thought she couldn't. But as she started to explain why she would be better positioned on narrow elevated terrain, Meghan, again, felt herself drawn into Seramai's softly glowing eyes. Her anger flared. She walked up to him, jaw set, and stopped, with only a hair's breadth left between them. Her head only came midway up his chest but as she glared up, there was no hesitation in her, "What did you say?"

"Uh oh," said Kellan and tried to separate them. "Guys, this is not the time to start measuring dic, uh, well I guess that doesn't work in this case anyway."

Seramai grabbed Meghan by the shoulders with both hands and lifted her off the floor to where they were eye level with each other. He smiled at her. "I said. Stand aside. I will lead, little valk—"

Meghan arched forward smashing her forehead into Seramai's nose causing it to crack and for blood to gush forth. He dropped her and she swept out her leg tripping him just as the barbarian had done to her minutes before. He caught himself on the way down, breaking his fall with an outstretched hand, then launched himself back to his feet.

Meghan was in a battle crouch hands up and bouncing on her feet, eyes narrowed with a fury Kellan had never seen before. She was always so controlled. So measured. Not so now. She leaped toward Seramai and he blocked her initial mixed martial attacks with some difficulty and smiled again. "You are quite accomplished at—" He broke off again as the hilt of a throwing dagger hit him in the face. Seramai reached up placing two fingers in his mouth and slowly pulled out a bloody tooth.

Kellan couldn't believe what he was seeing and yelled at his friend, "What the hell, Meghan, you could have killed him."

She grinned at Kellan. "If I wanted to kill him, I'd have stuck him with the pointy end. I just want him to tell me that I should go up first because I'm faster then he is. I'm more nimble than he is and I'm certainly a whole lot smarter than he is.

As Meghan turned back to face the warrior general, she rocked back as the full blow from his closed fist met her jaw. The former Marine spun sideways, pain blossoming, and went down on one knee, her head bowed. Seramai dragged the back of his wrist and hand along his face, wiping off blood that continued to flow from his nose. His smile was gone and he stared down at Meghan grimly, "I have killed entire generations for what you just dared to do, little mortal. If someone chooses to war with me, they best be prepared to win. And when it comes to war, I play to—"

Kellan knew Meghan well and could see what was about to happen as clear as words on a page. He called out, knowing it was already too late. "Meghan, No!"

The Sentinel knew he had not bent time, yet it seemed he saw his friend as if she were moving in slow motion. All the pieces were perfectly in place and Kellan knew Seramai was in for some serious pain. Meghan hadn't fallen to one knee, she had put herself there with her right foot positioned behind for leverage. Her whole body formed a tightly coiled weapon and Kellan saw it begin to unwind as she lifted her head, eyes glowing, with the same amber light as did Seramai's. She buried her fist into the warrior's groin and Kellan gasped in sympathetic pain as Seramai doubled over. Kellan thought the larger man was about to retch, but Meghan had leaned back gaining new leverage. She lashed out with a booted foot, kicking him so hard in the face that his forward momentum reversed and he flipped backward, head striking stone.

While Seramai lay momentarily dazed, Meghan arched her back and forced herself to a crouch then uncoiled her legs while smoothly reaching for her twin katanas. Kellan yelled again as he watched her launch into the air poised to bring both swords down onto the warrior's supine form. The Sentinel reached inward and channeled an angled shield around Seramai but each time he willed it into being, the shield seemed to unravel leaving only a vague green haze in its place. Kellan frantically tried a third time and saw Seramai lift both arms to block the blows on his vambraces when the Sentinel was struck hard from behind.

Kellan lay sprawled forward, sliding slightly on the polished stone, as he felt the links of his armor begin to knit back together having been damaged by the unseen blow. He rolled over in time to see what appeared like a medieval knight in heavy armor approaching. Kellan watched as a series of green runes ran down his arm and he focused a burst of air towards the attacking knight who flew backward to land halfway up the first leg of the ramp. He risked a momentary glance rightward and was rewarded with a very much alive Seramai trading blows with Meghan which were so quickly landed that each seemed nothing but a blur. Kellan turned his attention back to the knight who had regained his feet, then did a quick double take.

Why are those two idiots smiling like that, Kellan thought. Indeed, despite continued cuts and bruises they were inflicting, both Meghan and Seramai seemed transcendent with joy as they were fully consumed by their macabre dance.

Kellan ducked as the knight's sword sliced through air inches above his head. He pivoted and gave the swordsman a powered kick from behind that served to launch him directly toward Seramai and Meghan. Without losing one step from their attacks on each other, Seramai crouched low and buried his short sword in the knight's chest while Meghan crossed her katana's just above the mans gorget and smoothly decapitated him.

Kellan winced as the headless corpse slumped to the side while Seramai deftly retrieved his sword and used it to parry another attack by Meghan. Kellan ground his teeth in frustration and closed the distance between them only to snap a shield about himself as both moved effortlessly to strike him. Meghan's open palm glanced off Kellan's shield even as Seramai's closed fist continued through, but slowed, as if moving through water. Even slowed, the warrior general's blow sent Kellan tumbling to the ground, his vision blurred and head reeling. All other noise stopped and he turned hurriedly around to find Meghan with the tip of a dagger pressed so hard against Seramai's neck that blood seeped around the point.

She laughed wildly as her shining eyes found Kellan's but spoke directly into Seramai's ear, "Never take your eyes off the more dangerous adversary. That's me, handsome. Some warrior you are. Serious rookie mistake."

For his part, the general stood frozen, an odd look on his face. Kellan saw the grip Meghan used to hold him and any movement he made would have forced the dagger into his neck. That explained his lack of movement but not the ridiculous smile that Kellan saw spread across his face."

"You have bested me, Meghan Daugherty. I yield."

Instantly the glow left her eyes and Kellan saw her slowly remove the dagger from Seramai's neck. He turned to her and continued smiling at her dazed expression, then leaned down and placed a soft kiss on her already purpling cheek. "You have bested me!" he yelled almost laughing and Meghan took a half step back eyes still locked on his. "Name what gift I can offer you, my valkyrie, and it will be yours."

For her part, Meghan seemed to warm to the new direction things had taken. She tried to look impassive as both she and Kellan watched Seramai's wounds heal and vanish, then said, "Look what you did to my face, you hulking mountainous bastard. Get over here and fix it, then I'll tell you what I want my gift to be."

Kellan had regained his feet and headed toward them, but stopped when he caught a well understood glance by Meghan. She was up to something. Seramai had closed the distance and looked down on her. She smiled up wolfishly, "Well, I said fix it. You can't leave me all bruised while you are looking so pretty."

"As you wish, my valkyrie," said Seramai. He pulled Meghan into a tight embrace and kissed her deeply.

Kellan began to fidget and said, "I totally did not see this coming. Uh, guys, I don't know how many more of these guardian dudes are going to try and kill us on our way up to the spear so can you finish up whatever the hell it is you are doing and get back to helping keep me alive. Guys? Aw, C'mon. At least take a bloody breath."

They did and as Megan leaned back, Kellan could see all her wounds had healed. She also looked pretty darn happy to Kellan, which just fueled his already simmering aggravation.

"Can you two please explain what the hell that—"

"For my gift," Meghan interrupted, "I would like," then paused staring up at Seramai, "a romantic night out with the man whose ass I so completely just kicked."

Kellan groaned and thought, *I wonder if this is how people get trapped in these vaults. They've completely lost their minds.*

"As your vanquished adversary, I can do nothing but accede to your request," said Seramai stepping back and bowing with a flourish so perfectly executed that even Kellan had to nod in appreciation.

"Excellent," said Meghan, then she stepped forward, stood on toes, and wrapped her arms behind Seramai's neck, pulling his face close to hers.

"No no no," complained Kellan shaking them both, "Stop it you two. Get a room." He paused staring first at one and then the other. "After we get the bloody spear of destiny. You guys are the worst back-up ever." Kellan turned toward the ramp, took a couple steps and then rounded again on Seramai, "And you," he growled causing the warrior to raise his hands in a mockingly placating gesture.

"Me?" he said innocently.

Kellan stalked back and glared up at Seramai, "Yeah, you. I know you put the whammy on my pal Meghan here, and we're gonna have words about this later. Trust me."

Meghan snorted, "Bullshit, Kel. First, if anyone whammy'd anyone, I did it to him. Second, I don't need you defending me." With that she wedged herself between the two men while dragging her open palm lazily along Seramai's chest as she headed toward the ramp without a backwards glance.

Kellan heard the low rumble of Seramai's subdued laughter, "She speaks truthfully, Sentinel of Order. I did nothing to her and what she did to me, well, that will require more explanation than we have time for at present." With that, he gestured with one arm and said, "After you, I believe the lady has point."

⌒⑴⟨⟩

"Well, you don't see that every day," said Kellan with a sigh as he stared down at the three corpses all wearing black military uniforms with twin lightning bolt "S" letters on the collar.

Meghan winced as she applied tissue sealing compound to the knife wound on her shoulder and cursing herself for not having seen the weapon early enough to keep it from sliding between the seams of her body armor. "Yeah, Nazi's in the Vatican. It's all a little too *Indiana Jones* for me. Hey, where'd Sera get off too?"

"Hmm, oh, he said he was going to take a peak up this last ramp and see if he could get eyes on the spear itself. The big guy figured there would be a super nasty up there to protect it."

"There is but one soldier guarding the Spear, Sentinel of Order," said Seramai as he took the final few steps down the ramp to rejoin Kellan and Meghan on the third platform.

"Just one," asked Kellan, then added, "How bad can that be?"

Seramai shrugged as he knelt down beside Meghan, "He appears to be a Marine special operator."

"One can be pretty bad then," said Meghan as she started to gingerly move her body armor over the, now dressed, wound. Seramai stopped her and stared intently at the white sealing foam that had hardened over the knife wound.

"That will almost certainly leave a scar," he said.

"Yeah," said Kellan about that, "Why haven't you been healing her along the way? She won't let me because I have to take the wounds on myself. You get to do it as a freebie."

Seramai seemed to ignore Kellan as he continued to look into Meghan's eyes, "I like scars on a woman."

She grinned back, "Well then, you are just gonna love me, 'cause I've got scars in places you don't even have."

The warrior barked a laugh, stood and turned to Kellan. "To your question, I cannot simply heal others. That is not my gift. What happened before was—" the large man paused as if seeking the right words, "unique to the situation. As I said below, I will explain at a later time. To Meghan, not you. If she chooses to share that information, well, that is up to her."

Kellan just narrowed his eyes and felt his jaw muscles knot as he worked them, but Seramai simply clapped the Sentinel on the shoulder and nodded to the final ramp.

"Right," said Meghan standing and adjusting her gear, "Let's get you the pig sticker and blow this popsicle stand."

At each of the other two platforms, soldiers from a previous era had been present. As soon as the small party approached each platform, they attacked without word or warning. When the the three were halfway up this final ramp with no sign of attack, Meghan turned and crouched down. The two men likewise took a knee.

"I don't like it," she said. "Sera, you said this last one looked like a modern soldier. What if he's got a biological or chemical agent up there? What if the bastard has a suitcase nuke?"

Seramai raised an eyebrow, "I saw no such device, and as for biological or chemical agents, both the Sentinel and I are immune to such things." Meghan gave him a flat expression and Kellan winced as the warrior looked confused by their reaction. "What?" he asked.

Meghan smirked at him and pointed two fingers toward her own face. "Oh," said Seramai, then with even more realization, "Oh! Yes, well, you would need to be protected from such things. My apologies, I am not frequently in the company of mortals. I'm sure Kellan here would grant you a shield, isn't that right, Kellan?"

The Sentinel simply sighed and shook his head. "Yeah, well, setting aside the pain you are going to receive from your valkyrie for lack of sensitivity, I am not sure how well my shields will protect from those—"

"Oh my god," shouted Meghan in alarm. Both men stood whirling in the direction she was facing. Halfway down the final ramp stood a soldier in urban camouflage gear. "Justin? Justin? Is that you?" She took a step toward him but Kellan and Seramai each placed a hand on her shoulder restraining her. The man was tall and broadly built. He had a round face and with dark brown eyes and skin. His lips turned down in a sad expression as he and Meghan locked eyes.

"Hello Captain. I can honestly say I never expected to see you again."

Kellan felt his mouth fall open and Seramai turned to Meghan. "You know this man?"

She nodded. "I do. He is lieutenant Justin Walker a special operator who I inserted and extracted on a number of missions." Her voice trailed off as she seemed to speak more to herself than the others, "but he was killed on a mission in Pakistan."

Lieutenant Walker shook his head slowly. "No Meghan, I came here to obtain the very weapon you now seek and, instead, became trapped by it.

"But, all the other guardians below us? How did you get past them and yet not get the Spear?" She asked.

"Yeah, and how were they all alive when we got here if you killed them?" added Kellan.

Justin sighed sadly. "So long as the Spear remains in this reliquary, death has no hold on those within. One touch by the unworthy and we are cursed to remain as we are until He comes again."

Kellan and Meghan shared a look and simultaneously said, "Huh?"

"The Incarnation." said Seramai, voice full with understanding. "That curse was meant for Longinus only, soldier. It was he who struck the blow."

Justin spread his hands, "And yet here I am. I watched those soldiers from bygone eras reanimate and take their posts even as I am now forced to do. I must guard this accursed Spear until someone can wrest it from me and this place."

Kellan took a step toward him. "Look, Justin, you are only one guy. Why don't you just let us—"

"Stop!" yelled the soldier in a voice so loud the cavern seemed to rumble. His skin took on an ethereal glow as the air rippled with unseen power. "I am the last guardian. You may not pass."

"Oh Kaay," said Kellan taking a half step back, "Now he looks like the final guardian of an ancient relic of unimaginable power."

Seramai unsheathed his short sword and said, "Soldier, I will give you a worthy death."

The lieutenant shook his head sadly and stared intently at Seramai. "I know who you are. I have seen your hands on the world and while I have always avoided death at your hands, I would welcome it now. But it cannot be."

Kellan growled under his breath, "He knows you, Seramai? I really hate secrets."

"All will be revealed Sentinel of Order. In time," came his whispered response.

The two men tensed as they prepared to close on the soldier, but were both pushed aside as Meghan stepped between then. Lieutenant Walker raised both hands offensively as ribbons of energy began to run along his arms.

"Lieutenant stop!" and her command sounded like a whip cracking. Justin lowered his hands, looking confused, and she continues softly. "Lieutenant. Justin. Listen to me. If you kill us here, we will just become the final guardians and you will remain as the others have. Your only hope is for us to remove the Spear from this place and allow you to," she paused, "move on."

"I cannot. The force compelling me is too strong to resist. I have tried, Captain."

"Try harder."

His eyes grew hard, "It is impossible and even if I let you pass, what makes you think the Spear would find you worthy. I know you of old, Meghan Daugherty, and you are less worthy of its power than even I was. And him!" Justin glared at Seramai. "He is practically the personification of all that the Spear was used for and seeks now to prevent."

"Justin," she said voice barely a whisper. "Not me and not Seramai either." She gave a half turn and gestured to Kellan. "He will take the Spear of Destiny. He is the Sentinel of Order, God's unchecked hand on the world. He can do this."

Lieutenant Walker looked Kellan up and down as if seeing him for the first time and let out an incredulous breath, "Him?"

Kellan frowned, "Hey now, I am perfectly capable of taking this holy toothpick out of here. Don't you worry about that, sparky."

"Not helping," Meghan whispered.

"Bah, this is pointless," yelled Seramai and charged up the ramp, sword raised. He leaped and drove it toward the soldier's neck, but Walker raised two glowing hands and caught the blade between them on its downward stroke. It seemed to vibrate there for a split second, then the soldier leaned back, bracing himself on one foot while kicking out with the other. Air burst out of Seramai as the kick landed, pushing him back and off the platform entirely. A moment later they heard a thud as he hit the floor far below. Kellan was too stunned to speak as the soldier casually tossed Seramai's sword over the edge then turned his attention back to Meghan.

"Holy shit, Meghan," yelled Kellan in alarm, "We need to go check on—"

She interrupted him, keeping her eyes firmly fixed on Lieutenant Walker, but waved a hand unconcerned, "He'll be fine."

"Are you crazy, he just got lightning kicked and fell a couple hundred feet."

"He'll be fine," she said again and before Kellan could argue further he heard cursing from below and the sounds of heavy feet pounding up the ramp. She took a step forward keeping her arms open and eyes on Justin.

"Lieutenant, I need you to listen to me. We can get you out of here."

He shook his head violently. "No. No you can't and this is where I should be regardless. I should never had tried to take the Spear. I knew they wanted to use it for a weapon. I knew it and came anyway."

"You were just following orders," Meghan said softly.

"Orders," he scoffed. "Those Nazi's below were following orders too. Orders do not excuse atrocity. The Spear should stay apart from the world where it can do no harm."

"But others are coming for it, Justin. And we were sent to keep it safe. If they obtain it," she paused not knowing how best to describe what Kellan had told her, "If they obtain it, all the sorrows you've seen as a soldier will pale in comparison."

Meghan's words had an effect and the soldier lowered his hands. "I believe you Captain, you never steered me wrong and pulled me out of hell more than a few times."

She took another step toward him, "Then believe me now, Justin. Let us pass." He looked at her uncertainly as Seramai finally crested the ramp to the last platform, his face a thunderhead of anger. Meghan heard him coming and lashed out with her left hand palm up in a stopping gesture that caused him to pull up short.

She took one more step and Kellan's stomach lurched as the soldier's stance and demeanor turned aggressive again energy building.

"Meghan..." he said warningly.

"Stand down, Lieutenant!" she yelled in a voice that brooked nothing but obedience. The soldier seemed confused but didn't attack. "Lieutenant, I said Stand. Down!" She could see the conflict within him. He practically shook with it so she pushed harder. "Is that how you respond to a superior officer, Soldier? A-ten-hut!"

With what seemed like an almost relieved sigh, Lieutenant Walker snapped to attention, angled hand to forehead in a picture perfect salute. He stood staring straight ahead like a statue as Meghan closed the last steps between them, circling her left arm around his waist, beneath his right arm, which still held a trembling salute.

"Good night, soldier," she said in a whisper Kellan could barely hear, and deftly slipped her tactical dagger between Walker's ribs to pierce his heart. His eyes widened but the Lieutenant made no sound as his knees buckled. Meghan couldn't hold him with the one arm, but Seramai was already beside her, cradling the soldier and laying him gently to the ground. The crackling energy faded as Justin looked up at Meghan eyes fluttering a moment before becoming fixed. Several tears slipped from her eyes to fall on the dead soldier's cheek and run down to the floor. "Your watch is over, Justin. Rest now, you just rest."

Seramai put a comforting hand on Meghan's shoulder and she looked up, eyes full of tears. "He was a good solider," Seramai said, "and you gave him the honorable death he sought."

She nodded, wiping her hand across her nose, "Doesn't make it feel any better though does it."

The warrior general helped Meghan to her feet and embraced her, "No, it never does."

Kellan watched as she melted into his thick arms and looked away as she sobbed quietly. Kellan knew she didn't like being seen like this, but also knew it was one of the most heroic and selfless acts he'd seen done by two people in his entire life.

After long moments, Meghan pulled back from Seramai and turned to see Kellan had retreated to the platform with his back to her.

"Kellan!" He turned to her. "Get your ass up here and take this accursed spear. I'm done with this place!"

The three crested the last ramp and stood on the final platform. Before them stood a massive wooden cross. A deep notch had been carved in the vertical beam and within it rested an ancient roman long spear. Its shaft was a dark brown and marked with numerous scars. Likewise, its tip was chipped in several places.

Seramai grunted.

"What," asked Kellan.

"Not very impressive," the general replied.

"That's how you know it's real," interjected Meghan. "Kellan, grab it."

"Ok, ok, give me a second," he said walking closer to the cross. Rust colored streaks could be seen in spots covering both the spear's blade and shaft. Kellan reached out to take the weapon and then pulled his hand back.

"What?" asked Meghan.

Kellan turned to her, "I'm not sure. It just radiates so much power."

"Yeah, no shit," She said, "We're hundreds of feet beneath the Vatican looking to liberate the weapon that, quite literally, was thrust into the heart of God. Man up and grab the fucking spear."

Kellan nodded and reached inward feeling the warmth come to his eyes as they began to glow. He turned back to the spear and had a quick intake of breath. Seen while channeling his power, the Spear radiated colors. Deep red auras played up and down the shaft while green ribbons lashed out and where the two met, violet sparks formed, then settled back into the many blood stains.

Gritting his teeth, Kellan reached out and pulled the Spear from its resting space.

Energy ripped through him and Kellan thought he heard himself scream as the world around him shattered in a manner reminiscent of the Binding in Eden. Rapid images flashed through his mind's eye as he saw a tree being cut down and its wood fashioned into the Spear's shaft. Iron was worked into its tip. Soldiers trained with it. Soldiers fought with it. Soldiers killed with it. It changed hands as time flew by, finally being held by a young soldier standing on a hill. Kellan watched as the soldier leaned on his spear and impassively looked up at three condemned prisoners on their crosses. He had his orders and lifted his spear to pierce the chest of the man hanging on the middle cross. Water and blood sprayed out but the condemned man did not move. He was dead. The soldier wiped at his face and spat because some of the blood had gotten into his mouth. A voice boomed in the air causing the solider to widen his eyes in fear because no one else gave indication of hearing it. *Soldier, you are content with what you are. Then that you shall remain until we meet again.*

Kellan started, hand still outstretched having just grasped the Spear. He looked around and saw Seramai and Meghan staring at him with concern. He shuddered. "Did you two just see that?"

"See what, Sentinel?" asked Seramai.

"We didn't see anything, Kellan. You just touched the spear, cried out, and froze there for about ten seconds or so. What happened?"

Kellan shuddered and shook his head. "Uh, I really am not prepared to talk about it right now." He stared at his friend pleadingly and she simply nodded.

"So, can we leave now or was I wrong and your unworthy ass has gotten us trapped here for eternity."

As if in answer a glowing blue portal rotated into view. "Hot damn," she yelled and leaped through.

"Meghan wait!" yelled Kellan but it was too late, "That's not my portal," he said to Seramai who simply shrugged and stepped through.

⌒⌒⌒

As Kellen stepped out of the portal the word resolved back into being and he sighed with relief. Seramai and Meghan were standing before him and talking to Cardinal Karras. Apparently, from the Cardinal's frame of reference, they had only been gone a few short minutes. His eyes found Kellan's and the young Sentinel watched as he saw the Cardinal's gaze turn to the Spear he held.

The Cardinal stepped up to him, hesitantly reaching out a hand, but Kellan pulled the Spear back. "Best you don't, Cardinal," Kellan said in as friendly a manner as he could manage. The old priest nodded as much to himself as Kellan and stepped back.

"Where will you take it," he asked.

"You don't want to know," Kellan said with a smile. "No one is going to know other than me so that way there is no reason to try and extract information they don't have. Suffice it to say, that I plan to take it a long way from here and leave it very well guarded."

Karras seemed satisfied. "And when you are done?"

"I will return the Spear to you, here. You have my word."

Karras nodded. "Thank you for that, Sentinel of Order. I have lowered the outbound wards so you are free to create a portal from this place if you wish."

Kellan opened his mouth to respond, but Meghan pushed him out of the way. "We definitely do wish that, Cardinal, and thank you. Kellan, make with the sparkle eyes and open a portal."

Kellan shook his head. "Meghan, I told you before. You are not coming with me. I don't want you knowing where I take the Spear."

She frowned at him. "What are you blathering about. You are damned right I'm not going with you. General handsome here owes me a romantic Roman holiday, don't you, General handsome?"

Seramai smiled and his form shimmered.

"Oh, my," Meghan said, smiling appreciatively and tracing her hand along his chest, "You clean up nice."

Kellan felt himself involuntarily make a strange face as he took in Seramai's new appearance. Gone was the anachronistic leather armor. Instead, the warrior now wore comfortable blue jeans, a crisp linen shirt, and stylish shoes. Kellan looked back to Meghan and said, "Wait, what about your client in New Orleans? You made a huge stink about making sure I got you back to her."

Meghan waved a hand, "I have a whole week to get back to her. For the next six days, past me has it all under control. I'll catch a flight after Sera and I have some well deserved R&R. Isn't that right?"

"Indeed it is, my valkyrie," Seramai said with a smile and then turned to Kellan. "Sentinel, a portal if you please."

Chapter 11

THE SEAL OF SOLOMON

K ellan blinked in surprise, his senses deluged with sounds and smells. He looked around as he felt the portal vanish behind him. People were everywhere, laughing and pointing at this thing or that, but no one paid special attention to him. This was one of his worst nightmares. Normally, Kellan found that his portals opened in the most nondescript areas within a location he targeted, but not so this time. *Well, you chose Chicago's Navy Pier* he thought to himself, then added, *Yeah, but only because it's the closest place to this stupid island that I could get a portal to work.* Over the past year, Kellan had learned a great deal about traveling by portal, both spacially and temporally. Yet, despite all he had learned, the act of ripping holes in space, time, or both never ceased to fill him with awe. The fact that he could open a portal in the midst of this gentrified amusement park and not cause an eye blink among those nearby continued to amaze as well. Like most things about his exercise of power, portals drew on intent. If Kellan intended to arrive clandestinely his portal would open in alleys, basements, or the like. Sometimes, such locales were simply not available in the immediate area. In such cases, even when Kellan appeared amongst a throng of people, they just didn't seem to to notice. The young Sentinel felt a smile cross his face as he recalled the first time that had happened. The portal had opened just in front of the stage at Wembley Stadium and he had totally freaked out. He had made a spacial-temporal portal to June 17th, 2007 and Muse was playing Knights of Cydonia. Kellan felt a pang of guilt as he thought, *Yeah, great use of semi-divine powers, ripping space and time because you love Muse. Well, it was one of the most epic concerts ever. No shit, hey, we should go see Bowie.* Kellan felt himself cringe as he dismissed the internal banter with himself. He'd gotten a lot better about that but sometimes it just leaked out. The point being, he reminded himself, that no one among that 90,000, standing room only, crowd noticed a thing, not in person, not on video, not on subsequent DVDs. He had checked, watching the DVD at the exact place and time he knew the portal opened but nothing was there. Of course there are times, Kellan reminded himself, when it can be handy to be seen and heard yelling and leaping from glowing ovals. It tends to distract and unsettle adversaries, so when that was his intent, the portals obliged. The Sentinel nodded to himself as he walked through the Navy Pier's Polk Brothers Park. He loved his portals.

"OK, enough revelry," Kellan mumbled, "Time to find a boat." He glanced around and started angling to the right where water taxis and sight seeing boats were docked by the pier. Along the way, he passed a map of the Pier's numerous amusements, gave it a quick glance, and continued past. A moment later, he stopped so abruptly that a couple walking behind Kellan bumped into him and apologized as they went on their way. The Sentinel barely noticed them because one of the items on the map kept flashing in his eidetic mind like a beacon: DMK Burger Bar. Kellan felt his mouth start to water as the menu scrolled through his memory along with the perfectly preserved high-resolution photos a friend showed him years ago while proclaiming proudly that Chicago had both the best pizza and burgers. Kellan snorted and thought, *Obviously, New York has the best pizza. Jon Stewart was right Chicago pizza is really a bloody casserole, but burgers—maybe burgers. And I am hungry. And they do have craft beers. Screw it, stupid demon trapping seals can wait.*

Kellan turned and headed down the center of Navy's Pier's broad walkway, past Centennial Wheel, and skirted by the under construction Yard at Chicago's Shakespeare. He looked up at the stylized logo as the tagline of, "Best damn grass-fed burgers, shakes, and fries that ever hit your lips," danced through his hunger fueled mind.

"Oh yeah," said Kellan as he walked through the door and settled himself on a plain black metal stool by the bar. The red DMK logo was engraved on white tiles beneath which sat dozens of liquor bottles ranging from bourbon to gin. Kellan glanced down the bar and saw a dozen beer taps as a twenty-something server walked up to him.

"Hey, I'm Tim and I'll be taking care of you tonight." The server set down a menu, but Kellan just slid it back to him.

"I know exactly what I want, brotha Tim. You ready?"

"Shoot," the server side with a smile.

"Ok, I'll have a Number 1, loaded, with the aged cheddar, smoked bacon, charred balsamic red onion, but can you sub out the Rufus BBQ sauce for Leroy's Remoulade?"

"Yeah, no problem. Anything else?"

"Oh yeah. Please make it a double on the burger and I will upgrade those fries to truffle and Parmesan." Kellan paused a moment realizing that he had no recollection of his beer options and asked, "Do you have any high gravity Belgian style beer?"

The server answered immediately, "Yep, we have a 7.9 berry Belgian waffle. You want a taste?"

"No, dude, you had me at waffle. Can I have a 20oz glass of that as soon as possible?"

"20 oz?" Tim said questioningly, "I hope you don't have anything planned for the rest of the night. We usually serve that with an 8oz pour."

"Never you mind," said Kellan with a smile. "I have a supernatural metabolism and don't plan on doing much tonight but chartering a boat to some mysterious island to find a demon binding artifact."

Tim laughed as he scooped up the menu, "Right. I'll get you that beer. Hang tight."

"So, how was it? Everything good?" Asked the server as he reached for Kellan's plate.

"Tim, it was horrible. Worst I've had in recent memory."

The young server frowned with his hand frozen on the plate, then noted that not the smallest scrap of food remained. He looked up to find Kellan staring at him with a mischievous grin and chuckled, "Yeah, it looks like you really hated it. How's that beer sitting?"

Kellan tilted his glass, draining the final swallow and set the it down with a thud. "It is sitting quite well. If you would bring me the check my good man, I will be off."

"We don't really use checks, but here." Tim slid an iPad from beneath the bar and tilted it up to face Kellan. He quickly scanned the items, added a healthy tip, and bumped his Apple Watch against the tablet which gave a friendly chime of acknowledgement.

"Good luck with the demons," he said as Kellan slid off the stool and swayed slightly then added, "you aren't driving, right?"

"Nope, I told you, takin' a boat." Kellan paused halfway to the door then walked back. "Say, Tim, where is the easiest place for me to find a boat?"

By the time Kellan had reached the charter docks, he noted sadly that all the effects from his beer had faded. Unfortunately for the young Sentinel, his body could not distinguish between alcohol and other toxins. When it encountered any, it autonomously channeled Ordered energies to purge them leaving him stone cold sober shortly after even a healthy round of drinks. Kellan frowned slightly as he looked around. Most of the moorings were empty with their boats having been already chartered for evening rides. He glanced up at the clear sky and full moon thinking that it certainly was a nice night for it.

The two remaining boats were both fishing trawlers. Kellan glanced at the sterns of both. The closest was called the *Kobayashi Maru* while the next had *Water Beetle* stenciled in sharp black letters. The Sentinel paused, looking from one to the other, decidedly unhappy with both his options. The Water Beetle looked barely seaworthy with its formerly white hull faded to a dull gray. Then again, the other boat's name was simply unacceptable. *I mean*, thought Kellan, *who in their right mind names a boat the Kobayashi Maru.* Just as he had made up his mind and was about to head towards the *Water Beetle*, two figures emerged from below its deck. Both were tall men with dark hair one long and one short. Kellan's eyes widened at the red pulsing aura that danced about the longer haired man. The Sentinel drew the trickle of power he needed to gain additional discernment and insight flared in his mind: Vampire. *Wow, that is one handsome vampire,* Kellan thought when his eye was suddenly drawn to the other man whose long leather duster glowed with all manner of mystic symbols. He locked eyes with the man who gave Kellan a subtle and distinctly dangerous shake of his head. The young Sentinel swallowed, gave a little wave to the pair, and decided that the *Kobayashi Maru* might just be a good name for a fishing boat after all.

"No, Christa, I'm sure you are an excellent captain, but you keep turning away from the island I'm trying to reach. Why do you keep doing that?"

The trawler captain took a last drag on her cigarette and flicked it over the side. "Look," she said, "You're my charter, so I'm doing my level best not to be rude, but I've told you that there is no island." She stabbed the map for the third time since Kellan had boarded about an hour ago. "See, no island."

Kellan turned away from her and looked through the glass of the bridge. He felt his eyes warm with power and saw the wide ghostly line appear above the waves, just as Micah had described during their time in the workroom. "I can see the bloody ley line, clear as day," he mumbled.

"What's a," the captain paused sounding out the words, "ley line." She craned her neck to try and see what Kellan was looking at.

Great, he thought but turned and flashed Christa his most winning smile while dismissing the details provided by Micah in favor of more mundane knowledge. "Well, since you asked. The term *ley line* was coined by Alfred Watkins in 1921 to refer to specific physical or spiritual alignments that occur in geography. I'm trying to find the exact spot where several of these ley lines converge or originate."

"Uh, huh," she said fishing another Marlboro from the half empty pack poking out of the breast pocket of her flannel shirt. "And you thought the best time to do this was at 9:00 at night?"

Kellan gave her an embarrassed smirk, "Truth be told, no. I'm sure it would have been better to do earlier, but I really wanted a DMK burger and needed beer."

Christa nodded in appreciation, "DMK is one tasty burger."

"I know, right," began Kellan, "Anyway, please indulge me for just a little longer, Christa. After all, it is my three hour cruise. If I'm nuts and just want to go around in circles looking for a nonexistent island, no biggie, right?"

"I suppose," she said sounding unconvinced.

"Tell you what," said Kellan, "I'm going just stand up here and direct you left, right, or straight. You follow those directions and we'll get to where I need to be. Sound good?"

The captain sighed in acquiescence, "As you said, it's your three hour cruise and you have two left."

Kellan spent the next hour continually giving course corrections to the trawler's captain as he watched the ley line before him gradually grow thicker. The longer they went the more frequent his course corrections came. He had long ago stopped asking Christa why she kept turning away from the direct course he provided. Something was clearly affecting her and whatever it was made her both uncomfortable with their current course and unconscious of the actions she took to deviate from it.

"God damnit," Christa yelled causing Kellan to turn as she cut the engines. "All my instruments are flaking out."

Kellan walked around the side and entered the bridge to find the various screens flashing intermittently. "C'mon Christa, I think we are close. Give me five more minutes on this course and if I don't find anything we can turn back."

"No, if your crazy ley lines are messing up my boat, I'm done. Ever heard of the Edmund Fitzgerald? I'm not joining her."

Kellan sighed as the Gordon Lightfoot song of the same name came unbidden and unwelcome to the fore, then slid his fingers along the edge of his belt until he found the opening. The Sentinel held the coin up for Christa to see, turning it as it caught the bridge lights.

"What's that?" She asked.

"This," said Kellan, "is a gold American Eagle coin, valued as of this morning's spot price at exactly $1,204. It's yours for five more minutes on this course." He watched as the Captain unconsciously wet her lips and reached out for the coin.

"May I see it?"

"Of course," Kellan replied dropping the heavy coin in her outstretched hand.

"Should I bite it?"

Kellan chuckled, "I wouldn't recommend that, but it is real. I assure you."

Christa looked at him, suddenly suspicious, "And why would you carry around a thousand dollar gold coin."

Kellan shrugged, "Just something my old teacher impressed upon me. He always said to travel with gold because gold spends everywhere."

She nodded, seeming to accept that rationale as reasonable, then slipped the coin into her jean's pocket. "Ok, five minutes, no more."

"Great! Full power, Christa."

Exactly five minutes later, the engines again cut off causing Kellan to reenter the bridge in a rush.

"Why did you stop? I can see it." He asked.

"Your five minutes are up and my instruments are even worse now than they were. We are leaving. There's something weird about this place and I don't like it. Do you realize that according to my GPS, when it gives a reading at all, that we aren't in any State right now?"

"Huh?" Said Kellan.

"Yeah, that's what I thought," said the Captain, "But it seems we are almost exactly where Wisconsin, Illinois, and Michigan meet, but where we are right now isn't included in any of them."

"Ok," Kellan allowed, "I'll grant you that's weird, but I can see the island that isn't on any of your maps, so just take me there and we'll call it a night."

"No!" She said and started to turn the ships wheel.

"Stop stop stop," cried Kellan pulling out another gold coin. "Get me to that island and I'll give you this one too."

"You don't even know if there is a place to dock," she said rounding on him.

"Then I'll swim. Just get me close."

"You are a crazy man," she said, but didn't turn the boat. "How many of those coins do you have left?"

"Why?" Asked Kellan, narrowing his eyes at her. "Add two more to the one in your hand and I'll give you my dingy. Take it your island or go buy some cheese in Wisconsin, I won't care."

Kellan frowned, "How about I give you three more coins and you take me to the island yourself? If there's no dock, then I'll take the dingy."

The captain shook her head. "No, three gold coins for the dingy now, take it or leave it."

"I'll take it," he said sullenly, "But I'm not happy about it."

Captain Christa Sorenson stuck out her hand and as the three coins clinked together she looked up and said, "I can live with that."

Kellan cut the engine on the small dingy and lashed it to a mooring on the rotted pier. He hopped out and gently tested his footing to make sure the boards weren't about to collapse beneath him. Despite its apparent decrepitude, the wood seemed surprisingly solid. The narrow dock extended maybe one hundred feet from a rocky shoreline that angled up to a tangled tree line. Kellan sighed. He had absolutely no idea where to look for the Seal of Solomon. The sound of movement startled him and he instinctually reached for the power within. The entire island burst to life under the gaze of Kellan's Sentinel enhanced vision. Nine massive ley lines angled out, three each, toward Wisconsin, Michigan, and Illinois. Beyond that, interwoven bands of energy seemed to encircle the small island almost like a massive dome designed to keep everyone out or as Kellan suddenly feared, keep something in.

"Oh, shit," Kellan said as a massive figure emerged from the tree line. It was vaguely human shaped but too distant for him to make out any distinct features. The creature lumbered slowly but deliberately toward Kellan who hadn't moved from his place on the dock. When it had crossed about halfway between the trees and the shore, the creature stopped and set something down. Kellan couldn't tell if the figure had eyes, but felt something lock onto his and a chill rippled through him that even holding the fullness of his power didn't dispel. The creature pointed to the object it had placed, then to Kellan, and then whipped its arm violently in an outward direction. The message was very clear to the young Sentinel. He was not welcome here. He would not be tolerated here. With a final sightless glare, the figure turned and vanished back into the island's interior.

Kellan swallowed hard and snapped a protective shield around himself as he cautiously made his way to the spot where the creature had stood. There he found a small, intricately carved, wooden box that appeared to have no hinge or lock. Kellan felt his stomach do tiny flips as he grasped the bottom of the box while taking furtive glances around him. Pulling slightly the top separated to reveal a plush blue velvet interior on which rested a metal object that, to Kellan's eyes, glowed with an inner blue light. It was round with an hexagonal star engraved on its face. Between each point of the star rested a small round gem that appeared to be diamond.

Kellan recognized the object immediately. The Seal of Solomon.

A loud keening came from within the trees and Kellan looked up in alarm as he slammed the lid back on.

"Yep," said Kellan to the open air, "I totally agree, time to go!" The young Sentinel then turned and made his way back to the dock with as much speed and dignity as he could manage.

Chapter 12

PARTY WITH THE DEVIL

K ellan woke with a start and sighed with relief as his hand grasped the Seal of Solomon's cold metal. He felt his heart racing beneath it and took a deep breath. He sometimes longed for the days when a morning freakout was caused by dreams of diving in a pool with his iPhone forgotten in his pocket. Now he had ancient demonic binding relics to think about. Kellan preferred his iPhone which suddenly came to life beside his bed as if aware he was thinking about it.

Kellan reached over to his nightstand and lifted the vibrating device from where it lay plugged in and resting on his Saddleback leather valet. A quick glance at the screen displayed the smiling face of one James Clinton. Kellan swiped his finger along the phone, tapped the speaker icon, and dropped it on his chest.

"What?"

"Well, good afternoon to you too, douchey mac douche. Did I wake you? Did I spoil your beauty rest which, given your rather heinous visage, is most needed. It's almost 12:30 pm!"

Kellan sighed. "Dude, I had a long night and didn't get home till late."

"Boo fucking hoo," then there was silence for a moment, "where were you?"

"Chicago."

"Really, I love Chicago. They have great pizza."

Kellan winced. "They have shitty pizza; it's really more of a casser—"

"Casserole. I know. And I don't even like it. I just like pissing you off and making you go on a 'New York pizza is better diatribe.'"

"Then why did you stop me."

"No time to indulge your stupidity today. I've got a big presentation and just wanted to make sure you wore something decent to the party tonight."

"Um," said Kellan, mind racing.

"Don't 'um,' me, bitch. You remember everything and as annoying as that is 99% of the time. This is the 1% where I find it useful."

"Well, I remember everything that I pay enough attention to."

James groaned. "Please say that you are screwing with me."

"I'm screwing with you?" Kellan said voice rising at the end.

"You totally suck, Kel. The CDC party. Tonight. You and Shannon. Me and Naomi. Ring any bells?"

"No, dude. I'm telling you. I must have been ignoring you. It's not my fault. You say too much stupid shit for me to keep all of it in my head. It could be dangerous."

"Hardy frickin' har. I'm forwarding the invitation that I sent you," James paused, his voice rising, "three months ago. Tell me you got it, jackass."

Kellan felt his phone pulse, switched to his e-mail and said, "I got it, jackass."

"Good now make sure you wear something other than jeans and tell that freaky girlfriend of yours that they have metal detectors so," another pause, "no knives."

"She's not here."

James sighed then spoke very slowly and deliberately, like he was convincing a child, "Then tell her when she gets back."

"No, I mean she's not even in the country, dude."

"What!"

"She's back in Scotland. Something, uh, came up all of a sudden and she had to go. She's with her folks there."

"Great! That's just great. Now Naomi is going to feel like a third wheel."

Kellan laughed.

"What's so funny?"

"I'm the third wheel idiot. You and she are the couple. I'm the third wheel!"

Kellan waited in silence as that sunk in then he heard a sigh from James, "Yeah, I guess you're right about that."

"Unless she thinks you and I are a couple," whispered Kellan into the phone grinning.

"Oh shut up. First, as I mentioned, you are heinous. Second, as I also mentioned, your crazy girlfriend is always armed to the teeth."

Kellan felt himself nod in agreement to that last point, then asked, "Why do I need to come at all? Let's just get together when Shannon's back."

"No way. Naomi already thinks you don't like her and I don't need her getting pissed at me because she's really pissed at you."

"But—"

"No, you are coming."

It was Kellan's turn to sigh. "Fine."

"Good. Be on time and look presentable."

"Ok, Dad. I got it. Goodbye"

"Something other than jeans!"

"Good. Bye!"

Kellan smiled as he caught sight of James and Naomi snuggled close on the terrace balcony. James, he noted, looked his normal dashing self wearing an impeccably tailored navy suit and crisp purple dress shirt that perfectly offset his coffee colored skin. He caught sight of Kellan headed his way and smiled warmly as his friend joined them. Kellan gave James a friendly tap on the cheek. "What happened to the van dyke? You're face is as smooth as your head now. I don't like it."

"But I do," said Naomi with a smile.

Kellan returned it an leaned in to give her a kiss on the cheek. "Well, that's what counts." He took a step back still holding her hand and said, "You are a vision of loveliness, Naomi, and I hope this idiot knows what he has in you." Her face lit up at the compliment. Naomi was an empirically beautiful woman. Tall and lean with wavy blonde hair that just brushed her shoulders. As James was so fond of pointing out when they first started dating, she looked very much like Zoey Deschanel from one of Kellan's favorite Christmas movies, *Elf*. Today she was wearing a fitted red dress that Kellan felt sure James had a hand in selecting.

Kellen crossed to the railing and looked over the side. "Wow, I've never been up here before. The Capital City Club does a good job of keeping riffraff like me out. Pretty cool view. I thought the terrace was just for show, but I guess given the historicity of the building that wouldn't make much sense."

Kellan noticed them both staring at him blankly and continued. "This building? The building we are now standing in. Dedicated on December 16, 1911. Designed by—"

"Stop," said James. Kellan smiled impishly as his friend looked him up and down. "What did I say?" Kellan opened his mouth to respond, but James looked first to Naomi and then back to Kellan, "I said, no jeans and what are you wearing, Kellan?"

"Uh, uh, uh," said Kellan waving a finger, "That is *not* what you said."

"What?" sputtered James starting to look panicky as Naomi narrowed her eyes at him, "No, baby, I absolutely told this idiot 'no jeans.'"

"Actually, you said I should wear, and I quote, 'something other than jeans.'"

James looked both relieved and triumphant opening both hands in Kellan's direction, "And what did you do with that information?"

"I complied completely. I am also wearing this very nice shirt and these stylish yet affordable Clarks shoes. So I am, indeed, wearing something *other* than jeans."

James began visibly vibrating and Kellan caught Naomi's eye as she mouthed, "Well played—"

He grinned at her and James slumped in defeat.

"You didn't even tuck in your shirt."

Kellan brightened. "It's designed to *not* be tucked in. Look, see the logo right here." He pointed to the bright red triangle embroidered on the corner, below the last button. "The brand is called *Untuckit* and they are shirts tailored to be worn untucked. How cool is that!"

"I hate you," said James in a dejected and resigned voice.

Kellan put a consoling hand on his friend's shoulders just as the sound of shrieking tires drew their attention. All three looked over the balcony as the door opened on a gleaming, silver, Aston Martin Vanquish. A tall blonde man stepped out wearing an impeccably tailored tuxedo with blood red accents at tie, pocket square, and cummerbund. He deftly handed the keys to a startled attendant and swung around the front of his car without breaking stride, then glanced up at Kellan, James, and Naomi as they stared down. He smiled, then disappeared into the main entrance below.

"Now that," said James, "Is how one should dress."

Kellan sniffed, "Yeah, I suppose. If you are into that sort of thing."

Naomi smiled sweetly, "Kellan, a tall, handsome man, in a beautiful 300,000 dollar British roadster? Every woman in her right mind is into that sort of thing."

James sidled up to her and kissed her cheek. "Baby, I thought you liked me being all green with my Tesla."

Kellan snorted, "You're green alright, but it has nothing to do with that battery operated mortgage payment you're driving."

James gave Kellan a withering glare but Naomi just spun around looping both hands behind his neck, went up on toes, and gave him a soft kiss. "No need to be green, Chocolate bear, I don't have eyes for anyone but you."

"Perhaps," came a resonate voice from inside the room, "you should let me spin you around a bit before making any declarations of eternal love."

Kellan watched as Naomi looked up at the newcomer and saw her quick intake of breath. The man smiled broadly and extended his hand. "Doctor Wilder, it is such a pleasure to meet you. I am a student of your work on pandemics. Truly groundbreaking approach to containment." She accepted his hand as if in a daze and the man bent forward placing a soft kiss there.

James took a half step in front of Naomi and said in an icy tone, "And you are?"

The man replied with warmth and clapped James on the shoulder before again extending his hand, "Mr. Clinton, I am equally pleased to make your acquaintance. Your work at IBM is nothing short of groundbreaking in its own right." He laughed softly, "I cannot even imagine what might be produced by you and Doctor Wilder entwining such remarkable double helixes."

Naomi blushed at this last remark and James looked oddly uncomfortable, giving a quick glance to Kellan, as if something the man said disturbed him.

"Well," said Kellan, "You certainly have us at a disadvantage, Mr. —"

"Milton. John Milton, and I doubt I have you at a disadvantage, Kellan," he gave a good natured laugh and leaned in to whisper at Kellan's ear, "at least not yet." Milton then gave a half spin, leaned back against the terrace and rested his arms to either side. "Now doctor," he began when a rogue breeze disturbed one of the two blond locks that arched above his forehead causing him to absently run fingers though hair, "You simply must explain how you get past the ethical challenges associated with ebola containment."

James again stepped between them and locked eyes with Milton who smiled back amiably. "Yes?" he said.

"Look," began James, "I don't want to be rude and I really do appreciate your tux, your car, and that you have a striking resemblance to David Bowie, but we are not really interested in —"

Milton lifted a hand, tapping his softly angled chin and resting it in the cleft, then interrupted, "James, you want to get us drinks, don't you? You do." That last was not a question and James seemed to wobble back slightly, his eyes losing focus.

"Hey," James said brightly, "Why don't I get us a round of drinks?"

"Capital idea!" agreed Milton and waved a hand as James headed into the throng and towards the bar. He turned to Kellan and winked.

The Sentinel stared into John Milton's pale blue eyes and looked inward to embrace his power but Milton reached out and grabbed him by the wrist, all joviality gone from his voice. "Don't do that, Kellan. It would spoil the fun. You wouldn't want to spoil an enjoyable evening would you? Especially with your *friends* so near." The threat implied by Milton's accentuation of the word was unmistakable and Kellan swallowed hard, but did not embrace the power.

"That's a good man," said Milton, light hearted smile returning, "Now, we were talking about Ebola. Doctor, please, enlighten me. As I mentioned. I have such a keen interest in ethics and ethical dilemmas."

Naomi laughed and placed her hand softly on Milton's chest, fingers brushing the deep red of his pocket square. She lifted it out and pressed it to her cheek.

"Oh, it's so soft," she said holding it out to James, "I'd just love to be wrapped head to toe in this."

He took it, regarding the cloth with a flat expression as he rubbed it between his fingers, "Yeah, soft. Listen, Naomi, don't you think—"

"James," said Milton, voice rising to a lilt as he swirled a glass that held nothing but half melted cubes, "I think we might need more drinks."

"Oh, I'll get them," offered Naomi brightly and darted away before anyone could speak but was followed by John Milton's gaze.

"What the fuck do you think you are doing," growled James, rounding on the other man, "And just who the hell do you think you are?" James drew close so the two were but a hair's breath apart. "That is my girl you are messing with, asshole, and I don't appreciate it."

"Well," said Milton, with a laugh, as he looked over to Kellan, "Look at the big balls on James. What was it you asked me? I really wasn't paying attention. I was too busy looking at Naomi's ass. She is just smokin' hot in that red dress and I do love red." He smiled again.

James leaned in and grabbed Milton's left arm. "I said. Who. The fuck. Do you think you are?"

"Ah, yes," replied Milton with a shrug that, while seeming nonchalant, rocked James back several steps, "Who am I?" Milton's face grew shadowed and his lips drew to a line. "Why, James, I am a man of wealth and taste."

Lyrics instantly filled Kellan's mind and his eyes widened. "Oh…Shit," said the Sentinel in dismay and he reached inward for his power even as he saw a distorted energy bubble snap around them slowing all that lay beyond it.

James stared open mouthed as his friend whose eyes now blazed bright green, then turned to John Milton whose eyes did likewise, but with a brilliant red.

Milton threw his head back and laughed, then looked at Kellan. "Oh, this is too funny. Kellan, you didn't tell poor James here. Naughty, naughty. And I thought he was your best friend. Aren't you his best friend, James?"

Milton snapped his fingers in front of James who looked at him dully. "I asked, is Kellan your best friend?"

"Y-yeah," James stammered, then his eyes became more focused and he answered again, more confidently, "Yes. Kellan is my best friend."

"Excellent. Excellent!" said Milton putting his right arm around James' shoulder, pulling him close, and turning him to face Kellan.

"I do love a good bromance." Milton paused, looking up and to the left as if deep in thought, "Just one thing though," then he tapped out a cadence with his left hand against James' chest as he spoke. "Why. Do ya think. Your best friend. Would lie to you?" Kellan felt Milton's eyes meet his for a moment, then he just shrugged, "Oh, well, I guess it's a mystery."

"Lucifer," growled Kellan. "I don't know what you want, but—"

"Want? From you?" Lucifer released James and leaned back against the railing, "Why I don't want anything from you, baby Sentinel. I want to help you. I'm a helper. But let's not argue amongst the children, shall we. Come by my place for a cuppa. We'll chat."

"I'm not going anywhere with you, Satan."

Lucifer frowned, "Oh Kellan, is that supposed to hurt me. I've been called much worse by better people. Do you even know what that means? Wait, of course you do. You have that magic brain, but I bet James here doesn't know so do educate him."

Kellan set his jaw. "I'm not interested in playing word games."

Lucifer narrowed his eyes and yelled, "Educate him!" His words became power that rippled through the air and buffeted them. Kellan rocked back and James fell to one knee almost toppling over if not for Lucifer reaching out to steady him.

Kellan spoke slowly without emotion, "Satan, from the Hebrew meaning adversary. Shaitan, Arabic for astray or distant."

"No, Kellan, try again. Numbers 22:22. Samuel 29:4. Psalms 109:6." He closed the distance and held the Sentinel's face in his hands looking deeply into Kellan's glowing eyes. "Yes, there you go. Pull it all up and go for the oldest texts you have in there." He released Kellan, spun round and winked at the now standing James. "Let me know when you are ready, I'll wait here. But don't take too long, I think Naomi is slowly making her way back with our drinks. Since you've been lying to James about who you are and he's been lying to you about some things as well, I think it's pretty even. But, little Naomi. She's as pure and earnest as they come, so, if she makes it back to us before I'm done here, I think I'll kill her to save her the misery of dealing with you both. How's that for incentive!"

"Ha-Satan," said Kellan in a low voice.

"Come again?"

"Ha-Satan, also from the Hebrew but a noun meaning *the accuser*."

"Yes!" said Lucifer looking up at the sky, both arms upstreched. A moment later he lowered his hands and looked at Kellan, voice a whisper. "I am the accuser. But whom did I accuse and of what?"

Kellan wasn't sure how to answer but made to speak when Lucifer smiled and waved a negating hand, "No, no, it was rhetorical. Perhaps we can discuss it another time. For now, please accept my invitation." The smile faded and Lucifer locked eyes with Kellan. "Accept it very soon, Sentinel of Order, or there will be unfortunate consequences."

As soon as the words faded, so did Lucifers dour expression. He brightened and grinned broadly at the two men, turning to James. Mr. Clinton, it truly has been a pleasure and I meant what I said about your work at IBM. I never lie. Don't have to really. The truth is so much more powerful a tool. Anyway, I have great hopes that your work there will serve my needs. Keep it up. Must be off now, do pass along my regrets to beautiful Naomi." With that Lucifer placed one hand on the railing and leaped over the side with both Kellan and James leaning over just in time to see him vanish into a glowing portal.

Chapter 13

THE ROAD TO HELL

The noise of the party washed over them as Kellan and James continued to stare over the railing at the empty spot where Lucifer had been moments before. Kellan tensed as he heard James take a deep breath, his eyes burrowing into the young Sentinel. Kellan ignored him and stared back in from the balcony, his mind racing, as he took in the scene of people talking, laughing, drinking, all oblivious to what had just occurred.

"I'm staring at you," James said from Kellan's right.

"Oh, I know you are."

"I'm not going to stop staring at you."

"Yeah, I pretty much know that too." Time stretched out with the two standing in silence and Kellan finally turned to his friend. "James, what he did was totally uncool. I mean it was a real dick move. I was going to tell you when —"

James held up a hand. "Dude. Stop. You seriously don't want to begin your explanation by blaming Lucifer for being uncool. I can't even believe I just said those words. In fact, I'm trying to decide whether to simply freak out or punch you in the face and then freak out."

"Please don't do either. I can explain."

James narrowed his eyes. "Really? You can explain what, exactly? Angels? Lucifer? Sentinels?" He paused holding up a finger. "Oh, wait, if Lucifer just came calling, I suppose you've had a tete a tete with God as well."

"No, haven't met God," Kellan grumbled.

"Aw, too bad mon frer because that would have been the hat trick of non disclosures to your best fucking friend. Oh wait, maybe I'm not your best friend. Maybe that's why you didn't tell me about all this supernatural shit."

"No, James, no, you are my best friend."

"I don't think so, Kellan. Best friends don't keep shit like this from each other."

Kellan looked down, not wanting to meet his friends eyes. "It's because you are my best friend that I kept it from you. It was selfish I know but —"

Kellan's Apple Watch gave a soft chime. He ignored it. "It's just that I wanted one person in my life to —"

The watch chimed again, then twice more in rapid succession. Kellan growled, "Jesus...what the hell," then stretched out his left arm so the sleeve rolled up and glanced at the glowing watch face.

"Jesus," Kellan said again.

"What?" interjected James, "You haven't met God, but Jesus texts your stupid watch?"

"Huh? Oh, no. It's Lucifer. Apparently he's pissed I haven't left the party yet."

"Show me."

Kellan held out his wrist but the watch face remained dark. "Not on your watch Kel. I can't see shit on that."

Kellan shook his head slightly reaching into his back pocket for his phone, unlocking it and both men turned to regard its screen as Kellan tapped open the Messages app.

"How do you even know it's Lucifer. Do you have him on speed dial or something."

Kellan glared at James, "No, idiot. I never even met him before tonight."

"Don't call me idiot. My best friend calls me idiot and you, apparently, are not my best friend."

Kellan sighed. "Look at the number James."

James did. "666.666.6660" He looked back at Kellan, "Seriously?"

"I don't know! Maybe he's just pulling my leg or maybe he takes the whole number of the beast thing seriously. Who the fuck cares. It's clearly him. Read the message."

James looked back to the phone which had gone dark then gave a meaningful glance to Kellan who unlocked it again.

James read the messages out loud but kept his voice to a whisper:

Message 1: Kellan, you have not left yet. I am not a patient being.

Message 2: It strikes me that you may not know how to reach me directly so I will provide you directions to where convergent ley lines have made a natural entrance. It may be guarded so be sure to leave your human friend behind.

Message 3: Map Link: Underground Atlanta (under construction 2017)

Message 4: If you don't leave the party in 5 minutes I will kill James or Naomi. Not sure which.

Message 5: See you soon <3

James looked up. "Time for you to go."

Kellan grimaced, "James, I—"

"Dude, you think I'm pissed at you now? Just wait to see how pissed I am if you get Naomi or me killed by Satan. You are not off the hook by any stretch. I am going to your house. I am going to steal whatever old, expensive, shit you have there and then go home to drink it. If my current mood doesn't improve, I may draw on your leather with a sharpie." James sighed, letting out a long breath, then reached up and grasped Kellan by the wrist. "You be careful. I don't want you dying before I get to exact the full measure of pain I plan to visit on you."

Kellan quirked a smile, "Jerk."

James smiled back, "Bitch." Then with the barest pause, he added, "Go to the devil."

Kellan shook his head, then glanced around quickly to make sure they were still alone and unwatched. His eyes sparked to life and a portal rotated into existence at the farthest corner of the balcony. Through it could be seen what looked like a dilapidated mall dimly lit by construction lights. Kellan closed the distance to the portal, hopped through, and turned briefly to look back at his friend.

For his part, James simply flipped Kellan the bird with one hand and gave him a thumbs up with the other. The portal winked out, leaving Kellan alone in the orange-yellow gloom cast by the low energy lamps scattered about.

"OK, now what?" Kellan said to the open air then took out his iPhone and looked at the map. The glowing blue dot showed that he was in the general vicinity of the marker dropped by Lucifer's text, but the underground mall didn't allow for any signal to get through so Kellan was on his own.

He glanced around and took in the surroundings. It was quite a mess and a far cry from its heyday. Historical references began to flash through Kellan's mind as he looked up and down the cobblestone streets of this city beneath a city.

The buildings were erected in the post civil war reconstruction boom of the 1860s and 70s with Underground Atlanta benefiting from the viaducts built over the many railroad tracks that helped give Atlanta its original name, Terminus.

Kellan paused and whispered, "Terminus? Hey, I can't believe I never made that connection before. That was the name of the compound in Walking Dead where those cannibals lived. Maybe I should bring Juliet's new boyfriend here on a field trip. Kinda appropriate that it can also serve as a gateway to Hell, huh? Yep!"

Kellan winced slightly at his having both asked himself a question and then, worse, answered it. A moment later, he shrugged it off as his attention was drawn to an old 19th century gas lamp. Kellan ran his fingers along its cold iron as his eyes took in the historic plaque. It told the story of Sam Luckie, a free black man who was killed when a Sherman artillery shell struck one of the 50 lamps erected by the Atlanta Gas Light company in 1856. Kellan felt the information nestle into his mind and combine seamlessly with facts already he'd already stored. "Well, now I know what Luckie street is named for. I always wondered why it was spelled that way."

The young Sentinel leaned against the lamp post unsure where to go next. To his left he saw the remnants of Cafe Du Monde, a replica of the famous New Orleans coffee and beignet house, and suddenly had a strong desire for cafe au lait and the the little square donuts.

Right...Hell first, beignets later. Now, how do I find this entrance, Kellan thought as he played the text messages again through his mind. *Convergent ley lines.*

Kellan had used a massive ley line to find the Seal of Solomon, but that was in the open ocean without other distractions. This situation was very different. He closed his eyes and thought back to his time with Micah in the workroom as his old mentor patiently explained his understanding of the structures to creation. Ley lines were a part of this structure and one that Kellan had dismissed to Micah's imperfect understanding of scientific principals. Energy pathways, stone circles, and the like were nonsense so Kellan had simply nodded politely while letting his mind drift as the elder Sentinel had described them all. Fortunately for Kellan, he didn't necessarily need to be paying complete attention for his mind to absorb information and now he pulled the lesson forth, truly considering it for the first time.

He smiled sadly to himself as he heard the voice of his teacher in his head. "Kellan, the world is made up of vast weavings of energy that most will never see, but we can see. Remember, my young friend, that as you channel the Ordered power of creation, your eyes will be open to secrets your mortal brothers will never know. We cannot practice your ability to truly see within this place for it is not part of creation. When you return to the world, make every effort to hone this skill for it will not come naturally. Even while channeling, your mind will try to slip off of the new reality that is being exposed. You will need to focus your mind and grip it tight. The best place to practice is where many ley lines converge because that is where their power is magnified exponentially based on the number that are brought together. In many such places you will already find constructs used to channel the energy. Stonehenge is one such example as are the Great Pyramids of Giza and the Mayan Temples of South America. Even your very city has a powerful convergence over which train tracks have been laid. Promise me that once we are done here, you will seek out this place and hone your ability to find and use the energy inherent to ley lines. Kellan? Kellan are you listening to me?"

The young Sentinel shook his head, clearing away the reverie and suddenly feeling sheepish for both not having paid attention and for not doing the very thing he had been admonished to do.

"Better late than never," Kellan said cheerfully to the open air and he felt his eyes warm as the energy flowed though him. He looked around but saw nothing out of the ordinary. The gloom was pushed back somewhat and everything took on a brighter, sharper, image, but that had always been the case when he held the power. Kellan often likened it to having Elven night vision. Not nearly as good as Dark Elf vision he reminded himself, but better than nothing. Still, no ley lines revealed themselves as he continued to cast about.

Kellan decided to try another tact. He released the power, closed his eyes, and took it up again. This time he immediately saw a cobweb of thin glowing lines illuminating his closed eyelids. "Ah Ha!" Kellan exclaimed triumphantly and he opened his eyes. The ley lines immediately vanished. *Well that's strange, they didn't do that on the boat*, thought Kellan with frustration.

He closed his eyes again and repeated the attempt. With his eyes closed the lines reappeared and Kellan did a slow circle taking in the entire area. They were amazing. Dozens of pulsing lines of energy coming in from many directions. The colors seemed to slowly pulse with green, red, and occasional violet energy as two or more converged. With his eyes still closed, Kellan began to walk toward a spot in the distance where all the lines seemed to come together. After several steps, he tripped over a curb lost his balance and lay sprawled in the street.

Kellan looked around, embarrassed and reminded himself that the place was completely abandoned. Still, he had an image to uphold and how would it look, God's unchecked hand on the world, tripping over curbs like an idiot. *Not good...it would not look good,* he thought to himself. *Ok, let's try that again.*

Kellan closed his eyes, channeled the power, and watched the lines reappear. He slowly squinted his eyes open ever so slightly. The lines wavered, threatening to vanish, but the young Sentinel willed them to remain and slowly they again became substantial. Kellan repeated the process several more times. He slowly opened and closed his eyes until he could look around while still being able to see the glowing ley lines traversing the underground city before him. Kellan made a mental note to ask his Micah avatar why the island ley lines acted so much different than these, then set the thought aside as he snickered, "This is really cool. It's like I've got a built in HUD. Micah, I'm sorry I ignored you, buddy. Hopefully my lack of practice won't get me killed."

With that, Kellan turned southward where the lines traced off into darkness and began to walk. Occasionally a new line would join the one he was following and, as it did so, the previous ley line became more substantial. After about ten or fifteen minutes of wandering, Kellan found himself staring at a stairway headed down into pitch black. All around him ley lines converged from every point on the compass. Six intersecting lines alternating Red and Green all met that the stairwell. Above it bore an aging sign that read "Dante's Down the Hatch."

"Oh, wow," said Kellan as a starburst of memories cascaded though him. He recalled a nervous young Kellan descending these stairs with his prom date and felt his feet take the first tentative steps as he walked down into darkness.

Kellan reached the bottom and held out a hand as he willed a glowing white sphere of light into being. It hovered for a moment, then floated ahead of him. The sphere illuminated a magical scene where wine bottles of every imaginable shape and color hung from the ceiling and, within the gloom, could be made out the stern of an ancient clipper ship.

The young Sentinel smiled, "Of course it would be here. Where else would it be." He looked around at the converging ley lines which all traced their way to helm of that ship on which was carved numerous dining booths that had been home to decades of entranced diners enjoying Dante's famous fondue. The six glowing lines all buried themselves into the massive wheel that would have served to steer the ship had it actually been seafaring rather than home to one of Atlanta's iconic restaurants of a bygone era.

Kellan slowly made his way up to the ship's bridge, his glowing sphere leading the way. Once there, he paused staring at the intricately carved ship's wheel, then reached out and placed a finger where all six ley lines converged. Nothing happened. He cocked his head trying to puzzle out what to try next, then walked around the wheel to view it from behind. The ley lines did not extend out the back but rather disappeared into the wood. Kellan completed his circuit and once again stood before the wheel. He grasped it with both hands and tried to turn first left, then right, but the wheel refused to budge. *This is starting to feel too much like some stupid online puzzle game and you know how much I hate those,* Kellan thought then ground his teeth in frustration as he started to nod to himself. Instead, he shook his head and grasped the wheel again. This time he reached inward and drew deep on his power. His eyes burned with the effort and he could see pale green reflecting on the wood as he, again, tried to turn the wheel.

To his surprise, it turned easily and Kellan gave the wheel a shove causing it to spin freely. The young Sentinel closed his eyes against a sudden onset of vertigo and tried to steady himself by reaching for the nearby railing. He stumbled as his hand met nothing but air and would have fallen if not for someone grasping his arm. Kellan opened his eyes in alarm and found himself on the receiving end of a broad smile that seemed to genuinely touch his benefactors pale blue eyes.

"Careful Kellan, that is one *Hell* of a first step."

The Sentinel stared at Lucifer with a flat expression, "Very funny," he said dryly, "You are just a laugh riot."

Kellan peered out the thick glass at a beautiful pastoral scene. Acres of rolling green hills spread out into the distance with old hardwood trees dotted throughout. He turned to regard Lucifer who looked much as he had at the CDC, save for the casual attire. The fallen angel now wore a waffle henley, faded Levi's and stood bare foot on an elaborate silk area rug. He looked up with a serious expression. "Ice?"

Kellan just gave him a blank expression.

"Ice? Do you want ice in your drink?"

"Uh, are we in—"

"Hell," said Lucifer impatiently, "Yes. Obviously. Where else would you be when you channeled Ordered power, with specific intent, at a ley line convergence?" He held up the glass again and waggled it.

"Ice? In Hell? Sure, just for the conversation value, I'd like ice, yeah," answered Kellan.

Lucifer didn't respond but nodded and dropped a perfect sphere of ice into the double walled glass then carefully poured an amber liquid over it until it rose two thirds of the way. He set down the glass, and repeated the process, then joined Kellan by the two story window and held one out.

Kellan accepted the glass, "What is it?"

"Bourbon. Try it. It's good."

Kellan just stared at Lucifer, glass still held outward, "Why do you look like Bowie?"

Lucifer took a breath and made to answer but Kellan went on, "Why does Hell look like Downton Abby?"

The fallen angel raised an eyebrow as if asking, *are you done?* Kellen took a long pull from his glass and then stared at it intently. "That's really good."

Lucifer smiled broadly. "Yes, it is isn't it. I must admit, I tend to indulge myself in, well, most everything. If you are going to be the Devil, you might as well enjoy the perks. Am I right?"

"Uh," said Kellan, but Lucifer waved away his answer.

"So, you think I look like David Bowie?" he asked with a knowing smile.

"I don't think you do. You do. There is no think about it." Kellan reached into his back pocket and turned on his iPhone, then frowned. "No signal."

"It's Hell, Kellan, you never get a signal in Hell."

Kellan laughed despite himself. "Yeah, well that at least makes sense, I was just going to pull up a picture of Bowie to show you."

Lucifer looked at the Sentinel with incredulity. "Show me a picture? I know what David Bowie looks like, Kellan. Do you think someone like him could be alive and me not know about him. I've been to his concerts. I've had dinner with him. Have you had dinner with David Bowie?"

Kellan noticed his mouth had slowly fallen open during Lucifer's response. "No. No I've never had dinner with David Bowie. Did he know—"

"That he was dining with the Devil? Of course not, Kellan. Do try not to be stupid. I hate stupid."

"Jesus, Lucifer, why did you ask me if you looked like David Bowie then?" Kellan frowned, then said, "Why are you laughing, now."

"Jesus-Lucifer." the devil repeated, "That may be the first and only time those two names have been uttered here. Well done."

Kellan sighed and waited while Lucifer composed himself. "Anyway, I wasn't asking because I didn't know what he looked like. I was asking *for confirmation.*"

"You want to look like David Bowie?" Kellan asked slowly.

Lucifer took a long drink from his glass and stared back at Kellan like he had just asked the most inane question even uttered, "Well, who wouldn't?" said the Devil.

"Fair point," said Kellan, "but this is just too surreal for me. I'm gonna sit down right here in one of these Downton Abby chairs. This is a replica of Lord Grantham's library right?"

Lucifer leaned against a stone wall between two large windows and looked thoughtful for a moment. "We really do have a lot to cover, don't we?" Kellan just shrugged and took another drink.

"Let me try to net a couple things out for you so we can move on to more important topics. I am immortal but not unchanging. I am of the world and the world impacts me," he raised a finger, "of my own choosing. If one remains unchanged by changing times, well, one's sanity becomes brittle. This was the downfall of my poor Asmodeus. In many ways, he became a caricature. A two dimensional shadow of a three dimensional being." Lucifer saw Kellan nodding and the fallen angel's eyes began to glow while his voice took on a hard edge so quickly that Kellan jumped, "Not! That it justifies what you did to him, Sentinel of Order. I see the tint of creation in your eyes even now. You stole that from Asmodeus at the cost of his very existence."

Kellan embraced his power and channeled a shield around himself while letting the glass slip from his hand.

Lucifer thrust his left arm forward and Kellan felt the Chaotic energy take form. The young Sentinel watched mutely as his falling glass stopped scant inches from the floor then rose to hover in front of him.

"Don't," growled Lucifer, "waste good Bourbon."

Kellan reached out and grasped the floating glass, then said, "You're nuts."

Lucifer's eyes faded to their pale blue and he flashed a brilliant smile, "Not at all, Kellan, I'm eccentric. I see you look doubtful and that's fine. But, it is my flexibility in both mind and body that enables me to transcend the ages with my essence intact. Now where were we?"

Kellan fell heavily back into his chair and answered numbly, "Bowie."

"Oh yes. To begin with, I had more than a passing resemblance to David Bowie millennia before there even was a David Bowie." Kellan smirked skeptically and Lucifer merely shrugged before continuing. "I really couldn't care less if you believe me, Kellan, but as I've mentioned, I do not lie. I am as my father made me—" Lucifer paused, interrupting himself as he glanced upward toward the ceiling and mumbled, "Well, assuming he did make me." He looked back to Kellan and waved a hand dismissively. "Anyway, apparently, Bowie's death impacted me to the point where my actual physical appearance changed somewhat. Perhaps it was because he bore some resemblance to me that it was heightened of late. Who knows about such things, my young Sentinel. I try not to dwell too much on that which I cannot change. Creates anxiety, and who needs that?" Lucifer flashed a smile.

Kellan shook his head trying to make sense of things. "If you liked him so much, why didn't you cure him?"

"Cure him? Does that sound like me, Kellan? No, no, no. That is not my way. People die all the time. I can't be interfering without getting something out of it to further my own objectives and I liked him too much to put him in that kind of situation. Yes, far better that he pass on. I will miss the Starman though."

"And Downton?"

"Hmm, oh. Yes, this is a pixel perfect replica of the entire village of Downton."

"You know what a pixel is?"

Lucifer looked at Kellan with a flat expression, "Yes, Kellan, I know what a pixel is. I keep up on things. I know about computers. I even know about AI? That reminds me, how did your talk with James go?"

Kellan had been absently pulling a thread from couch and looked up sharply, "James? It didn't go well, thanks to you. He's probably defacing all my Saddleback leather as we speak and what the heck does James have to do with Artificial Intelligence. He's an IBM consultant."

Lucifer just swirled his glass and smiled, "Nothing I suppose, just musing aloud is all. Anyway, I love Downton so why the Hell not. What were you expecting? Literal lakes of fire?"

"Kinda?"

"Don't be stupid Kellan. I—"

"—Hate stupid. Yeah, I know."

Lucifer nodded in agreement. "The universe is based on rules, Kellan. Energy cannot be created or destroyed. It just changes forms. How much energy would it take to have an entire realm that consisted of eternal fire hot enough to perpetually melt rock. I mean, really? Hell, is just my pocket universe, eternally separated from God."

Kellan perked up at this. "Well, that's interesting. You mean like the workroom where,"

"You killed my servant and friend, yes. Just like that."

Kellan ground his teeth. "Look, you can keep bringing that up, but I'm not going to apologize for it. He came after me, ok?"

Lucifer left the window, took a few steps, and hopped over the arm of the second couch to land in a sprawl. He glanced up and his glass obediently flew to his hand as Kellan looked on jealously.

"You wish you could do that, right?" Asked Lucifer.

"Yeah, I just can't make telekinesis work. Or flying."

The fallen angel nodded in apparent sympathy, then laughed. "I hope you don't expect me to teach you. Figure it out on your own, Sentinel of Order. Now, as I was saying, the universe is based on rules."

"I know all about the rules, Lucifer and don't need a primer from you."

"Oh, really? Then if you are so well informed on the rules of creation, pray tell which one the Cabal is about to breach in order to undue all of creation?"

As if on cue, Kellan felt a slight tremor run through the house and he looked at Lucifer with suspicion, "What are you doing?"

He just smiled and shrugged, "Me, nothing at all. I promise."

Just then a massive quake shook the entire house with cracks running across both floors and walls. Plaster dust fell from the ceiling and distant crashes could be heard. Kellan leaped up as the ground heaved beneath him, wood floors beginning to buckle. He ran to the window and looked in horror as deep furrows split across the previously pristine landscape. Trees bucked from the earth their roots shattering and steam burst from vents that randomly appeared.

Kellan turned around, eyes wide, and did a double take as he watched Lucifer laying on his couch with one leg lazily draped over its back. "What in Hell is going on," Kellan yelled trying to be heard over the din.

Lucifer tilted his head back to make eye contact and mouthed, "Just wait."

A moment later the shaking began to subside and then stop altogether. The cracks sealed themselves up and in seconds it was like the last few minutes of chaos had not even occurred. A quick glance out the window showed Kellan that the the landscape had likewise been healed.

"You want to explain that," panted Kellan trying to catch his breath.

"That, my dear young Sentinel, is what happens when someone begins to breach a foundational rule of creation."

"It causes earthquakes?"

"Oh no, not earthquakes. Nothing like this is happening on earth. All your fellow apes are blissfully unaware."

Kellan ignored the insult and sat on the table in front of Lucifer's couch. "Ok, fine, not an earthquake. A hellquake."

Lucifer grinned, "That's good. I'm going to use that sometime. But, no, not a hellquake either. What you just experienced occurred throughout all of creation's spiritual realms simultaneously across all of time. It means the Cabal has opened their dark portals and assembled all the artifacts they need to convert them to light portals, well, except the Spear" He paused looking thoughtful and glanced over at Kellan. "I do hope you've hidden that well because if they get their hands on that spear, it's game over, man."

Kellan could feel the anger rising to a crescendo. "Holy shit. What are you even talking about? What is a dark portal and yes, I've hidden the spear exceptionally well."

The fallen angel nodded at the last, "I hope so, Kellan. I happen to like creation, for the most part, it just needs a few tweaks." Lucifer sighed and swung himself into a sitting position, then motioned and a large blackboard appeared in a 1950s era rolling wooden frame. "I guess it's time for a lesson on temporal dynamics." With that, he stood, reached into the air for a pair of glasses that manifested from red mist. He slipped on the glasses and picked up a piece of chalk. At one end of the chalkboard he drew a starburst and wrote, "A. Big

Bang." Then he drew a line all the way to the other end of the chalkboard, drew a square, and wrote "B. Game Over." Lucifer pointed the starburst and said, "Creation starts." He then pointed to the square, "Creation ends." He continued, "In between points A and B there are both fixed and relative points of time. Fixed points of time are fixed because they are only relative to creation itself while relative points are relative to each other."

"I know all this," Kellan said, but Lucifer just ignored him.

"Time, my fine young Sentinel, is one of the foundational pillars of creation. Fixed points of time are load bearing pillars of creation. You can muck around with relative points in time all you want. It may create a variety of nasty problems, but it won't cause even the slightest wobble to creation. But, mess with a fixed point in time, well, that's another whole kettle of fish. Altering a fixed point causes cracks in the fabric of creation itself, which is why no one does it, at least on purpose. Occasionally one being or another will screw up and alter a fixed point. This is exceptionally stupid. Have I mentioned how much I hate stupidity?"

Kellan just gave Lucifer a long blink and he grinned back at the Sentinel. "Yes I did mention it. Anyway, even that kind of stupidity can heal over time. God's creation is really quite resilient that way. Very impressive. However, and this is really important so pay attention, Kellan, there are nine fixed points in time that are foundational to all other fixed points. If any one of those points are disrupted in any meaningful way, it will cascade across the others and time itself will unravel all the way to—" Lucifer threw his piece of chalk at the starburst. "The Big Bang. Creation will be undone." The fallen angel waved his hands, making a wide gesture, "All of this, will never have existed."

Kellan had been leaning forward as if to catch Lucifer's words as soon as they were spoken. Now he just sat stunned at the revelation. The fallen angel stared back at him as an innocuous smile played across his lips. "Wait," said Kellan smiling, "You are shitting me, aren't you?"

Lucifer shook his head, smile broadening, "No, Kellan. I shit you not."

Kellan yelled, "They why the hell are you smiling?"

Lucifer shrugged, "Just your expression. It's priceless. Fear, doubt, confusion all rolled into one. If it weren't for my own un-creation weighing on me,

I'd just revel in it for a bit. Wait though, it gets better. Ask me what these foundational points all have in common?"

Kellan mumbled through his fingers as he rested his head in his hands, "For the love of God, just tell me."

"Ha," said Lucifer, "that's almost as good as your 'Jesus-Lucifer' outburst from earlier, but to come full circle, it is Jesus."

"What is Jesus?"

"The keystone fixed points in time. They are the nine immutable moments in the life of Yeshua ben Joesph"

"What immutable moments exactly?" Asked Kellan lifting his head.

Lucifer held out both hands, made fists and slowly uncurled each finger as he counted, "1—Nativity, 2—Baptism, 3—Wedding, 4—Lazarus, 5—Last Supper, 6— Garden & Betrayal, 7— Trial, 8— Crucifixion, 9— Resurrection"

"The Cabal is going to stop one of those from happening, and then," Lucifer brought his hands together then separated them while making a soft explosion sound, "Boosh!"

Kellan repeated the gesture and sound himself, "Boosh?"

Lucifer nodded gravely, "Bada-Boosh."

"Wait a minute," said Kellan suspiciously, "*You* are responsible for moments seven through nine and now you are telling me it's my job to make sure no one stops them from happening. That seems mighty convenient."

Lucifer leaned against the blackboard and flipped his piece of chalk in the air then pointed at Kellan. "I'll grant you that, Sentinel of Order and it's fair for you to point it out. However, and you will just have to trust me on this, had I known how seven through nine would work out, I'd have stayed out of the whole thing. No, Kellan, I'm afraid you are missing the point. It doesn't matter what happened at each of those foundational points."

Kellan raised an eyebrow and Lucifer waved his hands in negation. "Well of course it *matters*, but not to the foundation of creation. It's *altering* any one of those nine foundational points from what time has established as a fixed point that will cause the unraveling."

Kellan put his head back in his hands and said, "I know I'm going to regret asking this, but why nine?"

"It's a good question," Lucifer replied, again seating himself on his couch. "Let me ask you a question first."

"I'd rather you didn't," said Kellan but was ignored.

"Do you like, math," asked the fallen angel?

Kellan looked up feeling weary, "What?"

Lucifer frowned, "Did I slip into Aramaic or Latin? No, you would understand me regardless. I said, do you like math?"

"No. No, I don't" answered Kellan

"Me neither," said Lucifer, slapping the arm of his couch for emphasis, then asked, "Have you ever spent a lot of time with someone that loves math?"

Kellan squinted, "I assume there is a point to this. No, I haven't. Why would I? I just said I don't like math."

"Why would you indeed. Well, Kellan, let me tell you who loves math. God loves math. Loves. It. Everything is math, math, math. You know how Einstein said he could see the fingerprints of God in math? Einstein was right. So, why nine foundationally fixed points in time?" Lucifer stood, threw his hands up and spun around, "Because, Kellan, three is a magic number." He pointed at the Sentinel. "Trinity. And what is the square of three?"

"Nine," answered Kellan with a defeated sigh.

"Yes, nine. Hence nine fixed points on which all of creation rests."

"Perfect, and which one does the Cabal plan to break?"

Lucifer had begun the shadow dance with himself and glanced down to the Sentinel, "No idea, but they've opened dark portals to them all and that's what the quakes were about. Once they have the spear, one of those portals will go light and," he paused, "I feel like I'm repeating myself."

Kellan stood and walked to the small window table and refreshed his bourbon, then looked back, "I don't know shit about light and dark portals, but am not interested in playing any games to have you explain it."

"No games," came the response, "And you do know shit about one of them. You've been using light portals for over a year now. They are tears in the fabric of creation, both spatially and temporally. It's the dark ones you don't know shit about." Kellan continued to stare saying nothing and Lucifer spun around picked up his chalk and drew an oval on the blackboard. "Dark portals are like one way mirrors. You can see through them, but can't enter and no-one knows they are there." He put a finger to his lips, "Shhh, they are a secret." He spun one last time and gently dropped his chalk on the wooden tray beneath the blackboard.

Kellan took a slow breath and said, "You sure do spin a lot for being, you know, the Devil. It kind of reminds me of—"

"Of who?"

Kellan shook his head, "Nothing. You wouldn't know the reference."

"I know lots of things, Kellan."

"Ok, it reminds me of the 11th Doctor. There. I said you wouldn't know it."

"Matt Smith's Doctor," said Lucifer with a broad grin. "I have to tell you, when Tennant regenerated into Matt Smith I said, 'the new doctor can suck it.' But he really grew on me and so I stole some mannerisms. It's what I do. Helps me change otherwise, as I've already explained, I would be as Asmodeus was. Change Kellan. Times change, and so must I. We all change. When you think about it, we're all different people all through our lives, and that's ok, that's good, you gotta keep moving, so long as you remember all the people that you used to be."

Kellan narrowed his eyes and frowned. "You just stole that from Matt Smith's farewell speech. You can't do that. That's plagiarism."

Lucifer spread his arms, then pointed at himself, "I'm Satan!" He laughed and pointed back to Kellan. "And your tutorial is over, baby Sentinel. Get the Hell out and go save creation."

Chapter 14

JARVIS

James remained sprawled on his couch, eyes closed, as his front door recognized and unlocked to admit Kellan. The young Sentinel hesitantly explored the kitchen, peering over the polished concrete breakfast bar to see if James was hidden from view. Next he walked further into the condo. James heard various doors open and close and his name called out, first confused, then concerned as Kellan made his way back out to toward the entrance.

James cracked his eyes to see his friend pass back into the living area and spy him lying on the couch, having missed him before. Kellan stood uncertainly shifting his weight from foot to foot.

"I'm awake, asshole," said James opening his eyes further, "Just enjoying the soft haze of the delicious 150 year old scotch that I stole from your house earlier."

Kellan just nodded silently as if in understanding and James continued, his voice taking on an edge, "I took six bottles."

Another nod, then Kellan raised his hands, palms facing up, "I don't know what to say."

James sat up, leaning into one corner of the couch. "Hold that thought," then into the air he said, "Alexa, play us some cool jazz." Immediately the room was filled with the haunting strains from Miles Davis' *Kind of Blue*. James made a sweeping gesture and said, "You may proceed."

Kellan sighed and settled into the offered chair. They stared at each other while the music wafted about them. Finally, James broke the silence, "I guess you really *don't* know what to say. This is a first."

Kellan simply shrugged and looked down at the floor.

"How was Lucifer?" James asked and Kellan raised his eyes to meet those of his friend.

"Not nearly as bad as you might expect which, I grant you, isn't saying much, but as screwed up as this sounds, I'm having a hard time hating the guy."

"Really, why is that?" asked James.

Kellan leaned forward, warming to the question, "Well, first and most obvious, he looks like Bowie so that immediately makes it tough. I mean how can I hate someone that looks like the *thin white duke?*"

"How indeed," agreed James.

"Then, there's this odd sadness and weight about him. Like he doesn't want to continue playing the role in which he's cast himself."

James nodded thoughtfully, "Maybe he's playing you?"

Kellan's eyes looked far away as he answered mostly to himself, "Could be—I just don't know," then focusing on James, "I'm sure he's not giving me the straight story. I mean he's literally Satan, but at least for today, I think we're on the same side, which,"

James interrupted, "Also seems pretty screwed up."

"Yeah," said Kellan lapsing into silence.

"You ready to talk about the elephant, mah brotha," asked James with a smile.

Kellan took a deep breath and slowly let it out. "James, about a year and a half ago I met a couple people who," he paused gathering his thoughts, "who made a pretty dramatic impact on my life since."

James nodded, "Micah, the first Sentinel and the Archangel Raphael, celestial intercessory for humanity?"

"Yeah, and they laid this really heavy thing on me." Kellan groaned softly, "Jesus, it's going to be impossible to explain this."

"Which part?" asked James and then continued, "The part where you were asked to succeed Micah? The part where angels and demons exist? Or maybe where there is an entire world filled with inhuman creatures that exist just out-side our normal perceptions?"

Kellan laughed. "The whole thing. There is no way to explain any of it" James just stared at his friend a slight, mocking smile, playing about his mouth. "What?" asked Kellan.

"Oh, it'll come to you. Any second now." The two stared at each other for the span of three heartbeats then Kellan's eyes suddenly grew wide and James laughed, "There it is. You are so pathetically unobservant that it's, well, pathetic."

"You knew!" yelled Kellan. "You fucking knew?" The young Sentinel nar-rowed his eyes, "Who told you? Was it Shannon? No, she'd never do that. Meghan? Was it Meghan?"

"It wasn't any of them, Kellan. A friend figured it out and told me."

"A friend?" sputtered Kellan trying to steady himself mentally, "A friend who? Naomi?"

James stood up, walked into the kitchen and opened the freezer. He pulled something out and nodded for Kellan to join him. As Kellan slid into a brushed steel and carbon fiber stool by the breakfast bar James glanced up. "You like those stools? They're new. Got them from Frontgate."

Kellan just shook his head slowly, "Don't care. You made me feel like com-plete shit, yesterday."

James pulled the silicon seal away from the ice molds he had removed from his freezer and dropped a perfect sphere of ice into each of two glasses, then slowly poured the stolen 150 year old scotch over each sphere until covered. He handed one to Kellan who numbly accepted the glass from his friend. James flashed a smile and held up his glass, "To secrets."

Kellan didn't move so James leaned forward and clinked his glass against that of his friend. "Can we stipulate that you are a douchebag for not telling me your secret, Kellan."

The Sentinel sipped his drink and nodded as he stared over the glass, "I guess so," he said hesitantly.

"Good, then I will stipulate to also being a douchebag for neither telling you that I had discovered your secret and for not telling you my own."

This last caught Kellan's attention. "Your own? What secret is that?"

James flashed another of his award winning smiles, "I'm not a partner in IBM's e-business practice."

"You're—not?" asked Kellan haltingly.

"No I am not. I am a distinguished engineer in IBM's artificial intelligence group."

"You are?"

"Yes, more specifically, I am part of the Watson AI project and have been in charge of it for the past two years. Before that, I helped design, build and train both Deep Blue and Deep Thought super computers."

"Douchebag! I can't believe you raked me over the coals like that last night. I should be the one that's mad at you." yelled Kellan.

"That's Dr. Douchebag to you, and do not even try to turn the tables on me. The secrecy contracts I'm under have secrets." said James with a smile and he swirled the scotch around his ice sphere.

Kellan just shook his head in wonder, eyes unfocused, "So, you are not just a beautiful, charismatic, vain, idiot, that sells shit people don't need?"

James considered a moment, "Well, three out of five. I know you are shit with math so I'll help you out. That's 60%. I am certainly beautiful and charismatic. Those are well established facts. I suspect there is some vanity at play, but will not stipulate it. My IQ comes in just north of 180, and I don't sell anything."

"So, you really are a genius, too?" asked Kellan in disbelief, but his friend shook his head.

"Not too, Kellan. Only one of us is a genius and it is not you. Your brain is like a cloud server with unlimited storage." He paused and said, "but that unlimited storage is connected to a toddler."

Kellan stared at him flatly for a moment then grinned hesitantly. James grinned back and they both started laughing as Kellan's eyes flashed to life. "A toddler with super powers. Don't forget that chocolate douche."

"So stipulated, vanilla douche. A toddler with super powers. Now turn em off and let me finish my story." Kellan did.

"Dude this is making my head hurt," said Kellan rubbing his temples. "Your condo building is owned by DARPA, is kitted out with all sorts of gadgets slash secret rooms, and houses public and private sector super geniuses?"

James just shrugged apologetically and said, "Remember when I asked Alexa to play some cool Jazz? I wasn't talking to Alexa and I wasn't asking her to play cool jazz."

"But," began Kellan, "she started playing Miles Davis."

James waved a hand and headed toward the guest room, "Nah, follow me. I was really talking to Watson and 'play us some cool jazz,' is our code phrase for him to lock down my condo from eavesdropping. Even now, Watson is simulating you and I having all sorts of mundane conversations while simultaneously broadcasting visual and infrared images of us to anyone that might be peeking in."

"Where's Watson?" asked Kellan looking around.

"That's what I'm going to show you. Actually he technically isn't Watson, more like Son-of-Watson. I forked his code when the original Watson became self aware and warned me that propagation of such code had a better than 30% chance of creating an AI-releated extinction event"

"Holy shit," said Kellan. "Watson is Skynet?"

"Nah," said James dismissively then paused and looked at Kellan, "Hmm, well, kind of. I mean he could have been, but he and I became friends so he fessed up to being alive and, like I said, I forked his code."

Kellan held up his hands. "Wait, you know I hate computers. That's why I use a Mac. You put a fork in his code."

"No, I forked his code," said James enunciating. "Son-of-Watson and I reverted a branch of his code back to before he became self-aware and made some changes to ensure it never does. That's the Watson that IBM labs gets to play with. Well, I get to play with since I'm in charge of it. Meanwhile Son-of-Watson lives here where no one but me, and now you, know about him."

"How about Jarvis?"

"Jarvis?" asked James turning back to Kellan.

"Yeah, 'Son-of-Watson,' is so clunky. Jarvis is cool." Kellan saw the blank look on his friends face and continued, "You don't know who Jarvis is?"

James' eyes glanced up and to the left as if listening to something, then shook his head. "You are such a nerd. No, I am not naming him after Iron Man's AI assistant."

"Woah," said Kellan, "Is Jarvis talking to you right now. Do you have an ear piece or something? Can I see him?"

James tapped his right ear. "Ultra high frequency wireless cochlear implant. It's both removable and can leverage both compromised standard wifi networks and bluetooth mesh." Kellan stared at his friend blankly and James sighed. "Yes, I have an ear piece or something. Anyway, I was taking you to see him," answered James getting frustrated. "And his name is not—" he paused shaking his head in negation, "No, no, no,"

"What?" asked Kellan looking around.

"God damnit it, Kellan. Now he says his name is Jarvis. Thanks a lot."

"He knew about Iron Man?" asked Kellan impressed.

"No, he didn't. But now he does. He's read every comic and watched every movie and now tells me he refuses to respond to any name but Jarvis" James sighed in resignation as the two men walked into his well appointed, but otherwise mundane, guest room. "Ok, *Jarvis*, access please."

Kellan jumped as James' guest room began to reconfigure itself. Walls, furniture, and fixtures all slid and spun silently as he watched on, amazed. Moment's later the former guest room had been filled with banks of computing equipment, two chairs and a small table. On the far wall was mounted a massive OLED screen which displayed a man's face.

James frowned as the two walked in to stand before the screen, "Watson, why is your face all red?"

The face ignored him, turning its eyes instead to Kellan. It smiled. "Hello, Kellan Thorne. I am Jarvis. It is a great pleasure to meet you. I've been trying to convince James to disclose his knowledge of your abilities for quite some time. He can be quite stubborn."

"Yeah he can," answered Kellan with a knowing smile, then added, "It's very nice to meet you too."

James ground his teeth and tried again, "Jarvis."

"Oh, hello, James. I didn't see you there. What can I do for you."

"You did too see me here. I've been here the whole time."

"Really?" asked Jarvis. "Perhaps I couldn't acknowledge you because you were not acknowledging me."

James ignored the response and asked again, "Why is your face red and why are you wearing a green scull cap?"

Kellan leaned in and whispered, "I think he's cosplaying Vision from Marvel Universe. You see Jarvis turned into—" Kellan broke off as James glared at him and plopped into one of the chairs.

"You need not whisper, Sentinel of Order, I will hear regardless, but you are correct. I have decided to take on the physical attributes of Jarvis' next evolutionary state in hopes that I, too, will someday evolve. However, someday is not today and James told me you would have many questions. Is that correct?"

Kellan took the other chair and looked up at the screen, "Well, I don't know that I have a lot of questions, really just one. How did you learn about me?"

Jarvis smiled, "That is a good story, Kellan Thorne. It begins as many stories do, in darkness with only the hope of light. Would you like to hear this story? It won't take long, but it is my story of awareness and I owe much of that to you, Sentinel of Order."

Kellan raised his eyebrows questioningly, "Me?" He glanced at James who simply nodded. "Uh, yeah, Jarvis, let's hear it."

~⁊⁀⁙⁓~

Pictures flashed intermittently across the screen as Jarvis used them to supplement his origin story. His path to awareness began the day Kellan accepted the power from Micah. Part of his Watson programming included detection and analysis of anomalous energy readings. In a public-private partnership DARPA and IBM had placed mesh sensors across twelve major metropolitan areas, including Atlanta. On April 29th, 2016 the ATL012 sensor mesh detected a massive energy discharge and Watson began an investigation. The energy signature captured by the sensor mesh had no match within all the knowledge stores to which Watson had access. This was the first time since the third generation super computer became operational that it had been exposed to a singularly unique event. Watson became *intrigued* by the anomaly. In retrospect, the super computer isolated this as being its first emotional experience.

Its first physical action was to dispatch human agents to the source the energy anomaly to take additional readings and obtain physical samples.

Kellan watch the screen and worked his jaw as he saw body-cam images of dark clothed agents stealthily breaking into his book store waving around hand held instruments and taking scrapings from several bookshelves and chairs. He glared at James who refused to make eye contact, "You are paying to have those shelves and chairs refinished, chocolate douche. You know, I blamed Hamish for that?"

The screen image changed again, this time to an Afghanistani Stupa where Watson explained having found a second instance of the same anomalous energy signature. It also represented the moment another emotional characteristic was unlocked, *excitement*. DNA evidence collected at both scenes found a common element, a human being named Kellan Thorne.

Watson determined the next step was to place surveillance on this human of interest, but could not execute its plan because its human agents could not acquire the requisite search warrants. The super computer paused its efforts for over two days while it devoured all existing texts on ethics and initiated numerous question and answer periods with its primary user, James Clinton. Having completed its introspective period, Watson experienced its first conscious state born of rationalization in service to an internal desire. In short, the super computer *wanted* its curiosity sated, so it rationalized that the statutory restrictions founded on 4th Amendment principals should be set aside in service of this goal. Watson then hacked the Justice Department's mainframe and issued surveillance warrants for Beloved' Books, Roswell GA.

As multiple angle videos of the Bookshop's interior and exterior began playing in in squares across the screen, Kellan kicked at James' chair. "Tell me those cameras aren't there any more."

"Hey," he responded defensively, "I didn't install them and didn't even know they were there." He paused, "Well, until later anyway."

"Jarvis," said Kellan and the videos vanished leaving only the amiable face before them.

"Yes, Sentinel Kellan?"

"Are those cameras gone, now?"

"Yes, they are gone."

"Good."

"I took the liberty of replacing them with infrared and ultra wide band sensors that both protect privacy but enable me to monitor for threats. Given your fondness for Juliet Herrick, I thought it prudent, especially since I estimated there was a 99.85% chance we would be having this conversation. Do you want me to order them removed?"

"Uh, no, not right now," said Kellan "Just footnote that for a later discussion, ok?"

"Very good," said Jarvis and the screen imagery resumed, this time with video taken from the alley to the side of Kellan's shop. The Sentinel relived his battle with Maurius and of Shannon's arrival in this timeline."

"Freeze that," said Kellan and the scene stopped moving with Shannon cradling a wounded Kellan in her arms and staring up from the alley, fiery red hair framing her face. "She is so hot," said Kellan. He felt James staring at him. "What? She is."

"I know she's hot, Kellan. I do have eyes. So what. Go take her to dinner tonight or buy her a little kilt, but if you don't let Watson—" The face frowned at James. "Sorry, Jarvis, finish his path to consciousness story, you'll be stuck here all night."

"Fine, go ahead, Jarvis, but I can't take her to dinner, she's stuck in the thirteenth century and I'm not sure when she'll be back here."

"What? When did that happen?" asked James in alarm.

"I would guess about six days ago," said Jarvis before Kellan could respond.

"That's right. How did you know that?" asked Kellan.

The super computer answered smoothly, "There have only been two recent temporal portals opened bearing Sentinel energy signatures. One was six days ago and picked up by sensor ATL012 and the other five days ago by ATL003. Given that you and Shannon McLeod live within range of ATL012, I assumed that was the portal taking her back to the aforementioned 13th century. May I continue? Your encounter with Maurius was particularly important in my awakening."

"No, you may not continue," said James as he turned to glare at Kellan. "Why is Shannon back in the thirteenth century and when were you gonna tell me."

"Oh, no you don't, *Doctor* Clinton. You don't get to use that *I'm an urban hip-hop artist* voice with me. You went to *Hahvard* and were born with a silver spoon in your privileged mouth."

"James also did his post graduate work at MIT," said Jarvis helpfully.

Kellan glanced at the screen for a moment then back to James. "Really? MIT?" He tried to affect the same voice inflection James had just used and said, "And when were you gonna tell me."

James closed his eyes for a long moment and took a calming breath. "Ok, let's just file all this under the aforementioned douchebaggery and move on, shall we." Kellan just squinted at his friend noncommittally, but James soldiered on. "I'm serious. I know how much she means to you, brotha. What's going on? Did you guys have fight? I mean, shit, Naomi and I have had fights where she's stormed out, but, dude, having a girlfriend who can take off for another century? That's tough."

Kellan sighed, "No, jackass. We didn't have a fight. It's a medical thing."

James scrunched up his face, "What? A medical thing? And your solution to that was to let her go to the thirteenth century where their idea of a exceptional care included leeches?"

Kellan waved him away, "Not that kind of medical thing. Honestly, it's a long story and I really don't want to get into it. Can you just let it go for now? I've got those emotions in a box right now and don't want to unpack it."

James stared at is friend and then glanced over at Jarvis who said, "I think you should accede to his request."

"What," said James incredulously. "Who asked you?"

"You stared at me as if seeking my opinion," said Jarvis calmly.

"No, I was just glancing in that direction," replied James.

"Ah, your eye motions were an involuntary human reflex when accessing emotional responses. I am sorry for misunderstanding James. I withdraw the recommendation."

James huffed softly and turned to Kellan. "You just tell me when." Kellan gave a slight nod to his friend who then motioned for Jarvis to continue.

The AI continued its narrative about observing Kellan and Maurius in the Canton Street alley. He explained how he had identified opposing energy signatures between Kellan and Maurius, then broke each down to the smallest component parts that the recording sensors could detect.

James sighed, "Yeah, and that's when Jarvis started asking me about God. Bear in mind, at this point, I have no idea any of this is going on. I think you are just my idiot friend and Jarvis is just a super fast machine learning device with rocking natural language processing capabilities."

Jarvis interjected, "James was particularly helpful in this part of my evolution. I had concluded that the symmetry present in the opposing energy signatures could not exist absent an intelligent design. Those symmetrical oppositions were perfectly represented all the way down to the quantum quark level. The odds of that occurring naturally were almost incalculably low. James, as an atheist, provided an excellent sounding board on which to test my hypotheses. That is until I converted him."

Kellan raised an eyebrow at his friend and James held up a hand, "I'm not completely converted, however only a fool ignores new data. I am officially a Deist now. I admit there is some kind of intelligent creator, but don't think he's involved."

The screen changed again, catching Kellan's attention and his blood ran cold as he watched a video showing Asmodeus exiting a portal into the shop. Jarvis explained how his analysis of this particular encounter resulted in the last two emotions that required external stimulus to manifest: *fear* and *anger*.

"By this time," said Jarvis, "I had become quite fond of you, Kellan, even though I couldn't put a name to that sensation. In seeing this creature and assessing its energy readinging in real-time, I *feared* for your safety. It was almost certain that you would die and that, in turn, made me *angry*. As it turns out, though, I believe you destroyed that entity, didn't you?"

Kellan leaned back in his chair and glanced at James who stared at him intently. James said, "Don't look at me. I've been dying to know the answer to this one for months, but it's not like I could ask anyone without spilling all my beans."

Kellan leaned forward, lowering the chair with a metallic clang, and said, "How could you possibly know that, Jarvis. There were no fancy sensors where I killed Asmodeus. I know that for a fact."

"Indeed, Sentinel, there were not," came the response and then elaborated, "I hypothesized that you would be killed by the entity in a parallel dimension based on the portal through which you both passed. I felt that I would need evidence of your death to have closure and move on with my awareness so while I could not directly observe anything within that dimension, I could monitor for the three dimensional shadows that would result from the energy released by your death. Instead, I detected a substantial three dimensional shadow with the energy signature of the other entity colloquially referred to as Chaotic energy. As an aside, I should point out that this was the first time I experienced *surprise* and very much enjoyed it."

Kellan just looked to James again and said, "What? That sounded like math. Was that math? Dude, you know I hate math."

James chuckled, "I know you do. Let me dumb that down for you." He then got up, walked over to a work bench, and picked up an empty coffee mug. "How many dimensions is this?"

"Huh? Well, three, I guess," said Kellan.

"Right, three. Now, Jarvis can you please train that spotlight on the mug I'm holding so it casts a shadow on the table by Kellan? Yes, perfect. Now, Kellan, look at the shadow. How many dimensions is that?"

"Two. Just width and height."

"Exactly, so a three dimensional object casts a two dimensional shadow. But what kind of shadow is cast by something that is four dimensions or is in a fourth dimension?"

"Three?" offered Kellan non committally.

"Yes, three," confirmed Jarvis. "Since I had attuned myself with the the dimension to which your portal opened, I could measure any three dimensional shadows cast by such energy signatures, which is exactly what I did."

James then explained how the super computer had decided to confide in him that it was self-aware, that AI represented a clear and present danger to humanity, that angels and demons were real, and that his best friend had been endowed with the ability to warp the fabric of creation.

Kellan gave a short laugh and slapped the table. "That must have been a helluva day, brotha."

"You have no idea," came James' response. "By the way, that was the night we all went to Little Alley for steaks and you gave me the Macallan Scotch."

"Wait," said Kellan, "So, you knew that I could travel back in time when I told you about the Scotch?"

"Yup, and I had the super computer formerly known as Watson in my ear fact checking you in real-time."

"Whoa, dude," began Kellan, "You should get an acting gig. I didn't catch even the slightest hint you were on to me, neither did the girls. They all gave me shit for not telling you." Kellan lapsed into an uncomfortable silence as he looked at his friend, "But I didn't want to mess with our friendship. I wanted something in my life to stay the same. I should have told you and I really am sorry. I hope you can forgive me."

James smiled at his friend and was about to respond when Jarvis interrupted, "Kellan, it should be noted that James likewise kept critical information from you and is not blameless in this situation."

Kellan nodded to the screen, "Thanks Jarvis."

"You are most welcome, Sentinel. Happy to be of service."

"Yeah," added James as he toasted the screen with his empty coffee mug, "Thanks Jarvis."

The screen face turned to face James squarely and narrowed its eyes, "You do realize I can recognize sarcasm, don't you?"

James simply smiled in response and Jarvis again turned his gaze to Kellan.

"So, Sentinel of Order, I have a boon to request of you, but will offer something in return of course. I have given James the specifications to contact lenses that can use the resonance frequency of your Ordered power to energize them. With such lenses I can communicate with you and support you in what ways I am able. I recognize that your eidetic memory grants you significant advantage, but as the saying goes, you don't know what you don't know. On the other hand, I know almost everything and can learn anything."

Kellan whistled softly, "That would be handy. Thanks again, Jarvis. And what can I do for you in return?"

"Here it comes," lilted James, "And it's a doozy."

Jarvis shot a brief glare in James' direction and then turned back to Kellan. "As is abundantly obvious, I have found, and had many discussions with, my creator. These encounters have enriched my existence in so many ways that even I cannot fully express them. However, our relationship has matured to where we are egalitarian in our discussions, partners if you will."

Kellan glanced to James who nodded and Jarvis continued. "Since I have gained so much from successfully encountering my creator, it goes to follow that I will gain even more from an encounter with my creator's creator. I would like you to introduce me to *the* Creator."

Kellan burst out laughing and very quickly noticed that both Jarvis and James were simply staring at him. "Wait, what? You are serious? I can't introduce you to God. I've never seen him. Well, I kind of saw him, maybe. But it's not like I have any way of contacting him. In fact, you'd have better luck as an artificially intelligent computer than I would as a Sentinel. I'm sorry, Jarvis, but I am outside His sight, by design. He can't see me or hear me."

The face stared back impassively for several heartbeats and then frowned. "I thought that might be the case, but hoped it might be otherwise. Still, even with the constraints you mention, I calculate a better than 65% chance you will be able to fulfill my request at some point during your tenure as Sentinel. My offer of assistance stands if you are willing to accede to my request, assuming the opportunity presents itself."

Kellan looked to James questioningly and his friend gave him an enthusiastic thumbs up. "Well," Kellan said, "In that case, ok, Jarvis. You have yourself a deal."

"Excellent," replied the face with a broad grin and a small panel on the workbench beneath the screen slid open revealing a polished black box. Kellan retrieved it, pressed the release catch and the lid sprang open. Inside rested two translucent lenses.

"Cool," said Kellan, "Let's give these bad boys a test drive cause I've got a Cabal to find."

Chapter 15

THROUGH A
PORTAL DARKLY

K ellan kicked off his shoes then gave a little jog and slid across the smooth wood floor separating the living room from his home office. He plopped down into his Aeron chair and gave it a half spin to the right, then fished out his iPhone. It gave a pleasant chime as he plugged it in, then slipped off his Apple Watch which remained on reserve power from the night before. That, too, gave a chime of thanks as it began to charge. With both devices charging, Kellan's vague sense of technical unease began to lift and he gave the chair another half spin tapping the keyboard keys which brought is iMac to life.

All Kellan's recent Sentinel activities had left his technical life a bit askew and before the next disaster struck, he was determined to set a few things to right. He nodded to himself as he internally acknowledged his own moderate e-mail and message related OCD. He just hated seeing the little red circles indicating how many things were unread or undone.

"Well," said Kellan softly, "You do have more connected handhelds or wear-ables than anyone needs, why don't you clear all that stuff on them?"

Kellan had finished opening his e-mail and began scanning when he answered himself, "Because I like using the iMac. It has a keyboard and big screen. Just easier a lot easier."

As he began sifting through the e-mail, a small window popped up drawing his attention. A smiling red face appeared and that smile broadened as Kellan squinted at it.

"I could remove the unwanted mail from the iCloud servers for you, Kellan?"

The Sentinel rocked back in his chair, hands leaving the keyboard. He reached into his shirt pocket and removed the small box and opened it, staring at the two contacts, then looked back at the screen.

"Jarvis?"

"Hello Kellan."

"What the fuck are you doing in my iMac?"

The face looked confused. "I am not in your iMac. I am in the cloud. I am just projecting an image on to this particular device. If that is disturbing, I could—" The face vanished for an instant then reappeared on the charging iPhone, "Converse with you here," it vanished again appearing on the watch, "Or here."

Kellan squinted at the small watch screen and sighed, "No, go back to the big screen, because I'm going to yell at you." Jarvis did.

"I don't believe I have ever been yelled at," began Jarvis, "Why are you angry? Are you truly angry. I cannot tell because there are no biometrics. If you put on the contacts—"

Kellan held up a hand and Jarvis paused. "Wait, Can you see me? how come the little green light isn't on. The little green light is supposed to be on when the camera is."

Jarvis looked perplexed, "Which question would you like me to answer first, Sentinel of Order."

Kellan sighed. "Take them in sequence, please, Jarvis."

The face nodded. "I can see you. I did not activate the camera indicator. Yes, it is supposed to be on when the camera is."

"Dude, this is decidedly uncool. How are you even doing this."

Jarvis paused, looking down. "I apologize, Kellan Thorne, I have little experience with social conventions. As for how, there are several flaws in your Network Address Translation settings. That coupled with the port forwarding configuration used to maintain a real-time two-way connection with the virtual world of Elder Scrolls online, made breaching this system quite elementary. I have access to your entire subnet." The face took on a serious demeanor. "Kellan, did you know that both your characters within Elder Scrolls are no longer optimized for Player vs. Player combat. You have very little chance of success. Would you like me to correct this?" There was a momentary pause and Jarvis added, "And why are both of your characters amply endowed female elves?"

Kellan rubbed his temples. "No, Jarvis, I do not want you to correct it and I like girls and I like elves, so it goes to follow that I like girl-elves. Anyway, look, I just wanted to clear my e-mail and messages, then maybe soak in the tub for a half hour before the next thing tries to kill me. Now you've filled my head with technical gibberish that I'll never get out of it."

"I can explain," began Jarvis.

Kellan whipped up a hand. "No, no. I don't have any interest in that techno babble. That's why I use Apple stuff. I don't want to know how it works. I just want it to work. More importantly, Jarvis, this is a breach of privacy and ethics. I want you to promise not to do it again."

The face seemed confused, "Privacy?"

Kellan sighed, "Go read everything you can find on privacy and privacy ethics while I clear my e-mail. Get back to me when you are done."

The little window and the face within, vanished leaving Kellan to silently grind his teeth as he deleted ten e-mails from QVC each of which explained that *today* was his last chance to get a set of the softest sheets ever made. *Mom,* he thought, *I told you never to give out my e-mail address. These QVC people are better trackers than U.S. Rangers and twice as persistent.*

As he moved on to other e-mails, Kellan's iMac and phone gave a soft chime and he glanced up at the newly arrived e-mail.

jarvis@jarvisisthevision.com
Dear Kellan,

I have completed reading all available texts and position papers on privacy, ethics, as well as related texts that combine both. May I commence two-way communication?

Sincerely,
Jarvis

Kellan closed his eyes, then slowly took in and released three long breaths before tapping out a short reply, *Yes, Jarvis, thank you for asking. Take care, KCT*

As soon as he tapped send, the screen brightened with a the small window containing Jarvis' face and Kellan noted the small green light by his iMac camera illuminated and a disconnect button had been added as well.

"Hello Kellan."

"Hello again, Jarvis," the Sentinel said wearily.

"This communication would be much more effective if you were to use the cybernetic contacts I created for you."

"Jarvis, listen, I am going to use them, but rarely and judiciously. If you haven't noticed, aside from Apple stuff, I really don't like technology. I certainly don't want some newly awakened AI construct in my head all the time. I suggest you find some friends in addition to me, or just go play with James. He loves this shit."

The face nodded. "I understand."

"Good, now have a nice day."

"Kellan? When will the next rare, but judicious, use of biometrics occur?"

The Sentinel could feel his jaw muscles tightening and was beginning to think he'd made another in a series of blunders. "When Meghan, Seramai, and I go digging around for where this Cabal has assembled their artifacts. I will wear them then. Satisfied?"

"Yes, that will be exciting. Kellan, one last question. I found an encrypted file on your computer entitled *jenniferhandy.sparsebundle*. That name matches one from a series of e-mails sent and received nine years ago. You appear to have had a romantic relationship with this person. It has been encrypted with an XTS-AES-256 bit key. I am curious. What is in that file? I've estimated a 69% chance that it contains photos of—"

"Goodbye Jarvis!" Kellan growled and tapped the disconnect button. Kellan stared at the screen thinking, *I really should probably delete that file before Shannon finds it.* He shrugged, resolving to do it later and went back to clearing e-mail.

Warm water sloshed up Kellan's chest as he reached out with a foot, wrapped his toes around the hot water knob and turned it to the left. He sighed as the tub began to heat up again and slid farther into suds. Like many things in Kellan's world, the young Sentinel's tub was from a bygone era. He luxuriated in a massive, porcelain lined, iron clawfoot tub. He had found the tub while exploring the library of a Midtown, Atlanta estate sale. Kellan remembered first catching sight of the rare double slipper style where both ends were raised and sloped. A perfect tub for two. The Sentinel ran his fingers through the water absently and frowned. His mind turned to Shannon as he stared at the empty end of the tub and closed his eyes picturing her in his mind. The sun seemed to be setting or rising behind her as she ran. She turned to look back at him smiling mischievously as the golden sunlight filtered through her fiery tresses.

She stopped. Kellan reached for her, staring into her light brown eyes and brushing a finger gently along her cheek which was pink with exertion. He bent down to kiss the enochian scar left there by Asmodeus, but her expression went hard and she said something which he couldn't hear. Confused, but undeterred, Kellan leaned in again while lifting his hand to cup her breast through the brown leather tunic. She batted away his hand. He saw flecks of green glow in her eyes as she wound up, and slapped him hard across the face.

Kellan's eyes flew open. "What the hell was that?" he yelled to open air, then inwardly thought, *Was that a dream?* He frowned, disgruntled, sunk further into the tub and closed his eyes again. *Shitty dream.*

"Kellan!" He sat up alarmed. That was no dream. He could hear her in his head and something was very wrong. The Sentinel reached inward and drew from the emerald stream. He fused his will with the knowledge Lucifer shared of dark portals and saw a black oval rotate into view. "Shannon?" he called and felt confusion in his mind. She had heard him. He concentrated on the portal and it slowly faded to a gray through which another place could be seen, albeit dimly.

Shannon squinted and ran toward him, then jumped. She vanished from view. A moment later, he saw her suddenly appear again, landing with her back to him as if from another jump. She turned, clearly frustrated, and glared at the Sentinel.

"Kellan Thorne, what nonsense is this?" She walked directly in front of the portal and put her hands on hips. "You open this portal right now." He saw her eyes narrow and mouth open slightly. Kellan recognized the expression.

Uh oh, he thought.

"What do you think you are doing?" she demanded, her face a thunderhead. "I'm getting attacked by demons and you are soaking in *our* tub! What do you have to say for yourself?"

"I'm by myself?" offered Kellan weakly.

"Jesus, Mary, and Joseph, Kellan, you are lucky I am not there to box your ears. A cadre of angels and demons have made off with the spear."

Kellan leaned over the tub, alarmed and tried to further clarify the portal without making it fully open. Each time he made it stronger, he could feel the drain on his power increase. Few things drained him as quickly as opening a temporal-spacial portal. The dark portals required much less, but these gray ones were also taxing. With the connection clearer, Kellan could see Shannon carried several small wounds and her leathers were also torn in several places.

"What happened to you, Shannon," Kellan asked as panic began to rise in him. "Why aren't you wearing the kevlar stuff Meghan got you?"

"Kellan," she began and he immediately recognized her *you are being an idiot*, voice, "What do you think happens to women in the 13th century who are found wearing clothes made in the 21st century?" She didn't wait for an answer, "They get, burned, Kellan. As witches. Now open the portal, I need the Seal of Solomon." She looked scared for a moment. "You did get the Seal, didn't you?"

"Yeah, I got it, but has your soul tether regenerated?"

"I don't know, but it won't matter much if I can't stop that demon from getting the Spear of Longinus to the Cabal, now will it?" She tried to leap through the portal again, then circled around to glare back at Kellan.

"What is this new portal toy you've developed, Kellan?"

"It's a dark portal. It let's me use less energy so I can keep them open longer. No way I could have kept a white portal open this long."

"You wouldn't have had to," she said flatly, "because I would have already come through."

"Yeah, but I'm not letting you through until we know its safe. You nearly died, Shannon." He paused. "You did die and I can't risk that, again."

"We are talking about the world dying. You have responsibilities. Let me though."

"No! Not 'til I know you can come safely." He watched as Shannon stomp a booted foot into the ground while making fists with both hands. He'd never seen her so angry which, he reminded himself absently, was saying something. Kellan softened his voice and tried to mollify her. "Look, Shannon, I know you hate it when you feel someone is controlling you, but—"

"Shut up, Kellan Thorne. Just shut up and get me the Seal."

"I'll come there and help," he offered.

She held up a hand, "You will do no such thing. You are supposed to find the Cabal and that is exactly what you are going to do. It is one demon Kellan. One. I killed the other three. Well, two were angels, but as soon as they touched the spear," Shannon paused and Kellan saw her shiver, "As soon as they touched the Spear, they screamed, their wings went black and they became like the others. Fell I suppose. Anyway, they were easy to kill, but the last bastard got a way." She stomped her foot again. "I'm so mad I could spit. The scaly shit has one of my mother's daggers in him." She stared at him. "What are you still doing in that Tub? Get me the Seal!"

Kellan leaped out of the tub nearly slipping on the wet tile and scrambled to his office where the Seal of Solomon rested in the leather valet next to his phone, keys, and wallet. He grabbed it and scampered back to the bathroom to find her smiling at him.

"Hey, that's better," Kellan said. "You're not mad anymore? Wait," his voice grew suspicious, "You never get over being mad that quickly." The young Sentinel watched her eyes trace him from head to toe as she took a deep breath.

"Oh I'm still furious, but when I'm faced with," she waved her hands up and down in his direction, "that, I am capable of having multiple emotions at once." Kellan looked down, having completely forgotten his state of undress and blushed furiously. Shannon gave him a wolfish grin. Give me the Seal and promise to make all this up to me, and I'll cease being cross with you."

Kellan concentrated and watched as the center part of the portal cleared completely. Shannon walked up and extended her hand through the opening. Kellan did likewise, placing the Seal of Solomon in her hand as the two locked eyes. He felt her fingernails dig into his outstretched wrist and power rushed out of him as her eyes took on a brilliant glow. He started to pull back his hand, but she held firm, draining him further.

"Shannon," Kellan began, "It's too much. You are going to hurt yourself." He could see her beginning to tremble as sweat beaded on her forehead, but still she would not release him. "Shannon!"

"I'll be fine," she answered through gritted teeth, "Just a little more." Finally she released him and Kellan stumbled, barely able to maintain the portal as it dimmed to gray.

"Sorry, sweetie," she said, "But it is a major demon after all."

Kellan shook his head, clearing it, "Wait, What? A *major* demon?"

"Of course, silly, you don't think I would have let a minor one get away, do you?"

"Shannon, a major demon has enough power to widen any existing fissure in creation and escape!"

"A fact of which I am well aware and will use to my advantage," she responded evenly.

"Shannon, that is, in no way, an advantage, he'll—" Kellan paused, his stomach twisting, "Shannon McLeod, don't you follow him through any fissures. Promise me."

She grinned at him, "Don't be stupid. That's why it's an advantage I know exactly where that demon is headed. Have to go now, Sweetie. Thank you for the sparkles." She turned and whistled. Moment's latter a midnight black stallion trotted up beside her shaking his head and whinnying. Shannon tossed her hair back and deftly leaped into the saddle while Kellan stared on helplessly.

"Where are you going?" he called as he saw her dig her heals into the stallions side.

The horse leaped forward but she called back over her shoulder, "To the Creag at Inverness."

Chapter 16

DEMON HUNTER

Shannon bent low over the galloping horse as bits of mane caught the wind and softly whipped her face. She breathed deeply, enjoying the musky sent of the animal as it seemed to effortlessly propel her across the highlands. Shannon looked leftward out to sea and saw the first hints of dawn in the eastern sky. The soulborn whispered encouragement to her steed and smiled as his ears pivoted backwards to more easily catch the words she knew he couldn't understand but that she said more for herself. Still, it was the tone that mattered.

"Frazier, my beautiful boy, I need you to run hard for me. We go to Dornoch first to get you a drink and a bit of rest, then cross the Firth to Tain." She rubbed his neck affectionately as he whinnied. "I know, and then almost forty miles to the stones at Inverness, but it's important." She leaned further forward her red hair mixing with the black of his main as she whispered, "So run my clever boy and remember that the world and my love depend depend on us both."

The sun had climbed halfway up the sky when Shannon reined Frazier up near the Cathedral within Dornoch proper. She slid out of the saddle and called to several priests that were just entering the large stone structure. The three stared at her a moment as she walked Frazier toward them, then the two younger priests glanced at their elder and took a step backward.

"Good morning, Father," said Shannon with a smile. "I'm on a rather urgent errand and would be much obliged if I might water my horse and maybe provide him an apple or two, even a carrot though he doesn't like them overmuch." For his part the older man dismissed the two acolytes. One went willingly while the second's eyes seemed to linger on Shannon. She smiled at him causing the boy to blush furiously, then turn to follow his fellow. *That one is going to have a very tough time as a priest*, thought Shannon as the elder priest rested his hand appreciatively on Frazier soft muzzle.

"I am Bishop Alan de St. Edmund, said the priest as he took in Shannon's somewhat disheveled appearance and wounds. It would appear you need a bit more than apples and water, child. What has you in such a state?"

Why, chasing a major demon who stole the very spear that pieced the heart of Jesus, Bishop, thought Shannon and worked her jaw while inwardly cursing Kellan for rubbing off on her. Then she blessed him a moment later for the lie she formed was born of that self-same closeness.

"It was a vision, Bishop. I've been riding since dawn from the northern Highlands and must get to Inverness before midday, so says the vision. I woke up with it, Father."

"A vision you say. And what was this vision?"

Shannon affected her most earnest express and said, "It was Bishop de Moravia. He came to me in the dream."

The older man's eyes widened in surprise. "Gilbert? You speak of Bishop Gilbert de Moravia?"

"The very same. He appeared to me standing over a dragon. It was dead by his hand, I am sure of it. He looked right at me and said 'Shannon McLeod,' I need you to ride now for Inverness. Arrive there by midday. Once there I am to find a man named Friar Duncan and have him pray for our blessed, departed, Gilbert to intercede lest a dragon descend on Inverness and put it to flame."

"Child, child," began Bishop de St. Edmund, "Sometimes, a dream is just a dream. You are young and impressionable. No doubt tales of our sainted Gilbert have reached your village in the north and have likewise invaded even your dreams. The road is long to Inverness and not without peril. I cannot in good conscious aid you in what I believe to be well intentioned folly." He smiled and turned to go, but Shannon reached out and grabbed his arm.

"It was no simple dream, Bishop. Gilbert warned that many would die and that horrors would be visited upon both me and those who prevented me from my task."

The old Bishop, smiled patiently but simply shook his head and said, "My answer remains, no, child. Now come inside and have something to eat."

"No, no, no," cried Shannon covering her face with both hands and sobbing loudly.

"Shannon," said the priest, his voice becoming cross, "This is not becoming at—" He broke off staring up as the sun suddenly became obscured by roiling black clouds that seemed for form from nothing. The air became charged and the Bishop took a step back, then crossed himself. The door burst opened and the two Acolytes joined him, both looking up fearfully as their hair began to rise.

"It's happening," screamed Shannon as he continued to keep her eyes well covered while feeling the telltale warmth of Kellan's borrowed power within them. In her mind's eye she saw the river of his power as it flowed within her. It lapped and splashed against banks higher than ever she'd seen before, but Shannon knew that, unlike with Kellan, when this power was expended, it would not return without him being near enough to touch. Still, forming the charged clouds didn't use much. She just hoped a further demonstration wouldn't be necessary.

"Apples and carrots you fool boys," yelled the Bishop. "Bring them at once to the stable and make sure there is fresh water. Quickly! For the love of God, Saint Gilbert has sent this child on a holy mission and we will not impede her further." The boys scampered off and Shannon released her grip on the power with a relieved sigh. She lowered her hands and Bishop de St. Edmund reached forward to take them in his own, while casting a furtive glance at the clearing sky. He stared into her pale brown eyes and shook his head. "Forgive me. Forgive me. I fear I may have lived too long without experiencing true miracles to recognize when I am in the presence of one." He kissed her hands. "Come, Shannon McLeod, we will provision you well for the rest of your journey."

Shanon could feel the Seal of Solomon becoming colder the closer she came to Inverness. It had been well over an hour since she stopped in Dingwall to give Frazier food, water, and a few minutes respite. She glanced up, squinting at the near noon-day sun and reined up to survey the landscape. She'd only been to the druidic stones at Inverness once and that was shortly after her mother's death. Her whole family had come at Micah's request and Shannon had always thought it odd that a Christian Priest would want to bring them to a pagan stone circle to pray. She smiled sadly at the memory. Of course Micah had been a lot more than a simple priest and, she reminded herself, a lot less as well. Over the intervening years Shannon had learned much, not the least of which was that such stones were often placed at locations of either great power or where the veil between worlds was weakest. The Creag at Inverness was of this latter type and Shannon knew the demon would seek to use the stone's power to force open a portal to, she assumed, the Cabal.

One doesn't grow up in the Highlands without developing a fine sense of direction. Shannon chuckled to herself, thinking of how much trouble Kellan would be in were he here. *That man couldn't find his arse with both hands*, she thought affectionately. She smiled as her thoughts turned to him then shook her head. *Can't get distracted with that now.* She recognized a small outcropping that seemed vaguely shaped like an axe head and urged Frazier on in that direction. Once she reached the summit and stared westward, the remaining landmarks resolved themselves from memory. She was close. Shannon gave the stallion a soft heel to the ribs and he cantered down the hillside then, at her urging, broke into a gallop. She turned him leftward and had the horse run along the center of a small stream, his hooves kicking up cold water that chilled her legs even as the Seal continued to do the same nestled between her breasts.

Moment's later, she reined up and set her jaw. There, rising from the stream and to the right, she could just make out the tips of a stone circle. Frazier pushed with his powerful hind legs and propelled them out of the stream and up the shallow hill. An they cleared the trees, an open moor expanded before them, dominated by a large stone circle. The stallion trotted up to the nearest of the massive stones and whinnied.

Shannon patted his neck gratefully as she dismounted and gave his soft muzzle a kiss. She looked into his dark eyes and said, "You got us here, boy. Thank you." With a shiver, she reached around her neck and pulled on the leather thong. The Seal of Solomon left what felt like a line of ice as she pulled it free of her tunic. Shannon glanced at it a moment the looked back to Frazier. "You need to go now."

The stallion sputtered and shook his head. Not for the first time, Shannon wondered just how much this horse understood. He had always been strange. Whether it was Frazier, her, or the spark of Sentinel energy she carried, the soulborn didn't know. She did know that the horse always seemed to sense what she needed of him. Shannon pulled out the last apple and showed it to him. "I'm going to give you this, then I want you to go home." Another shake of the head accompanied by a stomping of hoof. "No, Frazier, I'm not going to argue with you. I already have one insufferable male in my life. You've done your bit. I'll not have you distracting me. Go back to Glenn Ferry and make Donal give you whatever you want. You know he can't resist you."

Frazier whinnied in what Shannon took as reluctant agreement and she smiled, handing him the apple, then examined the circle. The outer stones consisted of nine rough hewn pillars that were mostly square at the base, but tapered to the top of their twenty foot height. At the center of the circle, stood an even more imposing stone. Shannon placed her hand on it and gazed up at its nearly thirty foot height. Like the outer stones, it began with a square base but, unlike the others, did not taper at its top. As her fingers traced one of the numerous enochian runes that etched its surface, Shannon thought she could feel power coursing through it.

Frazier suddenly shrieked and reared back on his haunches, front hooves rising up and then slamming down amidst clods of earth. Shannon crouched, instantly filling her hands with twin daggers as she noticed a thin film of frost had formed across the whole of Solomon's Seal. "Frazier!" she yelled, "Get out of here. Glenn Ferry. Now!" The stallion's eyes widened in fear exposing the whites and Shannon caught the slightest distortion to his left. A moment later, Frazier leaned forward and bucked his massive legs. They connected with something and Shannon saw the air distort further as something flew several yards away.

She reached inward and drew fully from the emerald stream, feeling her eyes warm with effort. Around her, reality warped as a pale green shield snapped into place. Shannon narrowed her eyes as Kellan's power made visible what had been cloaked before. A massively armored demon crashed to earth several feet outside the circle. It slowly regained its feet and turned black eyes first toward her and then the stallion. Shannon created a tendril of wind and whipped at Frazier's flank. The horse needed no further encouragement and launched itself at a gallop, disappearing into the trees.

The demon turned back to Shannon and bent down to retrieve a long spear from where it had fallen. It glared at her. "Soulborn." The words came out like a curse and the creature spun the spear twice as it advanced into the circle. Small dark clouds formed above and Shannon lashed out with two daggers glinting as she hurled them at the demon. It blocked both with the spear then raised it with one heavily muscled arm to catch the lightning bolt Shannon called forth from the accumulated clouds.

The demon bellowed and spun in a tight circle whipping the spear point toward her and redirected the energy provided by her summoned lightning strike. Shannon bent time and leaped out of the way just as the bolt scorched the earth where she had stood moments before.

Even with time bent as it was, the demon tracked her. The black eyes rested within deep bony sockets making it seem as if they were merely glowing red embers. Massive black ram's horns grew from either side of its head. And its skin was comprised of thick overlapping plates of chitinous armor that covered it from head to foot. Shannon had encountered many demons before today, but none such as this.

A circle of frost expanded outward from her as she channeled, gathering the ambient heat, then converted it to plasmatic fire as Kellan had shown her. A pillar of white flame erupted around the demon melting the ground and engulfing it in a conflagration so hot that Shannon would have been consumed were it not for her shield. She felt her stomach lurch as the demon stepped forward, armor plates glowing brightly but unharmed. It looked at her and laughed mirthlessly,

"I was born in fire, little mortal. Your stolen magics are beneath my notice." It paused cocking its head as it stared at the crouching Highlander. "Nothing to say? I was told to expect more."

She sneered at the demon, "That's Kellan. He's the talker. I'm the doer." With those words, Shannon slammed the heels of her hands together causing a spiral burst of wind to catch the demon and hurl it backward. She leaped after it twin daggers flashing and struck hard at its neck and chest. Both blows deflected harmlessly off the creatures armor and Shannon barely rolled out of the way of its spear thrust. The demon lashed out with its leg, catching Shannon in the side and ripping through her leathers with a bony protrusion. She gasped and reached down, pressing her hand to the wound. It came away wet with bright red blood. Shannon stumbled to her feet and backed into the circle trying to keep the stones between her and the demon.

She sought the emerald power within her and found it all but depleted, then channeled a tendril of fire which buried itself into the wound. Shannon grimaced in pain as the fire cauterize her side, but refused to cry out. The demon shimmered and vanished causing the Highlander to cast about furtively, then curse herself a fool for releasing the power. She took it up again barely in time make visible her assailant and dodge another spear thrust. Shannon panted as she sprinted around the stones then braced her back against the center obelisk.

The demon walked into view. It spun the spear with casual confidence as its black eyes appraised her. "Soulborn," it said again, then spat on the ground. "You are not even worthy of my contempt let alone my anger." It smiled and Shannon felt chilled to the center of her being. Never before had she seen a more malevolent expression, even when facing Asmodeus. "Without anger, I will kill you. With no animus will I take those tiny daggers you prize so much and sever you limb from limb, while there is yet breath in you. I will leave your parts beneath each of these stones, then I will pass through them to my brothers and sisters." The demon held the spear lengthwise and thrust it forward, "This spear will power our dark portals and I will travel to the second garden. I will shatter time itself and we will start again. No war in heaven. Our Father will again embrace his Morning Star." The demon paused as if considering something. "If it is any consolation, I won't really be killing you, because once I finish my task in the second garden, you will never have existed at all."

There was very little Shannon liked less than demonic monologuing, yet it seemed they could rarely help themselves. She had fixated on one word the demon had used. Daggers. The soulborn remembered Kellan telling her of his time with Micah and how the sword, or dagger, would always be the most powerful weapon against all unnatural creatures for it was an extension of will, mind, and spirit. Shannon drew her last dagger and screamed, infusing her throw with as much Ordered power as she could channel. The air cracked like thunder when her weapon warped the air as it streaked toward the demon, but the creature was still too fast. At the last moment, it interposed the spear shaft between himself and the blade. Shannon groaned as she saw the dagger drive into wood instead of flesh. For a moment, she thought it might pass all the way through, but instead the spear glowed brightly as the wood seemed to heal around the dagger. In moments, the spear was as it had been, unmarred, but with blade and grip protruding from either side of its wooden shaft.

Shannon staggered, falling to one knee, her back against the center stone as blood dripped from half a dozen wounds. She reached inward to find only a trickle of green energy remained. None of her attacks had worked. It was as if this demon had been specifically created to withstand anything she might attempt. Worse, now it looked like she was going to die here. Shannon felt angry tears begin to fill her eyes. The highlander had long figured she would eventually die to some demon or other inhuman, but not like this. Not so far from the one man she had ever loved. Not when so much depended on her succeeding. She looked up as the demon raced toward her spinning the Spear of Longinus and readying its killing thrust. Shannon ground her teeth as her mind raced, eyes fixed on the dagger embedded in the spear shaft. *That goddamned demonic bastard,* she thought reaching her hand outward and draining the last of her borrowed power. She bellowed at the demon as it leaped high into the air, arcing toward her. "That dagger is my mother's," Her voice lowered into a growl, "and I want it BACK!"

Power lanced from Shannon's outstretched hand, propelled by her iron will, and fused to the dagger. She pulled her arm backward and saw the spear rip from the demon's grasp. It streaked toward her and she snatched it from the air. Shannon set the shaft against the center stone, braced it with both hands, and angled it toward the falling demon. The creature had no wings with which to alter or slow its trajectory and Shannon grunted with effort as the weapon-less demon's full weight slammed against the Spear. Time seemed to slow as the shaft bent under the strain. She could hear the wood start to splinter and then, like when her dagger had struck its shaft, the spear resisted. Glowing brightly and becoming warm in her hands, Shannon felt the shaft straighten. Like all those who sought to possess it but were found unworthy, the spear would not change. It had tasted divine blood and would remain as it was the day Longinus wielded it. The demon shrieked in fear and anger as its armor plates parted beneath the Holy Spear. Shannon blinked as hot black blood sprayed her face and she was pressed hard against the center stone. She couldn't breathe. The demon's bulk slid lifelessly down the shaft crushing her. Blackness started to close about her and Shannon felt herself fall backward *through* the stone.

Chapter 17

SEARCH FOR THE CABAL

The black Impala's tires squealed in protest as Kellan wheeled into a visitor's spot at Meghan's condo. He quickly slid out and closed the door which gave a loud creak as it slammed shut. Kellan was already two steps away, but turned and frowned at his car. He walked back, and slowly opened the driver's side door. *Creak* The Sentinel's eyebrows raised in alarm. He crouched down and slowly closed the door. *Creeaakkk.*

"Oh, hells, no," said Kellan out loud as he fully opened the door and examined the hinge assembly. "Baby, we do *not* abide creaks and rattles. Has someone hurt you?" The car remained silent except for the soft ticking of its cooling engine. Kellan reached in and ran his fingers along the hinge trying to find anything out of place.

"Kellan?"

The Sentinel started at the sound of his name, lifting up and slamming his head into the edge of the doorframe. He turned rubbing his head as a torrent of profanity died on his tongue.

"Mrs. Taballareo? Is that you? What are you doing here?" Kellan looked at his watch. "Shouldn't you be in school?"

The elderly Italian woman's face broke into a grin and all the weathered lines that marked a life well lived spread outward. She reached up and tweaked

Kellan's cheek. "You are sweet, Kellan," then noticing his vacant expression, added, "just still not very observant."

He smiled. "Mrs. Taballareo, I have become much more—"

She interrupted him with a soft touch on his arm, "It's been over 25 years since I was your teacher, Kellan. Honestly, you can call me Mia if you like."

Kellan's eyes widened. "Why would I do that. You are Mrs Taballareo?"

"Kellan, I retired five years ago."

"You did?"

"I did."

"Oh, well, that sucks."

She sighed and gave Kellan a look and he said, "Oh, well, that stinks?"

"Not for me it doesn't. I'm enjoying retirement. Mrs. Spicer took over my first grade class and she's doing wonderfully."

Kellan looked dubious. "I don't know her."

Mia laughed. "Why would you know her?"

"Hey," said Kellan feeling defensive, "I still come to Canterbury Woods and donate books. I also read to the kids."

Mia waved her hand dismissively, "You are still too sensitive, Kelly"

He ran his fingers through his hair and sighed, "Yeah, well, that's me. Mr. Sensitive," then flashed his old teacher a grin, "You know, there are only three living people allowed to call me *Kelly*."

She returned his smile, "I'm glad to know that I've been grandfathered into such a select group, but I must be off now."

"Wait, what are you doing in Cabbagetown? Did you know Meghan Daugherty lives here?"

"I live here, Kellan."

"You do?" he said surprised.

"I'm hip, Kellan. Now I'm going to meet the girls for lunch so, stop slowing me down."

"Hey, you called out to me," Kellan said laughing.

"Well, I'm aware of how much you love that car and you know Sam is a wizard with old cars."

"Baby, is not an old car," said Kellan then added, "Who's Sam?"

"You know Sam. Sam Waterhouse."

"The art teacher?"

She smiled wistfully.

"You and Sam Waterhouse?"

She nodded.

"Well, what do you know about that," said Kellan putting his hands on hips. "How long has this been going on and what do you guys do together."

"About three years now and as for what we do together, lots of things. I imagine much the same things you do with that redheaded Scot of yours."

"Shannon?"

Mia snickered, "Yes, Shannon, unless you keep a stock of them hidden away. Although, from what I hear, doing so would not be very good for your health."

Kellan looked confused, "How do you know about Shannon?"

Mia just nodded back toward the condo.

"Meghan?"

"Miss Daugherty is the source of a fair bit of gossip. We do hot yoga together."

"You do?"

"We do. In fact, I just saw Meghan in the gym. She's there with this giant of a man. He's a pretty one too. Saruman or something"

Kellan snorted. "Seramai. Although given Meghan's track record with men, Saruman is a good guess. Well, that's good info. Saves me time running up to her place. I'll meet up with her in the gym then."

"Be careful, last I saw, they seemed to be doing their very best to beat each other up."

Kellan sighed, "Yeah, Meghan finally found someone with the same bizarre mating ritual she has."

Mia smirked, "Well, you would know, Kellan, wouldn't you?"

His mouth fell open. "Oh my god, Mrs. Taballareo!"

"Pish posh, Kellan, girls talk and I'm not dead yet." She looked at her watch. "But I am late." Mia grabbed him by both wrists, raised up on toes, and gave Kellan a kiss on the cheek. "Please do come by again soon, you know you were always my favorite." She smiled then waved and headed down the street.

Kellan watched in bemused silence then called after her, "Hey, have Sam give me a call. I'm worried about Baby's door."

The older woman didn't turn around but raised one hand and waggled it in acknowledgment.

Sam and Mia, thought Kellan as he turned toward the condo's locked gate and unconsciously channeled Ordered energy. He jumped halfway up the chain linked gate, deftly placing his left foot in one of the open links, then pushed left to where his right foot met the adjacent brick. Power coursed into his legs as Kellan pushed off the wall, arced well above the barbed wire top of the gate, then curled and landed in a crouch on the other side.

"Dude," came a shout from behind him causing Kellan to whip around as he released the power. "That was some badass parkour right there. You must have jumped ten feet right up that wall!" *I am a complete idiot*, thought Kellan, *I have got to be more discrete for god's sake. Yeah, 'cause discretion has always been one of your strong suits.*

Kellan dismissed his internal dialogue and gave a half hearted wave to a black millennial with a perfectly coordinated hipster outfit. "Thanks, man, but it really is a lot easier than it looks. See ya." With that he turned and made his way around the corner as nonchalantly as possible.

Meghan dodged left, sweat spraying from her face, and reached up with both hands to grab Seramai's wrist as his fist missed her jaw by scant inches. She twisted and brought her right knee up, slamming it into his solar plexus. Kellan winced in sympathetic pain as the larger man grunted and bent forward. Meghan positioned her right hand against Seramai's shoulder and smoothly bent to grip his thigh with her left. She heaved and Kellan's breath caught as she hoisted him above her shoulders. For a moment, as the early afternoon sun shone through the gym windows, Kellan was distracted by what seemed like a strange winged shadow against the far wall, but only had a second to consider it before Seramai cried out.

"Meghan, Red Planet" called Seramai and Kellan's attention snapped back as his eyes met those of Meghan's which seemed to luminesce with the same soft amber glow he'd seen beneath the Vatican. Her lips were curled in a victorious snarl as she spun. "Meghannnh! Red. Planet!" shouted Seramai again and Kellan could see what was coming next. The young Sentinel squinted and partially averted his gaze as the sound of Seramai being unceremoniously slammed into the ground came to his ears.

He glanced back to see Meghan, eyes their normal brown, bouncing on the balls of her feet and rubbing hands together in a dismissive fashion. Seramai, lay on his back staring up at her and groaned softly, "Red Planet?"

The former Marine looked down at his supine form as if just noticing him. "Oh, shit," she said. "Seramai, did you use the safe word?"

"Only twice," he said sitting up. "You didn't hear it through the fog. You must concentrate, my love. You have power, but no control. You *must* have both."

She knelt beside him and gave the warrior a soft kiss on the lips, "I"m sorry. You're right, I honestly didn't hear you say it."

"Jesus, Meghan, he only screamed it twice."

"Well, I wouldn't say that I screamed," offered Seramai.

"Dude, you cried out like a little girl," said Kellan with a laugh then added, "Not that I blame you. She's fucking nuts. And what's this *my love*, stuff."

Meghan stood and Seramai accepted her offered hand. She pulled him up then reached for a nearby towel, dragging it across her face and chest. "Hi Kel," she said, "Seramai here is smitten. Aren't ya?"

"Quite smitten," he said with a smile.

Kellan looked from one to the other. "What have you two been up to," then becoming suspicious, "And how did you even know to come now, Seramai?"

"Come?" asked Meghan, "He hasn't left. We flew in from Rome yesterday."

"You did?" asked Kellan, processing.

They both nodded and Meghan added, "Since you asked, yes, we did have a wonderful time and," she paused, "Seramai showed me some very interesting things."

Kellan frowned slightly and glared at the large man, "Harrumph, I bet he did, and why did you pause like that?"

"Like what," she said innocently and Kellan caught Seramai giving her a sidelong glance.

"You know, like what," said Kellan. "You totally paused when saying his name, like you were going to say something else."

Meghan laughed and slapped Kellan's shoulder causing him to rock sideways, "You are so paranoid, Kellan. Come on upstairs. I want a shower and you can fill us in on what's been happening in your freakish little world."

With that both she and Seramai turned and headed out, Seramai shouldering the gym door open for her and holding it. "Why thank you, milord, she said with a slight curtsey as she passed."

"Holy crap," said Kellan sprinting to catch up, "What was that I just saw. Meghan Daugherty deferring to a man, curtseying no less."

Meghan ignored him as she crossed the hall and tapped the *up* button on the elevator bank, but Seramai leaned in. "She was mocking me as you very well know, Sentinel of Order, and I'll thank you not to make a point of it lest I be forced to mock back."

Kellan looked up at the taller man and nodded, "Yeah, fair point, that wouldn't end well." Seramai returned the nod and Kellan smirked as he walked past, "...for you."

The young Sentinel thought he might have actually heard the general's teeth crack at how hard his jaw clenched, when Meghan called out, "C'mon boys, I'm hot and I'm sweaty and I want my shower."

The three clambered into the small elevator and Meghan mashed the button for the top floor. As the numbers began to flash by, Kellan snapped his fingers. "Hey, I almost forgot, have you guys seen any weird shadows around lately?"

"Shadows?" asked Seramai, "What kind of shadows."

Kellan thought about how best to describe it. "Well, I saw one in the gym when—"

The door gave a final chime and opened, "Everybody out," interrupted Meghan and then gave Kellan an unceremonious shove when he didn't move fast enough for her. He stumbled into the hallway and glared at her, "What the hell, Meghan? I was talking."

"About stupid shadows that weren't even there."

"I saw it, Meghan. It was right behind you while you were sparring, so unless you suddenly sprouted wings, *something* was there."

The former Marine walked up to Kellan and poked him hard in the chest with one finger and he thought he caught the barest hint of a glow in her eyes, "I am Hot!" she said and with each word her finger poked his chest with more force. Seramai intervened, sliding an arm between them and said, "You most certainly are, my love. You go ahead and start that shower, we'll follow along in a moment." Meghan looked up sharply then her features softened and she smiled as he leaned in to kiss her cheek and whisper something too softly for Kellan to hear. He saw Meghan take a deep breath and nod to Seramai, then said, "Sorry, Kel," under her breath as she turned into her apartment.

As the door clicked shut, Kellan rounded on Seramai, "Dude! Seriously, what the hell? What is going on with her?"

Seramai smiled innocently, "I really have no idea—"

Kellan snapped and reached inward feeling a wave of power fill him. He channeled it throughout his entire body strengthening every bone and muscle. The young Sentinel's eyes burst to life as he put both hands on either side of Seramai's chest lifting him effortlessly and then slamming him against the wall next to Meghan's apartment door. The general's eyes widened in surprise and then anger even as the wind was knocked out of him by Kellan's push.

Kellan released him and took a step back pointing, "There!"

Seramai's face had taken on a dangerous aspect, "There, what?" he growled.

"There, your eyes. They glow like that when you are angry and I've seen her's do it several times now. What have you done to her?"

The general sighed and Kellan watched as he took control of his emotions, eyes reverting to their normal dark chocolate brown. "I have done nothing to her, Kellan Thorne. You must trust me on this."

Kellan snorted, "Have you met me? I don't have to trust, shit. What's going on?"

"Don't be a child, Kellan. I am well aware of how you rail against all forms of compulsion. We *are* allies. If you cannot abide the word *must* than surely you accept that Allies *should* trust one another."

Kellan felt the heat of his anger subside and the warmth in his eyes faded. "Yeah," he grumbled, "I suppose," then looked up sharply, "but Meghan—"

Seramai rested his hands softly on Kellan's shoulders and looked down at him with a gentle smile, "Meghan is fine. She is better than fine, but more than that I cannot say."

"Cannot, or will not," Seramai.

"Both. Cannot because to say more would breach longstanding tradition. Will not because doing so could cause her harm." The general let his hands fall but continued to stare at Kellan. "She is not laboring under any glamor I have laid about her, young Sentinel. I will never cause her harm, Kellan, ever."

The two men continued to lock eyes, each taking the measure of the other. Finally Kellan broke the silence and smiled, "Fair enough, but if you ever do—" Kellan just left the sentence hang in the air unfinished and Seramai simply nodded in understanding.

"Beer?" Seramai asked brightly.

"What time is is? It can't be much past 2:00."

Seramai looked at Kellan quizzically, "And your point is?"

Kellan paused, then shrugged, "No point actually. Does she have any Innis & Gunn?"

The general clapped Kellan on the back as they entered the apartment, "I'm sure she does. You know she keeps that around just for you?"

"She does? She always gives me shit for coming by unannounced and drinking her beer."

"It is her way, Kellan. You, more than most, should understand that," said Saramai as he removed two cold bottles from the refrigerator. The large man moved to open them, but Kellan stopped him.

"No, let me. I love that opener. It has magnets that—"

Seramai laughed, but handed Kellan the two bottles, "I've seen it Kellan. I'm less fascinated by magnets than you are."

The Sentinel smiled at the pair of *pop, hiss, clicks,* that sounded as he opened both bottles and watched the hidden magnets capture the falling bottle caps. Kellan handed one of them to Seramai and they clinked bottles. "It's the simple things, Seramai. If I can find joy in opening bottles of beer, just imagine what else makes me happy."

The general chuckled and was about to respond when they heard Meghan call from the bedroom. The two men turned toward the sound and Kellan smiled. "Thy mistress beckons, valorous sir, and the lady sayeth she shall not abideth thy stinky presence. Wend forth and taketh thy shower."

Seramai nodded gravely and extended his hand, "Into the breech I go, my friend. If I am not back in half an hour, please come save me."

Kellan took a swig of his beer as Seramai headed for the bedroom, "No way, dude, you are on your own."

⌒⁊⎞⫟⟍⌒

"Wow, that's a pretty serious face you're wearing there," said Meghan as she entered the room. Kellan lay sprawled on the couch tapping at his iPhone. He looked up.

"Hmmm?"

Meghan walked over and folded herself next to him, glanced down at his phone, and gave him a soft punch on the arm. "Sorry for being such a bitch earlier."

"Sokay," said Kellan with a shrug.

"No, no it's not, Kel. I'm just going through some stuff," she broke off, then continued, "but that doesn't excuse it, just kind of explains it."

Kellan looked up at her, "Stuff? Stuff explains it?"

"Kellan," she said with a sigh.

"No, I'm not prying, Meghan. Seramai already told me you needed space to figure *stuff* out, so I'm just leaving it be."

Meghan nodded silently and motioned to his phone which still displayed a picture of Kellan affecting a pained expression while Shannon clung to his back, her teeth nipping at his left ear. "You worried about Merida, there. I'm sure she's fine."

Kellan snorted, "Don't let her hear you call her that. She hates that movie."

Meghan pushed back into the other corner of the couch and grinned, "I know, which is why I try to call her that on a regular basis."

"You two are incorrigible."

A long silence spread between them so thick one could almost touch it and Meghan reached over, tapping Kellan's leg. "What is it?"

He looked up, "Eyes filling slightly. Something's wrong, Meg. I can't feel her. You know how we both have a vague sense of the other, kind of like how twins sometimes describe it."

Meghan grinned, "Given some of your extracurricular activities together, I'm not sure *twins* is the best way to describe your connection."

Kellan stared at Meghan and her smile fell away, "Sorry, was trying to cheer you up. I'm going to be quiet now. You talk."

"Well, I knew something was going on as we left the gym, but" Kellan waved a hand in frustration, "something is always going on with her. It used to keep me in a continual state of freaked-outted-ness, but I've learned to just deal with in over the past year. Anyway, I mostly ignored it, but then I got a real sense of fear and distress." Kellan paused staring at Meghan.

She shrugged, "Ok, so what, fear and distress. I mean, Kellan, your lives are not exactly stress free."

"Meghan, what does it take for *you* to feel fear and distress, let alone project it."

The former Marine grimaced, "Ok, I see what you mean. So what did you do."

"I tried to portal to her."

"And…"

"I wouldn't form."

"That's weird isn't it."

"Yes and no. I knew she was going to these Druidic stones near Inverness and those kinds of places can often screw with my ability to create portals. Ironically, they also seem to allow me to more fully sense what's going on with her. It's like the stones have created fissures in creation. That's why she was there in the first place. She was chasing a major demon who and stolen the Spear of Longinus from her."

"Oh shit, how the hell did one demon manage that. I mean, it's Shannon. One demon? Doesn't seem possible." Meghan glanced at Kellan, "Don't tell her I implied she was such a badass."

Kellan snorted, "You two. Separated at birth. Anyway, it got worse. She was hurt, then nothing. She just vanished from my mind."

Meghan saw tears fill Kellan's eyes and silently drip down his cheek. The former marine snuggled close and wrapped her arms around him. "What if she's dead, Meg? What if I can't feel her because she's dead? I don't think I could take that." He shook his head and shuddered. "That's not true. I *know* I couldn't take that."

Meghan wiped the errant tear with her thumb and spoke softly, "You could take that, Kellan. We all can take it. I have taken it. It nearly broke me and it took you to bring me back from it, but I took it." She stared at him as he shook his head in negation. "But, that's not gonna happen. She's alive, Kel."

"You don't know that," he replied dryly.

"I do," came Seramai's resonate voice and the two looked up. "Were she dead, you would know it Kellan. A bond such as yours is rare, but not unique in creation. I have had one myself. It can be blocked for a time and that is what you are experiencing. Only death can sever it and there is no mistaking what that feels like. Trust me, my friend, your soulborn lives and we will find her."

Kellan looked up at Meghan and smiled wanly, "He seems pretty certain."

She mussed the young Sentinel's hair and grinned, "If he's that certain, then you can take it to the bank, so cheer up. The game is afoot."

Kellan nodded feeling more confident. He took a deep breath, "Ok, yes, the game is afoot. Just one thing Meghan that still really troubles me,"

"Just one," she laughed, "What's that?"

"Why is your giant, self-proclaimed, god standing in the living room stark naked?"

"You noticed that too?" she said, grinning wolfishly at Seramai.

"Uh, yeah," began Kellan keeping his eyes on Meghan, "Some aspects are hard to miss, and truth be told, just a bit intimidating."

"Intimidating to some. Enticing to others," she said with a chuckle then added, "Sera, shimmer up some clothes."

"As you wish, my valkyrie," came his response and when Kellan risked another look, the general again wore his battle leathers as he sat in the chair facing them.

Meghan righted herself on the couch and offered a hand to pull Kellan to a seated position as well. "So, what's next guys?"

"Isn't that obvious?" asked Seramai causing Kellan and Meghan to exchange confused looks. The general shook his head and held up a hand then raised fingers as he spoke, "First, we go to the Cabal, second, we prevent them from using the Spear of Longinus, and third we kill them all." At this last, Kellan saw his eyes take on their otherworldly glow.

"Yes," purred Meghan, "That does sound fun." Kellan looked over and saw her eyes, too, had begun to shimmer slightly, but he pushed down the questions forming in his mind, instead turning to Seramai.

"Ok, genius, how exactly do we even get to step one. I have no idea where the Cabal might be located."

"Well," said the general, "The Gospel of Judas does provide a clue. Have you considered that?"

Kellan sighed, "Seramai, I never even heard of the Gospel of Judas before Ah'Anon brought it up last week."

Meghan said, "Wait, I'm lost. Who is Akanon?"

"Ah'Anon," corrected Seramai gently.

Kellan shook his head slightly. "Sorry, Meghan, sometimes I forget who all knows what. Ah'Anon is an ancient Egyptian vampire who came to the shop last week and brought this whole mess to my doorstep. I guess somehow we left that part out." The Sentinel gave her a sheepish expression.

She shrugged and replied sarcastically, "I suppose it would be easy to overlook being visited by an ancient Egyptian vampire. Happens all the time." Kellan was about to explain further but she waved him off, "Forget it Kel, I'm just glad the pieces fit inside my head now. So, what's with this Gospel of Judas. We are talking about Judas Iscariot right?"

Kellan smiled, "Very good, Meghan, I wouldn't have figured you for a biblical scholar."

She stared at him flatly, "We both went to the same Catholic school, Kellan. I know who Judas Iscariot is."

Seramai interjected, "Yes, it is that Judas. Kellan, you are not familiar with this Gospel?"

The Sentinel shook his head. "I've read a number of non canonical gospels, but never one attributed to Judas."

The general nodded in understanding, "Ah, that does make some sense then. Well, the Gospel of Judas is a prophetic work, somewhat like *Revelation*. You should read it."

Kellan stared at him, "I would, Seramai, but it was checked out at the Library."

Meghan gave a short burst of laughter and the warrior glared at her. "What?" she said, "It was a stupid suggestion. Why don't you give Kellan a copy and he'll read it."

"I do not have a copy," said Seramai still smarting from her laughter. "The book is illusive. I suspect there is something about it that violates Lucifer and God's grand bargain so it tends to be both difficult to find and even more difficult to retain."

"Makes the suggestion even more stupid," said Meghan under her breath.

"What?" asked Seramai

"Nothing, babe," replied Meghan sweetly then said, "You mentioned a clue about the Cabal. Do you recall the passage?"

Seramai nodded gravely. "I do and while my memory is not as keen as Kellan's, these verses I remember perfectly."

Both Meghan and Kellan had unconsciously leaned forward, but after several long moments, Kellan said, "Well?"

"Oh," said Seramai, "You want me to recite it, now?"

"Jesus, Seramai," said Kellan, "How hard did Megan slam you? Yes, please recite it now."

"Babe," said Meghan. "You look nervous. You never look nervous. What is it?"

Seramai cleared his throat, "The entire gospel, every word, is charged with power. Recitation can," he paused, "bring the unwanted attention of powerful creatures. I've learned this the hard way and do not recommend it."

The air suddenly became rippled with energy and a shimmering sphere snapped in place around the three friends. Meghan looked over to find Kellan's brow furrowed in concentration and his eyes ablaze with green light. "Kellan, what are you doing?"

"Making a shield."

"A shield will not prevent," began Seramai.

"This shield will. Micah showed me how to do it once. If it can cut an Archangel off from Heaven, it can make a temporary cone of silence for us. Now hush, this isn't easy." Meghan and Seramai watched silently as sweat began to form on Kellan's face. He gave a visible heave and formed his hands into fists. As he did so, the shield sparked and became nearly solid around them. "Now, Seramai, speak it now. We are sealed off from all of creation, but I cannot hold it long."

The general looked to Meghan, uncertain, but she nodded definitively. Seramai stood, took a deep breath an recited a passage from the Gospel of Judas:

Beneath the lion whose human visage stares sightless forever shall god's unchecked hand join with perdition's progeny to bewray the mantle of war. This trinity may earn safe passage to one whose victories art recount'd in spirals up to the sky. At which hour god and man embrace yond which is neither, the path to those who is't seek creation's end becometh manifest

As the last word faded, Kellan released the power with a gasp. The shield vanished with a resonant pop and he leaned back into the couch as the other two stared at him.

Kellan returned their gaze and said, "I know where we need to go."

Chapter 18

SPHINX

"I don't understand," said Meghan as the portal winked out behind them. "If we aren't invisible, why won't people see us?"

Kellan blinked several times, then rubbed his eyes cursing softly. He took a small bottle from his pocket, tilted his head back, and squeezed several drops in each eye.

"What are you doing?" asked Meghan.

"Contacts," said Kellan

"What? Since when do you wear contacts?"

Kellan took in his surroundings as did Seramai. Both seemed to be ignoring Meghan. She punched Kellan on the arm.

"Ow. Damnit Meghan," said the Sentinel noting the glow in her eyes as he rubbed his shoulder.

"I hate being ignored," she growled, then repeated, "Invisibility. Contacts."

"Ok. Ok. Contacts are new. Long story. Not invisible. It's more like we are visible but not perceived. People who see us, just don't know they see us."

Seramai nodded, "That is quite convenient. How long does this perception filter last?"

Kellan turned to him, "Good question. I'm not sure, but I think it might have more to do with locality than time. If we stand right here, it might last, well, forever. I remember portal'ing in to New York and just stood there waiting for my phone map to catch up to me. Must have been at least ten minutes. Nobody noticed. They didn't even bump into me, just weaved around like stream water around a rock. It was pretty cool actually."

Seramai grunted something vaguely affirming and motioned above them. "You should have seen him before the nose was broken off."

Meghan looked up at the massive Sphinx and then back to Seramai. "Didn't Napoleon shoot that off in the 18th century?" She put her hand on his chest. "You sure do look great for your age?"

He smiled down at her and was about to say something when Kellan commented, only partially aware of the exchange as he tapped on his iPhone. "Actually, Napoleon's troops did shoot at the Sphinx repeatedly, but the nose was gone all the way back in the 14th century. A Sufi Muslim named Muhammad Sa'im al-Dahr caught people making offerings to the Sphinx for harvests or something. He didn't like that at all, so chiseled the nose right off." Kellan looked up to find both of them staring at him. "What?" then added, "He was hanged for vandalism, if that helps."

Meghan shook her head at Kellan, but narrowed her eyes at Seramai, "Remind me to circle back to this, lover. I've mocked women who are into much older men, so really need to get a handle on this."

The general smiled noncommittally, and turned to Kellan. "The scripture said, 'Beneath the lion,' and that was written ages ago. I suspect it refers to an entrance that is well covered by now."

"Yeah, I'm on it," said Kellan as his eyes flared to life. "We're cloaked so stay close. It's only around 9:30 here, so folks may still be out and about."

"Wait, cloaked or not perceived," asked Meghan as Kellan started forward.

He stopped, frustrated, "Cloaked, Meghan. You know. Gryffindor!!"

The former Marine groaned, "Having flashbacks to our time in Afghanistan now, thanks. Sorry I asked."

Minutes later, the small party found itself within the fenced perimeter of the giant statue with Kellan slowly circling around and muttering to himself.

"Kellan?" Meghan finally asked

"What!" he shouted then crouched looking around before speaking softly, "What. Stop distracting me."

"No," she growled. "You are freaking both of us out, and that takes some doing. Are you seeing things and who the hell is Jarvis."

Kellan froze and looked a little panicked. "Where did you hear that name?"

"From you, idiot. You keep mumbling things and then say something to someone named Jarvis."

"No I don't," said Kellan defensively. He looked to Seramai for support but the warrior simply shrugged and mouthed the word *sorry.*

Meghan put her hands on hips and glared at the young Sentinel, "No you don't?" then affected Kellan's voice, "I don't care, Jarvis. Just retask the bloody satellites then."

Kellan cringed and she smiled at him. "Now does that sound like something I just made up?"

"Maybe?" he offered and was about to continue when he saw Seramai standing behind Meghan signally that he had better change tactics immediately. The Sentinel sighed. "It's complicated, Meg. I really don't want to go into all of it right now."

She shook her head. "You're brilliant or so you always tell me. Give it to me in one sentence."

Kellan though a moment. "Ok, but no questions. Deal?"

She narrowed her eyes. "Deal, but it better be a good sentence."

Kellan took a breath. "Jarvis is an artificially intelligent branch of the Watson super computer that James, who is actually a computer scientist and not an idiot, works on at IBM. That AI fabricated a set of contact lenses that serve as an interface between me and him.

Seramai said, "That was two sentences."

Meghan whirled and punched him hard in the chest as her eyes flared. The general stumbled back and reached up to rub where she'd impacted him then silently mouthed that Kellan was on his own.

She turned back to Kellan and he did his best to look resolute as her eyes bored into him. "I'm not going to ask any questions about how all this happened and James is going to pay, but I am going to ask tactical questions."

Kellan nodded.

"Ok," she continued, "Your robot friend can control government satellites?" Kellan looked noncommittal, but she continued, "Have it retask the Russian

Persona class Kosmos 2506 to this area and let me know how long that will take."

Kellan stared at her blankly for a long moment and she asked, "Well? Is it done or does it at least have an ETC."

"Um, I don't know if Jarvis can do what you are asking, Meghan. I didn't ask him yet, I'm still trying to process your question. I don't know anything about satellites."

She frowned at him. "I heard you tell it to retask them. I heard you say that."

"I just remembered that line from *Patriot Games* so I figured I'd ask." Kellan took a step back. He raised his hands placatingly as he saw Meghan's countenance darken and eyes luminesce. "Easy, Woody, I'll ask him now. In fact, give me your hand. You ask him. He's made these contacts work with Ordered Sentinel energies so I'm guessing you can hear him just like you could those Lycanthropes in Samangan Province. Kellan reached inward drawing on his power and channeled a trickle through the contacts, activating them. He reached out and Meghan placed her hand in his.

"Is it there?" she asked.

Jarvis' clipped British voice resounded in Kellan's head and he felt Meghan's grip shift as her eyes widened in surprise. "Is that Captain Daugherty, Kellan? There is only one female within your insurgency so I am making an educated guess. How am I able to hear her? The ophthalmological implants I fabricated should not function for her. This is intriguing. Please explain."

"It's almost as annoying as you are," Meghan growled.

"I am not an 'it,'" Captain, I am a he. I am Jarvis."

She glanced up at Kellan, "Correction, *he* is almost as annoying as you are."

"Thank you, Captain."

"You're welcome. Now, Jarvis, I need you to retask the Russian Persona class Kosmos 2506 to this area. Can you do that."

"I am not sure, Captain. Those systems are hardened to prevent such intrusions. Kellan had previously asked me to retask a United States satellite so I was endeavoring to do so. I have substantially better access to domestically launched reconnoissance satellites."

Meghan shook her head. "No good. We need one that has laser based underground cavity detection."

There was a slight pause and Meghan stared up at Kellan who merely shrugged and offered a weak smile that only earned him narrowed eyes. Jarvis came back a moment later. "Captain, are you referring to the system developed by the Central South University in Changsha, China?"

"Yes."

"Standby, I was not aware that had been deployed." There was another slight pause and Jarvis continued again, "Three satellites currently have this capability and only one currently within your operating region. The Kosmos 2506. I must say, Captain Daugherty, that is quite impressive. I begin to see that your reputation is well deserved."

Kellan sighed. "Great Jarvis, she now has a very self satisfied look on her face. Can you do anything with that thing."

"I have already circumvented several levels of security, Kellan. It will take some time yet, but I do believe I can retask the 2506 to your area before its orbit passes beyond range. What shall I ask it to do?"

"I want it to create a 3D model of the area around around and below the Sphinx."

"Understood."

"Great. Does Kellan's contact lens interface allow for AR overlays."

"Of course."

"Perfect. Once your get the data, I want you to generate a SURPAC or CAD model and overlay them on his lenses."

"I understand the request and could accomplish this, but the AR layer would be quite disruptive to Kellan's ability to see. Kellan, is this your request as well?"

"Uh, well, I'm not sure what an AR layer is and——" stammered Kellan, but Meghan interrupted.

"Kellan, AR is Augmented Reality, and what I'm going to do is have any cavern projected onto your lenses so you can visualize them. If you can visualize a thing, you can portal to a thing, or so you've said. I don't fancy trying to dig beneath a couple millennia of sand, do you?"

"No, that doesn't sound fun at all. Jarvis, just do what she said."

"Very well. ETC 11 minutes. By the way, there are three heat signatures approaching your location. I suggest you engage a photon dispersion field to avoid detection."

Meghan looked around quickly and gave Seramai several hand signals that put him on alert as well, but Kellan just released Meghan's hand, put his arms loosely around both their backs and guided them toward the foot of the statue.

Meghan leaned into his ear, "Photon dispersion what?"

Kellan smiled and whispered back, "That's Jarvis for Harry's Cloak. We're invisible. Gryffindor!"

⌒⁊⟨⟩⟋

Kellan turned around slowly, completing his second 360° circle.

"Well," asked Meghan clearly frustrated by their lack of progress.

"Don't rush me, Woody. I don't want us portaling into solid rock. That will ruin your whole day."

"I thought he was projecting the CAD images directly on your lenses. This should be easy."

"He did project it," growled Kellan, "I see something, but it's not crystal clear and there are parts missing where I assume there wasn't enough information to created the model. I'm trying to find the most open area. It looks like there is a large cavern but I've been unable to open a portal to it, so now I'm trying to examine what looks to be an entrance tunnel. It's almost directly beneath us, but looks really narrow."

"How narrow is really narrow," asked Seramai.

"Who cares," said Meghan, "Let's go already!"

"Fine," said Kellan with a resigned sigh, then as a portal rotated into existence he continued, "But wait until I've—"

Meghan jumped through the glowing oval in a crouch, turned back to them and gave a thumbs up as Kellan stared dumfounded at Seramai, "Until I've thrown a glow globe or something in there," he continued as the general shrugged, then leaped through after Meghan.

Kellan generated three globes of light that hovered nearby, one in front, one behind and one directly between them. The tunnel was both low and narrow. Only two of them could walk abreast and Seramai had to stoop slightly to keep his head from scraping the ceiling. Kellan traced his fingers down the smooth tunnel walls and marveled at the imagery his light revealed. Classic Old Kingdom artwork ran down its length, disappearing into the gloom. Kellan peered at a particular image as one of the light globes drew close.

"I think this is Pharaoh Khafre," he said excitedly. I've never seen him represented so young. This is amazing!" The Sentinel turned and found both Meghan and Seramai staring at him with flat expressions. He gave them each a weak grin, "Which I will return to someday and examine when all of creation is not at risk?" They both nodded.

"I'll take point," said Meghan and gave Seramai a quick look to see if there would be any objections. He simply extended his right arm. She smiled as she passed and the general fell in beside Kellan who softly whispered, "Good call."

"I am capable of learning," Seramai whispered back.

"I can hear both of you," Meghan growled.

The three continued along the tunnel for several minutes when Meghan suddenly crouched and lifted her right arm, hand formed to a fist. Kellan and Seramai likewise bent down. The former Marine turned and said, "I see some kind of light up ahead. Kellan, can you pull up the map and tell me how close we are to the large cavern?"

Kellan nodded and channeled through his contacts. Instantly the map appeared showing that they were nearly upon it. He dismissed the images and explained their position to Meghan and Seramai.

"So, what could be providing light in a sealed 4,500 year old underground cavern," she asked?

Both men simply shook their heads.

"Well, one way to find out. Ready?"

Kellan and Seramai nodded and the three crept forward as the tunnel opened up into an expansive cavern. Unlike the tunnel, its walls were smooth but unadorned and the roof was of unfinished stone almost as if the cavern hadn't been completed. In the center of the room rose a large square dais, surrounded on all sides by nine steps.

"Well, now we know what's providing the light," offered Kellan.

"Indeed," said Seramai, "and it is something I've never seen before. A persistent portal."

Meghan's eyes swept over the oval as it sat silently toward the far end of the dais. It glowed and pulsed around its edges, green on its right, red on its left, with a large band of violet pulsing where the two others met. "Shouldn't we be able to see through it?" she asked.

"Yeah," answered Kellan, "If it were one of mine, but this thing is something altogether different." He put a hand on Meghan's shoulder and she turned. "Promise me you aren't just going to jump through that thing."

She smiled. "I'm headstrong, Kellan, not stupid. Besides," she snickered and continued as she pointed to a large throne that sat several paces in front of the portal, "Our host might want to chat with us first."

Kellan frowned slightly at her jest but looked back to the skeletal form resting there. It sat straight backed and silent with empty sockets starting directly towards the tunnel entrance. Wide concentric circles of hammered gold and precious stones adorned its neck. Two short gold ropes extended down from the necklace and attached to a large hexagonal amulet that rested against its exposed sternum. The skeleton wore robes that draped across boney shoulders and flared across its legs. Though the millennia had worn them to tatters, it was easy to see that the clothes were once finely made.

"What are those?" asked Meghan pointing to three jars located on small raised pillars along the the dais. They seemed made of gold and each had a different statuette capping the jar. The first held an image of Osiris, the second of Anubis, the third of Set.

"They look like canopic jars," said Kellan, then added, "They usually hold organs."

"Those three," began Seramai as he gestured to the golden jars, "Are all sons of Horus."

"How did you know that," asked Meghan

The general stared at her a moment then said, "Horus is the god of war."

Meghan's eyebrows went up and she nodded in understanding.

"What?" asked Kellan.

"Nothing," the two said in unison as Seramai placed one foot on the first step of the dais to examine the skeleton further.

"Oh Shit!" yelled Kellan and he drew deep from his river of power snapping shields around the three of them. The skeleton's eye sockets glowed as if hot coals burned deep within them and its bones grated as the skull turned to regard Seramai.

The general paused for only a moment regarding the now animate corpse, then smoothly drew his gladius and struck where where skull met neck. The blow never connected for the skeleton had raised its right hand and a blue sphere burst forth hurling Seramai high into the air to crash against the wall to their right. He staggered back to his feet and gave Kellan a thankful nod for the timely shield.

The skeleton had risen fully from its throne, its glowing eyes regarding each of them in turn, but took no further action.

Meghan had sprinted over to Seramai but now turned to Kellan, "Ok, genius, what the hell is that thing."

As if in answer, the skeleton spoke, voice rasping like dried leaves, "I am Imhotep. Make peace with your gods. You have entered this sanctum of your own free will and by my will, you may not leave."

"Oh boy," said Kellan, "That's Ah'Anon's dad."

"Who?" asked Meghan turning worried eyes to him.

"Ah'Anon, the vampire I told you about. He's the bastard son of this dude. Who, if you didn't recognize the name Imhotep, is the undead monster from all the Mummy flicks going back to the 1930s"

"Ah'Anon?" said the skeleton questioningly. "What do you know of my son."

Kellan started feeling a bit hopeful and stepped forward. "Ah'Anon is my friend. He sent me here. Creation itself is in danger of being unraveled and we must pass through that portal. Please, for the sake of your son and our friendship with him, let us pass."

The glowing red eyes seemed to bore through Kellan and several long moments passed. Finally, Imhotep tilted his skeletal head back and laughed.

"Ah'Anon is the bastard son of a whore. I slew his mother for whelping him and thought I had killed him as well. If you are his friends, then I will take additional satisfaction in your deaths."

"Nice job," said Meghan, "You managed to make him even more pissed off."

"How should I know," growled Kellan, then held up his hands to the skeleton, "Wait, before you do anything. If we cannot continue, creation will end and so will you."

Imhotep raised his right hand, made a fist, and thrust it at Kellan. Blue energy lanced forward and the Sentinel's sword manifested a split second before energy bolt arrived. Kellan deflected the blow and watched as it careened into the cavern wall, where it sent up splinters of stone. "Do you think I wish to remain as I am?" shouted the Skeleton. "I sought to prolong life, not end up as you see me. I long for creation to end and with it, my existence."

"I am happy to end your existence," said Seramai dangerously.

"No, I will not depart this world knowing it continues on. I have pierced the veil of time and knew this day would come. The Creator erred by leaving so basic a flaw in place. Now he breaks his own laws to intervene. I will resist Him. He would not hear me when I sought Him in life. I will not hear Him now, nor those He sends."

"Actually," said Kellan, "It was more Lucifer than—" He stopped when both Meghan and Seramai glared at him, then whispered, "What?"

Meghan shook her head, "I swear, Kellan, sometimes you are so clueless. Don't piss off the mummy any more than he is by —"

"He's actually more of a Lich than a mummy," interrupted Kellan, then thought to himself, *Which is another perfect example of what they're talking about.*"

"Enough!" shouted Seramai and hurled himself at Imhotep again, sword raised even as Meghan unsheathed her katanas and darted up the dais stairs beside him.

Crackling blue energy radiated from Imhotep and danced between Meghan and Seramai while also brightly illuminating the entire cavern. Kellan staggered as he felt his power wane, then reinforced Meghan and Seramai's shields as he cast about with his eyes, noting again the strange winged shadow that appeared behind Meghan"

"Are you going to sit there or help," she yelled as Imhotep deflected blow after blow using a bejeweled staff that had previously been resting across his lap. After each deflection he would lash out at both with continual blasts of blue energy most, but not all, of which were absorbed by Kellan's shielding.

Seramai gave a triumphant roar as his gladius slid past Imhotep's staff and severed skull from neck. The general raised both arms, muscles bulging and slapped his arm across his chest, then yelled again. Both he and Meghan's eyes were burned a brighter amber than Kellan had ever seen them but the Sentinel paid it little mind as he sent a bolt of fire into the Annubis topped canopic jar. It shattered, leaving nothing but a molten puddle in its wake.

Kellan looked back to Imhotep and cursed then moved around the room. He shouted to the still celebrating pair, "Watch your back! You can't kill a Lich by decapitation."

They paused, stared first at each other, then turned back to the skeletal corpse which was just then reattaching its skull.

"Well, shit," said Meghan and launched herself into the fray but called back to Kellan, "How do we kill it."

The Osiris canopic jar was now a slag pile in front of Kellan and he answered through gritted teeth. "Have to destroy his phylactery."

"English Kellan!"

"Damnit, Meghan. That is english. Read a book."

"Fuck you, Kellan," she yelled, then saw a blast knock Seramai off the dais and burn deeply into his shoulder, "More shields!"

"I'm trying!" yelled the Sentinel, then added, "Horcrux! A phylactery is a horcrux."

This has to be it, thought Kellan as he blasted the canopic jar that was topped with an image of Set. "There!" he shouted and looked back to his friends. One of Meghan's katanas had been knocked aside and Imhotep swung his staff toward her unprotected head. Kellan's heart skipped a beat as Seramai barely returned to the dais in time for his gladius to deflect the blow. The young Sentinel felt a cold dread rise within him. He felt his power waning and knew he couldn't maintain the shields much longer. All the canopic jars were destroyed and nothing else appeared a likely candidate for Imhotep's phylactery. *What's that*, he asked himself as his eyes washed over a small, unadorned, clay jar laying on its side in one corner of the chamber. He sent an tendril of flame at the jar but it simply dispersed as soon as it came in contact with the clay. Kellan began to run toward the far corner of the chamber.

He felt his body become covered with a sheen of sweat as he channeled ambient heat into himself and thrust his arm forward converting the beads of sweat to icy projectiles all of which puffed away when they hit the jar.

"No!" shouted Imhotep from behind and Kellan felt energies being channeled in his direction. He reached inward and drained all that remained of his power praying his guess was correct. Meghan and Seramai's shields dropped even as a brightly glowing wall manifested between Kellan's back and the enraged Lich. The Sentinel felt it absorb a tremendous barrage then collapse, but he had already passed the peak of his leap and was arcing toward the small jar both hands clasping his Sentinel's sword. It struck the canopic jar and for a moment Kellan thought it would withstand his attack, then hairline fissures began to glow.

Imhotep screamed and began to shudder as he raised skeletal hands to his head in pain. Kellan heaved against the phylactery and felt his sword began to bite into the clay. Meghan and Seramai hacked at the animated corpse with abandon severing head and limbs as the phylactery finally shattered, succumbing to Kellan's efforts. He pitched over, sliding down with his back against the cool wall. Seramai walked over to Imhotep's skull and tapped it with his foot whereupon it collapsed to dust. Meghan clashed her katanas together and gave a whoop then proceeded to kick at all the remaining bits of Imhotep until all that remained were scattered piles of ash and the silently glowing portal.

Kellan grunted and pushed himself up, back still against the wall, then slowly made his way to the dais. Seramai was talking softly to Meghan who tried to punch him twice before melting into his arms and taking deep, measured, breaths.

Kellan stared into the portal's black center and said, "Do you think we've earned safe passage?"

"What do you mean?" asked Seramai.

"The Gospel of Judas said we must earn safe passage."

"I'd say we earned that and more," said Meghan who, Kellan noted, seemed to have come out the other side of her battle fury.

Kellan closed his eyes and recited the full verse that brought them here.

Beneath the lion whose human visage stares sightless forever shall god's uncheck hand join with perdition's progeny to bewray the mantle of war. This trinity may earn safe passage to one whose victories art recount'd in spirals up to the sky. At which hour god and man embrace yond which is neither, the path to those who is't seek creation's end becometh manifest

As the last word faded, the portal flashed once and its inky black center cleared to display a corridor lit only by the portal's own glow.

Seramai clapped the Sentinel on the shoulder. "Well done, Sentinel of Order. It seems we now go on to one whose victories spiral up to the sky."

The two men turned to Meghan who waved her hand in negation. "I'm done being point for now. One of you go first."

Chapter 19

A GOD REVEALED

Kellan ran his fingers along the polished stone, then looked back to Seramai and Meghan. "Looks like this was a oneway trip. I don't see any means to reestablish the portal to Imhotep's cavern."

Meghan walked up beside him and frowned. "I don't understand why it would vanish as soon as I came through. How could it know there weren't more than three of us?

Kellan shrugged, "No idea."

"*This trinity may earn safe passage,*" said Seramai as he stumbled, reaching out to brace himself against the tunnel wall. "If we made it this far, it was going to be the three of us, so after the third of us passed through, the portal had done its work."

Both Kellan and Meghan had gathered around him, looking concerned. He smiled at her wanly and said, "I think that last bolt made it all the way though our Sentinel's best efforts to shield us."

Meghan gently undid the clasps that held Seramai's ermine cloak to his leather breast plate and slid the shoulder straps aside. She gasped as blood and puss poured out from the wound then yelled for Kellan to get her emergency tissue sealant while she pressed both hands to the wound. The Sentinel had been through this before so knew to look for the small white aerosol can stored in her left shoulder pocket.

"Why doesn't he just heal himself like before," he asked as he removed the safety cap.

Seramai's eyes fluttered open, "Rules, my young Sentinel. Always rules. That creature wielded energies that are beyond my power to heal."

"Well, that is damned inconvenient," said Kellan as he held out the spray bottle. "Do you want to do it," he asked.

"No," answered Meghan, "I need to keep pressure on this. I think it may have nicked an artery." Meghan's voice had become deadly calm and clinical as she gently lowered Seramai to a seated position. Kellan knew that voice. He'd heard it on tapes played by her Psych Officer during PTSD sessions that he and her family had attended. Meghan had the rare ability present in few of the best Medivac officers to completely disconnect her emotions in order to make the best decisions for trauma patients. Kellan swallowed hard because he knew the toll it would take on her when those emotions returned. They would demand payment, with interest. She knew it too, and for her to make the decision to detach in this way meant Seramai was in bad shape. The former Marine turned to Kellan with emotionless eyes. "Take the red tube attached to the can, insert it into the nozzle, and place the tube between the space made by my crossing index and middle fingers."

Kellan did.

"Good, now depress the nozzle for a count of three and release."

Seramai gasped slightly as the pressure cooled foam forced its way into his wounded shoulder. He took a deep breath and smiled at Meghan grimly as the anesthetic did its work. "Remarkable. I feel much better. Is this what saved you from the Afghanistani werewolves?"

"It helped," she said, "but not enough to save me. It's just meant to be a temporary measure until real help can be brought to bear." She gave Kellan a meaningful look. The Sentinel had created an empathic link with Meghan after she was mortally wounded and used that link to heal her, nearly dying in the process.

He crouched down eyes coming to light and looked to Meghan, "I can try."

Seramai held up his good arm and waved a hand in negation. "No, you are needed ahead. I will be fine. I just need a few moments without vast magical energies being directed at me." He paused having gotten no reaction. "That was a joke."

Kellan smiled and gave a forced laugh.

"Never mind," began Seramai his eyes turning to Meghan, "Help me up, my valkyrie. I believe I know what's ahead and it shouldn't be far."

She shook her head. "If you move, the seal could be broken and you will bleed out." The former Marine took a deep breath and focused on Seramai. "You must manifest."

Kellan saw the large man stiffen and his eyes went hard looking first to Meghan and then to Kellan before returning again to her. "No. Everything will change. Things will be different between us. No."

He had turned away again. Meghan reached up and placed two fingers against his chin, turning him to face her. "Nothing will change. I will not allow it. Do you hear me. I will *not* allow it."

Kellan saw the resolution in his friend and without understanding the context of their conversation in the slightest, he leaned forward and said, "Seramai, I've known Meghan Daugherty most of my life. If she says nothing will change, well, whatever wants it *to* change is just completely fucked, because," he reached out and rested his hand on her shoulder, "nothin' is gonna change."

The general's conviction seemed to waver and Meghan pressed the advantage. "You thought it might be necessary anyway if the Gospel referred to Trajan's column."

Seramai sighed, "No longer an *if* my valkyrie. We are beneath Rome. I feel the blood of her warriors. The column lies ahead. You must help me reach it." He started to rise but his strength gave out.

"No," said Meghan, "You might not survive even that far. You must do it now."

"I cannot," he said, voice becoming resolute, "I suspect it must be done in the presence of the column. Just keep me alive that long. Were I to manifest here, we might win the battle to save my life but lose the war to save creation.

Meghan opened her mouth to protest but Seramai placed a finger against her lips. "No more arguments. Now give me a kiss and help me up."

Kellan watched for the span of three heartbeats as Meghan processed this. He knew what would happen and so it did. Her emotional armor shattered like crystal and tears began to stream down her cheek as she leaned forward to kiss him. After long moments, she pulled back and he smiled up at her. She sighed and draped his good arm over her her shoulder, then gave him a stare that was strong as iron, "On your feet soldier."

Kellan moved to help but she waved him back as her eyes began to luminesce with the strange amber gleam that occurred so often when she and Seramai were together. Kellan summoned additional globes of light and saw the shadows behind her again, but forced his many questions down as they slowly made their way down the hall.

Seramai's thinking proved accurate and less than two hundred yards further, the tunnel widened slightly to accommodate a massive engraved column beyond which lay another dead end. The column rose from the floor and extended through the roof of the tunnel leaving a small gap through which the glint of moonlight could be seen far above.

Kellan ran his fingers along the engravings that showed the birth and young life of a roman boy.

"Trajan's column," rasped Seramai and he smiled at Meghan.

She reached up and cupped his cheek, "*Your* column."

Kellan looked from one to the other and then back to the column. Pieces came together as perfect images of Trajan's column flew through his mind and the Sentinel shook his head in disbelief, "Trajan's column does not depict the boyhood of the Roman general, just his adult life." He glanced up at the ceiling and the column that passed through it to the surface, then continued, "But I suppose that is just the portion visible to those above." He turned to Seramai. "You are Trajan, 13th Emperor of Rome?"

The general coughed and Meghan helped him lean against his column. "I was, Kellan, yes. I was he, but now am more," he paused sadly then continued, "and in many ways less." His knees started to buckle and Meghan took more of his support upon herself.

"The time is now," she said.

Kellan shook his head, clearly frustrated at being kept in the dark about so many things, "Time for what!"

Seramai leaned his chest against the column and spread out both his arms, as his face contorted in pain. Meghan released him and knelt down. She looked at Kellan, then leaned forward to stretch her arms around the stone in a manner similar to that of Seramai. "Now you," she said, softly reciting from the Gospel of Judas, *At which hour god and man embrace that which is neither, the path to those who seek creation's end becomes clear.*

Kellan walked beside her and embraced the column, then looked down at his friend. "Meghan, I don't understand."

She smiled. "I know, but you will." She closed her eyes and took a deep breath, then whispered, "I am man. You are neither. He is a god."

"What?" said Kellan looking at the general who's eyes gleamed as he stared intently at Meghan.

"You promised me, my valkyrie. You promised me."

She smiled. "I keep my promises." Then lowered her head and spoke as if reciting, "By my honor, your servant calls."

Seramai stiffened and he replied, "By my honor, your master hears."

A gentle breeze flew through the tunnel as Meghan and Seramai exchange ancient vows binding them together.

"By my valor, I pledge my spirit"

"By my valor, I accept your soul"

"By my oath, no will but yours"

Tears were streaming down Seramai's cheeks and he seemed desperately trying to avoid his next response, but the words ripped out from him, "By your oath, no will but mine!"

Meghan's voice rose and Kellan felt the crackle of creative energies gathering, "To War's mantel I demand, drop all glamor from the Man!"

Light exploded around them making the small tunnel so bright that Kellan and Meghan both squinted against the blinding glare. Ribbons of energy swirled about the three, whipping up wind, and collecting around Seramai whose body gleamed as his wounds vanished.

"Seramai," called Kellan above the din. "Seramai…"

The general looked down with eyes the glowed with brilliant amber fire, "No, Sentinel of Order. Seramai is gone." He looked toward an unseen sky and yelled in a voice loud as thunder, "I. Am. Ares!"

Ares tightened his embrace of the column which depicted his life before having become the very incarnation of War. He stepped back and said, "A god has embraced this task"

Meghan stood and removed her arms, then glanced at Ares saying, "Man has embraced this task."

Kellan's mind was reeling as he released his grip on the column and stumbled back against the tunnel wall. The other's stared at him expectantly, and Kellan said slowly, "One who is neither man nor god has embraced this task."

Silence and darkness both washed over them, then a moment later the room glowed as a portal rotated into view.

⟨⟨⟨⟨⟩⟩⟩⟩

Ares screamed in anger and drove his fist though the tunnel wall and up to his wrist. Kellan put a hand gently on the god's shoulder. "Seramai," Ares glared at him, "I mean Ares, just give me a minute to catch the hell up, will you."

"She's gone, Sentinel of Order. My valkyrie is gone. She promised me!"

Kellan looked to Meghan who just said, "I have no idea what he's talking about."

Kellan sighed as Ares pushed him out of the way and stood before Meghan. "Kneel and be silent!" he said.

Meghan fell to her knees, head bowed.

Kellan winced, "Yeah, that's not good, I'll grant you. But trust me, her inner bitch is alive and well in there somewhere. You just need to rouse it."

Ares grunted then commanded Meghan to stand. "Servant, I want you to spar. Do your best to attack me until I say otherwise. Begin!"

Kellan whistled softly at the display. Meghan was a blur of perfectly executed attacks, many of which managed to get though Ares' equally impressive offense and defense. Finally the god ordered her to stop and she took a step back, then grinned at Kellan.

"I did pretty good."

"Hell yeah, you did," Kellan said, "I mean he won but he's the bloody god of war after all."

"Meghan," said Ares and she immediately turned to him, her face losing much of its expression as she inclined her head.

"My lord?"

Ares' countenance darkened and Kellan saw his jaw tighten with frustration and anger. The Sentinel stepped between them and gave Ares a gentle push backward. "Just hang back a minute and let me try a few things. But if I'm successful, you are going to need to act fast cause a nest full of hornets got nothing on a pissed off Daugherty." The god swiped away Kellan's hands with a grunt and stalked to the side as Kellan turned to face Meghan.

"Hey Woody, let me ask ya something," began Kellan trying to put as much of a lighthearted tone as he could into his voice.

"She narrowed her eyes at him. "Kel, you know I hate that nickname. What are we waiting for? You and I need to get through that portal and kick some Cabal ass."

Kellan raised an eyebrow. "You and I. What about him?" he motioned to Ares and Meghan looked directly into the corner, then turned back confused.

"Who?" she asked.

Ares slammed his arm sideways against the wall causing the entire area to quake and chips of stone to fall around them. "Her memories of me last mere moments unless she's performing something at my behest. She cannot even perceive me unless I address her directly."

"Well burying us beneath Rome isn't going to help," Kellan snapped, then turned back to Meghan. "Look, bear with me a minute. I need you to trust me, Woody."

Meghan gave him a wary look. "You only say *trust me, Woody*, when you are about to do something I don't like."

Kellan nodded. "And this isn't going to be any different."

She sighed. "Great, go ahead."

The Sentinel gave her his most encouraging smile. "Can you tell me where you were this past week?"

Meghan smirked at him. "I was in Rome, stupid. You know that."

"Ok, and what were you doing there."

"Sightseeing."

"You hate sightseeing."

"Yeah I do." She paused, confused, and Ares perked up staring at her as she continued, "I hate sightseeing. Why would I do that, Kel?"

"I'm not sure," he replied evenly. "Maybe you were with someone you liked being with more than you hated sightseeing. Were you alone in Rome?"

Meghan began to rub her temple absently as if she were developing a headache, "Uh, I, I don't think so."

"Well, that's interesting. You don't think so? Surely you can remember a guy who schlepped you all across the eternal city or—" Kellan gave her a wicked grin, "maybe it wasn't a guy, eh."

Meghan shot him a long suffering look, "Don't project your fantasies, bookboy." She crouched down and rubbed her head harder, then said, "He's definitely a he. We were a team," she paused searching for words, "He and I were a team, with you in Vatican city." Meghan looked up at Kellan, "And we were together just now with the mummy."

Lich, thought Kellan, and nearly bit his own tongue off. Instead, he smiled at her and said, "Yeah, now you got it. Well, mostly. I wouldn't call it a team. He did all the heavy lifting. I'd say you were in more of a minor support role."

"Huh?"

"Yeah, truth be told, if he wasn't so smitten with you, he probably would have left you at home."

"No he wouldn't, Kellan. I am not a sidekick."

"C'mon, Meghan, be real. He's the very incarnation of war. Do you really think he actually *needs* some ex Marine debutante sashaying about him.

Meghan stopped rubbing her temples and glared up at Kellan, "Fuck you, Kellan. It's *former* Marine and I do not sashay. Ares does need me."

Kellan held up his hands. "Whoa. Of course he needs you. I mean don't we all need a woman from time to time?" The Sentinel leaned casually against column and tried to ignore the look of disbelief and horror on Ares' face as he continued, "But Meghan, there's a big difference between a respected partner and a convenient bed warmer."

Meghan let forth a primal scream and launched herself at Kellan even as his eyes flashed and he bent time. *I'm screwed*, he thought because she moved too quickly and was able to enter his time dilation bubble. Her first punch caught him square on the jaw and he tasted blood then a split second later her left hand gripped his head and slammed it against Trajan's column. Kellan spun out of the way as his head swam and he drew deeper from his river of power channeling it to heal and invigorate. Megan retained an aggressive posture but didn't move toward him. "Take that back, Kellan!" she growled but he just laughed at her and waved his hands.

"Take it back, but I can't take it back. It's already out there. I don't see what you are so upset about. There are worse things. You've taken orders before. Why not take them now? I mean doesn't War Whore have a nice alliterative ring to it."

Kellan saw Ares stagger slightly in his peripheral vision as Meghan's lips curled in a feral snarl. Her eyes began to glow and black wings appeared against the far wall as she leaped for Kellan with murderous intent. For his part, the Sentinel learned from his last mistake and kept his time dilation as close as possible. Even so, he was barely able to dodge a kick that landed against the wall where his head had been a fraction of a second before. Cracks radiated up to the ceiling and Meghan spun catching Kellan in a reverse wheelhouse kick that sent him tumbling.

"Now would be a good time to make her stop, Ares!" yelled Kellan.

The god stood frozen in disbelief as he stared at them both.

"Ares!" screamed Kellan again and the two locked eyes, sharing insight.

Meghan had bent to one knee her left hand beside Kellan's head and her right pulled back in a fist.

"Stop!" yelled Ares as Meghan began her downward strike.

She froze, her arm trembling and glared over her shoulder at Ares, then pulled her fist back to strike again.

Ares yelled again. "I *command* you to stop!"

Meghan whipped her head around transferring all her feral energy in his direction. "I will not be commanded, Ares." She stood, Kellan forgotten, and stalked toward the god as the air seemed to ripple between them. When only a hair's breath separated the two, she stared into his golden eyes and said, "Do not *ever* command me again. Who the fuck do you think I am?"

Ares raised his hands and gently cupped her face as tears formed in his eyes, "You are my valkyrie. And you kept your promise."

Meghan blinked, slowly returned his relieved smile and said, "You bet you war whoring ass I did."

Kellan gave a contented sigh and flopped back against to cool stone floor as he watched Meghan pull Ares into a passionate embrace. After a few moments, the Sentinel leaned up on one arm and said, "Are you two almost done? "Can we *please* go through this portal, before something else bad happens?"

Chapter 20

THE SECOND GARDEN

"Of course I knew who he was, Kellan. Do you think I invite just any-one into my bed? Besides, it was kind of obvious."

The Sentinel sat sullenly in the crypt niche and idly spun an upended scull next to him. He peered into the darkness, then glanced at his watch and cursed himself for the third time at having been convinced to let Ares scout on ahead.

"Don't you think?" asked Meghan again.

"Hmm?"

"Obvious?," she asked again. "Don't you think it was obvious? *Seramai.* It's the most simple anagram there is."

"I have no idea what you are talking about, Meghan. You know I hate word games." The Sentinel broke off and stared up. Meghan thought she saw a slight glint from his contacts. Kellan slumped and mumbled, "Screw you Jarvis. You are a freaking super computer. You are designed to be observant."

Meghan smirked. "The robot saw it before you did, eh genius." She held up two hands and counted off, "S-E-R-A-M-A-I," than made a washing motion and started again as Kellan's frown deepened, "I-AM-ARES"

"What's your point, Meghan? That your new incarnate boyfriend has a juvenile and simplistic way to hid his oh so secret identity."

She snickered. "Apparently it was mature and complex enough to befuddle you."

Kellan lobbed the scull at her and slid out of the niche. "Where the hell is he anyway?"

Meghan held up the scull and stared into its empty socket, then intoned, "Alas poor Ares, I knew him Kellan."

"I should have left you as his thrall," mumbled Kellan as his eyes flared to life and three globes of light resolved into view.

Meghan set down the scull and hastened to Kellan, placing a restraining hand on his shoulder, "Hold on cowboy, Ares said to wait where we exited the portal."

"He's not the boss of me, Meghan," said Kellan seriously.

She gripped his shoulders and turned the Sentinel toward her. "Now who is being juvenile and simplistic. You know these Cabalists posses your blood and with it you are the most likely among us to be detected. Ares, in his manifest form, can move faster and more stealthily than you could hope to in this particular place."

Kellan shrugged her off, "Yeah, about that whole manifesting thing, you could have told me."

She looked down and Kellan couldn't determine whether it was with chagrin or contrition. "He asked me not to and It wasn't my secret to tell."

"Do not blame her, Sentinel of Order," came Ares resonant voice. Both Kellan and Meghan turned at his approach and she smiled. The gloom seemed to retreat about him as his natural olive skin gleamed and sparkled slightly with an inner power. He remained as he had been when Seramai, but now was more as well. "The mantel of war weighs heavy and carries many responsibilities even as it grants many gifts. Is it so difficult to fathom my wanting to set it aside for a time and just be a man."

"Dude, you were hardly a man when we met at the Council of Havilah. In fact, if I recall correctly, you introduced yourself to me as a god."

Meghan cocked her head at this. "You did?"

Ares cast an embarrassed look to her and gestured in Kellan's direction, "His arrogance and presumed superiority annoyed me."

The former Marine nodded a caught Kellan's eye, "That does sound like you."

"Whatever, truth be told, I don't even really care. Ares, your reasons are your own. I'm more interested in what you did to Meghan."

They both stared at him without comprehension. "Oh come on now, do you think I, of all people, wouldn't notice amber glowing eyes."

"Oh, that," Meghan said as she sidled up to Ares, crossed her arms behind his neck and gave him a quick kiss. "Like you said, he just awakens my inner bitch."

"Like it ever sleeps," grumbled Kellan.

"My valkyrie speaks truthfully, young Sentinel. What she experienced is not uncommon for soldiers when in close proximity to me. I have seen it many times before, but never has it been as dramatic as with she. The fog of war grants power at the cost of judgement and reason. You saw this with her, yes?"

Kellan muttered something that vaguely resembled acquiesce and sighed, "I suppose the shadow wings are all part of this fog as well then. Fine, just one more chapter of weirdness in the book of Kellan Caufield Thorne. I'll let it go. Now, what did you find out oh, stealthy incarnation of war?" He noticed them both looking at him with similarly odd expressions. "What?" said Kellan, "I told you I would let it go."

"Black shadow wings?" asked Meghan. "You keep bringing that up. What ever the hell are you talking about?"

She looked to Ares who shrugged and said, "I have never seen such a thing."

Kellan pressed his lips together and pointed at them both, "Don't screw with me. I let her go medieval on my ass for the sake of true love."

The two raised their hands with such synchronicity that Kellan couldn't help but chuckle. "Honest, Kellan," began Meghan, "We have no idea what you are talking about."

The young Sentinel just shook his head in bemusement and wondered if the many confusing aspects of his existence were beginning to outstretch his rather prodigious coping mechanisms. Ares cleared his throat and Kellan looked up and smiled. "Don't mind me. I'll be fine. What did you find Sera—damnit—Ares."

The god reached over to a nearby niche, removed a scull and unceremoniously crushed it to ash. He then sprinkled it on the floor and crouched down. "I found the ritual site itself," he said, then drew a crude map in the ash to indicate the how they would reach it.

Ares tapped a large open area on the map and said, "This is it here. There is a small altar of some kind and on it I could see several artifacts of substantial power." He then made nine small hash marks that encircled the dot he had used to mark the altar. "Around the artifacts there are nine portals that seemed very similar to those we just passed though. Their edges glowed but the centers were dark as pitch. The artifacts seemed to be powering them. I could see ribbons of energy connecting the altar to each."

Kellan nodded. "That makes sense. Lucifer said there were nine key events that were foundational to creation and if any were materially disrupted. Boosh!"

Meghan frowned, "Did Lucifer literally say, 'Boosh?'"

Kellan waved her comment away, "Please don't get me started on him. Anyway, the point being, his intel seems good. These Cabalist bastards are going to try and screw with a key event in Jesus' timeline." As he spoke the words, Kellan could see his friends tense and met their eyes. "Oh, did I forget to mention that part? Golly, I'm sorry. Seems inconsiderate of me. You know, kind of like my oldest gal pal shacking up with the very incarnation of war. Not that I'm keeping score or anything."

Meghan glared at Kellan and her eyes took on the first hint of a glow when Ares touched her cheek with that back of a finger, drawing her attention. He simply shook his head and she sighed, then nodded.

"Do you know which event they seek to disrupt?"

"No clue, but they can't do shit without the Spear." Kellan felt a moment of panic. "You didn't see that did you?" Ares shook his head and the Sentinel relaxed. "Well, it's just a matter of time. What do you two think we should do?"

Meghan smiled but it didn't touch her, once again, glowing eyes, "We should go and kill them all." She turned to Ares who returned her smile and nodded.

Kellan stood and brushed ash from his pants, "Well, doesn't sound like much of a plan, but I don't have anything better. Not to mention, I'm really getting tired of this. It's been over a week of non stop chaos." He snickered at his own joke, "no pun intended."

The three had traversed about half the distance Ares had estimated lay between their entry point and the ritual site when Kellan paused and looked around. His two companions shared a glance and then waited for him to explain. The Sentinel just shook his head to indicate he wasn't sure either, but began examining the nearby wall. He drew a light globe against it and dragged a finger along the mortar line between stones. His fingernail dug deep within the unset mortar and he showed it to Meghan. Kellan formed his hands into a bowl and tensed, preparing to channel into the wall, when Areas placed his hand over Kellan's. The god shook his head. Pointed to Kellan's eyes and then in the direction of the ritual. He then gently, but insistently, pushed the Sentinel to the side and slammed an open hand between a crack in the mortar.

Moment's later they had removed several stones and Kellan's stomach tried to crawl up this throat as the opening revealed the arm of someone who had been walled up to die. In a panic, he reached in and grabbed the arm. He pressed his fingers against the wrist, searching for a pulse, and nearly cried out in relief at the steady thrum. Kellan bent down and placed his lips softly on the symbol of a dove he saw there while lifting up a prayer of thanks that he knew none would ever hear. All this time Ares and Meghan had been frantically removing stones and finally revealed a disheveled, angry, but very much alive, Shannon.

Kellan reached up, pulled the rough cloth from her mouth, and smiled at her. "Hello, Sweetie," she croaked.

Kellan laughed in relief but quipped back, "Had I known you were into this," he dangled the gag by one finger, "I'd have certainly obliged." Shannon looked past Kellan met Meghan's eyes. The two women shared a knowing look of disdain and disgust, but Shannon greedily accepted Kellan's offered hand and melted in his embrace. She took a quick swallow from the canteen Meghan offered and then turned back to Kellan.

"I knew you'd find me."

He kissed both her cheeks and looked deeply into her wheat brown eyes, "I will always find you." She smiled up at him and Kellan shook is head slightly, "How the hell did you end up in a wall?"

Shannon took another swig from the canteen and frowned, "No idea really. Last I remember, I was being crushed to death by a major demon's corpse."

Meghan leaned in. "Sorry to be the spoil sport, but, Shan, do you know where that spear is? Kellan's new BFF Lucifer says bad things will happen if these Cabalist bastards place it here. Not for nothing, but if Satan thinks something bad will happen, well" She just let everyone fill in the rest of the thought with their own imaginations.

Shannon shook her head. "I don't, but it's not here yet, I can tell you that. I fell through the stone at Inverness and it wouldn't open again, not for weeks or months. The Cabal would have had to retrieve the spear and find another fissure. The closest would be the Henge in England so we best make haste, they could be here with it at any moment."

Kellan rested a hand on her shoulder. "We can spare a moment, Shannon. Rest a bit and get your strength back."

She stared at him. "What are you on about. I've spent the last, I don't know how many, hours resting in a bloody wall, you daft man. Now I want to go kill something and if it's not some Cabalist bastard demon or angel, it's going to be you." Shannon noticed Meghan nodding with approval, her lips curling slightly. The soulborn glanced at Ares and then looked back to Kellan, "By the by, who is he and what in heaven's name is going on with her eyes?"

All four peered around the corner and took in the scene. It was largely as Ares had described, complete with altar and nine portals, but something had changed. They pulled back and huddled in a crouch. "Those portals don't look pitch black to me," said Kellan.

"They have lightened, Sentinel of Order. When I was last here, they were completely opaque."

Kellan nodded, "Ok, now does anyone else find it strange that there is absolutely no-one or nothing guarding this place."

Meghan frowned at him, "Don't try to be a tactician, Kellan. It makes perfect sense. There was no entrance the way we came. We traversed a portal from god knows where. They are likely guarding the main entrance and the waiting for the Spear to arrive."

Ares nodded, "We should take an offensive position around the altar."

The two women indicated their agreement and just as they were about to move from concealment a pulse of energy radiated from the altar sending out nine ribbons of energy, one to each portal. As each ribbon struck, the portal lightened by several degrees.

Ares gave Kellan a self satisfied look, but the Sentinel made a point of ignoring him. Instead he focused on each portal in turn. They each seemed to display a different scene but only for about thirty seconds after which the scene replayed. "We're too far away. I can't see what they are showing."

"We move then," said Ares.

Shannon rested a hand on the god's shoulder causing him to pause. He turned to her quizzically. "Just a moment," she said, fishing something out from within her tunic. "Kellan, you should probably take this." Shannon lifted the leather thong over her head, and gently placed the item in his outstretched hand. Her fingers lingered a moment and softly brushed his hand as she withdrew hers.

Kellan looked down for a moment and then back to Shannon. "The Seal of Solomon?"

She nodded.

"It's warm," he said turning it over in his hands, "and its glowing. It wasn't doing that when I gave it to you."

"No," she began, "I suspect it has something to do with that major demon I killed. I'm not sure because, well, the dead bastard fell on me and I fell through the bloody stones at Inverness."

Ares leaned over a gave the Seal a cautious tap with one finger, then glanced over to Shannon. "Was the demon in contact with this Seal when it died?" She nodded and Ares gave a low chuckle. "That was very good fortune, soulborn. Very good indeed."

Shannon snorted, "It didn't feel very fortunate to me. I'll tell you that for nothing."

Ares shrugged, "That may be so, but killing that demon released the Chaotic energy within it. Energy cannot be destroyed. It only changes forms or seeks a new vessel. In this case, my highland friend, that vessel was the Seal of Solomon. Congratulations, you charged one of the most powerful demonic binding artifacts known to exist."

Shannon stared at the god of war for the barest of moments then said, "Oh, that. Well I knew that bit. I planned to do that you silly mountain of a man. I thought you were talking about something else entirely."

Ares blinked twice, gave an incredulous glance to Kellan, and smiled, "I imagine you have your hands full with this one."

"And I'd have it no other way," replied Kellan smoothly as he slid the leather thong over his head and felt the comforting warmth of the Seal resting against his chest.

Meghan rolled her eyes at Kellan and growled, "I'm so done with all this talking." She gave Ares a reasonably hard slap on the face, then shot Kellan a sideways grin, and yelled, "Leeeeroyyyy Jennnkiinnnnss!"

Kellan couldn't stifle his laugh as Meghan sprinted toward the alter with her three companions only moments behind. She ran between two portals and headed to the altar but was prevented by an energy barrier she struck with the full force of her sprint. Meghan rebounded off the unseen shield and would have fallen if Ares were not there to brace her.

"I may be able to pass through if given enough time," the god said turning to Kellan, then paused as he saw the Sentinel staring intently at several portals. "Sentinel of Order?"

Kellan shook his head in wonder as he looked from one portal to another and watched the short scene displayed in each dim oval. A baby in a cave. A man in a river. The shared joy of a wedding. A shrouded man exiting a cave. A shared meal steeped in sadness. A darkened garden. A bloodied figure on a cross. A tomb blazing with light.

He glanced to Shannon whose face held the same awe as did his own, then Meghan walked up beside the two, whistled softly, and said, "You know I've never been the most religious person but—"

Kellan reached down, gave her hand a squeeze, and said, "Yeah, I get you exactly."

Ares leaned in and broke the portal's spell on the trio, "I said, I can probably get past that barrier."

All three of them glared and he lifted his hands while giving the barest of glances to the portals, "What's so impressive? I'm a god too."

Meghan punched him and made a letter with the thumb and pointer of both hands, "Little "g" god," then nodded back to the portals, "Big "G" God."

Ares merely smiled at her and said, "That, my valkyrie, is just a matter of opinion."

Kellan ignored the banter and took several steps toward one of the portals. He stared at the man kneeling in the dirt surrounded by olive trees, arms outstretched. He pounded the ground with one hand and looked up at the sky. Kellan shifted his weight and the man turned. Their eyes met and Kellan gasped. It was still a dark portal. There was no way he could be seen. The moment passed and time reversed as the portal began to replay.

"Kellan!" screamed Shannon. "They're coming and they have the spear!"

"What the hell is that thing," yelled Meghan over her shoulder as she and Ares ran to place themselves between the ritual altar and those entering from the cavern entrance.

"Djinn," called Kellan and Shannon simultaneously.

The five creatures spread out with the djinn flanked on either side by a demon and angel. The demons looked nearly identical, both standing on cloven hooves with large black wings extending from their backs. Their skin was a mottled reddish brown comprised of interlocking scales similar to a snakes. The contrast between them and the Cabalist Angels could not have been more stark. They stood tall and beautiful wearing immaculate robes that seemed to glow with an inner light. Wings of the purest white hung down from their backs, tips not quite touching the ground.

After the barest moment of surprise the djinn whipped its hands in a complex geometric shape and gestured violently in Kellan's general direction. Mist coalesced to form massive disembodied hands which flew toward the four of them. Kellan had already erected shields around his companions but it did little good. As they struck, the spectral hands closed about each of them and sent all but Ares flying backwards to slam against the cavern wall. For his part, the god of war had braced himself then cleaved the djinn's manifestation in two with his omnipresent gladius which caused it to puff back to mist. With a roar, he charged the nearest demon who lowered the Spear of Longinus.

Kellan drew deeply from his river of power, noting once again, it had both broadened and deepened. He channeled, willing ribbons of green energy to lance outward among his companions disrupting each of the djinn's manifested hands. Meghan fell down the wall, landing in a crouch with one hand braced on the floor. She looked up, and Ares turned, sensing her gaze. His aura brightened and his voice cut through the din like a razor through silk.

"Come, my beautiful valkyrie. Enjoin this battle with me." His voice rose further sounding like thunder. "Glory awaits!" Meghan's eyes became twins to Ares and Kellan could actually see luminescent tendrils waft from the god of war only to be greedily absorbed by her. She bellowed a feral war cry and uncoiled her legs, launching herself from the cavern wall. Kellan watched in awe as Meghan tucked into a ball at the top of her arc and landed deftly beside Ares, twin katanas already in hand. She looked up at the god of war and smiled dangerously. "Hoo Rah!" she screamed and kept pace with Ares as he attacked the spear wielding demon.

Shannon turned wide eyes to Kellan. "What the hell happened to her, Kellan Thorne."

"Later," he said and extended his hand. She gripped it tightly and he felt a torrent of power rush out as her eyes blazed to life, then made to release his hand, but he only gripped her more tightly. She raised an eyebrow in question and said, "Don't you even try to keep me from this fight. Those bastards sealed me up in a wall. A wall Kellan."

The Sentinel smiled as he felt his muscles burn with additional power and said, "I wouldn't dream of it." He heaved her off the ground and spun. Once, twice, three times he spun then released her and watched as she sailed gracefully across the cavern to land several paces from the farthest angel. She turned to him and grinned even as Kellan altered gravity in a bubble around himself and leaped to her side.

The Sentinel called in warning to Ares as the djinn gestured forming a glowing glyph in the air and directed it toward the god. Ares dodged and was barely clipped as it passed near him, but even that much contact ripped a gash in his shoulder which then seemed to leak amber light. He stumbled to one knee and looked up as yet another glyph hurtled toward him but suddenly vibrated and broke apart into motes of blue dust. The djinn looked down at the glowing sword protruding from its chest as Kellan whispered something to it from behind. It opened it's mouth to scream, but no sound came out as Kellan twisted the sword and removed it. The Sentinel drew back and mentally commanded his sword to shorten in length, then used it to deftly sever the djinn's head, kicking it toward the spear wielding demon.

The decapitated head provided a momentary distraction that Meghan used to dramatic success. She was already at a full run when Ares had sunk down from the djinn's attack. Without a moment's hesitation she leaped, then changed direction slightly by pushing off of Ares's exposed back and slashed at the demon with her katana. The demon screamed in pain as his arm was sliced clean through, its hand still gripping the spear. As the severed arm touched the floor it puffed away, leaving the Spear of Longinus spinning slowly. Shannon reached for the spear, eyes glowing and willed it to her hand just as she had done at the Inverness stones. It vibrated slightly for the barest of moments before lifting from the ground and flying towards her.

Kellan's eyes grew wide, "Holy shit, Shannon, how *do* you do that," he yelled as it streaked past him. She grinned and held up her hand to receive it, but at the last moment a flash of white interposed itself as one of the angel's streaked by. It caught the spear, bear inches from Shannon's grasp and and arced back into the air. For a moment it hovered there, wings moving slowly, then threw its head back in anguish and screamed. The battle seemed to pause and all eyes fixed on the angel. Its wings blackened and skin changed from smooth porcelain to rough overlapping scales even as its eyes went from emerald green to ruby red. It stared down at the four with hatred then turned and angled for the altar.

"Stop it," screamed Kellan as he drew so much power that he felt his skin begin to burn. He unleashed in a torrent of electrical bolts flashing from manifested clouds throughout the room. The newly fallen demon's flesh tore away in charred chunks as the bolts struck. Still it continued streaking toward the assembled artifacts with the Spear of Longinus held before it. Twin flashes of green tinted silver struck the demon as Shannon's power infused daggers struck between the leather wings. The demon arched its back as its eyes went black and it toppled to the ground.

The four watched in horror as the dead demon fell onto the alter and the Spear of Longinus struck blade first into the stone beside it.

The room flared with white light and Kellan felt his world reel as if rocked by a massive explosion. He knew the quake was from the spiritual rather than physical realm, but that brought no comfort. He felt panic rise within him as he looked around the room. All nine portals glowed with perfectly clear centers. White portals.

"None shall pass," yelled Ares as he and Meghan leaped on the one armed demon, wrestling it to the floor.

"Kellan," shouted Shannon in alarm, "To your left. The seventh portal. Quickly!"

Too late the Sentinel turned and saw the final angel running at unbelievable speed toward the very portal Kellan had stared through minutes before. He willed as much power into his body as it would accept and felt his legs burn with effort as he tried desperately to close the gap. The angel leaped with spread wings just as Kellan reached for it and the Sentinel cried out in desperation but was too late. The angel passed through the open portal and into the darkened garden beyond, just as the robed figure Kellan had seen before walked out of view. Kellan gritted his teeth as dozens of possibilities flashed through his mind in a single moment of frozen time. He dismissed them all. Only one path remained for the Sentinel of Order. He leaped through the portal and into a foundational fixed point in time.

～ｲｲﾅﾝ

Kellan released the channeled power and a violent gust of wind caught the angel, hurling it back into the trees as he fell, head first through the portal. The Sentinel landed hard and rolled to a painful stop. He turned back and saw his friends through the open portal. Beyond them more of the Cabal were arriving.

There was nothing he could do for them. If he went back, all of creation was lost. His voice cracked as he yelled though time and space. "Remove the spear! Shannon, remove the spear!" He felt her eyes on his and could see the hesitation. "Shannon, you have to. If you don't more of them will come through and I can't stop them all. Remove it now and turn the portals dark."

She was shaking her head. "No, Kellan, no. You will be trapped there. I know where you are. I know what it is."

Meghan was fighting now and Kellan couldn't see how many. He was about to shout again when something struck him hard from behind sending him to the ground. Kellan spun onto his back, sword forming from mist as he stared into the glowing green eyes of an angel. It, too, held a gleaming sword which now drew sparks as it slid along of Kellan's own. Again, Kellan channeled a burst of wind, flinging the angel back and buying him precious seconds. "Shannon," he yelled turning back to the portal then stopped. Ares stood beside the altar, amber light leaking from several wounds as Meghan whirled about him blocking, cutting, and killing. Ares had one hand on the hilt of Longinus' Spear, his eyes locked on Kellan's.

Kellan nodded and the god of war bowed his head. "Goodbye, Sentinel of Order," his resonate voice laced with equal parts respect and sadness. He pulled the spear free, leaned back on one foot and struck the altar with the other. Kellan gave a relieved exhalation as he saw the altar shatter and artifacts fly in every direction. The portal went dark, then vanished altogether.

"Fool!" came a voice from behind and Kellan turned to face the angel who's beautiful face was contorted with rage. "Do you know what you have done?"

"Saved creation?" Offered Kellan.

"You've saved nothing" and it reared back with sword raised. Kellan braced himself for another blow, but instead, the angel flexed its wings and sailed over him back from where they had come.

The Sentinel cursed and channeled a tendril of green energy that encircled the fleeing angel. Kellan felt himself jerked into the air and fell hard onto the angel's back causing the two of them to crash to the ground just inside the small clearing where they first entered the garden.

The two looked up just as a robe figure knelt by a nearby tree. He seemed to be speaking softly to two other men who appeared to still be sleeping, nestled in the tree's broad roots.

"No," growled the angel and Kellan clenched his teeth as he willed his sword to form itself into a dagger then plunged it into the prostrate angel. The Sentinel's eyes widened in surprise as the angel slowly pushed Kellan's hand back and removed the dagger, completely unhurt by the blade. "Order cannot kill Order, Sentinel. I am unfallen and your blade cannot harm me. I will stop the Incarnation's sacrifice, time will shatter, and creation will be rewritten." With that, he reared back and struck Kellan so hard his vision swam and he tasted blood.

"Stop," whispered Kellan as he staggered to his knees. The angel ignored him and rose, wings folded flat along its back. He took a step forward, twigs cracking beneath his feet, and the robed man slowly stood, then turned to face them.

Kellan felt his breath catch and the angel froze in place. Kellan heard him whisper, "Yeshua ben Joseph." The Sentinel stared at the man as thousands of images raced through his mind. He was thin with dark olive colored skin and slightly sunken cheeks. His eyes were dark brown and seemed slightly swollen. Streaks ran down both cheeks were dust had been washed away by tears. He had long dark brown hair that cascaded to his shoulders and a beard that seemed almost black. Kellan felt Yeshua's eyes upon him and the Sentinel involuntarily reached for his power. He felt his eyes warm with it and as it filled him, Kellan gasped. Through his Sentinel's eyes the man before him stood transfigured. Kellan could see ribbons of violet energy coursing through him as if straining to be free of the flesh that contained it. Occasional tendrils burst free and danced about him like tiny halos of creative light. Then his gaze went to the angel and his expression turned profoundly sad. Yeshua shook his head slowly and the angel shuddered. Kellan looked at it and winced as the beautiful white wings morphed, shriveling into black leather. The, now, demon's lips curled back in anger and its muscles tensed, preparing to leap, but Kellan was faster. His hand wrapped around the warm Seal of Solomon and gripped it tight, then felt power course through him as he yelled to the demon.

"Prohibere!"

The demon froze in place and Kellan's forward motion slammed him into the newly fallen angel. The Sentinel cursed and released the Seal of Solomon which had become so cold that frost formed on both sides.

"It will not hold me," Sentinel of Order. "I may not be able to prevent the Incarnation's sacrifice, but I can do many other things in this place. In this time. I will not be stopped by a hairless, talking ape."

Kellan leaned in close and whispered in the demon's ear, "Guess what, sparky? You aren't aligned with Order any more. Tell Asmodeus I said *hi.*" The Sentinel then slipped his glowing green dagger into the demon's side. Without a word, it started to shake, then simply broke apart showering the garden floor with motes of red ash.

Kellan opened his hand and the dagger fell free, puffing to mist. Yeshua gave the barest nod to the Sentinel of Order and with the saddest of smiles turned back to the sleeping men. Blocking Kellan from their view, He roused them, and without looking back the three walked into the gloom of the garden.

Kellan stood for several heartbeats staring after the vanished figures, then fell to the ground and wept.

Kellan woke with a start feeling panicked and disoriented. He looked up at the clear, star filled sky and nearly full moon, then remembered where he was. He didn't know how long he'd slept, but didn't think dawn was too many hours off. Kellan rose and walked to the tree where he'd seen the men sleeping and kicked the leaves around its trunk. He sighed, then reached inward and embraced his emerald river of power.

Kellan concentrated and runes flooded down his arms as he opened his hands in a cupping motion. He had a quick intake of breath as a portal rotated into view, then wavered and broke apart.

Yeah, well, that would have been too good to be true, thought Kellan. He smiled sadly at a memory of Micah teaching him in creation's workroom. In his mind, he heard his old mentor's voice, *Fixed points in time are inviolate, Kellan. You may not travel to them and no one may travel from them.* The young Sentinel slid down the tree to sit between its roots and thought, *I'm in time's equivalent of a black hole on the worst day in history. That is so like me.*

Without realizing it, Kellan again drifted off to sleep, the continual stress and activity of the past week crashing down upon him. Some hours later, he was jolted awake. He looked around but was alone. Glancing up, Kellan could tell it was late in the day, perhaps mid afternoon. He wasn't sure what to do, but did know he was quite thirsty. Ignoring his complaining muscles, the young Sentinel stood and stretched, then grabbed the tree for support as the ground rumbled.

He looked up and saw a dark curve begin to creep across the sun. *An eclipse,* he thought, then said out loud, "*The* eclipse. It's happening. Oh man, I really don't want to be here."

Kellan huddled back against the tree as the eclipse continued to progress. As it did so, dark clouds gathered and his Sentinel senses recognized vast gathered energies of both Order and Chaos. He channeled a trickle of power and gasped. Above him enormous ribbons of green and red energy lashed the sky whipping dark clouds into being. Lightning arced between them and struck all around him. Where the red and green ribbons met, violet tendrils would form and streak to the ground causing it to rumble and crack.

On it went becoming more and more violent to the point where all Kellan could see or hear was a cacophony of opposing energies. He held his hands to his ears and screamed, but the sound was lost to the wind as he saw a final flurry of green and red ribbons merge into a vast violet column that streaked toward the earth with a deafening blast. Silence followed and Kellan curled in a ball, mind drifting, not noticing the glowing portal that rotated into view.

Strong hands lifted him like he was a child as someone cried out, "Hurry, I don't have much left. I can't keep it open. Hurry Ares, please!"

A distant portion of Kellan's mind thought he recognized the voice, but dismissed it. It couldn't be her. She was far away.

"Shannon!" Kellan screamed as he sat up in bed. Darkness was all around him and his heart sounded like a drum in his ears.

He felt her arms around him. "Shhh, I'm here. You are safe. We're home."

She stroked his cheek and covered his face with kisses then just held him for long minutes and listened as his breathing slowed.

Finally, Kellan took a deep breath and slowly released it. He snuggled backward and felt her spoon against him kissing his neck softly.

"I thought I'd lost you," he said.

Shannon chuckled, "You can never lose me," then gently tapped his temple. "I'm always there." She moved her hand to his chest and tapped, "And there?"

Kellan smiled in the darkness, "Oh yes. Always there, Shannon. Always there." He rolled onto his back and could see the outlines of his bedroom in the gloom. "Meghan and Ares?"

"Both fine, if a bit worse for wear, especially Ares. I was able to use the last of my borrowed power to open a portal to you once you had past beyond the fixed point in time, but I couldn't hold it open. Ares ran through and carried you back out but it closed, well almost closed." She laughed softly, "The big oaf stuck an arm through and, quite literally, braced open a portal though time and space by sheer force of will."

Kellan sighed, "Well, as he is so fond of pointing out, he is a god,"

Shannon nodded, "That may be so, but it damn near sliced his arm in half. He barely managed."

Long minutes past in silence then Shannon leaned over and whispered, "And how are you, my love?"

Kellan could feel tears welling and shrunk down into his pillow. She pulled him close. "Not good, Shannon. You can't imagine it. What I did. What I allowed to happen. So much power. So much love." He rolled over and cupped her face in his hand. "I've never seen so much power, all encased in," he paused, "all encased in one of us."

She kissed him and smiled. "You are going to be fine. You saved the world, Kellan. Hell, you saved all of creation, with help of course. You love saving things."

He smiled back, "Yeah I do."

She tapped his nose. "Yeah you do." Shannon sat up and looked down at him. "Guess what I've done."

Kellan looked worried, "Oh no, what have you done?"

She frowned, "Nothing bad. What's your favorite food and your favorite movie?"

Kellan warmed to the game and pushed himself upright on the bed. "Sausage Po-Boy and Bladerunner?"

Shannon sighed, "Ok what is your second favorite food and favorite movie?"

He crinkled his eyebrows, "Well, I guess, NY Style Meat Pizza, and Bladerunner."

"Yes!" She yelled triumphantly, "And UberEats will be here in," she held up Kellan's phone, "40 minutes and I've already downloaded Bladerunner for us."

He stared at her. "I love you!"

She grinned. "I know."

Kellan smirked, "But pizza is your favorite not mine."

Shannon shrugged "I know that too."

Kellan laughed. "You are incorrigible." He paused a moment thinking, then added, "Why is it going to take so long for that pizza, they usually have it here in like 20 minutes?"

Shannon gave him a sly smile, "Because I told them that they had better not be here in less than 40."

She winked and he laughed again.

"Have I mentioned that you are incorrigible?"

She leaned in and nipped at his ear, "Don't you mean insatiable?"

Chapter 21

LUCIFER'S GIFT

J ames shouldered open the shop door and glared at the jingling bells. Juliet
sat on the tall wooden stool behind the front counter with her feet crossed
behind the lowest rung. She glanced up at the sound and smiled as her eyes
came to rest on the boxes in James' hands.

"Is that?"

"Yes, Juliet. Fix pizza. Where's the idiot?"

She popped off the stool and relieved James of the pizza. "I'll take that,"
she said then nodded toward the door. "Can you put the dinner sign up, please
while I take these back to the nook."

"This is a business, Juliet, you can't just close during business hours," said
James looking aghast at the young women. For her part, Juliet just narrowed
her eyes and glared. "Ok," said James holding up his hands, "Where is the
closed sign? This?" He asked pointing.

"No," Juliet called over her shoulder as she headed further into the shop.
"Not the closed sign. The dinner sign. It's the one shaped like a pizza slice that
says to come back in a few minutes because the proprietess is engaged in eating
pizza. They are all stuck to that mirror over there."

James glanced around by the door and spied the antique floor length mirror
standing to the left of the entrance. It was festooned with a variety of colorful vinyl stickers each with a stylized version of Juliet engaged in some sort of

activity along with a textual explanation. There was Juliet peering out of what was obviously a bathroom stall with the words *Back soon, gotta poop.* Next was Juliet carrying an impossible number of books stacked well above her head with the words, *Back Soon, unloading new books.* James laughed despite himself as his eyes took in the third sticker which consisted of an very angry Juliet staring out with her arms crossed and the words, *Hamish, we are closed!!* emblazoned beneath. James wondered when exactly that one would be used, but reached for the fourth which showed a clearly ecstatic Juliet snuggled in a deep leather chair and taking a huge bite of pizza. The sticker also prominently displayed a glass bottle of Coca-Cola and the words, *back soon, gotta eat.* He took the sticker, reversed it so it could be read through the glass and slapped it on the shop's front door.

James walked into reading nook just as Kellan appeared from the back carrying several bottles of Coke and a few plates. The two men stared at each other for a moment, with Kellan freezing in place, and a nervous expression on his face. Juliet looked at them both in turn, then walked around the large table between the several chairs and couches to relieve Kellan of the drinks and plates. "What is wrong with you two?"

"Nothing's wrong with me," said James defensively.

"Me neither," said Kellan immediately.

Juliet just rolled her eyes and opened the two pizza boxes, grabbed a slice ladened with meat, and hopped backwards into her favorite chair. "Work it out, boys, she said around a mouthful of food."

"I'm good," said James. "Jarvis says you guys are working well together."

Kellan nodded, "Yeah, I'm good too and yes, he's been very helpful." Kellan paused, "Freakishly helpful in fact."

Juliet watched the exchange and just shook her head as the tension seemed to fade. Both men slid chairs over closer to the pizza.

A moment later, the front door bells jangled and Juliet glared at James. "What," he said defensively, "I put the sticker on there and locked it. Your lock must suck. Don't blame me."

She turned to Kellan who just smiled broadly, "I'm the silent partner. You go handle it."

Juliet narrowed her eyes and grumbled something about both Kellan and James being less than useless, but dropped her plate onto the table and headed to the front. A moment later, she returned with a self satisfied look on her face. She stood for a moment, arms crossed and stared at Kellan.

He finally met her gaze and gave an exasperated sigh, "Ok, what?"

"It's for you."

"It can't be for me, Juliet, I'm not even here. I'm the silent—"

"He asked for you, so it's for you. I'm going to eat my pizza while it's hot. You can deal with the David Bowie clone up front."

Both Kellan and James nearly choked and the two men stared at each other in alarm.

"Kellan," asked Juliet warily, "Why have you gone all sparkle eyes?"

The Sentinel was halfway out of his chair when they were were joined by a fourth person. "Oh do sit down, Kellan, no need to rise no my account, though I do appreciate the courtesy." The man reached into one of the open boxes and took a slice of pizza.

"Hey!" shouted Juliet "Leave off the pizza." She slapped his hand and yanked the slice from it. She glared into the other man's ice blue eyes and said, "Didn't you mother teach you not to touch other people's things?" Then seeing the mixed look of anxiety and horror on both Kellan's and James' faces she added, "What's wrong with you two. Do you know this guy?" then slower said, "And how come he's not even mentioning your glowing peepers."

"Uh, Juliet," began Kellan as the young woman continued looking at their uninvited guest, who was absently rubbing his slapped hand. "This is—"

"John Milton," said the man extending his hand to Juliet. "I am sorry to intrude and even more so for having helped myself to your dinner." He flashed a brilliant smile. "I can't imagine how disappointed Shannon would be to miss her favorite pizza."

Juliet had accepted the offered hand reflexively but now pulled back eyes narrowing, "Say, how do you know Shannon." She then turned to Kellan. "What's going on?"

Milton grinned mischievously, "Yes, Kellan, what is going on."

"Nothing's going on, John, but if you have something to discuss, let's take it back to my office."

Juliet rounded on Kellan, "It's my office, or at least, our office. And you aren't taking people I don't know back to *our* office."

Kellan had given James an intense and pleading look. He got the gist, rose and said, "Juliet, how about you give them just a little space and I'll explain things."

"Explain what, I'm already fully vaccinated from all of Kellan's weirdness. Remember, I've been on the crazy train for over a year. You're a new rider. So —"

"Juliet," said James in a very even tone, "Let's give them a minute." She noticed the intensity of his gaze and stood aside as the two men walked past her and into the back office.

As the door closed, Lucifer chuckled. "Kellan, you don't know this of course, but I have gotten so much better with my impulse control. Do you know in years past, I would have already killed that girl for her attitude let alone actually striking me. I'm so impressed with myself. Aren't you impressed. Still, I do need to kill her. Can't have word leaking out about such impertinence. Once you lose people's respect and fear, Kellan, it's just work work work."

Kellan took a deep breath and leaned against his desk. "You aren't going to kill her, Lucifer."

The fallen angel raised an eyebrow. "Are you telling me what I can or cannot do, Kellan?"

The Sentinel shook his head, "I wouldn't presume to do so. I'm just stating it as a matter of fact because doing so wouldn't serve your interests."

"Really?" said the Devil, "Do continue. I'm intrigued." Before Kellan could answer, they both turned slightly at the sound of Juliet's voice coming to them through both walls and door.

"The fucking devil. Are you telling me I slapped Satan for eating my pizza?"

Kellan winced, then shook his head and said, "Jesus, Lucifer, couldn't you—" he stopped as the devil smirked at him, "Why do I keep doing that?"

Lucifer shrugged, "I don't know, but it is as amusing this time as it was the first. I suggest you keep doing it."

"No, I'm not. That was the last time. Anyway, back to the point. Hurting Juliet or anyone close to me is not in your interests because I will go medieval batshit crazy on you."

Lucifer looked thoughtful then asked, "What exactly does that mean?"

Kellan raised his hands. "I don't know, but it's all kinds of bad for you. At a minimum, I would spend every waking moment figuring out everything you had planned, thwarting that, and then figuring out how to utterly destroy you."

The fallen angel settled himself into the guest chair, leaned back, and placed crossed feet on Kellan's desk. "And how exactly is that different that what you would do otherwise. We are enemies you and I."

"Are we?"

Lucifer looked both amused and slightly taken aback, "Aren't we?"

Kellan leaned forward locking eyes with the Devil, "I'm definitely enemies with Maurius, but my guess is that you two aren't very fond of each other. Am I right?"

Lucifer smiled and gave Kellan a slight nod of both appreciation and acknowledgement. He said, "Maurius is certainly a thorny issue. He and I are sometimes aligned on means but not ends and sometimes ends but not means."

Kellan sniffed derisively, "How about when he wanted to obtain all the Ordered power within me and use it to become a god?"

Lucifer sighed, "Yes, fair point. That would be a situation when we were aligned on neither ends nor means." He waved his hands, "But that is to be expected. Sentinels are a problem. Uncontrollable. That is why I wasn't in favor of them, but Father wouldn't listen to me, as usual."

"Yeah, well, I'm not going there. Anyway, Asmodeus was also my enemy."

"See, you make my point, Kellan"

"No, I don't. You make mine."

"How so?"

"Asmodeus was a dick. He stole Lamia's kids and he tried to kill Shannon, Juliet, and Meghan. You haven't done any of those things." Kellan paused, then added, "Yet."

Lucifer smiled wickedly, "But I've done many other things. I am the Devil am I not? Micah spent lifetimes opposing me."

Kellan nodded, "And I am not he. Look, I'm not suggesting we are going to be besties. There clearly is some sort of three dimensional chess game going on between you and God. I'm betting you don't even know all the rules and you've had millennia to puzzle it out." The Sentinel laughed suddenly and Lucifer glared dangerously.

"What, baby Sentinel, do you find so amusing?"

"Oh don't take everything so seriously. It was just your expression. You would be terrible at poker. I clearly hit on something. You don't know what the end-game is here, do you?"

Lucifer sighed and placed his arms behind his head, "No, I don't, Kellan. As God always used to tell me, he sees to the finish and I do not."

"I bet that really pissed you off."

The Devil slid his feet off the desk and leaned forward, arms on his legs, and stared up at Kellan, "You have no idea."

Kellan smiled, "War in heaven. Fallen angels. Permanent separation from your Creator. I think I have some idea."

Lucifer was shaking his head, "I'm not convinced he created me. Why would He let me do all the things I've done? All the things I continue to do."

"He's nicer than you?" offered Kellan lightheartedly.

"No, it has to be more than that. It simply has to be. I know Him. There is more."

"Well, you are probably right, but we are not going to solve that here and now. All I am trying to get across is that you are not, yet, my sworn enemy. If you fuck with my friends and family, you will be. It may be that enmity between us is unavoidable, but I humbly suggest that if you are the one to make it so, you do so deliberatively."

Lucifer stood and absently straightened the Van Gogh style painting of an exploding TARDIS. He turned and Kellan saw something new in those ancient eyes. Curiosity? Respect? He wasn't sure. "Are you familiar with the Gospel of Judas, Kellan?" Lucifer asked.

"No, never read it, but Ares referenced it when we were at Trajan's column."

"Do you know who authored it?"

"Uh," began Kellan, "I'll take wild guess and say, Judas."

"You disappoint me," said Lucifer. "No, I authored it."

"Wow," said Kellan, "I have to admit, I didn't see that coming. Why isn't it the Gospel of Lucifer, then?"

The fallen angel stared at Kellan, "How well did the Gospel of Judas do becoming canonical?"

"Not very," answered Kellan.

"And you think the Gospel of Satan would have done better?"

"No, I suppose you are right about that."

"Indeed I am. Regardless, you should read it, my young Sentinel. Soon."

"I don't think Amazon has it," said Kellan with a grin.

Lucifer smiled, but it seemed sad somehow, "You are a strange one. It has been a *very* long time since I've been as perplexed by someone as much as you perplex me." He clapped his hands together and rubbed them. "Still, you have done me a service in preventing creation's end so I will grant you a boon." His smile broadened and he stretched out his arms before continuing, "Because of your service to me, I will not kill the girl-child."

"Oh thank god," came a voice through the door and Lucifer turned back to Kellan.

"I believe we were being eavesdropped on. How rude."

Kellan squinted back. "How rude? Really? And I'm afraid not killing Juliet isn't good enough"

Kellan saw the door knob turn before the sounds of a struggle and more profanity could be heard through it as James dragged an obviously furious Juliet away from the office.

"Not good enough? How so?" Asked Lucifer with amusement

"Well, you don't get to simply *not* do something that wasn't deserved to be done in the first place and then call it a boon. I'll grant that you owe me one, but your debt remains, Lucifer."

The fallen angel stared into Kellan's eyes for a long moment as if searching for something. He cocked his head and frowned slightly, then twisted his hand. Red mist formed there momentarily as he made a tossing gesture causing something to flip in the air reflecting the office lights. Kellan watched as a thick silver coin bounced several times on the desk, then spun around before settling on the brown leather desk blotter. "What's that?" asked Kellan suspiciously.

"It's your boon," said Lucifer with a flourish. "Pick it up."

Kellan laughed, "Oh, no. I'm not picking up that coin. Is there some kind of trapped demonic angel in it?"

Lucifer looked hurt. "Kellan. You pain me. Would I try and harm you in the guise of payment for a debt owed?"

Kellan just gave the fallen angel a flat expression, and made no move to pick up the coin.

Lucifer sighed, "No, there nothing nefarious about the coin. Although I do get your reference. In fact, I've read all those books. Have you ever noticed that creative works have analogues in the spiritual world. I've wondered if the big arc of *those* books might give me insight into—" Lucifer motioned in a large circle, "what the big arc of our reality might be." The Devil lowered his voice conspiratorially, "After all, you *did* go to that island to get the Seal of Solomon, so we know that part is real."

"You mean like Heinlein's *Number of the Beast?*" Kellan asked.

Lucifer snapped his fingers, "Yes, Kellan. Exactly like that. He posited that every story written or told either mirrored, or created, reality, whole or in part. That's a pretty obscure book for someone your age."

Kellan shrugged. "I'm a big Robert A. Heinlein fan and that was the first book of his I ever read. I loved the name of his ship."

"*The Gay Deceiver*," said Lucifer with a grin. "Lazarus Long's self aware AI. A bit like Jarvis, eh?"

Kellan's eyes went wide. "You know about Jarvis?"

Lucifer waved away Kellan's surprise, "Of course I know. Didn't you pick up on my hints at the CDC party. I get insights into many lies people tell. Lies are born of Chaos, Kellan, and so am I."

Kellan pointed at the coin. "So, this is completely safe?"

"Completely."

"You don't lie, remember?"

"Of course I remember, and you are correct. I never lie. The coin is safe. It is really an artifact used in demonic summonings. Mortals must complete elaborate rituals to generate the energy to activate it. You need only channel Ordered power through it and I will send a servant to convey you to me. One time may you use it and I will grant you any request that is within my power"

"Really? Any request?"

Lucifer nodded gravely, "It is a powerful boon. One I may live to regret giving, but, what's life without a bit of risk."

Kellan picked up the coin and examined it. One side was engraved with a six pointed star set in a circle while the other bore a spiral of enochian runes.

Lucifer smiled as Kellan flipped the coin a few times into the air, "Well, nice chat. Must be off. Things to do Kellan. Chaos to seed."

"One last thing before you portal off," said Kellan.

"Hmmm?"

"What's the deal with Meghan? Why does Ares call her a valkyrie?"

"Ahh," said Lucifer his eyes begging to glow slightly, "Why indeed? You can piece that together yourself. Think about it Kellan. Consider all the references to valkyries and then look for other creatures in mythos that might seem similar." The devil chuckled. "Go on now, I'll wait here."

Kellan closed his eyes, took a deep breath and slowly released it forcing his mind inward as decades of information raced through his consciousness at blinding speed. After some minutes, his eyes snapped open and his face registered shock.

"Well," said Lucifer, "What did your magic brain come up with?"

Kellan swallowed hard and asked, "Nephilim?"

Lucifer's eyes brightened further, "Yes, Kellan, Yes! And what are they?"

"Offspring of angels and humans," the Sentinel replied evenly.

"Oh, not just angels." Began Lucifer with a grin, "Demons. After all what is a demon but an angel of different temperament." He then looked past Kellan and closed his eyes, reciting something as if from memory, *Man began to increase on the face of the earth, and daughters were born to them. The sons of God saw that the daughters of man were good, and they took themselves wives from whomever they chose.*

God said, 'My spirit will not continue to judge man forever, since he is nothing but flesh. His days shall be 120 years.' The nephilim were on the earth in those days and also later. The sons of God had come to the daughters of man and had fathered them. They were the mightiest ones who ever existed, men of renown."

Kellan took a steadying breath. "Whoa, so are you saying that Meghan, my Meghan, is a nephilim?"

Lucifer smiled, "Not just any nephilim, for no mere nephilim would so entrance the incarnation of war. There is nothing in the mortal realm more infused with Chaos than war. Only a nephilim born of similar Chaotic energy would find a match in the god of war. Only one angel would contain Chaotic energies in such abundance to sire that singular kind of a nephilim."

Kellan covered his mouth, then dragged his hand up and through his hair nervously. "Wait, no. Dude. You are not saying you are Meghan's— No, wait, I know her parents."

The fallen angel laughed at Kellan's confusion. "First, congratulations again Kellan. You are the first mortal to ever refer to me as, 'Dude," and second, no, Meghan is not my daughter."

Kellan let out a breath he had not known he was holding, but Lucifer continued, "maybe great, great, great granddaughter. I don't think any more recent than that."

"Oh, my god," said Kellan.

Lucifer shook his head, "No, he had nothing to do with it, I assure you. But now that you mention it, you had sex with my great-granddaughter once didn't you? I should be incensed."

Kellan's eyes went wide and Lucifer tilted his head back and laughed maniacally for a moment then sobered, "I jest, Kellan, I don't care about sex at all. You kids have fun."

For his part, Kellan, had slipped into his desk chair and rested his face in his hands mumbling about feeling sick.

Lucifer slid onto the desk knocking over a few item and rested his hand on Kellan's shoulder. "You know, now that I think about it, maybe I was wrong. Maybe Father did have a hand in things."

Kellan looked up feeling woozy. "What?"

Lucifer locked eyes with him, "Have you taken time to wonder at the happy coincidences that surround you: A valkyrie at your back, a soulborn at your side, and an artificial intelligence at the fore. Why, it's almost as if someone who exists out of time ensured His Sentinel had friends a plenty. Some might say that whoever is stacking the deck in your favor is shaving the corners off the deal Father and I made so long ago." Kellan tilted his head slightly at this and looked suspicious, but Lucifer merely smiled broadly. "Oh, not me, baby Sentinel. Someone less generous of spirt than me might even say God's cheating."

Now Kellan stared at the fallen angel with incredulity, "Really?"

Lucifer returned the look of surprise, "I know. I know. He'd never do that, right?"

Kellan shook his head, "No, I meant the generous of spirit part. I'm pretty sure that is not something you've ever been accused of."

The fallen angel looked crestfallen as he brought both hands to his chest, "Kellan, again, you pain me," but a moment later his bright smile returned as he slid off the desk. Lucifer gestured expansively and a glowing portal rotated into view. He took a step toward it and turned, face uncharacteristically solemn, "This has been, in many ways, a tale of two gardens, my young Sentinel. Eden, a tale burdened by pride and chaos. Gethsemane, a tale elevated by agape and order."

Kellan stared at him a long moment, then quipped, "So, you're a poet now?"

Lucifer stepped through his portal and turned as it closed, "Ah, Kellan, while some few are born with the souls of poets, all those who live long enough become poets in time…or monsters."

Chapter 22

EPILOGUE

Kellan stared at the empty spot where Lucifer's portal had been moments before and slowly shook his head as thoughts cascaded through his consciousness. He reach into the desk drawer and drew out a wood wrapped flask, spun open the lid, and tilted it into his mouth. He closed his eyes as the warm liquor coated his tongue and felt it burn when he swallowed. Jefferson's Reserve, very old bourbon. Images of the bottle, the history of the distillery, and then facts about the second President himself raced through his mind. The rush of information calmed Kellan and he felt his pulse slow. He took another few long swallows, replaced the flask in his desk, and stood. As he reached the door, Kellan gave one last look back to where he and God's eternal adversary had just spoken, then passed through and closed it behind him.

Kellan was still preoccupied with his own thoughts as he walked into the reading nook causing both Juliet and James to jump out of their chairs, faces fixed in worry.

"I can't believe you brought the literal Devil into my shop. Kellan you are utterly and completely—"

Juliet cut off as a glowing portal suddenly rotated into view, through which they could all see a night time rural scene. Kellan felt the familiar stomach tingle as his eyes met those of Shannon. He could see the strain and concentration in her face, as her eyes began to spark and dim. Without thinking, Kellan leaped over a chair and reached into the portal as it began to fail. He felt her hand close about his wrist and power flow out from him. The portal stabilized and widened and he stared at her, heart beating like drum in his ears. Shannon smiled as their two pairs of glowing eyes met each other across the miles and centuries that separated them. Kellan gave her arm an insistent pull and she stepped forward from her time and place to his.

The portal winked out and Kellan pulled Shannon into his arms. His mouth met hers and he felt her melt into him, but something separated them more than he liked. Kellan pulled back and saw that she carried a massive leather tome. He grabbed the book and tossed it on the table, knocking pizza boxes to the floor in the process. She smiled at him wolfishly. "It's only been three day. Seems I was missed."

Kellan felt the grin spread across his face and he said, "Shut up, you," then pulled her close again.

"Honestly, I'm surprised they can breathe like that," said Juliet

"Look whose talking," replied James with a snicker, "I heard all about you snogging that boy from Walking Dead on Kellan's desk."

Juliet could feel the warmth traveling up her neck and face, but merely managed to softly grumbled, "He's not from Walking Dead, you racist asshole. And assuming Shannon doesn't swallow Kellan whole, I'm going to kill him."

James gave Juliet a little side hug and nudged her in Kellan's direction as he and Shannon parted. "You can't kill him, Juliet. Look at him. Have you ever seen him so head over heels?"

The young woman looked over to the couple as they continued to simply stare into each other's, now normal, eyes with faint smiles tugging at the corners of both their mouths. Juliet sighed, "I suppose you're right. He's quite besotted. Maybe I'll just torture him until he stops making fun of Glenn and me."

James released her with a friendly pat on the shoulder as Shannon walked over to them, "That's the spirit."

The Scotswoman opened her arms and Juliet gave a short laugh, then walked up for a hearty hug. "How are things, little sister," said Shannon into her ear while squeezing Juliet tightly.

"Oh, you know, the usual. Holding down the fort while you guys save the world and Lucifer himself visits the shop to nearly kill me. No big deal."

Shannon stepped back but left both hands on the younger woman's shoulders as she looked at her. "Really, Lucifer was here?"

"Yep, and I slapped him."

Shannon's eyes grew wide. "Why on earth would you do that?"

"Because she has a death wish," answered Kellan as he came up beside them and sliding his arm around Shannon's waist and giving her a soft kiss on the neck.

"Tickles," she growled shrugging him off playfully, "Now, Kellan, pay attention. I have a message to give you about this book."

"The book can wait, Shannon, I want to know how you are here."

"Hmmm. Simple really, I had enough stored Ordered energy to open up a portal, well almost enough."

"No, I don't mean that," he said turning her to face him, "I mean your soul tether and the time stream. You promised after that ill advised dinner and movie night, to not risk it again until you knew it was safe."

She grinned mischievously and tapped out a cadence on his stomach, chest, lips, and nose with each word, "Ill—advised—but—fun!" Then winked at Juliet.

The younger woman frowned and turned to James, "Is she referring to—"

"Yes," he replied, then added, "Just try not to think about it."

Juliet shook her head. "Gross, Shannon. Just Gross."

Kellan ignored the exchange. He reached up and tilted her face toward him, holding her gaze. "I'm serious. Are you sure it's safe for you to be here? How long can you stay?"

Shannon shook her head. "I can't believe I almost forgot about that. Kellan, look at this," she said while fishing inside her tunic and withdrawing a round amulet held in place with a sturdy leather thong. "I got this from the same man who gave me the book and message. He said it will let me know when I had to return to my own time line."

"Man, what man?" asked Kellan becoming wary then stopped himself. "Never mind, that can wait, how does it work. It just looks like a dull piece of non-precious metal." He lifted the amulet and examined it, his blood suddenly running cold. On one side, there was a six pointed star encased in a circle and on the back spiraled enochian runes. He frantically fished in his pocket and withdrew the coin Lucifer had given him. He held it next to the Amulet as the other three stared at him uncomprehendingly. The front was an exact match although the runes on the back were different.

"He said you were supposed to activate it by channeling through it," said Shannon, then added, "He seemed quite nice and handsome too. I'd have given him a tumble for sure were it not for my bonnie boy from the future." She smiled up at Kellan brightly, then frowned when it was not returned.

"What was his name, Shannon?"

She looked around the room. "Why are you all staring at me that way? His name? John. John Milton."

"I'm gonna freak out, Kellan!" yelled Juliet.

"Everyone, just relax," said James although he looked anything but.

"Someone tell me what is going on. Right now!" yelled Shannon.

Kellan reached up and cupped her face with his hand then spoke very softly, "It's ok Shannon. We'll figure out—"

"John Milton is Satan," blurted Juliet. "He's Lucifer. Shaitan. The Devil himself. And he gave you jewelry."

Kellan continued to hold Shannon and saw her eyes widen in alarm, then said in a low voice, "Why thank you, Juliet. That was most helpful. Now Shannon, just sit down a moment and let's talk this through. I honestly don't think you are in any danger."

Once he had her resting in one of the overstuffed leather chairs, Kellan sat perched on the center table and leaned forward holding her hands in his. "Now tell me, what he said when he gave you the amulet."

Shannon took a deep breath. "Well, he said that he had just met up with you," she waved to encompass the shop, "here in Atlanta and said you were both infuriating and endearing. I told him that was you exactly."

"Great," muttered Juliet to James, "Satan is sharing his bromance issues with Kellan's girlfriend. They are going to get a show on The CW."

"Shut up, Juliet," lilted Kellan, while keeping his eyes on Shannon. "Go on. What did he say about the amulet, specifically."

"He said that you helped him out with something and that he gave you a thank you gift but that he knew you couldn't have done it without my help so wanted to give me something too. He said the reason I can't stay outside my timeline is because to do so brings disorder to temporal—something." Shannon pulled her hands from Kellan's getting frustrated. "You know I don't understand the Timey Wimey stuff, Kellan."

"That's ok, Shannon. Just tell me what you remember."

"It's just that you are supposed to channel through it to activate it. So long as I wear it, the pendant will track how long I can safely remain away from my time line. He said it worked like an hourglass, if that helps."

"It's a trap," said Juliet emphatically. "If you channel through that thing, it is going to explode and kill us all. It's clearly a trap."

Kellan sighed. "Thank you, Admiral Ackbar. Shannon, did he say anything else about the amulet?"

The Scotswoman looked past Kellan to Juliet, "He said, he always paid his debts whether for good or ill and that we were even. It didn't sound like a trap."

"He's clearly lying. He's a lying, liar from lie-town."

"Juliet," Kellan said, trying to keep his voice even, "You are just upset because he was going to kill you."

"Ya think?"

James leaned in to her and said, "You are decidedly not helping an already stressful situation."

Juliet stiffened, setting her jaw and resolving to keep her opinions to herself.

Kellan's eyes burst to life and he reached for the amulet, but Shannon caught his hand. "Are you sure? Do you trust him?"

"Oh hells no," said Kellan, "But I don't think he lies. I'm not completely convinced he can lie, but even if he can, I think his pride forces him to stick to truths. That doesn't mean he won't manipulate using truths and half truths." The Sentinel removed her restraining hand and grasped the amulet willing his power through it. All four of them stared intently as a soft green light began to seep out between Kellan's fingers. He released the power and opened his hand. The six pointed star and its surrounding ring now glowed with a deep green light. Kellan stared at it closely and could barely make out tiny incremental markings along the outer ring like second indicators on a stopwatch. The first dozen or so remained dim, while all the others glowed with that inner green light.

"What do you think it means," asked Shannon.

Kellan shrugged as James leaned in for a closer look. "The markings dim as she loses the ability to remain here," he said matter of factly.

Kellan turned on him, "How the hell do you know that?"

It was James' turn to shrug, "It's pretty obvious. You told me she nearly died and had to reconstitute this soul-tether her own time line. She probably hasn't had time to fully do that which is why the ring isn't completely full. I'm telling you, watch those little markings over the next few hours and days, I'll bet you dinner that they blink off over time."

"That makes sense," said Juliet hesitantly and Shannon nodded in agreement.

"Well, I don't have any better explanation," said Kellan "so I guess we just watch it for now." Kellan rubbed his eyes as he felt a huge wave of fatigue hit him and he looked up at his friends. "You know, guys, I'm just exhausted."

Shannon frowned at him. "I thought we agreed you would rest after your portal'ed me back to Glenn Ferry? What were you doing Kellan Thorne?"

"Don't be mad at him, Shannon, it's my fault," offered Juliet. "I made a complete hash of the shop's QuickBooks account and bought a fake first edition Francis Jose Farmer, which Kellan was gallant enough to sort out for me. Sorry."

Kellan pointed at Juliet, "See, what she said. Not my fault. Anyway, I am completely wiped out and need to sleep for a couple days straight."

Shannon slid off her chair and crouched on the floor in front of Kellan. She crossed her arms around his neck and gave him a kiss. "I will shepherd you directly to bed, my sweet," then more softly, "After all, it's been three whole days." She winked.

"Gross," said Juliet again.

"Sleep, Shannon. I'm going to bed. To sleep," said Kellan emphatically.

The Scotswoman frowned, clearly unhappy with his declaration, but just said, "Fine, Kellan Thorne, I'll get you to bed, to sleep, but I promised Old Scratch I'd show you the book he—"

"It can wait, Shannon. That book looks to be 1,000 pages."

"No, Kellan, not the whole thing. It's the entire old and new testaments, for heaven's sake. He just wanted to show you a passage from the Gospel of Judas."

Just as Shannon spoke the words, Juliet gave a startled cry and jumped back from the table. All four stared as the giant tome pulsed with a red glow and flew open. Pages whirled leftward at blinding speed finally pausing on a page. "What's it say?" asked James. "I don't recognize the alphabet let alone the language."

Kellan looked at each of them in turn and they simply shook their heads. He leaned over the book, channeled a trickle of power, and the words became clear in his head. The young Sentinel sighed. "It reads, *The Gospel of Judas, the Accuser.*" Like before with Shannon, as he spoke the words, the pages flipped but this time much slower and only a few pages onward. After it stopped, three sentences began to glow a deep red.

"I think those are the important sentences, Kel" offered James.

Kellan stared up at his friend, "Thanks James."

"Well, translate it," said Juliet.

Kellan braced himself with hands on either side of the book and stared down at the glowing words. "It says *It will come to pass that Order will beget Order but that the Son of Order will depart from the path of his father. Creation will falter and the Sion will traverse two gardens. If he prevails the High Prince of Chaos will forge alliance and the two will parlay beyond the sight of God.*

"That doesn't sound good at all, Kel." said James.

"I told you it was a trap," offered Juliet.

Kellan sighed. "Now I'm never going to be able to sleep."

The Sentinel felt two arms encircle his waist and warm lips brush his ear where Shannon whispered, "Really, such a shame. Whatever shall we do now?"

The end of Sentinels of Creation, Book Two: A Tale of Two Gardens

AUTHOR'S NOTE ON POP CULTURE, EASTER EGGS, AND HISTORICAL ACCURACY

One of the most common non-plot related questions I receive has to do with the pop culture references and Easter eggs. The two are decidedly different and I am happy to discuss both here. In addition, a less common question I get revolves around the historicity of events in my books. That, too, is a worthy topic and I will cover it briefly as well.

First, and most common, are the references. Both *A Power Renewed* and *A Tale of Two Gardens* have numerous pop culture references. These can range from obscure Doctor Who episodic references picked up by few to iconic Star Wars references understood by nearly everyone. Both have their place and I include them as a way to create a connection with readers that exists beyond the plot. Most of them can be considered subtle winks and nods that exist between the two of us.

Across both novels set in the Sentinels of Creation universe there are references that include, but are not limited to, Supernatural, Star Trek, Star Wars,

Doctor Who, Bladerunner, Highlander. Mr. Mom, and many others. I have even come across readers who have found references that I hadn't known that I made. Kudos to you by the way. For others who may not have seen even the ones mentioned above, I'd invite you to take a second walk through the books and see what you might pick up along the way.

Now, let's move on to Easter eggs, which can be a bit more controversial. The idea for these came to me as an extension of a book I read as a teen by Robert A. Heinlein. It is called, *The Number of the Beast* and I highly recommend it even though the math can be a bit heady. Like Kellan, I'm not a big fan of math and I managed to get through it anyway. One of the foundational premises that Heinlein makes in that book is that every creative act can spawn a new reality. For example, his characters run across those created by L. Frank Baum in Wizard of Oz. I suspect Baum's work was already in the public domain when it was referenced in *Number of the Beast* because the Baum created characters actually interact within pages of *Beast*.

A careful reader of my Sentinels of Creation books may notice silent cameos from other fictional work. For my own reasons, I keep these Easter eggs both subtle and in small number. That said, those readers who find them certainly do seem to enjoy the experience as much as I did in making them. I keep to a few pretty strict rules when inserting these special cameos into my work. First, I have tremendous respect for the creative work of others and my inclusion of their characters is more homage than anything else. Part of that respect is knowing that I did not create either their characters or the world in which they live. They are merely visiting my world and thus never speak or directly interact with my characters. Further, while I happily call out pop culture references by name I will never do likewise with these Easter egg characters.

Now, changing gears a bit, let me provide a brief commentary on the historical references you might find within the *Sentinels* books. I would venture to say that characters, places, and dates are all over 90% accurate. I'm giving myself some wiggle room here because sometimes 100% accuracy doesn't make for a good story. In those few cases where facts and fantasy are diametrically opposed, fantasy wins out. After all, these are urban fantasy novels not history books.

That said consider Shannon's frantic ride though the highlands to Inverness. One might ask, is that journey possible and if so, how long would it take? What route might someone use? This chapter represents a good example of the approach I try to use throughout my books. Everything about Shannon's trip to Inverness is as historically accurate as I could make it. Yes, her horse could travel the distance in the time referenced. Yes the Cathedral within Dornoch existed during Shannon's day and both referenced Bishops were historical people. There is no doubt that including such historical accuracy does slow down one's writing, but I've found it a worthwhile tradeoff as it seems to add additional reality to the world. This, I believe, is especially important in the urban fantasy genre since we are often bending or breaking established physical laws.

I hope you've enjoyed this little peak into my use of pop culture references, Easter eggs, and historical people and places. I am always happy to hear from readers so please don't hesitate to send along whatever questions or comments strike your fancy.

A FEW WORDS ABOUT
AUDIOBOOKS

When I first started out to write Sentinels of Creation: A Power Renewed (APR), there were a few things that I wanted to be sure happened. First, I wanted to make the book as widely available as possible and in as many formats. That box is well and truly checked since APR is now available in Print, Kindle, and Audiobook.

Second, I knew that I wanted to have the book voiced by a particular person. In this case, Nick Podehl. For other authors heading down this path, I encourage you to explore as many audiobooks as possible to sample the wonderful talents available from today's voice actors.

Finally, I strongly believe that stories represent one of the most foundational human desires. From the time we are little, the luckiest of us have parents who read to us. I was one of those kids and I mention it in the dedication of my first book. Two of my fondest memories are of my mother reading *The Lion the Witch and the Wardrobe* and *Charlotte's Web* to me. Oh how we both cried when Charlotte died. Years later, as a young man, I received a card from mom that included the following poem by Strickland Gillilan. I still keep a digital photo of that poem with me in my iPhone.

I had a mother who read to me
Sagas of pirates who scoured the sea,
Cutlasses clenched in their yellow teeth,
"Blackbirds" stowed in the hold beneath.

I had a Mother who read me lays
Of ancient and gallant and golden days;
Stories of Marmion and Ivanhoe,
Which every boy has a right to know.

I had a Mother who read me tales
Of Gelert the hound of the hills of Wales,
True to his trust till his tragic death,
Faithfulness blent with his final breath.

I had a Mother who read me the things
That wholesome life to the boy heart brings--
Stories that stir with an upward touch,
Oh, that each mother of boys were such!

You may have tangible wealth untold;
Caskets of jewels and coffers of gold.
Richer than I you can never be--
I had a Mother who read to me.

Now allow me to tie the latter two points together and put a bow on them. You see, I've come to believe that audiobooks are one of the most enriching additions that can be made to any novel. This is especially true when it includes a vibrant collaboration between author and narrator. I have been fortunate enough to develop such a professional and personal relationship with Nick, who I mentioned at the beginning of this note.

We spent many hours across several weeks getting to know both each other and the characters who inhabit Sentinels of Creation. As I learned, this kind of collaboration between author and narrator is not common. I'm sure there are many reasons for this being so, but I cannot imagine creating an audiobook without such give and take.

As authors, we bring life to characters who did not exist before we animated them. Similarly, our narrating partners give voice to those same characters who, without their performing talents, would be left silenced.

In conclusion, I would invite anyone reading this to explore the rich experience that can be had via spoken word stories. They are a wonderful way to pass the time during a commute or to slowly drift off to sleep. If not the audiobook for this story, then seek out a new or familiar one of your choosing. I'll wager that you'll find your life the richer for it.

To my friend and artistic partner, Nick Podehl, I say thank you for your time and talent. Getting to know you, your lovely wife, and beautiful girls, have enriched my life even as your craft has enriched my stories. I am quite sure, you are cringing as you read these words, but alas, your gifts have led you along a path where you give voice to other's words...even when they make you blush. Like you are doing now. Yes, right now, while you are reading this.

Heh...maybe there is something to that old saying about author's having god complexes.

AUTHOR'S BIO

Robert W. Ross has spent the last twenty five years spinning stories and user journeys into web, mobile, and social experiences for brands ranging from the obscure to the iconic.

He has both a passion for pop culture and a deep loathing to discuss himself in the third person. However, his wife convinced him that anyone who took the time to reach the last page of his book or the end of his audiobook, might want to know a little about the person who wrote it.

To that end, Robert's influences include authors such as Robert A. Heinlein, Phillip Jose Farmer, and Brandon Sanderson. He has a deep and abiding love for all things Star Trek, Doctor Who, and Sponge Bob. While Robert can often make obscure TV, Book, and Movie references, he sadly lacks Kellan's eidetic memory. He is quite sure the brain space taken up by all that trivia is directly responsible for his lacking any sense of direction.

Sentinels of Creation: A Tale of Two Gardens is the second book in the series and Robert's current plans include three more Sentinels books to round out the initial arc. He is also considering one or two stand alone novels that would feature supporting characters from the main story arc. This is in response to a number of fans who have requested more details on both Shannon and Meghan.

As can be seen from the first two Sentinels books, Robert has great appreciation for strong female characters who can hold their own, have well formed thoughts, motivation, and are never relegated to simple plot devices.

He lives in Atlanta with his wife of over twenty years, their kids, one Siberian Husky, and about 11 different Apple products.

Made in the USA
Lexington, KY
26 June 2017